I0653074

After

Janet Durbin

Whimsical Publications, LLC

Florida

After is a work of fiction. Names, characters, and incidents are the products of the author's imagination and are either fictitious or are used fictitiously. Any resemblance to actual events or persons, living or dead, is entirely coincidental.

If you purchased this book without a cover, you should be aware that this book may have been stolen property and reported as "unsold and destroyed" to the publisher. In such case, neither the publisher nor the author has received payment for this "stripped book."

Copyright © 2007 by Janet Durbin
Revised Edition

www.janetdurbin.com

All rights reserved

No part of this book may be reproduced in any form or by any electronic or mechanical means, including information storage and retrieval systems, without prior written permission from the copyright holder and the publisher of this book, except by a reviewer who may quote brief passages in a review.

Published in the United States by
Whimsical Publications, LLC
Florida

ISBN-10: 0-9787738-1-0
ISBN-13: 978-0-9787738-1-6

Printed in the United States of America

Acknowledgments

This book is dedicated to the ones who helped me with my journey:

Thanks Michele (may she rest in peace), Karla, and everyone on 2 North—in fact the whole hospital—for listening to my ideas and encouraging me to see them through. Your support helps me greatly.

Thanks Sharon and Gordon. Your willingness to answer my many questions help the growing pains lessen.

To my family. I appreciate all your support, whether by listening to me talk incessantly about writing, or by taking my mind off it through golf, tennis, or bowling.

And a special thanks to the most important person in my life: my son. Without you putting up with my constant badgering: "How's that sound?", "What do you think?" and my insistence on reading it to you, this story would not be here for all to enjoy. Big hugs to you, my bestest buddy.

Also by
Janet Durbin

Journey of Twins Series

AFTER
*STOLEN**

Nature Kranderson Series

INNOCENCE TAKEN

---

*Coming soon from Whimsical Publications, LLC

When one world ends, another begins.

Always

Janet Durbin

One

On a late summer night, in a city left barren and desolate by the ravages of time, a bum scrounged through the trash trying to find anything of value. An old tattered hat sat half-cocked on his unkempt gray hair; his faded and worn brown suit hung off his skinny body as if it had belonged to someone several times his size. The shoes on his feet had holes where holes were not meant to be; the laces long since gone. Everything on him was from a time long forgotten, just like him.

He knew better than to go out once the sun ducked below the horizon. Bad things came out after dark. Unfortunately, these were desperate times. The stores of food hidden in his small ramshackle home were all but gone. His stash of spirits was all but gone too. That would not help his aching bones during the cold months to come. He needed the warmth of the alcohol to make it through to spring, or at least that's what he told himself all the time.

The year was 2215. Technology had long since disappeared, although its remains were evident everywhere. Skyscrapers that once reached for the stars above now lay in heaps. Their rusty frames stood in the moonlight like sentinels watching over their beloved homeland. Foliage from neglected parks covered areas that had once been a thriving society. The remains of the dead city went on for as far as the eye could see.

The old man was bent over, digging through a pile of

crumpled boxes when a noise sounded behind him. He glanced over a stained shoulder with his bloodshot eyes.

Nothing.

He returned his gaze to the trash beneath his hands. He was in the remains of a store where alcohol was sold during a time much easier, a time 200 years in the past. The old man had been lucky to find an unbroken bottle here once before. He hoped his streak of good fortune would continue. If he couldn't find a bottle, maybe he could find something to trade for the spirits he so desperately wanted, in addition to some food.

He knew his chances were slim of finding anything else; he continued scrounging through the remains of the store anyway.

The face of the full moon glowed bright through the missing ceiling. Its rays reflected off the bits of broken glass, throwing a beautiful design on the walls. The reflections reminded him of when he was a boy. He smiled.

He heard the noise again. This time it was right behind him. He turned. A large silhouette of a man stood there, tall and still, his features hidden by the darkness. For an instant, a look of fear appeared on the wrinkled face. One of mistrust and anger replaced it.

"What you look'n at?"

He was anxious to get back to his search. His prize awaited him and he wasn't interested in wasting any more time on some mysterious stranger, especially one who showed up out of nowhere.

"Go back where you came from. I ain't got nuttin you want. And I ain't sharing nuttin I find wich you neither." He turned his back to the man, ignoring him. It would be the last mistake he made.

The stranger moved fast. A hand flew up and knocked the hat off. He seized the bum's hair and pulled back hard, knocking him off balance. An arm wrapped around the old man's chest, lifting him off the ground, pinning him against a muscular body.

The bum struggled. He tried to break free; but he couldn't. The grip holding him was too strong. His neck was fully exposed.

The old man whimpered as the dark silhouette leaned over. Hot breath blew on his cold throat. An intense pain coursed through his body as teeth sank into the soft flesh and ripped the neck open. A sucking sound followed. He twitched. His eyes rolled back until only the whites glowed in the moonlight. His death came quickly.

When a pulse was no longer evident, the stranger let the body fall to the ground. With a shudder, he turned and left the store, disappearing into the blackness of the alley, leaving the thick smell of death behind.

*   *   *

The sun shined bright in her eyes when Shyanne awoke. She stretched and rolled over to look out the window. A banner with a rearing stallion on it waved in the breeze. From the angle of the light shining in, she knew it was mid-morning.

Shyanne rode into town late in the evening. She liked small towns verses the big ruined cities. The people didn't have a haunted looks in their eyes, or jump at the least little noise. Several had even helped her find the stable and this inn. It was a welcome change.

"Drayco...where are you?" she whispered to herself.

She stared out the window a second longer before returning to her back. She thought about what had to be accomplished today before moving on. Restocking of her food and water supplies was foremost.

Shyanne flipped back the covers and sat on the side of bed. Her long strawberry-blonde hair fell over her shoulders and down her back when she stood up. Her small stature and slim build led some people to believe she was a mere female, until they saw her wield her sword.

Reaching her arms over her head in another stretch, she inhaled deeply. The breath left her in a whoosh. "Boy, do I need a bath."

She looked around the rented room. It reminded her of a cabin her family had used during their summer vacation so long ago. A stove, round table, barrel filled with water, and a bed were all that furnished it. The only window allowing light into the room was the one next to the bed.

"All the comforts anyone would want."

Chuckling softly to herself, she walked over to the pot-belly stove used to heat the room. The small fire inside was reduced to a few glowing embers. Two logs grabbed off the pile next to it rekindled the flame.

A beat-up metal pan hung from the side of the barrel. Hot water was a luxury nowadays. She relished every moment she got the chance to use it, even this little amount. Filling the pan to the top, she set it on the stove to boil.

While the water heated, Shyanne went to her travel bag and took out a fresh set of clothes. Her brush followed. By the time she finished halting the progress of the snarls making their way through her hair, the water was boiling.

She wrapped a rag around the metal handle before carrying the pan to the table. One leg was a smidge shorter than the other three. It rocked back and forth, causing some of the precious hot water to spill out. After making sure no more was lost, she shed her dirty clothes and dunked the rag into the pan. A sigh of pleasure escaped as the warmth of the water caressed her skin.

"What I would give for a tub full of this stuff."

She closed her eyes, relishing the warmth against the rest of her skin. Once every part of her grungy stinky body felt clean, she bent over and dunked her head into the water. Well-calloused fingers scrubbed the scalp. Afterwards, while she dried herself with a worn towel, her stomach growled, reminding her of the need for food.

"Ok, ok, I hear you."

Shyanne tugged on a pair of deerskin breeches and a pullover shirt. She wrapped a belt around her waist to keep the shirt from being too loose. Well-worn boots made of tanned leather followed. Finally, she pulled her long thick hair back into a braid.

She picked up her sword. It was like no other. The blade was double edged and as sharp as hag's tongue. The handle was shaped like a crouching puma, its fangs bared. She had found it in a weapons shop during her many travels. Out of all the swords there, this one seemed to draw her to it.

The role of women in this post virus society brought back memories of her history class. The women stayed home and cared for the children while the men worked and fought to keep their families safe.

She could be one of those women, the ones who

slaved to a husband; but it was not in her nature to do so. She could not see herself bowing to another's will. One day she wanted to find a good man and give him children. Now was not the time. She had her quest to complete first.

Shyanne positioned the scabbard across the middle of her back with the handle in easy reach over her right shoulder. Picking up her bag, she threw it over her left shoulder and exited the room. Her loyal friend and companion, Drizzle, a humecat, materialized next to her as she started down the hall.

He was large for a puma, thanks to mankind's tinkering. His body features were that of a mountain lion. The difference was the front hands and the mind was human in nature.

He walked on all four, making the pads of his hands as tough as his hind paws. Those hands, which were covered with the same tawny fur as his body, hid sharp retractable claws. Drizzle's mind was just as sharp. He had the ability to speak, yet, when he was happy, he purred like any cat. Shyanne remembered all the times he had comforted her with that purr.

"What are we going to do today?" Drizzle asked. His long tail waved in a leisurely manner as he kept pace with Shyanne.

"The usual, look for Drayco."

"I say again...are you sure he's still alive? It's been a long time."

"Of course he is, silly. I would know if something had happened to him." Shyanne tapped her chest over her heart.

*   *   *

Drayco and Shyanne were twins. They were born in the year 2002, a bustling time filled with modern conveniences: like cars, subways, and all night fast food restaurants. The big cities had millions of people coming and going to their destinations; the countryside filled with others trying to get away from it all. The Government did its political duty watching out for society. Or so they thought.

That was before the virus broke out; a virus so devastating that three-quarter of the people on the planet died before anyone understood what hit them.

It was created in total secrecy as a part of germ warfare, to be used 'just in case'. Nuclear power was available for weapons. It was expensive and under close scrutiny, making it hard to obtain. Biological warfare was inexpensive; it could be placed anywhere without anyone knowing who did it.

The geniuses who created the virus had not anticipated the uselessness of plastic seals. It ate through the joints of the suits worn by the workers as if it was dessert, then entered their bodies. The virus was supposed to be a contact one. It mutated into something far worse. It became airborne.

These same workers carried it home to their families. They falsely assumed the decontamination process worked. They were wrong; the world paid the price. Most thought it was just a cold or allergies. They ignored the need to see a doctor until it was too late. Whole families were wiped out in days, a town in a week. A big city was cleared in a matter of weeks.

The government tried to keep the information from going public; it was too late. The news media had discovered what was killing everyone and spread the information worldwide. The ones who created the virus died immediately, if not by the public, then by the virus. Any chance of a vaccine died with them. The geniuses had not bothered to write down how they created the killer germ. They preferred to keep that knowledge to themselves, just in case non-friendly nations illegally obtained the information. The government scrambled to find a cure with the data that was left behind. There was not enough to use. The virus continued its epidemic killing.

A few people became sick. After a couple of days, they recovered. Doctors learned that the lucky ones had high immune systems. Their white blood cells were extremely aggressive toward invading organisms like the virus, ending its progress throughout the body before it had a chance to establish. Shyanne had a high immunity. Her brother was the same. They recovered. They were lucky.

Those same doctors tried to use this information to help the people with inadequate immune systems. The virus was too fast. Young and old, rich and poor, they all died the same. Some tried to hide in fallout shelters made during the cold war. It didn't matter; the virus found them anyway. Out of the billions of people worldwide, only a few hundred thousand survived when the rampage stopped.

* * *

The virus died out when there were no more victims left to infect. Over time, Shyanne discovered that her aging process had slowed greatly. The virus had mutated her. She looked like she was still in her late twenties, even though she had aged 213 years. Her brother was not so lucky. The virus inflicted Drayco with the need to drink blood to maintain his youthfulness, and to stay alive.

"Before we go looking for him, we need to get something to eat," the cat moaned. "My belly is so empty I heard an echo when it growled this morning."

"Are you sure it was your belly that growled? I know about those wonderful dispositions you wake up with."

She reached out to pat him on the head. Drizzle ducked away before she touched him. He emitted a deep growl that would have made any other person pray for their survival. She shook her head, smiling.

They entered the dining area and found a booth close by. Shyanne tossed her pack down next to it and slid to the center of the bench. Drizzle crawled under the table. He was so quiet; no one noticed he was there.

While she waited for service, she looked around. She noticed a large burly man with scruffy hair and a shadow of a beard sitting at the opposite end of the room. He had the makeup of a body builder, except for his belly. Too many ales had made it grow and sag. A smaller man with shifty eyes and a beak shaped nose sat across from him.

Several animal heads decorated the walls and a fire burned warm and inviting in the large fireplace. An occasional spark floated into the air like the lightning bugs she used to catch as a child. Tables and chairs sat throughout the room, ready and waiting for patrons to have a seat.

"How are we this fine morning?" The innkeeper's wife asked as she walked up to the table.

Shyanne remembered seeing her briefly last night. A smile filled the woman's face and her eyes twinkled. She set down a large mug of hot cider in front of her.

She was a stout woman; her brown hair dusted with gray. The only noticeable wrinkles on her round face were the ones near the corner of her eyes, caused by lots of smiling. Though she had a stained apron over her worn dress, she gave the impression of being rich. Shyanne liked her right away.

Drizzle poked his head out from under the table. A friendly purr sounded. The sudden noise startled the woman; she recovered quickly. She was not the least bit afraid of the big cat hiding under the table.

"A humecat. I haven't seen one of them in a long while." She bent down and gave him a scratch under his chin. "I bet you're just as rough and tough as you look."

Shyanne was amazed to hear the wife had seen a humecat before. She had no idea others existed. She was glad, though. Maybe one day they would come across the other one so Drizzle would not be so lonely. He never indicated it, but Shyanne could tell.

"I can see Drizzle's doing much better," Shyanne chuckled. "I'm fine too."

The wife straightened and took her order. As she moved toward the kitchen, Drizzle watched her go. He sighed.

"Not all humans are bad." He lowered his head onto his hands, watching the kitchen door with a forlorn look.

Shyanne picked up the mug and sipped at its contents to prevent the laughter threatening to escape. She had no desire to hurt the humecat's feelings. Her eyes traveled around the room once more. The burley man continued to sit in across the way, drinking from a mug of whatever, probably ale. The man with shifty eyes sipped at his own mug. They glanced toward her but quickly looked away when they noticed her watching them.

Those two sure do look out of place. They must be travelers. Their mannerism says they don't fit in with the rest of the people here.

The men had an obvious nervousness to them, a complete opposite to the other patrons. Occasionally, a burst of laughter or a loud debate about someone's farm doing better that someone else's rose above the drone. Overall, a feeling of warmth and friendliness flowed about the room.

Except from those two.

"Here we go." The wife set the food down on the table.

Shyanne nodded her head in the direction of the pair across the room. "Who are those guys?"

"Trash!" she spat. "They rode into town yesterday and been up to no good since. They caused a big ruckus here last night." She cast a scornful look toward the kitchen. "All the money they flashed around was the only thing that kept my husband from tossing them out. Best watch yourself, young lady. You never know what will come out of a pair like that." She bent over and placed a bowl filled with chunks of raw meat on the floor in front of Drizzle. Straightening, she wiped her hands with her apron.

"Don't worry," Shyanne gave the wife a comforting smile. "I will."

*   *   *

While they ate, she started thinking about her brother, Drayco. They were twins, yet nowhere near identical. She was a foot shorter, pushing the hell out of five foot two, with lightly tanned skin. A peppering of freckles covered her nose and cheeks and her hair was strawberry-blonde.

Drayco, on the other hand, was tall. His hair was as black as a raven, falling just past his shoulders; and he had a dark tan. They both were slim and muscular, but not to the point of being bulky. Shyanne took after her mother while Drayco had a lot of their father in him.

Their mother and father had been loving parents. They made sure their children had a well-rounded education. Camping and fishing trips turned into science events. Instructions on which plants and berries were safe to eat were commonplace. Fencing was something she and Drayco had taken as an elective in school. He sparred with her often, which helped develop their expertise with the sword.

Her parents had been amateur botanist and read every book they could get their hands on. The backyard became a classroom on the care of many plants, including spices. Shyanne had fond memories of those times, and was very thankful for them today.

Before the virus ended their lives, both parents had

worked for the government. They discussed their job very little due to its confidential nature. All Shyanne knew was they worked with DNA and other molecular structures, trying to find new ways to cure old diseases.

Shyanne remembered the day when Dad had surprised the family by coming home early from work. Mom was off, a rare thing for her, as well. He had a worried look on his face as he guided her into another room, closing the door behind them. Shyanne looked at Drayco. They were enjoying an afternoon snack while doing their homework. She shrugged her shoulders. Both were curious about what was going on so they quietly crept over to where their parents talked. Ears pressed against the door, they tried to hear what was said. All they heard was frantic whispering.

Suddenly, the door burst open. Their father almost fell over the two teens kneeling next to it. He ignored what they were doing and indicated for them to get up. He was coughing. His nose was running. His eyes were red and bleary, as if he had been awake for weeks without the benefit of sleep.

"Get your things together. In the morning, we're going on a camping trip. We won't be near a power source so pack things that don't require electricity." He and Mom went toward their room to start getting their things ready.

Later that evening, the twins were instructed to go to bed before 9pm. They had learned a long time ago not to argue with their parents. Shyanne remembered nothing out of the ordinary on the television when she and Drayco gave their parents a hug. Her father's cold seemed to be getting worse. She hoped he would be better before they left.

"Dad, you going to be okay? You have a really narley cold this time," Shyanne said. Drayco nodded his head in agreement.

"Yes honey, I took some cold medicine earlier. It will kick in soon. You and your brother go on upstairs and get to bed. I'll be okay by morning." He gave her a weak smile of encouragement.

"Love you Dad," They chimed together. "You too, Mom."

"Love you back. Now get!" Dad emphasized his words with a wave of his hand.

Mom stared at the television with a concerned look on her face. "Love you too."

The twins hoped Mom was worried about something else, something on the TV, and not because of Dad. Their parents had the usual number of colds throughout the year. They lasted a short while. Dad was resting his head on the back of the couch, his eyes closed, when they darted up the stairs.

Shyanne snuck into her brother's room after they finished changing into their nightclothes and brushing their teeth.

"What do you think is going on?" she whispered so they wouldn't be caught.

"I don't know, little sis," he whispered back. "They sure looked bugged about something."

"Dad sure has a bad cold this time, doesn't he? I hope he'll be okay."

"I hope so too." A frown covered Drayco's face. "That cold came on him pretty quick. He was fine before he went to work this morning."

"Yea. I hope Mom doesn't catch it. You know how Dad always shares all his colds with her."

"Yea. They can be such babies when they're sick."

The twins snickered. They covered their mouths to hide the noise.

"You'd better get back to your room. You know how they can be if they find us awake." Drayco pushed Shyanne toward the door.

"I know, I know. Just like when they have colds...real babies."

That brought on another round of snickers. Shyanne disappeared out the door before her brother could throw a pillow at her.

The camping trip never happened. By morning, their father was unconscious and having a hard time breathing. Their mother dialed 911 when she couldn't wake him. Before the ambulance got there, he stopped breathing. Mom checked him. She found his heart had stopped beating, as well, and tried to get them started again with CPR. Nothing seemed to work.

The ambulance arrived within minutes. A fire truck was right behind it. The paramedics gently pushed Mom out of the way so they could start working on Dad. She gathered the twins and stood watching in shock. She took them downstairs to the kitchen. After a hug for both of her kids, she picked up the phone and called the grandparents. Shyanne noticed she had a bit of a sniffle and an occasional cough. Her eyes were getting red and bleary.

One of the paramedics came in to get her as she set the phone down. They had Dad on the gurney, heading toward the ambulance. He had a tube in his mouth, a bag attached to it. One of the men squeezed it to push air into his lungs. Another person was compressing on his chest as best he could while the gurney moved.

"I want you two to stay here and wait for Grammy and Grampy. I have to go with Dad. I'll call you from the hospital as soon as I can."

Mom knew better than to talk to them as if they were little kids. She tried to catch herself whenever possible. For the most part, she was successful. Under stressful situations, like today, she reverted to old comfortable ways. They nodded their heads in silence. They were in too much shock over the situation to be able to speak.

The grandparents arrived in 20 minutes. They took the twins to their house instead of the hospital. They were of the old school: children were not need to seen in the hospital, no matter how seriously ill the patient was.

Later that evening, the call finally happened. It was not their mom. It was the hospital's Chaplin. Their mother was in the intensive care unit. Their father was dead.

The grandparents hugged the twins tight and went to the hospital, leaving them at home full of unanswered questions. Drayco and Shyanne had pleaded to go with the grandparents, to no avail.

While waiting for information, the teens decided to turn on the television. Breaking news was on every channel. Hundreds of people were flocking to the hospitals and clinics with a mysterious illness. Symptoms were similar to the common cold. People not sick were urged to stay in their homes and remain calm.

The twins looked at each other. Each was thinking the same thought...their parents. They returned their attention to the screen. Shyanne moved closer to her brother. She needed the comfort of his touch. Especially now. It was late into the night by the time they fell asleep, huddled together on the couch, waiting for the grandparents to return.

When the grandparents finally returned home early the next morning, grim looks were on their faces.

"What happened? We saw the news last night about all the people getting sick," they chimed together; a frantic undertone filled their voices. "How's mom?"

Grampy looked at his wife before speaking. With a sigh, he said, "We're so sorry. Your mother passed away this morning."

Grammy went to Shyanne and wrapped her in her arms. Tears flowed freely down both their cheeks. Drayco stood with his head hung forward, his hands buried deep in his pockets. Grampy walked up to him and gripped his shoulder. Drayco tried to hide his emotions. He was young; his emotions got the better of him. In an instant, he flung his arms around the older man and buried his face in his shirt. His shoulders shook with each sob that wracked his body.

Over the next couple of weeks, the news reporters talked constantly about the disease and its devastating impact on the world. People were dying anywhere from 24 to 36 hours after catching it. No one could figure out how or why it started.

At first, the Government remained aloof and denied any knowledge about it. After the news people learned of their involvement, they finally broke down and admitted it was a virus they had created. By then, it was too late. By then, millions of people had died and all attempts to stop the spread had failed.

The twins became sick shortly after the death of their parents. Their symptoms were light so the grandparents hadn't taken them to the hospital. At that time, to go the hospital was certain death. Within a couple of days, they recovered. Drayco was forced to live with the grandparents while Shyanne had to go live with an aunt in a nearby city. The advanced age and ill health of the grandparents made it difficult for them to care for two active teens.

Shyanne ran away after less than a month. The aunt became sick and couldn't keep track of her ward. She arrived at the grandparent's house just before they died. She comforted both during their final hours. Drayco was there a short time after their deaths, but the virus caused him to do terrible things, things he could not help. He had to drink blood to survive.

One night, he lost control and almost killed Shyanne. He left after that and she had not seen him since. Her heart yearned to know what had become of her twin brother.

*   *   *

A loud noise brought Shyanne back from her past. Looking around, she located the cause. The big burley man was coming toward her. He shoved other patrons out of his way, not caring if they objected.

"My, ain't you a pretty one," he slurred once he reached her table. He put both hands on the worn surface and leaned forward, raking over her body with his blood shot eyes. The shifty eyed man stood behind him, also drunk.

"Why don't you come upstairs with us? We can have us a real good time."

Shyanne sized up the situation and leaned back, arms outstretched on either side of the bench. A look of disgust covered her face. It was not even noontime and these two were already drunk.

"I'd rather swim in a lake in wintertime," she replied, distain thick in her tone.

Shifty eyes looked at her, and said, "You'd best reconsider, missy."

The burley man reached for her, intent on dragging her from her seat. He was too slow.

Shyanne jumped onto the bench. Her sword was out before he knew it. A resounding thud echoed across the room as it cut deep into his flesh. It stopped when it met bone. With a tug, she pulled it free. The burley man let out with a howl as he fell to his knees, hugging his arm against his body.

A shadow came out from under the table. In their drunken state, both men had failed to see the big cat when they barged up. The shifty eyed man let out with a yelp and jumped back. Seeing the situation, he turned to make his escape. Drizzle gave him a swat on his backside to re-mind him of his foolishness. Shifty eyes disappeared through the exit, his ripped pants flapping behind him.

Shyanne jumped down from the bench and stood with her sword held ready.

The burley man held his arm against his body; blood ran between his fingers. His breath came and went in a ragged hiss. By the time he looked up, he found he was alone. His partner was already gone.

He glared at her as he struggled to his feet. "This ain't over yet, girlie." He went out the door after his friend, leaving a bloody trail in his wake.

The innkeeper's wife watched the disturbance as it un-folded. Once the two men scurried out the door, she hur-ried over to Shyanne.

"You'd best be moving on, my dear. Those two will be nothing but trouble if you stay. I can feel it in my bones."

"I'm sorry for the mess," Shyanne said as she put her sword away. She tossed some gold coins on the table and picked up her pack. "I hope this will cover both the price of the meal and the cleanup." She was heading for the door when the woman yelled.

"Wait! You'll need this more than I will." She walked over and handed Shyanne the money from the table.

"I can't take this. I ate some of your food and helped mess up the place." She handed the money back to the older woman.

"My dear...watching those two bullies get their fannies whooped by a little bit of a girl was payment enough. Now take this...I insist." She grabbed Shyanne's hand, placed the money in the palm, and closed the fingers tight.

Shyanne smiled and hugged the woman. In a hushed tone, she said, "Thank you."

The innkeeper's wife was blushing when they broke apart. She turned Shyanne toward the door and gave her a gentle shove. "Now get on with you. You don't want to dally too long and give them shyster's time to think up something to do to you."

Drizzle rubbed against the wife in typical cat fashion before moving with Shyanne toward the exit. The other patrons backed out of the way. They wanted no part of this pair. They had witnessed what could happen if you crossed them and did not want the same treatment.

"I wish things weren't like this," she said with a heavy sigh after they were outside. "The virus changed so much."

"I understand," Drizzle answered. "Survival tends to bring out the worst."

She tossed her pack over her shoulder and walked down the road toward the stables. Children were running about laughing and pointing at them. Adults whispered to each other, or stared. Disturbances of this nature were unusual in their town.

"News sure does travel fast, doesn't it?"

Shyanne held her head high as they continued to their destination.

The stable was a large building nestled on the outskirts of town. It had ten stalls in all, two of which were big enough to hold more than one horse. Hers was in stall four, one of the larger stalls located in the back. At present, five other horses were boarded there. Drizzle waited for her outside, lounging in the sunlight. His presence frightened the animals and caused them to kick and buck in their stalls.

As Shyanne entered the building, the strong smell of horse and straw hit her nose. She loved that smell and stopped to take in several deep breathes. When she felt satisfied, she moved on. A big bay horse poked its head out as she walked past. Shyanne gave him a quick pat on the nose and continued toward stall four.

The stableman came up to her while she was leaning against the railing looking inside.

The man was tall and as thin as a pole, but handsome in his own way. His face was as long as his body; a solemn look covered it. He took off his hat, scratched his head, and then returned the hat to its original spot, covering the wisps of thinning blonde hair.

"I heard about the fight. Please be careful, those two can be mean ones." He remembered how they had treated him last night before heading to the bar. His left arm bore a large bruise from being shoved into a support post for one of the stalls.

Shyanne thanked him for his concern. She unlatched the door to the stall and went inside. A tall dark horse with white spots on its hindquarters stood in the farthest corner, his ears pointing toward her.

"Jack...how's my big man?"

He danced toward her when he realized who was in the stall with him, shaking his flowing black mane back and forth with every toss of his head. A smile crossed her face. Her heart filled with joy every time she watched him move. It was so fluid, especially for such a big animal.

The stableman watched as she hugged her horse. He leaned against the railing, but made no attempt to enter. "Sure is a loyal beast that one is. Wouldn't let me get near em for nut'n. Had to toss his grain into the bucket and run before he kicked the stuff'n out of me." He pointed to an old battered pail against a wall, grain spread across the floor in front of it.

She scratched the horse on the neck, and replied, "We've been together for six years now. Before that, he was with a man who abused and whipped him every chance he got. When I witnessed what this man was doing, I persuaded him to give me the horse." The smile on her face broadened while she recanted how she had changed the man's mind.

"He refused, at first. Some money and my sword helped him change his mind. It took lots of time and patience to win Jack over. Now that I have, he won't let any man near him."

"You did a fine job with him, missy. That you did."

Shyanne grabbed the halter and indicated for the tall lanky man to back away. When he was safely out of harms way, she led Jack into the walkway. The horse pranced around with excitement. He knew they were leaving and looked forward to stretching his muscles. The stall had plenty of room, but the wide-open spaces had more.

"Easy there, young man. We'll be going in a minute."

She reached over, grabbed the rope hanging off to the side of the walkway and secured it to the halter. She repeated the process for the other side. Picking up a brush, she started on his coat. Both were glistening by the time she finished.

She flipped the brush over and gave the pad draped over the railing a couple of resounding whacks. Thousands of tiny dust particles danced and twirled in the sunlight. They gently came to rest moments later as if exhausted from so much activity. She threw the pad onto the broad back. The saddle followed. After tightening it down, she secured her pack behind it with the attached straps. She worked the bridle onto Jack's head and wedged the bit into the open space behind his teeth. The reins were tied to a nearby post for extra security.

The stableman came up behind her, carefully watching the horse. He handed her a waterskin and a package wrapped in some white cotton material. "I wanted you to have these for your travels. It ain't much, but it will hold you for a few days. I know you didn't have time to resupply because of those idiots picking a fight."

"Thank you," she said as she took the supplies.

He looked down while shifting some straw with his feet. "You'd best get a move on. The more distance you put between you and those devils the better."

Shyanne hooked the waterskin over the saddle horn and placed the white bundle in her pack. She checked the belly strap one more time to make sure it was still tight. Before grabbing the reins and getting into the saddle, she hugged the tall man. Prodding Jack toward the main thoroughfare, she turned and waved. He followed her as far as the door and waved back.

"Good luck, and watch yer back," he yelled.

I wish I could have known these people better. Unfortunately, circumstances never seem to let that happen, she thought with a momentary twang of sadness.

Shyanne waved again and turned Jack toward the trail that took her in a westward direction out of town. Drizzle ran beside her. The horse was used to the sight and smell of the big cat; he paid no attention to the tawny creature next to him.

She never looked back as she rounded the bend. If she had, she would have noticed two battered and angry men watching her as she disappeared, vowing revenge for what they considered an extreme injustice done to them.

"She will pay, don't you worry none. She will pay," the burly man muttered as he watched her go.

Two

Drayco moved away from the section of the city where he had killed the old man. He did not want to be in the vicinity when the body was found. People were curious. They asked too many questions; questions he did not want to answer.

The old man's blood had helped, but at such a price. He remembered the many times he had not satisfied his need and how he had nearly died because of it. The thought of killing never sat well with him. Unfortunately, there was no option if he wanted to survive. He was worried, though; the thought of killing was getting easier.

Will this ever stop? Why did this have to happen to me?

The sun was reaching its orange rays over the horizon as Drayco made his way through the ruins. He was a tall man with a darkness about him, a darkness that made most people think twice before approaching. The sword swinging from his hip helped. He did not mind. It made it easier to avoid unwanted company.

The road he walked on laid broken and overgrown, grass sending out ever-reaching tentacles to take back what was once its territory. It ran through a big city, the city he and his family had called home. That was before the virus made a complete mess of everything, before chaos ran rampid. The monuments and statues that had brought so many tourists now lay in ruins. The White House destroyed.

The towering buildings reminded him of the haunted houses he used to enter at Halloween. Rundown stores with broken windows were everywhere. Dirt covered the glass panes that had somehow survived intact, hiding the contents inside from view. What used to be automobiles was nothing but piles of rusted metal, abandoned where they sat.

When the virus was in full swing, some made a mad rush to get out of the city, while others simply hid in their homes. The people fleeing blocked the roadways with their many cars, making it impossible for emergency personnel to get to the dead and dying. Some tried to carry their worldly possessions with them after abandoning their vehicles. They were forced to drop everything after the items became too heavy.

In the end, the virus found them. No one could outrun it.

Looting increased dramatically during the first few weeks. People grabbed televisions, clothes, jewelry, and any items they thought were important. Most were found dead with the 'important' things lying next to them. The police, or what was left of them, were unable to keep up. They were too busy trying to survive, like the rest of the world.

Descendants of survivors still lived in the city because they had nowhere else to go. Their ancestors had not left, and neither would they. They felt safe in the familiar environment.

Drayco looked at the different buildings as he walked down the road. One would catch his interest and he would enter, finding nothing of use. Looters, both past and present, had done their job well. Even though he needed blood to stay alive, he still needed to eat the same as any other person.

A rundown store stood at the corner of an intersection. A light breeze made the worn and weathered sign dangling in front swing around in a circle. The hinge squealed with every turn. The noise caught his attention; the message on it drew him closer.

"Groceries. I wonder if anything might have been missed this time." Shrugging his shoulders, he added, "Won't know unless I look."

The door for the dank and dusty building was jammed with pieces of fallen concrete. He peered through the broken window and saw a few canned goods and other items thrown all around. At one time, it was a grocery store; now, it was nothing more than a trash heap. The looters had ruined everything in their haste to get 'the good stuff'.

Papers lay scattered throughout the interior. Occasionally, a breeze would catch one just right, causing it to float in the air until a wall stopped its progress. Dust covered the floor where the shifting papers had not. Except for a random footprint from an animal, the dust had not been disturbed in quite some time. Most of the cans were rusted beyond recognition or destroyed. Broken glass from the overhead lights littered the room.

Drayco crawled through the opening and walked around the room. The sound of crunching glass echoed off the bare walls. On prior explorations, he had been lucky enough to find a can still in good shape. Maybe today would be as successful.

He was rummaging through the store when he found a doorway half hidden in a back corner. Beyond it, he saw a room with shelves knocked over. Boxes in various states of ruin were visible under them.

"This looks like the storage room," Drayco said to himself as he stood in the doorway.

He put his pack down and moved to inspect the boxes. Some had large holes in them. He discovered most were filled with partially eaten dry foodstuff. Dead bugs and their dropping confirmed his suspicions about what had caused the holes. It made their contents useless to him.

He could see the label of a favorite brand of cereal from his childhood, but it was hard to make out due to the bite marks made by the bugs. A smile came to his face as he remembered all the times he had nagged his mom to buy it whenever they went to the store.

Drayco moved some of the bigger boxes and discovered a smaller one hidden underneath. It looked like it was still new; the bigger boxes had protected it from the ravages of time. He pulled it out and knelt down to look inside. This was the prize he had hoped for. Pint-sized cans without so much as a single rust spot on them were inside. He pulled one out and read the brightly colored label. Five others remained wedged inside the partitions.

"Peaches," he read with excitement. "A prize for sure."

Drayco popped the pull-tab and tugged the lid off. Inside, he discovered the can was lined with a white material used in the past to prevent rust.

He tasted the contents carefully. Cans found on previous outings were opened and large mouthfuls consumed before he discovered the food inside was rotten. He learned his lesson about sampling with a very small amount from that point on. The fruit, and the juice it was stored in, tasted as fresh as when it had been canned.

"A little bit of heaven I haven't had in a long time." He closed his eyes and finished off the rest of the contents with a satisfied smack of his lips.

Nowadays, peaches were no more. For some unknown reason, the virus affected them. All the trees started loosing their leaves, then quit producing fruit altogether. One by one, they died out. They were the only fruit trees affected. The rest, like apples and oranges, continued to flourish and produce.

He had just finished putting the last of the cans in his backpack when a noise sounded behind him. He turned and saw a large head with beady red eyes appear over some crumpled, half-chewed boxes. It was a rat, though not like any rat he remembered. This one was about the size of a medium dog.

Where did that come from?

The dark man stared at the big rat in front of him. Almost immediately, he heard other sounds in the room. Parts of the downed shelves shifted as if something large was passing under them. He knew what it was; he could see their many glowing red eyes.

I must have stumbled into a nest of them, he thought.

The rats moved with lightening speed, darting from one bit of cover to another. Watching their movements, he realized they were positioning themselves between him and the door, thus cutting off any chance of escape. He had to get out fast, or he might not get out at all. He carefully picked up his pack and started backing out.

Hunger made the creatures bold.

A rat jumped onto his back from a pile of broken rubble. The weight of the beast almost brought him down; he managed to keep his feet under him. Pain shot through his shoulder as teeth sank into the flesh. Others attacked him from the front. Another bit his leg.

Drayco reached up to grab the one on his back before it bit him again; it was too late. Its teeth sank into the soft flesh of his shoulder once more. He bellowed with rage as he grabbed it and threw it across the room. It hit the wall with a thud. It did not get up.

He kicked at the other rats surrounding him. One let out with a squeak when he hit it. The rest backed off after he started swinging his pack. They watched the man with hungry eyes, waiting for him to tire. They had played this game before.

Some of the rats focused their attention on their wounded comrades. The one he threw against the wall remained where it had landed; the other was limping from the kick it had received. Hunger drove the rats to turn their attention away from the stronger prey onto the easier.

Drayco used that moment to turn and run. Squeals of pain filled his ears as the rats tore at the wounded ones. They now had the meal they so desperately wanted.

He slowed when he was several blocks from the store and bent over to catch his breath, hands resting just above his knees. "That was close."

The virus had caused mutations. Some were good; others were not—like the rats. The dark twin understood mutations. He was one. He needed to drink blood to stay alive.

Drayco pulled his shirt back to see a set of ragged tear marks on his shoulder. Blood oozed from the wounds. Thankfully, they were not deep. The bite on his leg smarted. It too was not deep.

"Damn. I hope they don't get infected."

He cleaned all the wounds with some water from his drinking pouch and covered them with pieces of cloth ripped from an old shirt. His body's defense system, which helped him survive the virus, would most likely prevent any infection from setting in.

"Feels better already."

Drayco straightened his clothing after he finished and placed the pack on his good shoulder. He continued through the city.

The sun was high in the sky when he entered another section where whole families were moving about. Some of the people in the cities had grouped together for protection from the awful mutations, and from other humans.

With the need for blood satisfied, along with his curiosity of finding useful trinkets and foodstuff, he tossed his pack on the ground and sat down in an open square to consider his next move.

He saw a family looking through the rubble close to him. There was a man, a woman, and two children. The man was dirty and skinny; his clothes looked like they'd seen better days. The woman was in a tattered floral dress with her long brown hair pulled back in a ponytail. The kids looked to be in the same condition.

The woman kept glancing over her shoulder toward Drayco. It was as if she thought he might become some sort of demon and eat her and her family. Her man looked at him once. He returned to his rummaging, ignoring the dark twin altogether.

The kids were playing with old broken toys they had found somewhere. After a few minutes, the boy went off to find his father who had disappeared from view. He left the girl standing alone with nothing to do but kick rocks. The woman had her back toward her daughter; she was bent over concentrating on a pile of rubble.

Drayco focused on his planning. He failed to notice the little girl approaching him.

"You're new around here, ain't cha?"

She appeared to be about seven years of age with long strawberry-blonde hair flowing down her back. It was wound into a loose braid. Strands on either side of her face waved with every breath of the light breeze. Freckles dotted her nose and cheeks. She was dirty, and skinny, but there was a sense of pride about her. She reminded him a lot of his sister, Shyanne. His heart wrenched.

"Yes I am."

"Do ya plan on hanging around?" She looked down and kicked a rock, sending it skitting across the road.

"I'm just passing through."

"You're cute." She turned her face away, hiding it behind her hands, giggling.

Drayco smiled. He picked up his pack and reached inside. When his hand reemerged, he held one of the small cans of peaches toward her.

She stood there, tilting her head this way and that in an attempt to see what he held in his hand. Hesitantly, she reached out and snatched the can before he could change his mind and take the offering back. She ran off a few paces and spun around.

"Thanks, mister."

The girl's mother was yelling for her. "Lishal! Get over here!"

Lishal ran to her, hugging the can against her body as if it was made of gold. He could hear the mother scolding the girl.

"How many times have I told you not to talk to strangers? You could be hurt!" She noticed her daughter holding something. "What have you got there?"

"Nothing." Lishal hid the can behind her back. "The nice man gave it to me."

Her mother reached toward the child. "Let me see it."

"No! It's mine!" She ran from her mother before she could take the prize away.

"Lishal! I just want to make sure it's safe, that's all."

Drayco rose to his feet and shouldered his pack. He moved away, smiling. Halfway down the broken, grass-covered roadway a small voice yelled to him. It was Lishal.

"See ya, mister!"

He turned around to see Lishal standing on her tippy toes. She had one hand in the air, waving it with all her might. The can of peaches was safely tucked away in her other. She was so much like Shyanne, so full of life. He hoped she would remain as full when she grew older. He didn't mind being around children. They saw him as a person, not as an evil entity.

Drayco decided it was time to leave the city. He needed to be back in the open spaces. In recent weeks, he had heard rumors of a woman with long strawberry-blonde hair who traveled in the company of a big cat. She could be Shyanne, his twin sister. It was beyond all reason, but something inside him told him it was so. He continued walking westward. In no time, he was far from a little girl enjoying a can of peaches.

Three

The rejuvenating rains of spring and early summer had come and gone, leaving its mark on the dirt road. Deep ruts created from the passing of wagons made it difficult for Jack to walk without stumbling. Shyanne moved him to the smooth grass covered edge to keep him from getting hurt.

She loved the openness surrounding her. Trees scattered throughout the fields danced as the breeze made its way through their reaching arms. Large fluffy white clouds floated lazily across the rich blue sky.

It was late in summer. The days were hot, the nights comfortable. Yellow, white and blue flowers dotted the fields that paralleled the road. Shyanne took in a deep breath and exhaled it slowly.

"Jack, this is living. I miss the modern conveniences. But I love nature when it's at its best."

The horse cocked his ears back toward the girl as if he was really listening to what she said. A butterfly flew in his face and distracted him. He focused on it instead, ears pointed forward, watching it as it floated past in an erratic pattern in search of nectar. His ears started swinging back and forth; first toward the woman on his back, then toward the delicate black and yellow thing flittering close to him. Shyanne chuckled. She really loved her horse.

It would be dark soon. She knew that staying out alone without a shelter of some kind was not a wise move. The world had changed. Savage mutations prowled in the night.

A few were cunning and very deadly. The manmade ones were worse, far worse. They would not mind making a meal out of a girl, her horse, or her cat.

A short while later, a road branched off to the right. It was wide enough to allow a wagon to follow it, though no ruts marred the surface. It led toward a thick growth of tall majestic trees. Since nothing was visible ahead except a few trees and open fields, she decided to chance it.

Tugging on the reins, she turned Jack in that direction with the hopes that an old hunter's shack or an abandoned house would soon appear. If nothing showed, at lease she would have the cover of many trees to hide in.

Drizzle had disappeared some time ago. Shyanne wasn't worried. She knew he would find her no matter where she went.

She rode for another half hour and was starting to wonder about her decision when she came upon a clearing with an old building in its center. She was glad to see the shelter.

From the looks of it, the roof had disappeared a long time ago. Only parts of the rotten rafters remained. It had four stone walls. A good thing since the red hue of the setting sun now blanketed everything. The remnants of a wooden fence marked the outskirts of the property. Tall ripe wheat covered most of the field. It waved as if inviting her to stay.

"At least the walls will protest us from the cool night winds. And whatever else," Shyanne said to her horse. She looked up at the clear sky. "I don't think we'll have to worry about rain tonight." She dismounted and walked into the building.

The door, like the roof, was long since gone. She entered what appeared to be the main living area. Another room was located in the back and was probably for sleeping. The floor was made of hard compacted dirt with patches of tall grass growing in both rooms. There was plenty of space for the three of them.

Only bare walls and bits of broken wood from the roof were evident. No furniture remained. The wall dividing the two rooms was in bad shape. The doorway was three times what it should have been. She gave it a quick shake. It held up against her rough handling.

Shyanne went outside and brought Jack into the back room and removed his saddle, bridle, and blanket. She brushed him down as best she could with some dried grass and fed him a handful of grain from the saddlebag. There was no need to hobble him; he never wandered off.

When she finished with Jack, she piled her things in the front room. Shyanne walked around, both inside and out, and gathered wood before it became too dark. She wanted to make sure there was enough to last the night. Afterwards, she dug a small pit. In no time, a fire was burning, the winding cloud of soot disappearing into the night sky above.

She moved her bag closer to the fire and took inventory of her foodstuff. She had had no time to replenish her supplies before the two men confronted her, and was thankful for the gift given by the stableman. She opened the white cotton bundle to see trail bread, jerky, a wedge of hard cheese, along with some dried apples inside. She still had plenty of rice, but it was nice to have something else to go with it.

A small battered pot emerged from her bag. She placed it on the outer aspect of the fire and poured water in to boil. Some rice followed, along with some of the jerky. The scent of a fine meal soon filled the air.

The pot was one of the few things she had managed to keep from the pre-virus time. When they were little, her parents had taken the twins to a used army supply store and bought each their own camping gear. The thought of parting with the old pot for a new one was more than she could bear. It had too much sentiment attached to it.

After finishing her food, she ate a few of the dried apples. She tucked the rest back into the cotton bundle.

These goodies are to be savored, not wolfed down.

Shyanne cleaned up and put everything away before spreading out her blanket. Drizzle had not returned yet, which was nothing out of the ordinary. He sometimes disappeared for days when hunting. She knew he would find her when he was ready.

She placed her sword on the ground next to her. Her boots followed. Crawling beneath the covers, one of her arms slid under her head like a pillow as she looked up at the night sky, listening to the crickets play their music.

She was eyeing the constellations above when she heard a noise outside. The crickets became silent.

"Drizzle, you ugly cat, have you finally made it back?"

The noise sounded again. This time, a strange snorting went with it. It was unlike anything the big cat would do. They had been together for a very long time and she knew what sounds he would and would not make.

Shyanne heard growling coming from several places beyond the walls. She had a feeling that whatever was out there, she wasn't going to like it. Frowning, she grabbed her sword and rose to her feet. A full moon shined high in the sky, casting enough light to see.

Her scent, along with that of the horse, was thick in the air. Without a doubt, she knew it would draw the creatures inside. A shadow stretched in from outside. A head appeared. The sight of it nearly took her breath away.

The beast was a cross between a wolf and a lizard. The head hung low to the ground, its ears twirled back and forth, listening for any movement as it slinked through the doorway. Its eyes were located on either side of the head. A long snout filled with razor sharp teeth extended below the eyes. Patches of gray fur showed between large areas of green scales. It was as large as a good-sized wolf. A second one followed. It was just as ugly as the first.

The government had experimented with the DNA of several animals to create 'better' ones. The animals were to be used instead of human spies because of their new capabilities, and, if captured, they were expendable. The experiments went awry though; it was a case of man trying to be God. Drizzle's kind was one of their few successful cases.

"Oh great. A rizbak."

She had heard about some of the mutations in her travels, but had never seen this particular one before. From what she saw before her, she understood why the information stuck. She also remembered that the rizbak were known to run in packs and be very aggressive and cunning.

"Man, are you ugly," she said as the stench of the beast hit her nose. "Phew...you stink!"

She gripped her sword firmly with both hands and wished technology had not died with the virus.

"What I would do for a gun right now."

Time had made guns and the ammo for them useless hunks of rust.

Shyanne backed up close to the wall. She knew the rizbak liked to get behind their prey and bite the hamstring to disable it. She was not going to allow them the chance to do that to her.

The creatures stopped. After only a few seconds, one rizbak came in her direction while the other went toward Jack. It was as if they had spoken to each other mentally before moving.

The walking nightmare approached with its head slightly angled, mouth hanging open. A long thread of dribble trailed from the mouth. It stank of dead animals. She wished she could plug her nose. The rizbak halted its progress when it was about two sword lengths from her.

For what seemed like only a second, Shyanne looked at the beast going toward her horse. The one in front of her attacked. It had been waiting for such an opportunity.

A sharp, burning twinge in her left thigh forced her attention back. It had raked her darted out of range before she could think to bring her sword down. The claws were as sharp as Drizzles. They cut into her pants and skin with ease. Blood flowed down her leg. She paid no attention to it. The pain was intense, but she ignored it as well.

"So fast," she whispered. "I'll have to give my full attention to this one if I want to survive this battle."

The rizbak turned and came in for another pass. Shyanne brought her sword up and felt it meet resistance. The creature jumped back before she was able to follow through. While it paced, its tongue hanging out, panting, she could see a trail of blood on the ground beneath it.

"I got you," she said as the trail grew with each pass.

A high-pitched scream sounded to her right. This time, she knew better than to look away. Watching the beast paced in front of her, she hoped Jack would be all right

"I won't be fooled this time, you son of a jackass!"

Suddenly, Shyanne heard a noise above her. She glanced up quickly then returned her gaze to the one in front of her before it could attack. A third rizbak was on top of the wall. It had climbed one of the fallen roof timbers and had worked its way around behind her. She knew she would not be able to watch two of them. They were too fast and worked too well as a pack.

"I'll at least take one of you scumbuckets with me! I won't go down that easy!"

She inched slowly away from the rizbak on the wall. The creature looked down with keen interest, crouching low in preparation of leaping.

Just as she thought the end was near, Drizzle appeared. He leaped up to face the rizbak above her. With his ears flattened against his head and a growl from deep in his chest, he attacked. The rizbak fell with a single swipe. It never stood a chance against the powerful speed of the big cat.

The one in front of her attacked during the distraction caused by the fighting above. Shyanne caught a glimpse of the leap from the corner of her eye and ducked to her right. She brought her sword up, felt an intense pain in her left shoulder and went down hard. The beast fell past her in a heap, dead, a pool of blood spreading across the ground from a gaping wound in its chest.

In an instant, Shyanne was on her feet. She had to see how her horse fared. Jack stood in a corner, a dead rizbak on the ground before him trampled and broken. He had several scratches on him; none looked deep or life threatening.

As she started to make her way toward him, an ever-consuming darkness seemed to get in her way. She shook her head to clear it. It only grew worse. She could not make sense of it. She knew the moon was shining bright, as was the fire in the pit. So why was everything so dark and fuzzy?

Shyanne tried to lift her sword. It hurt too much to do so. She grimaced, deciding to drag the weapon behind her instead. Something sticky and wet seemed to be all over her hand. It made it difficult to keep a grip on the handle. She refused to drop it. More rizbak might show up.

She was halfway across the room when it started to lean and the growing darkness finally consumed everything, including her.

Four

Several days had passed since Drayco left the ruined metropolis. He kept mostly to the well-traveled roads, occasionally taking the less used ones when he wanted to avoid people and the conversations that went with them. The road he walked on today crossed an open plain. A large grouping of trees was visible in the distance. No one else was on the road with him.

The survival training he had received from his father many years ago had paid off a hundred times over in this post-virus world. He missed his father dearly and wished he had been among the lucky few to survive. The outings they had taken, just the two of them, allowed him to have a bond stronger than most of his friends had with their fathers.

Thanks for getting me ready, Dad, even though you didn't know you were.

As he walked, his body started to let him know it would need blood soon. He tried to forget the many times he almost died before he recognized those signals. Exertion caused him to drink more frequently. The steady uneventful pace he set had not cause such an increase.

Drayco hated what the virus had done to him. His need for blood made it difficult to stay around others. In the past, he had had relationships. They always ended in disaster. His increasing need to see Shyanne and a strong will to survive were the only things that kept him from ending the madness.

Twilight was growing on the horizon. He needed to find shelter soon. Neither his strength, nor the sword he carried, would protect him from some of the things that came out in the night.

He was closing on the stand of trees when he noticed a twinkling of light through them. As he entered, Drayco saw several lavishly decorated wagons parked in a circular pattern in a clearing amongst the trees. A fire burned bright. People sat around the flames, laughter and conversations echoed from them. A cook pot bubbled; the scent of stew was everywhere. Near them, horses grazed.

The dark twin crouched low and watched how the people behaved before attempting to enter. In this day and age, people had to be cautious. Otherwise, they wound up on the wrong end of a sword.

The men wore loose pullover shirts with flowing sleeves gathered at the wrist. Leather straps created a crisscross pattern at the neck. Their pants were tight, yet the material flexed easily with movement. They belled out over their boots. A colorful sash wrapped around the waist. A couple of the men wore white sashes. Drayco assumed they were unattached. Some had moustaches while others were clean-shaven. None sported a beard. Every one of the men was stocky and muscular.

The women, on the other hand, came in all sizes and shapes. They wore long flowing one-piece dresses. A sash the same color as their man wrapped around their waist showing to whom they belonged. The laughter and the smell of the stew helped solidify his decision; he stepped into the clearing.

"Hello," he called out.

He did not wish to startle these people. Surprised people killed first then asked questions when it was too late. An elderly man with gray hair pulled back into a ponytail rose and came toward him.

"Welcome, young man. What can we do for you?"

"Your stew smells good. I was hoping I could impose on you for a hot meal and the safety of numbers from the denizens of the night. I have money to pay for it." He reached into his pocket and pulled out a couple of gold coins.

"No, no," the elder man said. He pushed the hand

holding the coins back. "You keep it. Come enjoy our food without the worries of paying for it." Drayco returned the coins to his pocket. "My name is Brind. And you are?"

"Drayco."

"What brings you out into this hostile environment alone, Drayco?" He started toward the fire, waving for the younger man to follow.

"I'm searching for my sister. I heard about a woman in these parts who might be her. I came to see if it is so.

"I wish you luck, my boy."

Brind sat down on a log and indicated for Drayco to sit next to him. After doing so, he was introduced to the rest of the group. Each acknowledged him, in turn.

One man in particular stood out.

Garrett was loud and tried to pick fights with the other men. He bothered the women in ways considered inappropriate. Drayco could tell Garrett felt himself to be a ladies man because of his long blonde hair and good looks. The sash around his waist was white. The rest of the people ignored him. His antics grated on Drayco's nerves. The dark man kept his face expressionless. He did not want to cause any trouble.

"We are a clan of Wanderers. We welcome others openly into our camp, especially in these hard times."

Brind opened his arms wide, indicating the people around him. He winked at an older woman standing close. Her sash was the same color as his. She nodded her head in understanding and reached into one of the pocket on her dress.

Drayco was looking in another direction and missed the exchange. He was surprised by the friendliness of these people. He had heard about Wanderers during his travels. None was mentioned as being this open toward strangers. Rather, it was more like the opposite.

The conversations continued while the women prepared the food. When it was ready, the old woman handed Drayco a plate heaped with stew and a large mug of wine. Setting the mug down, Drayco scooped up several pieces of meat and vegetables and put them in his mouth. The stew tasted better than he had imagined. He had his supplies, but a hot homemade meal was a rare treat. The plate was empty in no time. He followed it with a long draw of the wine. It had a bitter aftertaste. He shrugged it off to being not used to wine. More stew was offered; he refused. He continued to sip from the mug and enjoy the company of the Wanderers while the rest finished their food.

Suddenly, he felt very sleepy. He reached up to wipe his eyes. The hand was blurry and would not hold still when he looked at it. He tried to rise, but found that he couldn't. His legs felt like they were made of rubber. They would not support his weight. The mug in his hand clattered to the ground. The Wanderers gathered around him, anticipation on their faces.

"The wine," Drayco yelled. "You put something in it! Watch out for your fellow man, huh, only for what you can steal from them with tricks and lies." His words came out slurred; his eyes felt as heavy as lead weights.

He tried to fight when the men approached and quickly lost the battle. All the faces started to blend together. Hands grabbed him everywhere, taking his sword and pack from him. Two faces stayed clear in the sea of many—Brind and Garrett. The last thing he heard before the world went away was the sound of an old woman cackling.

*   *   *

Drayco awoke to the sun beating down on him. He had a headache that could knock a horse over and his throat felt worse than parched paper. He remembered the Wanderers with their drugged wine and sat up quickly. The sudden movement increased the throbbing to his head. The pain caused him to lean over and retch. When his body calmed down, he looked around. He was alone.

His body felt weak and shaky when he stood up, though he was once more in control of it. He felt his pockets. The money was gone. The knife stored in his boot was also gone. The place where his sword normally rested was vacant. It felt as if a part of him had been yanked out.

"They took everything," he said with disgust.

A dangerous look fell upon his face. He did not mind so much losing the pack or the other things, but the sword he carried was a gift from long ago—it was a gift from his grandfather.

Drayco remembered coming home after a particularly difficult match where he had lost. The older man met him at the door and took him into the living room. A wrapped bundle lay on the coffee table. The sword was inside. The thought of those Wanderers touching it with their thieving hands was almost too much for him to bear.

He began looking for their tracks. Horse drawn wagons filled with people and their belongings tended to leave marks in the soft ground. It was not long before he found what he was after. The tracks led westward.

The sun was shining high in the sky when he started out. He hoped they were only half a day ahead of him. If it were more than one, he would have a harder time catching up to them. But catch up to them he would.

The dark man's body needed blood. He refused to acknowledge it. His thoughts were on the treachery used, and how easily they had played him.

Those Wanderers have no idea who they are dealing with. They will understand fully once I'm through with them.

Drayco walked at a steady ground-eating pace. Sweat ran into his eyes, making them burn as if hot coals were imbedded in them. He used his sleeve to wipe off the streams flowing down his face. Even though the nights were cooler, the days were still hot.

No one was on the road, for which he was grateful. He did not wish to meet anyone in his present state of mind, only the ones he sought. His body started giving him stronger signals that it needed blood. He ignored it still. He would soon solve the problem when he caught up with the treacherous group.

The tracks stayed with the road. He kept an eye on them in case they turned aside. As dusk approached, the tracks did just that. The wagon wheels cut a path in the ground toward a clump of trees. The arrogance of this group was amazing. They made no attempt to cover their trail.

I guess they thought I would simply give up and go away, he thought as he crept into the woods. *How wrong they were for underestimating their victim.*

Darkness was upon him when he reached the camp.

Drayco had taken his time to keep from alerting the group of his presence. A cook fire burned, a pot of leftovers boiling over. The families were sitting around it laughing and kidding with each other, same as the last time he'd seen them. The conversation, though, was different.

"I still chuckle when I think about the look on that suckers face," one said.

"Yea, especially when he realized he'd been drugged," said another.

"This boot knife will sure come in handy," another in the group added as he held the weapon up.

The first man who spoke held something in his hands. Drayco could not make out what it was because the man's back faced him. His blood seethed when the speaker held the object high. Firelight reflected off metal.

Brind emerged from the shadows of the wagons. "Best be thankful for that sword, Garrett. They don't make 'em likes that no more."

Drayco crouched low behind some bushes and watched Garrett swing his grandfather's sword recklessly. His temper flared. Unfortunately, his body reminded him that he wasn't strong enough to take on the entire clan because of the need for blood. He'd have to wait for an opportunity to arise. Sitting down, he watched patiently as the group went about their business. Soon enough, he'd take back what was his.

Most of the Wanderers retired to their wagons once the evening meal was finished. After a while, only two remained by the fireside, drinking. Garrett was still held onto the sword, the sheath for it lying on the ground near him. Drayco's pack lay next to the sheath.

"I wonder how old it is, and how many men it's killed," he slurred, turning the weapon back and forth to admire the blade.

Brind glared at the younger one, and said, "Probably more than you'll ever know."

He reached into his shirt and pulled something out then leaned over toward Garrett. Drayco heard coins hitting together.

"We'll share these with the others...maybe."

They had apparently played this game before. Both men started to laugh as the coins were divided equally. A few more drinks followed. All the while Drayco watched and waited.

The pair was hitting the wineskins hard. A stack of empties lay discarded, testifying as to how much they had drunk. Full ones waited nearby to be relieved of their contents.

Brind threw another empty wineskin into the ever-growing pile and almost fell over with it. With some difficulty, he muttered, "I gotta go empty my own wine sack. Don't drink everything up before I get back."

"I'll make sure to leave nothin for ya, Old Man," Garrett slurred a little too loudly.

Brind stood and stumbled against a tree before getting his feet under control. He disappeared behind one of the wagons. Drayco saw his chance. Using the skill he was taught during his outings with his father, he crept in the direction Brind had gone.

He found the man standing with his back toward the woods, legs spread apart, relieving his bladder. One hand held tight to the large wooden wheel, thus preventing himself from swaying and wetting all over his boots.

"Boy, do I feel better," he said with a sigh as he finished. "Now I have room for more of that fine wine." He chuckled under his breath while he closed his breeches, almost falling against the wagon once he let go of the wheel.

All of a sudden, Brind had an eerie feeling that he wasn't alone. He had lived a long time in this harsh world and had learned to trust his instincts. He tried to turn around; he was too slow. A hand covered his mouth, cutting off any chance of crying out. An powerful arm wrapped around his chest, pinning him against another.

Drayco whispered into his ear, "No one takes something of mine without understanding the price involved with such foolishness."

Brind froze. He knew that voice. It seemed he had underestimated this one, and he might not get another opportunity to correct his mistake. His family had tricked many strangers using the drugged wine. No one had ever acted like this one. All the rest had licked their wounds and accepted their losses. This one, this dark man, was like a devil incarnate. He felt his head being tilted back, exposing the neck.

Brind didn't know what Drayco was going to do. Even in his drunken state, he had a feeling it wasn't going to be anything good. His breath came faster and faster as Drayco leaned close. He wanted to say something, anything, to get this man to stop. The hand over his mouth prevented it. He struggled against the arm holding him. Too much drunk made that ineffective.

Drayco bit deep into the exposed neck, allowing an artery to bleed freely. He drank the warm liquid without hesitation.

Brind struggled harder, to no avail. The last thought he had before death overtook him was that he should have followed his instincts and killed this man when he had the chance.

When the blood flow stopped, Drayco let the body slip quietly to the ground and vanished back into the woods.

Garrett was still sitting near the fire, his head nodding, a wineskin tucked under his arm when Drayco returned. His stolen sword leaned against a bent leg. The dark man slipped up behind him. Being a fighter, the Wanderer sensed someone there. Garrett jerked his head up and looked at Drayco. He grabbed the sword as he staggered to his feet.

"You!" He spat that single word out as if it was poisonous.

Raising the sword above his head, Garrett charged at Drayco. Halfway there, he stumbled and fell on his face. The blade clinked on a rock sticking out of the ground; sparks flew into the air. He tried to get up, but was too slow. He had had too much to drink. Drayco was upon him in an instant. He grabbed Garrett by his hair, pulling him to his knees.

"My Grandfather's sword is to be cherished and respected. It is NOT a toy to be played with." A dark and deadly look filled Drayco's face as he spoke through clenched teeth.

Garrett had forgotten the sword in his hand. He raised it in an attempt to slice at Drayco. It never reached him.

The dark man grabbed the arm and twisted it, causing the sword to fall from the hand. A pop echoed from the shoulder. Garrett opened his mouth to scream. A sharp yank on his hair snapped the head back, cutting off any sound before it came out.

Drayco sank his teeth into the exposed neck like a rabid animal. The soft flesh gave way easily, allowing the sweet juice of revenge to spurt with every beat of the Wanderer's heart. The dark twin drank like a man who had been lost in the desert without liquid for weeks. With every swallow, his body rejuvenated itself. When he had his fill, he dropped the body. It fell in a heap, leaving the ruined neck visible for all to see when they found Garrett's body.

After the rushing in his ears lessened, Drayco listened for any cries of alarm. The usual sounds of the night were all that filled the air. The brief scuffle with the younger man went unnoticed by the rest of the camp. Drayco went through Garrett's pockets, taking all the money found in them. Picking up his sword, he strode over to the fire and retrieved his pack and scabbard. Once the scabbard was in hand, he slid the sword inside with a silent prayer of thanks and returned it to his belt. The missing part of him was now filled.

The dark man looked inside the pack and was surprised to find everything still there. Garrett must have claimed it and all the contents for himself. Drayco put it on his back and returned to Brind. A quick search through the man's clothing located the rest of the money taken from him. The knife for his boot was lost. It could be replaced easily.

When he finished, Drayco disappeared into the blackness of the night. The revenge killing had his adrenaline pumping. He knew that if anything were stupid enough to mess with him tonight: man or creature, he would enjoy showing them the errors of their ways.

In the morning, the Wanderers found the bodies of their comrades. The look on both men's faces showed a horrible death: eyes wide with fear, their mouths open in an attempt to scream. Both had their throats ripped open. No blood surrounded their bodies, which was something very unusual. They wondered what manner of creature had killed them, and how it could have done so without waking the others. The Wanderers were a superstitious lot. Whispers of spirits and demons began.

The group refused to touch the bodies, choosing instead to burn them where they lay. The wagons were packed quickly and the horses hitched. Breakfast would wait; they wanted to be as far from this cursed place as possible before stopping again. Talismans were hung on the wagons in an attempt to keep both the evil thing that had killed the men from following.

They moved on, never to pass those woods again. They were afraid that if they returned, the demon would finish the job it had started, or the lost spirits would haunt them forever.

Five

Shyanne was running, her clothes and the skin underneath ripped, her hair flying loose about her face. Darkness without end surrounded her. The only light she saw appeared to come from the thick glowing mist around her. Wherever she went, the mist followed, wrapping itself around her lower body like a snake. It swirled into her face then fell back to the ground as is it was a demon-possessed thing of the night. She waved her arms back and forth, trying to clear it. The mist always returned.

She had been running for what seemed like an eternity, her cheeks wet with her tears. She was lost...and alone. She called out; no response came back.

"Drizzle! Jack! Where are you! I need you!" She spun around and around, causing the swirling cloud to spin like a tornado. "Drayco! Help me! I don't want to be alone anymore! I'm frightened!"

Noises started in the mist. The sounds were difficult to make out or pinpoint. The mist made them seem like they came from every direction. Shadows moved, but nothing solid ever materialized. She turned this way and that, trying to see what was in the swirling cloud. Outlines of huge grotesque creatures were in her peripheral vision. They faded when she looked directly at them, never becoming real. She had the feeling that a thousand menacing eyes were watching her.

Shyanne started running again, her breath in ragged gasps. Her chest and legs felt like they were on fire; her heart raced. Slowing to a jog, she panted, "I have to stop soon. But if I do, they'll find me and kill me."

A deep guttural growl sounded to her right. She jerked her head around. A shadow moved. It was so close she thought she felt its hot breath on her neck. She turned and ran with renewed vigor as if her life depended on it.

*   *   *

Drizzle watched Shyanne as she moaned and thrashed about. Her flowing hair was matted and wet with sweat. He tried to calm her by calling her name. She didn't seem to hear him.

"Shyanne, please come back. Jack and I can't go on without you."

Three days had passed since the attack. Drizzle had not left her side except for those few times when he stepped out to relieve himself. Hunger was ignored. Thirst was quenched with the water in the room.

After the Rizbak were killed, he watched as Shyanne tried to make it to Jack and went down in a crumpled heap. He was off the wall and by her side in a flash. Rolling her gently onto her back, he saw blood on her thigh and left shoulder. The thigh had clotted itself off. The shoulder was bleeding profusely. He held pressure to the area until the flow stopped. Her chest rose and fell in a rhythmic pattern. He was glad to see the motion continue.

Drizzle bit her shirt and dragged her closer to the fire. She was in shock, her skin so cold. He had to get her warmed up quickly or she would die before his eyes.

Several pieces of wood helped stoke the dwindling fire. A soothing warmth soon filled the area around the burning mound of orange and yellow. He carefully cut open the shredded breeches above the leg wound with his claws. Several gashes showed. Fortunately, the muscle appeared undamaged. He cleaned them as best he could and covered them with a cloth from Shyanne's pack.

He moved to the shoulder next, carefully removing the torn material. Several deep gouges showed. Again, no muscle appeared damaged, but he knew this wound would take longer to heal. He flushed the area with some water and covered it. Rizbak's were filthy animals. Their wounds usually became infected, no matter how quickly they were taken care of.

Sadly, the infection he tried so hard to fend off happened. That was three days ago.

Shyanne continued to burn with fever. He wet a cloth and placed it on her forehead. She tossed her head back and forth, making it difficult to keep the cloth in place. Drizzle watched her. He wondered what she was dreaming about, what made her so upset and restless. He heard his and Jack's name mentioned on a few occasions, and Drayco's once or twice.

He checked and cleansed her wounds again. The thigh was scabbed over completely. The shoulder remained open. They were healing faster than anticipated; and, thanks to his vigilance, all signs of infection were gone.

On the night of the attack, Drizzle had taken the bodies of the dead rizbak to the edge of the woods. The scent of so much available meat would bring many scavengers. He had not wanted to fight them off while trying to care for Shyanne. The scavengers had come, but they never strayed too close to the building. The idea of an easy meal of dead rizbak, versus a meal of very much alive Humecat, won.

Growls and battles over the meat continued long into the night. He wandered over to the door and looked out during the worst of the fighting. Animals that looked like a cross between a hyena and a badger nipped and bit at each other while others feasted. The scavengers kept at it until just before dawn. They faded back into the woods when the cresting rays of the sun hit them. They never returned. Drizzle went out the next day to discover nothing but bones left.

Drizzle focused his attention back on Shyanne. She seemed to be resting easier, her breath less ragged. He took the dry cloth from her forehead and wet it down again. Squeezing a few of the precious drops of moisture into her mouth, he watched to make sure she wasn't going to choke as she swallowed. He moistened her cracked lips before wetting the cloth again and returning it to her forehead.

The cat remembered when he had first met Shyanne. They both were very young. Shyanne's father had brought him home from work after getting permission from the government to continue his studies away from the lab. The 'big people' were interested in the learning capabilities of their newest genetic creature to be successfully created. They were trying to see how loyal and protective the cat would be and whether it would be worthwhile to continue with the project.

Drizzle stumbled toward Shyanne as soon as his feet hit the ground. She squealed with delight and ran over to him, trying to scoop him up with her tiny arms. He was already over 60 pounds and as big a Labrador. Shyanne was only 5 and small for her size. Her father laughed until tears rolled down his cheeks at her attempts to pick him up.

Drayco played with Drizzle almost as much as Shyanne, but he was a little more aloof than his sister. He was a boy, after all, and boys did not do those mushy things like hugs and kisses. The three of them ran around doing all kinds of things, as kids' do, with their father taking notes on the cat's learning progress the entire time.

When the twins grew into teenagers, Drizzle's body had aged the equivalent of only one year. It was discovered through testing that Humecat's had the possibility of living to a ripe old age of 500. He was about half that age now and considered himself to be in his prime.

The family had a great time in everything they did and all was wonderful—until the virus. He protected her through all the mayhem that followed. Drayco was there in the beginning. But the virus had changed him.

The need for blood became too much and he left one day when it almost cost Shyanne her life. She'd been searching for him ever since. Drizzle hoped, for her sake, Drayco had his blood lust under control. If it wasn't, he hated the thought of having to kill her brother, thus causing her to hate him for the rest of his life.

Drizzle lay down, resting his head on his hands, and resumed his vigilance. His stomach grumbled in protest at the extended fast. Unfortunately, he had become very good at ignoring the empty feeling.

*   *   *

Shyanne continued to wander in the mist, completely lost. She was exhausted from running. The fleeting shadows paced her every step, but they never came fully into view. She needed to rest, to regain her strength; the shadows would not let her. In total despair, she flopped down on the ground and cried.

Her shoulders shook with every racking sob. She did not care if the things in the mist got her anymore. All she wanted to do was sleep. The sobs became less as she closed her eyes, almost making it to the land of dreams.

A voice, soft and distant, brought her out of her despair. Her head shot up. She knew that voice. It was a voice not heard in a long time. It was her brother, Drayco.

"Shyanne.....Shyanne.... Where are you? I can't find you." The sound came at her from all directions because of the mist.

"Here! Here I am!" she yelled with all her might. Shyanne knew to stay where she was. If she moved, Drayco would never be able to find her. She continued to yell until a shadow broke away from the others. It took on the shape of a person.

"Drayco, I'm so glad you found me," Shyanne said as she leaped to her feet. She put her arms around him, resting her head on his chest. "I've been looking for you everywhere. I've been so scared."

Drayco folded her into his arms, and replied, "I've been looking for you too, little sis."

Shyanne's heart sang with those words. She and Drayco were twins, but he had always called her little sis because she was so much shorter than he was. She snuggled against his body. His mannerism was too stiff, too reserved. Sensing something was wrong, she looked up at him, their arms still wrapped around each other.

This was not her Drayco. She could see it in his eyes. They were cold and without life. His smile tilted in a sinister manner. She tried to push away, his hold on her tightened. She could not break free. He grabbed her hair with lightening speed and pulled her head back.

"I've been looking for you too, little sis," he said with the same ugly tone in his voice as was on his face.

The smile she loved to see when she was a little girl, now made her cringe. Drayco leaned toward her, his gaze locked with hers. She wanted to tear her eyes away from those horrible black pits, but couldn't. Her brain screamed for her to fight. Her body refused to respond. A sharp pain ripped through her body as Drayco bit deep into her neck. Her lifeblood started flowing into his mouth. Something inside her finally broke loose. The trance holding her disappeared. Shyanne started to scream and scream and scream.

*   *   *

Shyanne bolted into an upright position, screaming at the top of her lungs, clutching at her neck. Drizzle materialized next her in an instant. He crooned her name, trying to calm her down.

"Shyanne...Shyanne...shhhh, its okay. It's me. It's Drizzle, shhhh," he purred. This time she heard him. She focused her eyes on him.

"Oh Drizzle! I was so scared," she sobbed as she hugged his tawny neck with her good arm. The injured arm was in a sling strapped to her body. "It was Drayco...but it wasn't. Even though I knew it wasn't his fault, he hurt me."

She sobbed uncontrollably for a few minutes, her shoulders shaking. Slowly, the sobbing subsided. Shyanne slipped back into the land of sleep. The haunted look disappeared as she did. He laid her down and tucked the blanket over her. This time she looked as if she truly slept.

"Oh my poor Shyanne, everything will be better when you wake up. The nightmares are gone now and you're safe with us."

Drizzle stretched out next to her. He was relieved that the land of lost souls was not going to claim another victim tonight. He lay on his side and slipped into a much needed sleep.

The sun shining bright in her eyes brought Shyanne awake the next morning. Her throat was parched and every muscle in her body felt stiff. She looked around. Drizzle lay on his side, asleep, his ribs jutting out.

"So thin," she whispered.

She started to sit up. An overpowering weakness prevented it. Drizzle heard her move. He got up and sat beside her.

"Shyanne, I'm glad you returned to us."

Shyanne could tell by the looks of him that he was almost as exhausted as she was. "How long have I been out?"

"Four days."

"Four days! What about the Rizbak? What happened to them?" She tried to sit up again, without success.

"There were only three in their pack. I took their bodies to the edge of the woods. The scavengers took over from there."

He handed her a cup with a small amount of water in it. The cup shook so badly in her grasp that Drizzle helped hold it. She sucked the liquid down with a thirst that seemed to never end. She was exhausted and sweating by the time she finished the contents.

Shyanne curled over on her side. In the blink of an eye, she was fast asleep. He knew she was going to be okay and decided it was time to go hunting. When she woke again, she would need something to eat to build her strength. So did he.

*   *   *

Drizzle left the building, crossed the field, and entered into the woods. He passed by the bones of the rizbak on the way. Thank goodness only bones were left. No cat of his status would ever stoop so low as to eat rizbak, no matter how hungry he was. In his present state, he might have been tempted.

The cat continued into the forest. Pausing a short distance into the foliage, he held his nose up and inhaled the many scents floating in the air. A deer had passed by, but the scent was barely noticeable where it had brushed against a bush. He knew it was long gone so he moved on.

He soon discovered the fresh tracks of a rabbit. Looking around, he spotted it nibbling on some greens. Fortunately, he was down wind of it. He knew that once the rabbit caught his scent, it would flee. He did not have the patience or the strength to hunt for another.

As he crept toward it, the rabbit stopped eating. Drizzle froze, becoming one with the shadow covered scenery. His eyes never left the intended prey. His tawny colored coat allowed him to blend in with his surroundings. After a few wiggles of its nose, the rabbit went back to eating. Drizzle saw his chance and acted on it. He closed the distance between them quickly and with one swipe of his clawed hand, brought the rabbit to a quick and painless death.

The one thing he had failed to take into account was the bush behind the rabbit. It was a thornberry bush. His forward momentum brought his upper body right into it. He yowled with pain and bounded back. Thorns stuck out in various directions from his nose, face, ears, as well as his shoulders. Anyone looking at him would have thought he was half porcupine instead of all humecat.

"How humiliating," he growled.

He sat on his haunches and pulled them out one by one, a scowl firmly locked on his face. Thankfully, his fur hid any evidence of his run in with the bush. When he was finished, he picked up the rabbit with his mouth and started back to camp.

*   *   *

Shyanne was awake when he returned. She looked more alive than she had in four days. Dark circles lined under her eyes, but there was a bright clear look about her. A fire burned and the pot of water was just starting to boil.

"When I woke up and saw you were gone, I figured you were hunting. Thank goodness the wood for this fire was close." She reached over, grabbed another piece of wood, and worked it into the glowing mound. A look of pain flashed across her face as she moved.

"Man, this shoulder sure smarts. But, hey, I can move it better than when I first got up." She raised her left arm to about shoulder level before wincing with pain and lowering it. The sling lay on the ground next to her, discarded.

"The leg is a bit stiff too." She grinned at Drizzle. "I know it will hold me up without too much pain. I found out when I made sure Jack was okay."

Drizzle brought the rabbit over and set it on the ground. She picked it up and slowly skinned it with her boot knife, not to prevent damage to the hide, but to prevent excessive pain or loping a finger off due to her growing fatigue.

She saved a small portion of the meat for herself; the rest was thrown back to Drizzle.

"Here, you need this as much as I do. You look like a walking rack of bones."

"Thanks for the lovely compliment," he said. "You make a great pile of bones yourself."

She looked down at herself and laughed. "Yea, I guess your right."

He ate the rabbit in three bites, bones and all. He knew the meal would come back to haunt him later. Right now, he didn't care.

Shyanne cut up her share and put it into the pot of boiling water. She tossed in some rice and seasonings and wished there were some vegetables to go with the meat.

Stirring the concoction, she said, "Drizzle, you need to hunt some more or you'll be of no good to the both of us. I'll be fine now." The cat's situation was not bad yet. It would not take long if he didn't find something else to eat. Drizzle rose and moved toward the door. She added before he ducked outside, "Thanks, Drizzle, I owe you...again." Her voice was full of emotion.

He looked at her, and said, "Friends don't owe friends." He left without waiting for a reply.

Shyanne stood up on wobbly legs and made her way to her pack. She picked it up then returned to her blanket. The effort left her panting. Her breath calmed after a few minutes rest.

She tried to forget her dream, yet was unable. The feeling of Drayco biting her neck had been too real.

Oh, Drayco, I know it wasn't you. You could never do that.

The fire sizzled as the rice bubbled over the edge of the pan, drawing her attention away from the dream. Removing the pot quickly, she stirred the contents. The smell almost made her gag. She forced herself to eat as much of the meal as possible, even though she didn't have much of an appetite. Water washed everything down.

Her shoulder and leg throbbed from the increased use. As she lay down and slipped back into the land of sleep, she hoped the nightmare would not return.

Night was setting and a new day dawning when she awoke. Drizzle lay close, licking his hands with a contented look on his face. His belly bulged with his recent meal.

"Caught something good, did you?" She smiled.

"Of course."

The fire was almost out. Shyanne picked up some wood lying close and placed it on top of the glowing embers. Drizzle watched her.

"Thought I was going to lose you a couple times there to the land of lost souls. You really had me worried."

"It takes a lot more than a Rizbak to get rid of me."

She flipped the blanket back and inhaled deeply while she stretched. The stench of her body hit her nose. The breath escaped in a rush.

"Wow, do I stink." Shyanne gingerly rose to her feet and walked toward the door. "Where have you been getting the water for the waterskins from?"

"Close," he replied with hesitation. "You should wait until you're stronger."

"Drizzle...I'm strong enough to make flowers wilt. I can't stand the smell of myself any longer."

"Your scent is pretty bad." He held his nose to emphasize his point.

"Then help me get there, silly! We'll both be a lot happier after I wash some of this stink off me."

He went to her side and insisted she lean on him as they went through the door. They crossed the clearing and entered the woods by way of an animal trail. The burbling stream was close, like Drizzle had said. It was still far enough for Shyanne to be worn out by the time they arrived. She plopped down and panted like a gymnast after a grueling workout.

"Phew, I didn't realize how weak I was," she managed to say after several deep breaths to help slow down her rapid heartbeat and feed her oxygen-deprived lungs.

"I told you," the cat said with a satisfied look on his face. She gave him a dirty look and stuck out her tongue.

After a few minutes rest, she walked to the stream's edge. Fortunately, it was not too deep. Rocks of various sizes were visible throughout. Shallow pools swirled behind some of the larger rocks. The current was lazy, not rushed. From the looks of things, she would not have to worry about being carried away when she entered in her weakened state.

She undressed carefully, making sure not to open the partially closed shoulder wound, and eased herself down into one of the pools large enough to submerge completely. The water was tepid. Fall may be around the corner, but the water temperatures had not dropped yet.

"Oh my, does this feel wonderful. You're missing out, Drizzle."

Drizzle watched her from the shore, disgusted. "How can you stand having all that water on you? I just don't understand the fascination."

"It's better than all this dirt I have on me now."

Shyanne scrubbed her body with as much vigor as she could muster. There was not a soap bar to be found, but the mere act of scrubbing the head and body made it feel better. Closer inspection of her wounds showed that the thigh had closed nicely. The shoulder still had a few open areas. After completing the scrubdown, she stretched her arms out and floated with her nose barely out of the water.

After resting, she sat up. "Boy do I feel better."

"You smell better too," Drizzle said under his breath. She heard his comment though, and splashed water all over him. He leaped back, a look of shock on his face.

"How could you! You know I hate water!" he snarled as he walked away in utter disgust, shaking his legs alternately to rid himself of the excess fluid.

Shyanne laughed so hard her sides hurt and tears streamed down her face before managed to sputter, "How could I resist, especially with such an inviting target?"

"Great... Are you happy now?" He shook his droopy wet face, flinging water everywhere. He looked like a spiky wet mop when he finished.

This brought on another bout of gut wrenching laughter.

Once she was under control again, Shyanne said, "Thanks Drizzle. I needed that."

"So happy I could oblige."

She crawled out of the stream and lay on a bed of soft grass in a small clearing to dry. The sun beamed down through the trees, making the job faster. Once dry, she dressed in the same dirty clothes.

"I can't wait to get some clean clothes on."

Shyanne checked on Jack upon their return. He stood

in the field surrounding the building, grazing. As she walked up, he greeted her with a soft nicker. "Nice to see you too, young man."

She gave him a pat on the neck then ducked inside. Seconds later, she emerged with two handfuls of grain. Jack munched on this special treat as if was chocolate to a chocoholic.

She changed as soon as the horse finished, pulling a fresh blanket out of her pack afterward. The soiled items were tossed into the farthest corner to reduce the torture of having to smell them any longer.

"Tomorrow, I'll take the blanket to the stream and wash it. Right now, I need something to eat."

Shyanne made sure the fire was still burning strong before sitting down. Her strength and endurance were returning, but she still tired easily. She reheated the leftover meal from the night before. After she ate her fill, she curled into her blanket and was quickly asleep. Drizzle sprawled out next to her, content to stay in for the night.

Six

Drayco had walked through the night and the better part of the day since the vengeful encounter with the Wanderers. It was dusk when he made his way into town. The people went about their daily business, paying him no attention. They were used to seeing new faces. Travelers passed through on a daily basis while on their way to other destinations.

Life was different in the rural towns than the ruined cities. The people here were adapted to the changes that had occurred after the virus ended so much. They weren't trying to hold on to hopeless dreams, like the return of lost technologies.

A store clerk swept the front porch of his business. A woman hurried home, her arms loaded with food purchased for her family. Kids ran around in the streets playing tag, their parents close by, keeping an eye on them while they talked. Life with his family had been like this: loving and caring. He felt a momentary pang of loss, but shrugged it off. He could not continue living in the past.

Drayco looked up and down the main road through town, trying to locate an inn. All he could see were shops and a stable.

"Excuse me," he asked of a passing woman. "Where might I find an inn to stay at?"

The woman kept her distance, clutching the bag she carried close. She wore a long flowing dress that reminded him of an old school marm. A hat covered her brown hair.

"Keep going this way." She pointed down the road into town. "You'll see it on the right. You can't miss it. Listen for all the noise." She turned and hurried away before he could ask any more questions.

The dark twin looked where she pointed, then back to thank her. She was already gone.

"Sure did leave in a hurry."

He wondered what had alarmed the woman so. Looking down at himself, he laughed. "No wonder she was so nervous. I would be too if I looked like me."

He was filthy.

The faint tracing of a beard lined his face and the dust of the road was all over him, turning his dark clothes a shade of gray. He tried to pat some of it off. All he did was smear it around. With a weary sigh, he gave up and started toward the direction she had indicated.

About a block down the road, he heard loud laughing and singing coming from the right. Drayco followed the noise until he was standing in front of the inn. A banner with a rearing stallion on it hung near the roof.

He entered through the front door and looked around. A group of men were crowded around the bar laughing and carrying on. He walked to a table in the back and was sitting down when the waitress came over to him.

"Welcome! What'll you have?"

"A pint," he said as he put his pack on the floor next to him.

"Sure thing, sweetie, coming right up."

She flashed him a smile full of suggestion and turned back toward the bar. She swung her hips to attract his attention, making her skirt sway with every toss. He watched her for a short distance before focusing on something else. When she glanced over her shoulder and saw her tease wasn't working, she pouted.

Drayco noticed a big burley man with a bandaged arm standing near a smaller shifty eyed man at the far end of the bar. They looked his way several times, then at each other, moving closer to talk. Drayco ignored them. He was more interested in having his thirst quenched.

The waitress returned with his order and a wooden bowl filled with dried berries and nuts. She leaned over while putting the bowl on the table, allowing him to take a good long look at her chest. A very low cut shirt with a rounded collar made it easy for him to see.

Drayco acted as if nothing happened. He picked up the mug and took a long drink to wash away the dust in his mouth. He was familiar with her kind and wanted no part of what she had to offer.

She stood up, exasperated at his lack on response, and put her hands on her hips. "Anything else?"

"Have you heard of a woman around these parts traveling with a big cat?"

"She was here about five days ago.

"Is she still here?" He tried to keep his voice even. He succeeded.

"No." She smiled and leaned over again, still hoping to attract him. "If you're looking for company, I'm free this evening."

Drayco doubted she was free. "Do you know which direction she went?"

"Sorry sweetie, I don't. I wasn't working that day. But I heard she had a bit of a scuffle with some gents and left in a hurry."

"Was she hurt?"

"Naw. I think the gents got the worst of it."

The waitress snickered as she looked over her shoulder toward the bar. Drayco wondered who she was looking at. She was in the way so he couldn't see. A man yelled at her, preventing him from asking anything else.

"Hey Sheila! Get over here! Customers are waiting!" the man behind the bar yelled. "I don't pay ya to stand around gab'n!"

Sheila gave the bartender a dirty look after he turned his attention elsewhere. "He's such a slave driver."

Drayco slid two gold coins across the table toward her. "Thanks for the drink...and the information."

"Anytime, mister. If you need anything else, just let me know. I'm always available." She winked at him.

Sheila slipped one of the coins down the front of her dress and went back to the bar with the other. The burley man grabbed her around the waist, pulling her against him. She giggled and pretended to fight. Drayco could tell she wasn't trying very hard. Burley whispered something in her ear as he held out a coin. She whispered back, pulling the man's hand toward her exposed cleavage. He dropped the coin between her breasts and copped a feel before withdrawing his hand. They both started laughing.

Must be arranging for something else since I wasn't interested, he thought to himself. He finished his drink and stood.

The weariness of his sleepless night and all day trek was catching up to him, fast. The nuts and fruit he ate while drinking the pint had taken the edge off his hunger. After he slept, a large meal would be the next thing on the agenda. He was more tired than hungry, right now.

The eatery and bar were on one side of the building; the rooms for sleeping were on the other side. Drayco picked up his pack and went through the connecting doorway. A lad sat behind a counter. He walked up to him.

"How much for a room?"

"Three gold coins a night, includes breakfast."

"I only need one night. If I need to stay longer, will it cause any problems?"

"We're not crowded. If you have the money, we have a room for you."

Drayco yawned as he paid for the room.

"Room Four. Up the stairs and down the hall." The lad sounded bored.

The dark twin swung his pack over a shoulder and trudged up the stairs. He found the room at the end of the hall. Once inside, he turned and shut the door, locked it, and tossed his pack on the floor. After the recently taxing experiences, all he wanted was a good night sleep. He crossed the room and flopped down on the bed.

"Ah Shyanne," he sighed. "I always knew you were a tough cookie and could hold your own in a fight."

His eyes felt so heavy. With a groan, he sat up and peeled off his boots. He did not have the energy to undress further, so didn't. Unbuckling the strap to his sword, Drayco curled over on his side and placed the weapon next to the pillow, within easy reach. Snoring soon echoed throughout the room.

* * *

"Click"

Drayco was in a deep sleep and never heard the noise. The door slowly opened. The burley man from the bar peered into the room. The shifty eyed man was standing behind him.

"He's asleep. Let's do this now."

They entered the room quietly and shut the door, locking it again. Shifty set a pack on the floor next to Drayco's. Both men moved to either side of the bed. With a signal from the burley man, they attacked. Drayco woke up, though not quick enough. Burley punched the dark twin in the face and hit him across the back of his neck before he could counterattack. He went down, face first; knocked out.

"Tie him up," Burley said as he picked up Drayco's sword and leaned it against the wall.

The shifty eyed man pulled out some twine from his bag and went to work. He rolled Drayco over onto his back, tying his wrist together with the palms facing outward. The feet followed.

"Hey Brom, he sure does look like that girl we want, doesn't he?" Shifty said once he finished.

"Go through his bag, Moss. Maybe there's something in there that'll tell us who he is."

Moss rummaged through Drayco's bag. "Nothin here but clothes, some metal things, and foodstuff. I guess we'll just have to wait till he wakes up to get more information."

Brom wasn't in a waiting mood. "Throw some water in his face. I want him awake for questioning." He moved a chair closer to the bed and sat down. Grabbing the sword, he took a better look at it. "Nice piece of work. I'll just have to make this mine after we kill this guy."

Moss splashed water onto Drayco face. He came around, sputtering. With a glance, he took in the situation, and asked, "What do you want? Why have you tied me up?"

"I want information on the girl you were asking about downstairs. I owe her." Brom rubbed his bandaged arm while he spoke. "And we don't want you leaving until we have it."

"And I owe her cat," Sam threw in as he rubbed his backside.

"I don't know what you're talking about."

In the blink of an eye, Brom was out of the chair. The

sword clattered to the floor as he dropped it and grabbed Drayco by the front of his shirt, lifting him into a sitting position.

"Oh I think you do, my friend. And if you don't talk to us now, we'll make sure you regret it."

These must be the men Shyanne shuffled with, Drayco thought as he glared silently at them. *I won't tell them anything.*

The burley man became enraged. He hit the prisoner repeatedly. By the time he finished, Drayco had a busted lip, a bloody nose and a swelled eye, but he had kept his mouth shut.

"That's enough! You can't get any information out of a dead man!" Moss emphasized through clenched teeth.

"We'll have to take him with us then. If we stay here, we'll get caught...and I want that information." He glared at the beaten man with deadly intent.

Brom stuffed a wad of cloth into Drayco's mouth. He secured it with some twine to prevent him from spitting it out. Fresh blood ran down the side of Drayco's face where it bit into the split lip. The bonds around his feet were cut; his wrists remained tied. He winched with pain as he was yanked into a standing position.

"Don't try any funny stuff or I'll kill ya where you stand." Brom pulled out a small knife and held it at the dark man's throat.

Moss shoved Drayco's boots into a pack. Both packs were in his arms before he opened the door. The hall was clear. He waved them on. The burley man held the knife against Drayco's throat as they made their way through the halls to the back door of the inn.

Two horses waited, saddled and ready. A third was bare. The two men had obviously planned their escape before coming for him. Drayco was thrown across the back of the horse without a saddle. A rope secured to his wrists went under the belly of the beast, ending at his feet.

"Can't have you falling off now can we. You might get hurt."

Brom grabbed a handful of hair and forced the captive to look up. He slapped the dark man hard across the face before letting go. Both men chuckled as they got into their saddles. They rode out of town in the same direction they had watched Shyanne go five days earlier. Drayco's body bounced with the rhythm of his horse. He mercifully passed out when his bruised and battered body could take no more.

*   *   *

The ground beneath him was firm and steady when Drayco returned to consciousness. The continuous bounding of hooves as they hit the road was missing. Stars shined above. He was lying on his side, obviously left were he had fallen from the back of the horse. His wrist and feet remained bound, but the gag had been mercifully removed. The cut in the corner of his lip was sore from where the twine had dug deep into it, keeping it from healing. It was difficult to look out his left eye because of the swelling from the beating.

He turned his head. His captors were eating by a fire. Once they noticed he was awake, Brom came over to him with a cup in his hand.

"Have you reconsidered talking to us?"

Drayco shook his head no. Even if he had wanted to, the strength needed to talk was beyond him. His throat was parched and his belly growled. He had not eaten at the inn. Now wished he had.

"I bet you could use some of this food and drink." Brom put the cup close to Drayco's mouth but pulled it back when he tried to put his lips on the rim. "Not until you talk to us about the girl."

Drayco laid his head back on the ground and turned away.

"Suit yourself." Brom downed the contents of the cup in one swallow.

Moss sat by the fire shoveling spoonfuls of stew in his mouth. He looked at Drayco and swallowed. "You can have some of this too if you tell us about the girl."

The dark twin ignored both men. Brom rejoined the shifty eyed man by the fire. They ate their meal slowly, taking great pleasure in taunting their captive with loud sips and smacking lips. Drayco wished unconsciousness would end his suffering at having to listen to these men. His strength of mind remained intact; his strength of body was giving out.

No food and water was taking its toll on him. The lack of blood was even worse. What he had drank from the Wanderers would only hold him for so much longer, especially under this stressful situation. Drayco knew from past experiences what happened next.

The twine cut into his wrists. He gave no indication, refusing to give these men more pleasure at his expense. His feet and hands were like ice. The boots he had taken off back at the inn were in his bag. The captors hadn't felt he needed them. He tried to shift his position to a more comfortable one, but he was tied too tight and couldn't.

They had taken everything with them to make it look like he had left of his own instead of being abducted against his wishes. Since he was a stranger, no one would be the wiser. The two men sitting by the fire were talking about his sister; he lay still, listening to their conversation.

"When we find her, I'm going to cut her arm—and whatever else I want—like she did mine," Brom stated sourly.

"I plan on cutting that cat open."

"I can't kill her though, the Boss wouldn't like that. He needs her alive."

"Yea." Moss shuddered as he remembered what he had seen the in the past. "He'll see to it she suffers real good."

"Yea. He can be a mean one. I've seen what he's done to guys who try to cross him. It ain't pretty."

They both let out with a nervous chuckle and went back to drinking their ale.

The rest of their conversation was too low for Drayco to hear. He wondered who the Boss was and what he needed with his sister. These men seemed afraid of him, which led Drayco to believe that the Boss must be a very powerful and cruel person to cause such a reaction.

"We'd best turn in. We have a long ride ahead of us." Brom came over to Drayco and checked the twine holding his extremities together. He smacked him across the face before going back to the fire.

Moss threw some wood into the flames. The brightness would keep smaller creatures of the night away. Both men tossed a blanket over themselves and were asleep in no time. They didn't bother posting a watch over their captive.

They knew he wasn't going anywhere.

They left Drayco uncovered on the cold ground. He was too far from the fire to benefit from any warmth emanating from it, and began shivering within minutes. His belly growled constantly. His throat was so dry it was hard to swallow. He knew it was going to be an even longer and harder day tomorrow, especially since the energy in his body was almost used up.

When I get the chance, I will make those two pay the ultimate price. I only hope I get the chance.

He lay contemplating what he would do when a sharp pain reminded him of the agonizing death he would suffer if he didn't get some life sustaining blood soon. It was long into the night before he finally fell asleep.

The next morning the captors ate their breakfast, leaving Drayco to do without. Suddenly, Moss came over and helped the dark man sit up. Every muscle in his body hurt because of being in one position far too long. He kept silent, gritting his teeth, not wanting to give this man any pleasure by crying out.

The shifty-eyes man brought a half-full cup of water to Drayco's lips and poured it into his mouth. Drayco coughed as the liquid tried to go down the wrong way. He recovered and drank greedily. It wasn't much, but it helped.

"We can't have you dying on us before we get that information, now can we." He winked at Drayco.

"Don't waste the water on him! If he won't talk, let em suffer!"

Moss scowled, but didn't say anything. He knew better that to cross his partner, having received too many of the same blows given to Drayco. He stood up and went back to the fire.

When they were finished with their meal, they packed everything and readied the horses. They came for him and yanked him off the ground in a not so gentle manner. His body was stiff and weak from lack of food, water...and blood. He tried to stand on his own. Instead, he crumpled to his knees.

"Great!"

"Maybe we should give him something to eat, Brom."

"Naw. Let em starve. He'll be dead soon enough."

Drayco knew that to be true. He needed to drink blood

today or he would not see another sunrise. He felt light-headed. The muscles in his legs and arms were going in and out of agonizing spasms. His stomach continued to make its presence known. All of these were signs he had experienced before when he had gone too long without drinking blood. The lack of food wasn't helping either.

They dragged him painfully by the arms to the horse. Brom picked Drayco up and threw him over its back. The force of the landing took his breath away. If food had been in his belly, it would have come up. He lay there gasping while the men tied him to the beast. They laughed as his stomach rebelled, causing him to gag while they worked.

"I can't wait to get this job over and done with," Brom said. "I want to get back to that Sheila girl. She's a fine number. When I had my hands on her last night, I almost didn't want to do this job. Not right away as least."

He lifted his eyebrows a couple of times and flashed his filthy yellow teeth in a wicked grin. The fingers on both his hands flexed as if they were squeezing something soft. Moss smiled, flexing his own fingers. They got up on their horses, still chuckling, and rode off, tugging Drayco's animal along behind them.

Seven

Shyanne felt better than she had in almost a week. The defense system in her body that helped her to survive the virus also helped her heal faster than post-virus people. Drizzle lay next to her, keeping her warm. The bite of the coming fall was in the morning air.

She got up and restarted the fire. Because of her forced stay, she needed to gather more wood. The pile in the corner was all but gone. The waterskins also needed to be filled. She was pretty sure these jobs could be accomplished without too much difficulty.

After breakfast, Shyanne thought it would be a good idea to test her strength, and to build up her endurance. Spotting a piece of rotten wood hanging down from the roof, an idea came to her. She grabbed her sword and walked over to the beam, rotating the bad shoulder around in a circle to test its strength. The shoulder was still sore, but the wounds were now closed. She jabbed and thrust and with a swing of her sword hit the board several times, then leaped back. A piece of old tattered rope kept it tied to what was left of the roof.

Drizzle lounged by the fire and watched her with his half-opened eyes. He yawned as if completely bored with the whole process, and said, "You know....If you had claws you wouldn't have to do that."

Rising, he stretched himself out in typical cat fashion and straightened. He glided to the board and with a single swipe of his hand took off two inches from the bottom. The board swung about crazily but did not fall.

"Showoff."

He shrugged his shoulders and sauntered back to the fire.

Shyanne continued with her sparring for a short while longer. When she finished, she leaned her sword against the wall and flopped down on her back, panting, her body covered with sweat.

"Boy, did I need that. I was getting soft from lack of exercise."

She sat up and rotated her wounded shoulder again after recovering her breath. It was still sore, but it moved better. The wounded leg gave her no problems at all.

Looking at Drizzle, she said, "I need to wash that blanket when we fill the waterskins. The clothes are too torn up from the fight to be saved." Standing, she grabbed the tattered rags and tossed them onto the fire. Sparks and bits of ash flew into the air, flittering about like butterflies in a field of flowers. "Besides, it's about time we got a move on. I'm strong enough now to stay on Jack without falling off."

She put the carrying straps for the waterskins over her uninjured shoulder. Gathering up the blanket and a pack with some clean clothes in it, the pair walked to the stream. Drizzle sprawled under the wide overhang of a tree that was a short distance from the edge of the water. He remembered the last time they were here and did not feel it was time for another bath.

Shyanne undressed and entered the water, washing everything she brought with her, including herself. Afterwards, she dressed in the clean clothes from the pack and hung the wet items over some tree branches to dry. A warm gentle breeze caused the material to wave with its passing.

"This would be the perfect time to scout around and find some foodstuff to add to our supplies." She remembered seeing some bushes with a glint of red growing on them not far off from the path leading to the stream. "Maybe those were berries. Let's go check them out."

Drizzle cringed when he saw the bushes.

"Thornberry's!" Shyanne exclaimed.

"Oh great...those bushes," he grumbled under his

breath with a look of disgust.

"Why do you say that?"

"Never mind." He hoped no evidence was lying around to show his earlier disgrace with the rabbit.

She picked the berries, making sure to avoid the wicked thorns protecting the bounty. Several handfuls made their way into her mouth during the process. This time of year, close to fall, they were ripe and sweet. When she had her fill, Shyanne picked more and placed them in a small pouch she had brought. Drizzle stayed as far away from the bushes as possible. Tubers and herbs were located and added to the bag. She scouted around the rest of the area; nothing more was found.

The blanket and clothes were not quite dry when they returned. She flipped them over and sat down with her back against a tree trunk. A long piece of grass popped into her mouth, sticking out between her lips. Drizzle lay down next to her, his tail swishing gently. They both watched the leaves as they swayed in the breeze.

"I keep getting this feeling that something is wrong with Drayco." Her voice was soft. A frown settled on her smooth features. "It gets stronger with each passing day."

"What do you suppose it means?"

"I don't know. I feel that he's hurt and suffering." Looking at the cat, she asked, "Do you suppose he's close and that's why the feeling is getting stronger?"

"One never knows. The bond between twins was never fully understood."

"I wonder if that's how I know he's still alive, our bond as twins."

Shyanne rose and checked the damp things again. This time they were dry. She folded everything and placed the clothes in the pack. Then she went to get the waterskins. They were lying next to the stream where she had left them, filled. The straps went over her shoulder and she positioned them so they rested comfortably. Scooping up the folded blanket and pack, she and the cat started toward the camp.

"This stuff sure is heavy," she said to Drizzle as they walked. "Sure would be nice if I had help carrying it."

"I'm a hunter—not a pack animal," Drizzle responded.

Shyanne smiled, *Good ole Drizzle. Never changes.*

They heard voices coming from somewhere close as the clearing for the camp came into sight. They had not emerged from the woods yet and dropped to the ground quickly just before several people on horseback rode into view.

*   *   *

Drayco went in and out of consciousness due to his beaten and battered body, and the intense pain from lack of drinking blood. He felt so old. His head swung with every motion of the horse's gait. When the motion stopped, he turned his head to see why. The small effort used left him exhausted. A clearing with a run down building in its center was in front of them.

Moss looked at Brom. "What do you think? Do you think it's occupied?"

"Won't know till we check it out, will we?"

They moved into the clearing. The return of the swaying motion had Drayco wishing his journey would end— soon—one way or another. The trio pulled even with the building. Moss jumped off, his sword out as he landed, and ran up to one side of the doorway. With his back against the wall, he cautiously looked inside then ducked back again, reminding Drayco of the old time detective movies he used to watch on late night TV. In a flash, Moss disappeared inside. He came out a few seconds later with something in his hand.

"Someone's staying here alright. All kinds of stuff lay'n around inside, and a horse is housed in the back." He paused and gave Brom a slight smile. "And I found this." He held up a sword, the figure of a crouching puma with its teeth bared as its handle.

"That's hers! I'd know that blade anywhere!" Brom focused on his bandaged arm, then on Moss.

The burly man stood tall in the stirrups and looked around the clearing. Seeing no one, he got off his animal and led it into the building. "Get your horse inside, quick. I want to surprise her when she comes back."

Drayco felt his horse pulled into the building. Once inside, the bonds holding him to the animal were cut. He dropped to the ground like a lead weight. The pain caused from the hard landing ravaged his body more than ever. He lay where he landed, unable to move, grimacing.

"Stash them animals with the other one," Brom said as he inspected the items in the room. "We need to get him out of the way too." He walked over and kicked Drayco in the side, causing the dark man to draw himself into a ball.

Moss led the horses to the back room. The girl's horse acted somewhat strange and held its distance from him while he was there. When he came back to the main room, he watched as Brom grabbed Drayco forcefully by the front of his shirt and dragged him to the far corner. He threw him into it, causing the dark man's head to slam back hard into the wall.

White spots danced before Drayco's eyes; he was able to blink them away before the world of darkness settled in.

The burley man stood over him with his hands on his hips, and smiled, "When that girlie returns, we're gonna have a bit of fun with her. I want to remind her of her folly before we take her to the boss."

The words came out with such sliminess that an ugly picture forced its way into Drayco's mind. He hated this man more than ever and vowed he would kill him without an ounce of mercy when the chance arose. The intensity of hatred in his eyes made them shine.

"Who is this boss you talk about? What does he want with the woman?" Drayco managed to ask.

"What difference does it make? She somethin important to you?" The slimy smile never left his face.

Drayco held his tongue, glaring at the burley man towering above him.

"You do look a lot like her," Moss added. "I'll bet you two are related somehow. That's why you're so interested in her. It makes sense."

"Quit with all the chattering. How're we gonna surprise her with all this noise going on?" Brom growled, moving toward the doorway leading outside.

"We'll never be able to surprise her with you yelling like that," Moss whispered under his breath.

The two men took up positions on either side of the door and waited.

Drayco leaned his head forward, resting his chin on his chest; thinking. *What does this boss person want with my sister...and how much does he know about her?*

These questions would have to wait. He needed to concentrate on finding a way to warn his sister about what awaited her first.

*   *   *

Shyanne and Drizzle watched as the shifty eyed man went into the building and came out again with her sword held high.

"Damn."

She had left the blade in the building because Drizzle was with her, and nothing would mess with her when that cat was around.

"How stupid can I be?"

The only weapon with her now was her boot knife. It would be ineffective against their swords. Moreover, Drizzle could only do so much against two well-armed men. Shyanne watched as the horses were led into the building. The last animal had someone draped over its back.

"That's Drayco!" she hissed. "What have those things done to him?" She almost gave away her position at the shock of seeing her brother for the first time in so many years. "He looks like he's in bad shape. Drizzle, we have to help him."

"Those are the men from the inn, aren't they?"

"Yea."

"If we're going to help him, we have to do it fast. He doesn't look like he'll make it to morning. Do you have a plan?"

"No. But I'll think of one as we go."

Shyanne took the pack, blanket, and waterskins and hid them under some bushes. If these men went investigating, she did not want them to discover her things and know that she was here.

The woman and cat crept through the woods until they were on the opposite wall from the opening. Keeping low to the ground, they made a dash for the building. Once they reached it, they stopped and listened. No sounds of alarm filled the air. Shyanne hugged the wall as she slid around toward a hole they noticed while circling. She peeked in quickly. The horses were on the other side. Two animals were biting at their bits. Their heads hung low and sweat ran from under their saddle pads.

Just like them to not care about their animals.

As decided before they separated, Drizzle made his way around the building close to where the men were hiding. He crouched and waited for Shyanne's signal. He wasn't sure what it would be but knew it would come.

The hole was not very big. Nevertheless, she knew she could make it through due to her smaller size. She crawled in with the animals. Jack pushed against her with his head and whinnied. She rubbed his nose to quiet him.

"What was that?" Moss looked in the direction of the horses.

Shyanne flattened herself against the wall as best she could and prayed they would not come investigate.

"It's just the horses. Pay attention." Both men turned back to the entrance and resumed their watch for her.

With relief, she peered in Drayco's direction. His head leaned back against the wall; his eyes were closed. One of his eyes was purple and badly swollen. His lip was split near the corner; dried blood crusted his chin. He seemed so pale. Her blood boiled at the sight of the beating he had endured. She wanted to reassure him, to let him know she was there, but couldn't chance it. She was trying to think of her next move when a devilish plan came to her.

I hope Drizzle knows what to do when the commotion starts.

Shyanne hoped Drayco would be safe during the melee that was about to occur. He was in the far corner away from the other men, which helped her with her decision. She reached up and grabbed Jack's halter. With her free arm, she started to shout and wave it wildly. The other horses were so startled by the sudden motion that they bolted from the room. Moss and Brom were equally as startled. They recovered quickly, though, and threw themselves out of harms way. Or so they thought.

The horses started for the only exit to the outside world, the door where the men once stood. The animals had almost reached it when Drizzle blocked their way. He let out with a deep growl followed by a loud roar. The sight of the snarling humecat was too much for them. Their eyes rolled back until only the whites showed and they started to buck and rear in any direction they could, except the one where the big cat was.

The two men never had a chance. Shyanne turned her head away, unable to watch as they were kicked and stomped several times. Unfortunately, she could still hear their bones breaking. Screams bounced off the walls, then only moans when the men were unable to scream anymore.

Drizzle waited until he knew the men could not get up before herding the horses into the back room again. The cat stayed by the opening between the rooms. His presence prevented the horses from stampeding through the main room and hurting Shyanne or Drayco.

Shyanne waited with Jack until the animals were in the farthest corner, trembling with fear before she checked on the two men and Drayco. Her boot knife appeared; it sliced through the bonds holding her brother with ease.

"Are they dead?" he asked, barely able to speak.

"No. But they aren't far from it."

Putting the knife away, she grabbed his ice-cold hands and started rubbing them. He winched when the pinpricks of returning circulation grew in intensity. The hands remained as pale as the rest of him even after warmth had settled in. She poured a small amount of water into a cup.

"Here, drink this."

He tried to hold the cup but his hands shook uncontrollably. Shyanne took it from him and gently poured a small amount into his mouth. After a couple of swallows, he motioned for her to stop.

"The water is helping, but I need something else to get my strength back."

"Is it anything I can get? Bread, cheese?"

"No," he said in a matter of fact tone. "I need blood. It is the only thing that can help me at this point."

Using the wall as a support, Drayco struggled to his feet. He stumbled to the burley man's side, his weak and battered body fighting him the whole way. Brom lay sprawled to the left of the door, moaning. Judging from the odd angle of his arms, both were broken. Blood trickled from the corner of his mouth.

"What have you done? Why can't I move my legs?"

"My guess would be that your back is broken," Drayco

said calmly. "And I didn't do anything. The horses did."
Shyanne walked up behind her brother.

"You! I should have known you were behind this!" He
started to cough. Blood sprayed outward like a fan. He was
bleeding internally.

Moss started to whimper. Shyanne went to check on
him. He screamed with pain when he tried to move. "My
legs! My legs!" Blood spattered into the air with each word.
"Aaahh... my chest, it hurts so bad!" Tears mingled with
the blood on his face.

"If he can, I want him to watch what I'm going to do."
Drayco knelt beside the burley man.

Shyanne knelt beside Moss. The crying man looked
into her eyes. He was in a lot of pain, but he knew what
was going on.

"Don't move. You'll only make the pain worse if you
do."

She placed her hands on either side of the wounded
man's head and forced him to look toward her brother. Her
own head hung low, unable to watch what was about to
occur. It had been a long time since she saw this side of
her twin; the memories it brought back were frightening.

"I need information," Drayco said, "and you have it. I
want to know who this Boss is and what he wants with my
sister."

"I knew it! I knew you two were related! You'll get
nothin out of me!"

"Oh I think I can help you change your mind." Drayco
gave one of the broken arms a wicked twist.

Brom emitted a blood-curdling scream followed by
laughter. He looked at his tormentor with a crazy glaze in
his eyes, and repeated, "You won't get nothin out of
me...no matter what you do!" He spat blood at Drayco,
missing him by a mile.

"I guess since you won't cooperate with me, there's no
further use for you."

"What does that mean? What are you going to do?" A
glint of fear blended in with the crazy look. "You can't kill
me. If you do, you won't get the information you want!"

"You're not going to help me anyways so what difference does it make."

Drayco grabbed Brom by the hair and pulled his head

abruptly to the side. The dark man sank his teeth into the exposed neck. He ripped a chunk of flesh out and started to drink the life juices pumping from the wound. Brom tried to pull his head away. The condition of his body prevented it.

Strength returned to the dark twin with every greedy swallow. As the struggles grew less and less, so did the flow of blood. Drayco released his hold on the lifeless body when the struggles ceased altogether.

Shyanne tried not to listen to the slurping noises coming from the other side of the room. She knew what her brother was doing to the burley man. Moss' eyes were wide with fear as she forced him to watch what happened to his partner. She could imagine what was running through his mind. She had almost been a victim of Drayco's need when it first reared its ugly head. The dream from her fevered state came back in a rush. Because of it, she actually felt sorry for the shifty eyed man in her grasp.

Shyanne brought her head up to look at her brother when he stood. She released her grip on the injured man's head. Drayco's color was better, though he still looked pale. A small amount of blood ran down from the corner of his mouth. He left it there.

Drayco walked toward Moss; nothing of the unsteadiness from earlier showed. He stopped a few paces short. "I hope you'll be more cooperative than your partner was."

Moss looked up, his eyes still wide. He shook his head up and down.

"Who is this Boss you two were talking about?"

"I...I...I don't know."

"Don't play games with me." Drayco moved closer to the frightened man.

Moss' gaze went from the dark man's eyes, to Brom's blood in the corner of his mouth, and back. "I'm not! I really don't know who he is. We never met em. All I know is that he contacts us through a messenger whenever he needs a job done."

"Are you able to contact this messenger?"

"I can, but it ain't easy. It's done by code."

"If you value what's left of your life, you'll tell me what that code is and where I have to use it."

"My life ain't worth much, right now." He closed his eyes and seemed to ponder his next thought. Opening them, he said to Drayco, "You know...I never wanted to hurt you. I only wanted to get the girl and take her to the Boss." A grimace of pain swept across his drawn face. It disappeared before he continued.

"You have to go to a town far to the west of here called Grandfield. Find the inn. It's the only one there so you'll get the right one." He started to say more, but a sharp intake of breath cut his words off. He held it for a second then moaned as he let it out.

"My legs hurt real bad."

"Your legs are broken in several places and you're bleeding pretty heavily," Shyanne told him.

Moss looked down. Blood covered the skin surrounding the bone that was sticking out of the left thigh. The right one was at a weird angle. Large purple areas swelled through the torn breeches, showing bleeding under the skin. He paled even more and closed his eyes. A calmness settled over him.

"I'm not gonna to make it, am I?"

Shyanne shook her head no. Neither she nor her brother had the knowledge or equipment to treat wounds so severe in nature.

Moss turned his head toward Drayco, a knowing look in his eyes, "I'll give you the code if you promise to make my passing as quick and painless as possible."

Drayco nodded his head to the request. He understood what was wanted of him.

Satisfied, he said, "You have to talk to the bartender. The code you have to say is, 'The painted pony is prancing, but only in the morning.' He'll follow with, 'Have you traveled far on that painted pony?' All you have to do is shake your head no and walk away."

A wave of agonizing pain struck Moss so hard he had to stop. Tears streamed down his face when he was finally able to go on.

"Get a room and wait. The messenger will come," he whispered. "He will lead you to the Boss."

Shyanne gave his hand a squeeze. "Thank you."

Moss smiled at her. "I know I've done some bad things in my life...that I can never change. I only hope this makes up for some of em."

He tilted his head back, exposing the neck. Shyanne closed her eyes and held Moss' hand tight. Drayco took his cue. He leaned over and bit into the exposed neck, drinking the blood spurting out of the cut artery. In moments, it was over. He sat up when he finished and wiped his mouth.

"This man deserves a proper burial," Shyanne said. "He may have done some bad things, but, in the end, he made up for it."

Drayco nodded his head in agreement. "I only hope the information he gave us is correct."

"I think it is."

"I hope so, for your sake."

The dark twin made his way to the discarded packs and found his soft leather boots. After putting them on, he and Shyanne went outside and dug a shallow pit in the ground near the back of the building. Drayco brought Moss' body outside and placed in it within. They covered the grave with rocks and roof timber to prevent scavengers from digging it up once it was filled. After a moment of silence, the pair returned inside. They dragged the burley man's body to the edge of the forest and left it near a pile of dried bones.

Shyanne fetched the things hidden in the bushes prior to the incident and brought them inside. After putting everything away, she carried in some dirt and covered the blood on the floor. She did not want the scent to draw scavengers into the building. Her last encounter had almost cost her everything.

Drayco went toward the horses to check on them. The three newcomers had calmed down. Jack, on the other hand, went stiff legged and snorted a warning.

"Drayco...wait! Don't go near Jack. He'll hurt you if you do."

Drayco stopped at the entrance to the other room. "I need to check the horses and make sure they weren't hurt during their scare."

"Let me get them out for you. Jack will not let a man near him without trying to kick the crap out of him." She slipped past and grabbed the hanging reins.

"Great.....a sexist horse," he chuckled, shaking his head.

Shyanne led the three horses into the main area. Jack stayed where he was. He wanted no part of the strange man standing so close to his rider. The twins removed the saddles and blankets from each animal and went over their bodies, inch by inch, making sure they were okay. They were sweaty from their scare; otherwise, they were unhurt. Some dry grass gathered from outside was rubbed against their wet coats to reduce the moisture.

"How are you doing over there? How's your eye?" Shyanne asked. "It looks better."

"It'll be okay. The blood makes everything heal faster."

One of the horses, a big bay with a black mane and tail, seemed less skittish than the others. It was the one ridden by Brom. While Drayco worked on the coat, it kept nosing at his shirt, trying to find a treat hidden in the fabric. With an affectionate smack on the neck, the dark man decided to make the animal his.

Drizzle came in from outside and sprawled near the door. Two of the animals became restless and jerked at their reins. The bay remained still, looking over his shoulder with his ears pointed toward the cat, watching his every move. Drayco's decision to keep the animal was finalized.

"Shyanne, I'm going to let these two go and keep the bay. They're too skittish around Drizzle to be of any use to us." Stepping between the two excited horses, he warned, "Step back, I'm going to remove their bridles. Drizzle, you'd better move too."

After his sister was out of the way, Drayco pulled the bridle off both horses at once. Drizzle scrambled from the doorway before the two horses trampled him in their haste to get outside. The sound of pounding hoofs faded as they galloped off. The bay stood his ground, watching Drizzle as he moved around the room. Drayco whispered softly in his ear and gave the horse another pat on the neck.

"You're a brave one, aren't you? I will call you Bravaro."

He untied the reins and led the bay toward the back room where he removed the bridle and with a swat on the rump, put Bravaro in with Jack. The horse jumped at the touch. He turned on a dime to watch both him and the cat equally. Jack did the same, though only for him. Drayco remembered Shyanne's warning and stayed out of the area. His sister stood by the outside exit when he faced toward the main room again.

"We need to get more wood before dark. There isn't enough to last the night."

The twins went to the edge of the forest and picked up as much wood as they could find. After it was stacked in the corner, Shyanne rekindled the fire. Drayco sat down on a blanket and watched her while she worked.

"How are you doing? I heard about the run in you had with those two. Where you hurt?" he asked.

She chuckled. "No. I think they got the worst end of the deal." Her smile faded. "Your color looks better."

"Blood will do that to you." He wrapped his arms around his legs and drew them against his chest, withdrawing in on himself.

Shyanne paused to look at her brother. "I missed you, Drayco." She wanted to hug him, but was afraid. She didn't want the awful dream to become a reality.

He looked up at her, and said, "I missed you too, little sis."

The look of sincerity and pain in his eyes melted her fear. She went to him, wrapping her arms around him and hugging him tight. He buried his face in her shoulder, holding her just as tight. Tears ran down Shyanne's face by the time they separated. It felt good to have him back after so long.

Wiping the moisture off her checks, she said, "We need to get this fire going better. Nasty creatures roam around these woods at night." Without thought, she rubbed her left shoulder as she spoke. Drayco saw the gesture. He remained silent.

Soon afterwards, the wonderful aroma of stew, filled with tubers, rice, cheese, and trail bread thrown in for good measure, saturated the small area. Drayco practically drooled when he saw the heaping mound of food handed to him. It had been a long time since he'd tasted Shyanne's cooking. He looked forward to doing it again. Mouthful after mouthful was savored until nothing remained on the plate.

Placing the dish on the ground beside him, Drayco said, "After a meal fit for a king, dessert is in order." He retrieved his pack and pulled out two of the canned peaches. He threw one to his sister.

She read the worn label, and exclaimed, "Peaches! I can't remember the last time I ate some of these. Where did you get them?"

"I found them in one of the big cities."

"You were in a big city? You were brave—or maybe a little stupid. The virus turned them into havens for mutations and people who'd kill you rather than put up with you."

"If you remember, Shyanne, we're mutations too."

Shyanne looked down at the open can of peaches. "We could never be as bad as those people."

"Not all the people in the cities are bad." He remembered the vision of a smiling little girl with strawberry blonde hair holding a can of peaches.

Drizzle lounged near the fire, listening to their conversation. He remembered the time when Drayco had lost control and almost killed his sister. He knew if it happened again, he would not hesitate to kill the dark twin. No matter what Shyanne thought.

"Let's get some sleep. We have a long ride to this town called Grandfield," Drayco said.

"I'm going to hunt tonight." Drizzle started toward the door leading outside. "I'll be back before dawn."

"Be careful," Shyanne said.

"I will." He slipped into the darkness that had settled while the twins were eating.

Shyanne wrapped herself in her blanket and rolled over onto her side, using her arm as a pillow. She wanted to catch up with her brother and find out what had happened to him since he left. Instead, she fell asleep after only a few minutes of lying still. Drayco lay on his back, looking up at the night sky. Most of his strength had returned after drinking the blood, although sleep eluded him. He crawled quietly out from under the blanket and went outside.

A large tree with thick branches stood at the edge of the clearing. He sat down under its canopy, resting his back against the hard base. With his arms draped over his bent knees, he looked over the surrounding area. A noise in the forest behind him caught his attention. He wasn't concerned; he knew what caused it.

"I won't hurt her, Drizzle."

The cat materialized out of the darkness. "Don't worry, I'll be watching. I still remember what happened a long time ago. One wrong move out of you and you'll never have to worry about doing it again."

Drayco heard every word. He kept his facial expression blank, choosing not to respond to them.

Drizzle watched closely for his reaction to the harsh words. When none came, he said, "I know you and Shyanne have the gift of long life. But you are not immortal. I can kill you."

"Is it a gift...or a curse?"

"You decide."

The cat melted back into the woods, leaving Drayco to ponder the question.

Drayco bowed his head and sighed. The dark twin longed for an end to the suffering given to him by the virus. Yet, he knew it would not come. He had finally found his family, and the desire to stay with her was stronger than any longing for an end.

He sat under the tree for another hour before returning to the building. Shyanne's position had not changed during that time. He stretched out on the blanket vacated earlier. After what felt like an eternity, he fell into a troubled sleep; a sleep filled with dreams of the unknown boss and of losing control and killing Shyanne.

Eight

Several days after leaving the campsite, Shyanne still did not know much about what had happened to her brother since he vanished so long ago. He was quiet and solemn and when she tried to get him to discuss it; he stared ahead without answering.

It was mid-morning when they decided to stop and eat. After they dismounted, the horses moved into a field next to the road to graze. Drizzle was forced to stay away from the temporary camp. The horse Drayco had acquired still tensed when he came too close. He was getting better, though, and given time, she knew Bravaro would not even notice the cat.

No fire was needed for the meal break for it was to be a short stop only. They wanted to get as far as they could on their quest for the town called Grandfield before having to stop for the night. Shyanne pulled out some jerky and walked over to Drayco. He was sitting under a tree, his back against the trunk. His eyes were closed as if he was deep in thought; a line of sweat covered his brow.

"Here's some jerky." She held out the meat.

He opened his eyes and focused them on the offering; a haunted look filled them. "I have to drink again...soon. After what I've had to endure recently, the blood from the men helped, but it's not going to last much longer."

A chill ran up Shyanne's spine, making the hairs on the nape of her neck stand straight. She tried not to show it, and knew she'd failed. "Would it help if I had Drizzle bring you something?"

"Yes. However, it has to be alive. I can't drink from something that is dead." He closed his eyes again and tried not to think about what he had witnessed from his sister.

Shyanne put two of her fingers in her mouth and let out with a high-pitched whistle. Drizzle appeared, seeming to melt out of the countryside.

"Is everything okay?" he asked, looking in Drayco's direction.

"Drizzle, can you go hunting for Drayco. He needs to drink again and could use your help."

The cat never took his eyes off the dark twin. "If it will help him to stay in control, I'll do it. For that reason alone. I am not a nursemaid for his every whim."

"One thing," Shyanne added as he turned to leave. "The creature you bring back has to be alive. You can't kill it."

He stopped and stared at her. To his credit, he didn't say anything. Drayco kept his eyes closed and listened to the conversation. He knew better than to speak right now.

Drizzle grumbled to himself as he disappeared, bits of his words overheard by the twins. "Helpless....nothing but...not a nursemaid....get you something....get it back when you're done..."

"I don't think he likes you anymore, Drayco," Shyanne chuckled. She sat next to him in the shade under the tree.

"It's not that. He remembers the reason I had to leave in the first place."

"That was a long time ago. You're in better control of yourself now, right?"

"So far, little sis. So far." Drayco took the jerky from her hand and stared at it, unable to meet her eyes.

They ate in silence while waiting for Drizzle's return. Shyanne finally broke it.

"Drayco, why do you think this Boss wants me?"

"I don't know. I do know that we'll find out once we locate him." He was glad to have an excuse to set the jerky aside.

"I wonder if there are other people out there hunting for me, or if those two were the only ones."

"We'll worry about that when the time comes." He thumped her on the nose like he used to do, bringing a smile to her face.

A noise from behind caused them to glance over their shoulders. Drizzle was returning with something big hanging from his mouth. He dragged it awkwardly on the ground between his legs. It was a deer. The cat had somehow stunned it and managed to bring it back before it recovered. He brought the deer to Drayco and dropped it at his feet.

"I did what was asked. I kept it alive."

"Thanks, Drizzle. I'm sorry you had to do this."

"I'll do what I have to if it will keep you under control."

The twin nodded his head in understanding. He picked up the deer and threw it over his shoulder. A small stand of trees stood a short distance away. He disappeared around them to do what he must to survive.

Shyanne was glad she didn't have to watch what her brother did. She realized she had been holding her breath during the exchange and let it out slowly through pursed lips.

"I wish you didn't have to live this way," she whispered softly.

Many men had died over the years because of her sword. None of their deaths had affected her like this. Drizzle sensed her discomfort. He relaxed his head in her lap, purring in his soothing way. Shyanne scratched him affectionately behind his ears. Staring off into the horizon, she tried to think of better times, times before the virus ruined everything.

Drayco emerged after what seemed like hours, wiping at the corner of his mouth. The deer was not with him. The virus had made it possible for him to rejuvenate himself with any living creature's blood, regardless of what type ran through its body.

Shyanne put a hand to her neck when her brother appeared; the recent events were still vivid in her mind. Drayco grimaced inside. Things had changed between them. Love was still very much evident. Unfortunately, something new had entered. Fear.

"I left the carcass for you, Drizzle. It's the least I can do for you helping me." He walked over to Shyanne.

The cat waited until Drayco was next to his sister before he wandered over and disappeared behind by the trees.

The dark twin stretched out on the ground. He laced his finger together under his head, crossed his feet, and looked up at the sky. Shyanne stretched out next to him and assumed the same position. She remained silent, observing him with a sideways glance. His bad eye was back to normal and the bruises and cuts were gone, thanks to the rejuvenating powers of the blood.

The vision of his sister's reaction when he reemerged from drinking the deer's blood returned. He felt that once their mission to find the Boss was over, he might have to leave again—for her sake. He had finally found his family. But had he really found the missing part of himself, or was that part forever gone. Only time, and Shyanne, would tell.

When Drizzle was finished, the twins climbed into their saddles and started down the road. The cat ran ahead, scouting the area before them. They spotted him occasionally. For the most part, he remained hidden. Half a day into the ride, a thin trail of smoke appeared on the horizon. Drizzle returned and reported to Shyanne what he had discovered. He gave Bravaro a wide berth.

"A town ahead was attacked."

"Did you see who did it?" Drayco asked.

"No. The only movement I saw was the buzzards flying overhead or the ones feasting on the dead. The attackers were gone."

"Just in case, let's use caution. They could still be in the area." Drayco urged his horse forward. Shyanne followed.

As they topped the hill just outside the town, they stopped. They were looking down on absolute carnage. Some of the buildings were burnt completely to the ground; others were partially burnt, while others remained untouched. The source of the smoke became evident; the partially burnt ones were still ablaze. Bodies lay everywhere. The smell of blood, mingled with the stench of burnt flesh saturated the air.

Drayco and Shyanne rode into town with Drizzle leading the way. Buzzards disturbed by their arrival took flight. The ones sitting in nearby trees screeched their displeasure at having to wait, but wait they did, until they passed.

"Oh Drayco, even women and children weren't

spared." Shyanne felt a lump of bile rise in her throat. She manages to keep it down as they rode to the center of the town and dismounted.

"Let's look around and see if there's any survivors," Drayco said.

Shyanne walked over to one of the partially burned home and looked inside. She turned away quickly and stumbled from the door. The sight of what lay inside was more than she could take. Leaning against a post to support her wobbly legs, she vomited the little bit of jerky from the last stop, then dry heaved when nothing else came up. She knew without a doubt that there were no survivors in there.

A doll lay in the middle of the road, dirty and broken. She walked over and picked it up. Tears streamed down her face as she hugged it close; picturing the face of a smiling child it had once belonged to. Drayco came over and wrapped his arms around his sister in an effort to comfort her after having to see so many atrocities.

"Why would anyone do this? Why would they kill all these innocent people?"

"I don't know, little sis," Drayco said as he smoothed her hair. "I don't know." A moment later, he pulled back. "Shyanne, we need to check this building out. Are you able to go in, or do you want to stay out here?" It was one of the untouched buildings.

"I can go in. After 200 years, I'm used to death and dying...just not when it's so extensive...and so pointless. It caught me off guard, that's all." Shyanne wiped the tears off her face and set the doll down on a bench near the house full of death.

Drizzle stayed outside so he could keep watch. The twins went through the doorway and looked around. Everything from clothing to foodstuff to hardware items was visible. It was a general store. A splattering of blood covered some of the items on display near the back. Drayco moved farther inside to get a better look in that direction.

A middle-aged woman was on the ground near a back wall. Her clothes were torn and her throat slashed. A large pool of congealed blood surrounded her. A younger man lay face down next to her, also in a pool of blood. Something about him caught Drayco's attention. He went over and rolled the man onto his back. A moan of pain escaped with the movement.

"Shyanne! Get over here, quick!"

She ran to her brother's side and knelt next to the injured man. Several slices marred the material covering his chest and arms.

"A survivor," he told his sister. "I only hope he'll continue to do so. He's lost a lot of blood."

"We have to move him. We can't leave him here."

Drayco checked out a door he had seen in the opposite corner of the shop. He hoped the room beyond was what he thought it was. "Hey. There's a room back here. It looks like living quarters. We can move him in here."

He came back and reached under the man's arms, grabbing his wrists and pinning them against his chest. Shyanne moved to the feet. As one, they carefully lifted the survivor and carried him to the room. They laid him on one of the cots. Shyanne started peeling away the shredded shirt to inspect his wounds.

"Drayco, can you bring me the waterskins, then go and see if you can find me some bandages? I need to clean these wounds before they get infected."

The horses were where they had left them, but Drizzle was gone. Drayco got the waterskins from Jack's saddle. The horse seemed to understand the gravity of the situation and didn't give him a hard time. He returned to the main part of the store where he found the requested items and brought them to Shyanne.

The bloody shirt was off and lying on the floor. It resembled a pile of shredded documents from a time far into the past. Drayco could see shallow cuts all over the muscular arms and upper body of the unconscious man. A large purple stab wound partway down his left side looked bad.

He must have used his body as a shield for the older woman, Drayco thought.

"I got the water and found these in the shop." He handed her the waterskin and bandages and watched as his sister plucked out a cloth and wet it down. She began to clean the dried blood from the cuts.

"Thanks. The cuts aren't bad, but the one on his side will take time to heal. As far as I can tell, no major organs were hit. Most of the blood under him must have come from the elderly woman. He did add enough of his own to it though."

The man on the cot tossed his head back and forth with every stroke of the cool cloth on his skin.

"Do you need my help?"

"No. I can handle this. You should check the rest of the town for more survivors, just in case."

Shyanne whispered quietly to the injured man as she worked. His face relaxed and his thrashing reduced with the sound of her voice. Drayco stood at the door watching for a few seconds before he left.

He went from building to building, bypassing the completely burnt ones. All the people he found were dead. The most heart-wrenching find was when he saw a woman who had covered her child with her own body to protect it from the massacre, to no avail. The little girl was also dead.

"What would lead someone to do this...and why? This was a complete slaughter."

A grim look was locked firmly in place by the time he finished his search. He had seen death of this magnitude before, although it had been a long while. It affected him deeply nevertheless.

Drayco returned to find the survivor bandaged and resting peacefully. The man had sandy colored hair that fell to his shoulders. He appeared to be in his mid twenties and was as tall as Drayco. His face was strong, and yet, had a gentle look to it, his build muscular from years of hard work. Shyanne sat on a stool next to the cot, her head bowed. She looked up when she heard him enter.

"I didn't find any other survivors. I did see the tracks of many horses everywhere I went. Whoever did this, they were looking for something." Drayco nodded his head toward the cot. "How's he doing?"

"He'll live. We found him in time."

"We need to gather the dead and give them a proper sending."

Shyanne looked down at Drizzle. "Watch over him. If he wakes, come get us."

Drizzle had returned while Drayco was out; he was lying next to Shyanne. The cat repositioned himself so that he could see the man on the cot better. "If I need you, I'll call."

It took the twins the rest of the day to recover all the bodies and put them inside what was left of the stables. They were sweaty and their clothes covered with the blood of innocents by the time they finished.

Shyanne was leaving the building when she noticed a bandaged and battered man standing at the entrance to the store. Drizzle was next to him. The fair-haired survivor was looking in her direction, but not at her. His eyes were focused on the building. He swayed badly. The cat and the doorframe were the only things preventing him from falling.

"Drizzle! What the hell is going on?"

"He insisted on getting up! If I had left him to get you, he would have fallen down. Then you'd REALLY be happy with me, wouldn't you!"

She ran over, wrapped an arm around the man's waist, and ducked under his to support him. He leaned heavily on her and continued to look at the building she had just come from.

"They're all in there...aren't they?"

"Yes."

"No others made it?"

"No. No others."

A look of such anguish washed over his face. He bowed his head to hide it. "Did you see a middle-aged woman with graying hair? She was working in the shop with me."

"She was beside you when we found you." Shyanne felt his legs give a little. He managed to recover himself before he could fall.

His voice cracked as he said, "She was my mother."

"Let's go back inside. You need to get off your feet and rest." She turned him around gently and guided him back to the room with the cot.

Drayco watched the scene with Shyanne and the injured man play out. *I can understand what you're going through, mister,* he thought as he returned his attention to the building with the dead inside. *I've been through it myself.*

The wood for the walls was dry from the partial burning it had received earlier in the day. He heaped brush around the base to make sure it would reignite easily when the time came. Matches no longer existed; a piece of flint was needed now. In no time, a small flame ate greedily at the dry brush. It quickly made its way up the side of the building. Drayco put a piece of board into the flames, lit it, and walked around, igniting more areas.

The dark twin was forced back due of the intensity of the heat radiating from the roaring inferno. He watched as the flames danced into the sky. Glowing cinders floated upward like angels returning home; a thick billowy plume of smoke carried them higher and higher.

The darkness of night had settled in; it covered the ever-reaching plume with its blanket. He hoped the fire's glow would not draw unwanted attention. It was too late to think of about that now. Drayco watched as the roof collapsed, causing the building to fall in on itself. A mass of shooting embers leaped from the mayhem.

"Good luck and safe journey to you," he whispered to the embers as if they were the spirits of the dead.

Drayco returned to the horses and took them into the building next to theirs, which was also untouched by fire. Jack allowed himself to be led alongside Bravaro. It was as if the horse had called a temporary truce.

The main room was large enough for both horses after several pieces of furniture were shoved out of the way. He removed their saddles and bridles and put some grain from Shyanne's pack in two wooden bowls he had found. A barrel stood near the edge of what looked like a cooking area. He removed the lid and discovered it was half-full of water. He set the lid aside to allow the horses to drink. When everything was set, he closed the door behind him, thus preventing the animals from roaming into the treacherous night.

The survivor was back on the cot, a bandaged arm thrown over his pale face, when Drayco returned to the store. A candle burned in the corner casting light across the room. He noticed Drizzle was absent again. Shyanne had started a fire in the stove.

"He okay?"

"As okay as can be expected. He had to watch his friends and family get slaughtered." She put another piece of wood into the potbelly stove and shut the door.

"Do you know who he is yet?"

"He was too distraught when we came back. I let him

rest."

"I'm not an invalid. I can talk," the injured man said sarcastically. He sat up with a grimace and looked at the twins. "Joseph. My name is Joseph."

Shyanne moved quickly to his side. "You have to lie down. You need to rest." She pushed on his shoulders. It didn't take much to force him back.

Drayco moved to the cot and sat on the stool next to it. "What happened here?"

"Drayco, he needs to rest."

"Shyanne, we need to know what transpired here."

"It's okay, I can handle it," Joseph insisted. He sat up for a second time and cautiously rested his back against the wall.

"I was working in my store, like always. My mother liked to help out. She said the shop needed a female's touch, kept telling me I needed to find a good woman and make her my wife. She wanted grandchildren to spoil." He smiled faintly at the memory. "I heard a commotion outside and went to the window to see what it was. Many men and women on horseback were galloping into town. It was kind of strange to see such a large group of people together, especially here." He closed his eyes and leaned his head back. After a deep breath, he opened them and continued.

"The townspeople watched with fascination at what was going on until the slaughter started. Men, women, and children were chased down like animals and killed. A few were spared...mostly women. They were tied up and carried to the bar. I don't know what went on in there but I heard a lot of screams...and a lot of laughter."

A haunted look filled his eyes. "Some of the men separated from the main group. They started going through each of the buildings, looking for more people. I hid my mother before they got there."

"They barged in and came at me before I could make a move for my weapon. They were so fast. The men kicked and punched me. They kept yelling the same thing over and over as their blows fell: 'Where is she? Where is she? We know she's here somewhere?'"

His words came out in a rush, his breath ragged and coarse; his face sweaty. Shyanne started to tell Joseph enough; Drayco cut her off with a glare. "I kept trying to tell them that I didn't know who they were yelling about, but they wouldn't listen. They were lost in a blood lust because of all the killing and they wanted more."

"One of the men pulled out a knife and started slashing at me. I tried to block the blows with my arms, which drove them even wilder. It caused them to cut me more. They laughed. They were having such a grand time. My mother saw what they were doing. She ran out of her hiding spot to protect me. The men grabbed her and made lewd comments as they started cutting her too. I begged for them to stop, to leave her alone."

Joseph was crying now, his hands clenched into tight fists. Shyanne had tears running down her face, as well. She placed a comforting hand on his shoulder. He reached up and held on to it as if it was a lifeline, a lifeline to sanity. Drayco sat with his head bowed, his arms resting on his knees, listening. His face looked like it was made of stone.

"I was so enraged, I attacked without thinking. I never felt the blade sink into my side. All I know is that it became harder to stay on my feet, I felt so weak. After I went down, the last thing I remember hearing before I passed out was my mother crying. The men must have thought I had died. It's the only explanation I can think of for why I'm still here...and my mother...oh God..."

Joseph lay down. He threw an arm over his eyes, hiding them, crying softly. Shyanne's hand remained in his. After a few minutes, his breath went in and out with the slow rhythmic pattern of sleep. She eased her hand free when Drayco indicated for them to go to the outer room to talk.

They retreated to the far corner of the main room so they would not disturb the sleeping man. It had a sitting area for people to use when visiting the store.

"What do you think?" Shyanne asked once they were seated.

"His story explained what I saw at the bar. The people looked like they had been tortured before they were killed."

Shyanne stared at her brother, her thoughts far from where they sat. "Drayco...we can't leave this man here. We have to take him with us."

"That's up to him, little sis. We can't force him to come." Shyanne took in a breath to say something else. Drayco continued before she could speak, "Until that time, we need to get some rest ourselves. We can discuss it with him in the morning."

"You're right," she sighed. "I'll bring some of those blankets with us. That floor in there is hard and I want some softness for a change."

"Maybe we should change first." He pulled the front of his shirt away from his body. "I'm tired of the stink of blood on me."

Shyanne looked down at her own filthy clothes and made an ugly face. Drayco smiled at his twin. They found some clothes in their sizes and put them on.

Just as they finished, she remembered the horses. An ashamed look crossed her face. "I totally forgot about the horses. They need to be taken care of."

"Already done. They're in the building next door. I made sure everything was shut tight to prevent anything getting at them."

"Thanks, Drayco."

"Hey...what are big brothers for."

They gathered all the blankets they saw and took them to the back room. Joseph was rolled over onto his side, snoring. The twins made beds with the layers and eased themselves underneath the uppermost one. A sigh of relief escaped from Shyanne's lips. The candle flickered out with a huff of breath and all were asleep soon thereafter.

*   *   *

Brother and sister were up early the next day. They crept from the room to keep from waking the still sleeping Joseph. Once they were outside, Drayco led Shyanne into the building next door. The sound of nickering met them before they made it inside. Two horses nearly mowed them over in their joy at seeing them.

"Come on, you two, lap cats you are not. Time to go outside." Shyanne held the door open as her brother chased them out. "A house is no place for animals the size of you two behemoths." Returning her attention to the room, she said, "We need to make better accommodations for them. They can't stay in here." Shyanne held her nose; the stench of horse was strong.

"Where else can we put them? The stables burnt to the ground yesterday."

"We make a temporary stable behind the building we're in. I saw the perfect spot." Shyanne took Drayco to the proposed area behind the store. "I found this while you were gone yesterday. We'll be able to keep a better eye on them, and the fresh air will do them good instead of being crammed in that small space."

"I agree," Drayco said. "I saw a pile of lumber close by. There should be enough to do the job."

With some rope from the store, they erected a lean-to big enough to shelter two horses. Shyanne covered the ground inside with straw while Drayco tossed a bundle of hay in a corner. As the final touch, a trough dragged around from the front was filled with water from a barrel sitting under a drainpipe. Shyanne led the horses into the newly constructed area. They munched on the hay, ignoring the twins who watched.

Suddenly, Shyanne disappeared inside and returned with two oval objects in her hands. "They need a good brushing."

The pair attacked the coats of the animals until they glistened in the sunlight, as did the twins by the time they finished. Shyanne's stomach growled when she stood back to admire their work. Drayco smiled at her startled look. In their haste to leave without waking Joseph, neither had bothered to eat.

"I don't know about you, big brother, but I'm going inside. I'm starved."

"Right behind you, little sis." His stomach growled right on cue, causing both of them to chuckle.

The smell of food reached their noses as they neared the room. They glanced at each other before peeking inside. A pan with several slices of ham in it sat on the stove. Baked yams were already finished and set to the side. Joseph stood in front of the stove with his back to the door. Drizzle lay on the floor next to him, an expectant look on his face. As they watched, a slice of ham hit the floor in front of him. The cat picked it up and swallowed it in one bite. He returned to his vigilance, waiting for the next accidental drop of food.

Joseph was flipping one of the slices over when they entered. He glanced over his shoulder, and said, "You two are filthy. Go wash up. There's a small space behind a dingy gray curtain hanging near the sitting area. A bucket of water is tucked in there."

"What are you doing? You're not strong enough yet." Shyanne's voice was thick with concern. She glared at Drizzle. "And you. What are you doing encouraging him. You know he needs to rest."

The big cat wasn't the least bit threatened by his companion's tone. He yawned, ignoring Shyanne completely, and continued watching Joseph.

"I'm okay for the moment. But you best hurry; the food's almost done, and so am I." He smiled weakly at the pair and winked at Shyanne. She frowned, but held her tongue. Drayco turned away to prevent his sister from seeing the smile that crept onto his face because of the look on hers.

"Come on, sis, let's go clean up." He grabbed her arm and pulled her out of the room.

They found the bucket where Joseph said it was and washed the grit and grime off their bodies. Clean clothes replaced the dirty ones. They reentered the room to find two plates heaped with food waiting for them, mugs filled with warmed cider close.

Joseph had returned to the cot, sitting with his back resting against the wall. Drizzle lay on the floor; the lower half of his body sprawled under the cot.

"I think you've made a new friend," Shyanne said as she picked up the plate left for her.

Except for the occasional words of praise from the twins, all three consumed their meal in silence. Joseph picked at his. He did not have much of an appetite.

"How you doing over there?" Drayco asked when he noticed the distant look in the man's eyes, and the virtually untouched plate of food.

"I have to leave. I have to hunt down the people who did this to my town. I want revenge for my mother and friends." He looked up; determination replaced the distant look in his blue eyes. "I have nothing left for me here. I have to go after them before the trail gets cold."

"Do you think that wise in your present condition?"

"I won't let them get away with what they did."

"But you're still too weak to travel," Shyanne said.

"I'll make it. But I had hoped you two would help me."

"We have our own quest to complete. A person—this Boss—is after my sister, and we have to find him before he finds her. I understand what you want to do, but Shyanne is more important to me."

"I understand, Drayco, I really do." Joseph looked at his plate. "I just hoped..."

Shyanne felt her insides crack with the desire to help; he sounded so forlorn. Unfortunately, her brother was right. They needed to finish one quest before taking on another.

Setting his plate aside, Joseph said, "I'll go with you to find this boss. Besides, the attacker's trail is probably gone by now. It's been too long since they were here."

Joseph rose to his feet and with a determined stride walked into the main area of the store. The twins set their plates down and followed. Drizzle, who watched with interest as the scene unfold, padded after the trio. The fair-haired man stood in the middle of the room with his hands on his hips, surveying the contents of the store, his weariness forgotten.

"We'll need all the foodstuff and extra supplies we can carry. Weapons are in order too. You both have your swords. I need mine."

He went to the counter and reached behind it. A long object wrapped in cloth appeared. They watched as Joseph pulled a beautiful double-edged sword free from its worn scabbard. The handle was shaped like the upper body a boar.

"Long ago, my ancestors bragged about our ability to stand against any adversary, just like the wild boar. Swords were made to show off our pride. Over time, we grew placid and weak." Joseph paused for a second; a look of sadness swept across his face. He shook it off. "This one belonged to my father."

He slid the weapon into its holder and placed it on his back with the handle in easy reach. "Go through the stuff here and pack up whatever we can use. I'll go to the bar and fill some pouches with ale. I don't know about you two; right now, I want something other than water to drink."

Joseph picked up several watertight pouches and went out the door before any objections were raised.

Drizzle followed close behind. He stopped, and said, "I'll make sure he's okay," and disappeared through the exit.

"Now I know Joseph's made a new friend." Shyanne shook her head, wondering what it was about the fair-haired man that drew the feline so.

"Sounds like somebody else I know."

"You!" She punched Drayco on the arm. Her stern look turned into a grin at the hurt, pathetic look that appeared on his face. He grinned back.

The twins went through the entire store and put everything they felt they needed into packs. It took a while to go through it all. The store wasn't huge, but it had a lot of stuff crammed into every nook and cranny. Night covered everything with its darkness and three packs were ready when Joseph and Drizzle finally returned with the filled pouches.

"I was about to come looking for you to make sure you hadn't gotten into any trouble," Drayco said as he walked over.

"Thanks, Drayco. I needed to spend some time by myself." Joseph's words were thick with exhaustion.

"I understand. I would feel the same way if I were in your shoes." The dark twin slapped Joseph on the shoulder then turned him toward the bags resting against a wall. "I put some clothes and things in a pack for you. That way when we're ready to go, we won't have so much to do."

Shyanne was cooking dinner and listened in on the conversation between the two men. She was glad Joseph was coming with them. She felt he would make a great addition to their little troupe. Her logical excuse for wanting him along was that one could never have too many good swords available. Drizzle flopped down on the floor next to her. She bent over and scratched him behind his ear.

"Silly old cat. You really like him, don't you?" Drizzle arched his neck into her hand and emitted a never-ending rumble from deep in his throat.

"He sure is a great cat." Joseph came over and gave Drizzle a rub on the head between the ears. Their hands brushed against each other in the process. Shyanne felt a rush of energy surge through her body. She pulled her hand back, stood up, and turned away from the man still petting the cat. She did not want him to see how his touch had affected her.

"Dinner will be ready soon. I better not let anything burn."

Joseph stood and looked over her shoulder at the pans on the stove. "I bet you're a fine cook. My mother would have been proud."

He grew quiet after he realized what he had said and walked to the stool near the cot. He sat down with a weary sigh. Drayco watched the brief encounter while he finalized everything.

"Joseph, Shyanne, I think we should leave in the morning." He looked at the fair-haired man, and continued, "You seem stronger than you were earlier. I know it's only been a day since we found you, but I think you'll be able to handle the journey as long as we take it slow and easy. You can ride on Bravaro. I'll walk alongside."

"Nonsense." Shyanne turned and wagged a finger at her brother. "That bay's a big horse. He can easily carry the two of you. He carried that burley fat man didn't he?"

Drayco snickered. "Once again, little sis, you are right. I just didn't want to tire him."

"We'll be at a walking pace. He'll be fine."

"I can see this trip will be full of entertainment." Joseph turned to Drizzle. "Do you have anything to add to this conversation?"

"I've learned to stay out of any argument she gets into. I can never win—nor can anyone she argues with."

"Drizzle!" Shyanne's mouth hung open in disbelief.

Joseph and Drayco laughed. They quieted down when she focused her attention on them.

"If you two don't stop, there will be no dinner for you! And as for you—you bullheaded cat—I will hear no more about arguments!"

The smell of something burning hit her nose; she spun around toward the stove. "Now look at what you guys have done. You caused part of the meat to burn!" She jerked the pan off the stove and flipped the contents onto a plate as quickly as possible. The men couldn't help themselves; they burst out laughing again.

"Just for that, you two get the burnt ones." She shook the wooden spatula at them to emphasize her point.

Drayco walked over to his sister, put his arms around her waist, and said, "I love you, little sis." He snuggled his chin into her neck and hugged her tight.

"That won't help you any, mister."

The dark man started tickling her sides. Shyanne squealed and tried to get away, but he had a firm hold on her. Joseph stayed out of the way. He was too tired to participate. He leaned back against a wall and watched the antics of the twins with a faint smile. By the time Drayco let go, Shyanne's face was beet red and she had tears running down her cheeks from laughing so much.

"Alright! Alright! I give!" She pushed away from her brother once he opened his arms and returned her attention to the stove. "Let's eat before this slaved over food gets cold."

Drizzle got up before the first bite passed into their mouth. "I'm going to check out the area and make sure we don't have company. I'll return by morning." He padded through the door.

The three devoured the meal of warm bread, partially burnt meat, and corn on the cob. This time Joseph ate all the food covering his plate. Afterward, they cleaned up and put away the dishes. Drayco made sure the horses were doing all right before settling down for the night with the others.

"I don't know about you guys," Shyanne said with a yawn, extending her arms outward in a stretch. "But I'm exhausted."

"We all are. It's been a busy day, so let's get some sleep." Drayco yawned loudly. "We have a long ride ahead of us tomorrow." Joseph's only response was a yawn.

Soon, the only sound throughout the room was snoring.

Nine

The twins woke the next morning to sunshine glaring in their eyes through a window located in the back of the room. Drayco stretched his limbs as far as they would go before relaxing. Shyanne was covered from head to toe by her blanket. Only her messy braid showed she existed. The cot where Joseph slept had the covers pulled up also. No sound came from it.

Drayco sat up. "Wake up, sleepy heads, time to rise and shine!"

Shyanne peered out from under her blanket. "I'm up, I'm up. Don't shout anymore." She flipped it back over her head.

"Joseph, how are you doing over there?" No reply. "Joseph?"

"Joseph? Are you okay?" Shyanne, now fully awake, rolled onto her feet and went over to the cot. She pulled the covers off in one fluid motion. Pillows lay underneath, arranged in such a way as to make it look like someone was still in the bed. It was the oldest trick in the book, and they fell for it.

"He's not here."

Drayco was beside the cot in seconds. "That fool!"

"What? What's he done?"

He wasn't listening. A quick glance around the room showed him one of the packs was gone. He bolted through the building toward the back door, toward the temporary stables. Only one horse was inside. Bravaro was gone.

"Drayco! Get back here, there's a note!"

The dark man returned quickly. His sister stood holding a piece of paper. He watched as a wave of emotions flashed across her face. "What does it say?"

She read it aloud:

Drayco, Shyanne,

I'm sorry for leaving the way I did. I know you both will be mad at me, but I couldn't let those things get away with what they did to my people, my town, and my family. Drizzle returned while I was getting ready and decided to travel with me. By the time you find this note, you will know that the bay horse is gone. I promise to look after them both and keep them safe. I hope one day you will be able to forgive me. Thanks for saving me and being my friends.

Joseph

"I should have known something was up when he gave in so easily," Drayco said through clenched teeth.

"When I get hold of that cat, I'm going to skin him alive."

"I'm going outside to see if I can track which direction they went. You get everything ready. Will Jack let me get on him?"

"I'll make him. We need speed if we're going to catch up with Joseph and that foolish cat."

Drayco returned to the temporary stables and focused his attention on the ground. He walked around looking for any fresh tracks leading away from the enclosure. He found them quickly. Bravaro had a distinctive print. His left front hoof had a slice cut out of it in the shape of a vee. It wasn't deep enough to hurt the animal, but it left a mark easy to follow.

The tracks led in the same direction as the faded prints left by the killing party. The big cat's paw print was clearly visible in the soft dirt. They went in the same direction as the horse.

He must have gotten up sometime in the night. Damn him, Drayco thought as he looked off into the distance. *I hope he doesn't get himself or anyone else killed because of his stupidity.*

He hurried back when he didn't see anything on the horizon. Shyanne was out in the stables. The task of getting the remaining horse ready was already finished, the supplies attached to the saddle. Her sword was strapped to her back; she handed him his when he returned.

"Do you know which way they went?"

"The tracks are several hours old and went northwest. He must have gotten up shortly after we went to sleep." He buckled the sword around his waist.

"We'll find them. I know we will."

"Let's get moving. Little sis, get up on Jack and keep him steady for me. Maybe with you on his back, he won't try anything."

Shyanne got into the saddle and gripped the reins firmly with both hands. She braced her feet in the stirrups. Drayco came up to the left side. The horse snorted. He sidestepped away, but she pulled on the reins while talking to him. He calmed down. Drayco grabbed the back of the saddle and swung himself up behind his sister.

Jack froze, straight legged, his ears swinging back and forth. He didn't know what to do. If he tried to throw the man off, he would hurt the one who cared for him.

"Easy there, Jack, he won't hurt you. You're a big strong horse. You'll be okay," Shyanne cooed as she rubbed the muscular neck under the flowing mane. Jack relaxed with the sound of her voice and the gentle touch of her fingers.

"Great job, Shyanne."

Glancing over her shoulder, she asked, "Which direction do we need to go again?"

"Northwest."

Shyanne pulled the horse around to where her brother pointed and gave him a gentle nudge. He sprang forward, forcing her to ease him into a slower pace.

Drayco pointed out Bravaro's distinctive track as they went. "See that print with the vee in it? That's his. Keep that in sight and we'll eventually find our AWOL members."

After riding for an hour, Shyanne pulled something out of a small pouch hanging off the saddle horn. She handed it to Drayco. "Breakfast is served." Drayco took the jerky and bit a small piece off.

"Why do you suppose he did what he did?" Shyanne pondered.

"Revenge would be my guess. I would have done the same thing under the same circumstances. That's why I'm kicking myself for not seeing it."

"Joseph seemed so enthusiastic about wanting to go with us. I'd never have thought he would go for revenge instead." She paused. "I wonder what Drizzle was thinking when he decided not to alert us of Joseph's leaving."

"We can ask him when we catch up," Drayco said.

His thoughts wandered during the silence that followed. *When I get my hands on you, I'll show you what I think of your slinking away in the middle of the night.* He sank his teeth into the jerky and ripped a large chunk off. Shyanne heard the maneuver and ignored it. She understood.

The twins continued in the same direction as the ones who had vanished in the middle of the night. The trail, for the most part, was easy to keep in sight.

"It doesn't make any sense. He makes no move to cover his tracks," Drayco said. "He knows that when we catch up to him; I'll remove him from my horse, forcefully if I have to, and we'll finish our original quest."

Maybe he wants us to find him. Maybe he thinks we'll help him instead of turning off on another path. Or, maybe he's in too big of a hurry to care whether the tracks are seen or not."

"I still think finding this Boss person looking you is more important than any vengeful hunt."

"I agree," Shyanne said. "But for the moment, finding our lost comrades is more important than worrying about this Boss person."

They rode for the better part of the day, following the distinctive hoof print. The sun moved smoothly across the sky toward the west. The deepening shadows spread a blanket over the area. When the twins passed through a large grouping of trees, Shyanne pulled the horse to a stop. A vast rocky terrain lay ahead. The tracks disappeared completely.

Drayco slid off the horse and walked around. "I don't see a thing," he said, frustrated. *You stay on Jack. I'll walk in their last known direction and see if I can locate the trail* again."

He hiked forward until he looked over a small crest. Rocks of various sizes, shape, and color lay everywhere. Patches of long wispy grass broke the sea of stone wherever they were able to extend their roots into cracks and crevices. Birds with their wings open wide floated on the air currents like a kite. Nothing on the horizon indicated a man, horse, and cat were ahead.

"It'll be dark soon. We need to find shelter," Shyanne said.

"We may not have an option. We may have to stay out in the open tonight. I don't see any place to hole up in."

"What about over there?" Shyanne stood up in the stirrups and pointed to her right. "I think there might be a trail leading in that direction."

"We can check it out."

She directed Jack toward the gap seen in the boulders, Drayco followed on foot. The group made their way carefully down the rocky incline to the bottom where they found a trail wide enough to allow the horse to move freely. A smaller path branched off toward an enclosed area big enough to hold them for the night. They entered just as the huge orange ball ducked under the distant horizon.

The enclosure had tall smooth walls that reached well above Drayco's head. There was only one way in or out. They set up camp by the glow of the rising moon. No fire was started tonight to reduce the likelihood of being spotted by anything or anyone passing through the area. Shyanne removed the saddle from Jack and gave him some grain and water.

"I'll have to hobble him tonight. I don't want him to wander off looking for greener pastures. Get it?" Shyanne smiled as she glanced at the walls of stone, then at her brother.

Drayco shook his head. "Only you could think of something that lousy at a time like this."

Shyanne shrugged her shoulders and tried to give her best innocent look; she failed. They both chuckled quietly.

"We'll have to stand watch tonight. Without having proper shelter, we are open for attack." Drayco returned the conversation to the seriousness of the situation. "I'll take the first watch. In three hours, I'll wake you to take over."

They shared a meal of bread and dried meat. Afterwards, Shyanne removed her sword and laid it on the ground beside her. She pulled her blanket up over her shoulders to ward off the coolness of the night air. Supporting her head with her arm, she looked at her brother standing tall in the moonlight.

"Drayco, do you think we will find them tomorrow?"

"It depends on how much of a head start they had on us. I hope Joseph's weakened condition will make him need to rest often."

"Are we going to be able to find the tracks again?" A huge yawn escaped after the question.

"If we follow the same direction, I think so. He veered very little from the northwest path he was taking."

He realized Shyanne had fallen asleep when he heard the soft sound of snoring. Drayco looked down at her and smiled. He loved his sister more than anything else in this post virus world. Unfortunately, things were different. Time, and their lengthy separation, had seen to that. No matter how much she tried to hide it, the fear she felt for him shined in her eyes when he moved too close unexpectedly.

Drayco walked to the entrance of their camp and leaned his back against the cold stone. He crossed his arms in front of him and looked up at the night sky. Thick billowy clouds were rolling in rapidly from a southeastern direction.

"I hope it doesn't rain until we figure out the right direction to go," he muttered under his breath.

A chill ran up his back. He wasn't sure if the cold stone behind him, or a premonition he had yet to understand caused it. Returning to the blanket, he plucked it from the ground and threw it over his shoulders. Without a fire, the night was cold. He started to pace back and forth to warm himself; his breath looked like little patches of fog with each exhale. Jack watched him from the other side of the campsite, eyes glistening in the moonlight.

Drayco paced to stay warm for most of his watch. His thoughts were on the missing trio, and on the Boss. He wondered what had led the cat to go away with a stranger, and hoped that nothing else would get in their way to prevent them from going to the town called Grandfield. The information they needed on the person who sought his sister, the Boss, was there.

He was about to wake Shyanne for her part of the watch when the ground under his feet started vibrating. Jack looked toward the entrance of their campsite, ears pointed forward, listening. The sound of hooves thundering across the ground at breakneck speed echoed throughout the rocks. Drayco ran to the entrance and hid behind a boulder to see who was foolish enough to go so fast in the darkness. The thunderous sound drew closer. He could just make out the sound of voices shouting over the noise.

".... Caused lots of trouble... want to get ....to enjoy killing....going to be killed if you don't slow down..."

A blur of horses ran past the rock where Drayco hid. The words 'caused trouble' and 'killing' were still ringing in his ears. "I bet they were talking about Joseph and Drizzle."

He ran back to Shyanne and grabbed her shoulder to wake her. He had to jump back quickly to avoid being sliced in half by her blade.

"Don't do that, Drayco," she hissed as she rubbed the sleep out of her eyes. "I could have killed you."

"We have to go—now. A pair of riders just went past and I think they were talking about Drizzle and Joseph. They were heading northwest in a really big hurry."

"Isn't that the direction the others went?"

"Yep." He started shoving things into his pack as fast as he could.

"I'll get Jack ready." She leaped to her feet and saddled the horse in record time. She had a thousand questions, but knew now was not the time to ask them.

In less time than it took to get dressed, the twins were on horseback, heading in the same direction as the unknown riders. Their speed was at a much safer pace.

"What did you hear?"

"Something about causing trouble." Drayco kept the killing part to himself.

"That's probably our pair," Shyanne responded.

The surrounding landscape continued to be rocky and sparse of growth. Broken and gnarled trees grew sporadically; angled in whichever direction the wind blew them. The moon's soft light made it easier for the twins to see the path before them. The dark clouds Drayco observed during his watch had moved on without giving a single drop of moisture to relieve the parched land.

For the most part, the path stayed in a northwest-wardly direction. No others branched from it. Finally, after what felt like many long and tortuous hours, the towering wall of rock lessened in height. A faint yellow glow became visible on the horizon. If the twins hadn't known better, they would have thought sunrise was close.

"Could that be their camp?" Shyanne asked.

"It is in the right direction. If it is their camp, we'll have to be cautious from here on out. They'll probably have outer perimeter guards posted."

Another alcove was discovered between them and the glow ahead as they wove through the various rocks and boulders. The entrance was similar the one recently vacated, one way in or out. Drayco suggested they leave Jack inside. Shyanne led the horse into the area and put some grain out for him. The alcove was about the same size as the stall shared with Bravaro back at the ravaged town they had left only yesterday.

"Stay here, Jack. We'll be back soon," she whispered as she squeezed the big neck tight.

He ignored her completely and continued eating the grain. She laughed softly at his single-mindedness.

Shyanne noticed some broken bushes that reminded her of tumbleweeds trapped in the alcove. The twins used them to block the way out before moving quietly toward the camp. They had gone about a mile when the silhouette of a guard was seen standing on top of a boulder. The man was leaning against his sword, half-asleep. He was oblivious of the twins near him.

Drayco pointed to himself then circled his arm in a wide pattern. Shyanne nodded her head in understanding. The dark man disappeared into the shadows. She was unable to trace any noise from his passage. The guard was still there, but he had assumed a sitting position instead of standing. She crouched low and started moving closer to the man, as well.

She was about twenty paces away when she heard a shout. It was close. Too close. She crouched lower into the shadows and noticed another man standing on the boulder directly behind her. Her heart raced; it felt like it was going to come out of her throat. She held her breath, hoping she hadn't been seen. When no alarms sounded, she relaxed and started to breathe again.

"Whatcha doin, Brent? Ya sleep'n at yer post again?"

"Naw, I'm just sittin. I got tired and wanted to rest."

"Best not let Ruben sees ya doing that. He'll make sure ya never do it again." The man moved away. He added before leaving, "I'll send someone to relieve ya in about two hours."

"I'll be here," Brent grumbled softly so the departing man could not hear.

That's what you think, Shyanne thought.

Brent rose to a standing position with a groan. After a few minutes, she heard the coo of a night bird off to the right and knew it was Drayco. Shyanne hesitated only a second before she untied the leather straps on her shirt to show some cleavage and boldly walked toward Brent, swaying her hips seductively. She knew this wasn't part of her brother's plan, but distraction was needed if he was to sneak up on this man unnoticed.

Brent straightened up and shouted, "You there. Who are you? What are you doing here?"

"I came to be with you, Brent." Her voice had a soft silky edge to it.

"Who sent you?" He looked around, trying to find the culprit of the practical joke. His attention returned almost immediately to the beautiful woman walking toward him.

"No one, Brent. I'm here because I like you, and I want to get to know you better."

"How come I ain't seen you before?"

"I've been here. Maybe you weren't looking." She reached Brent and put her arms over his shoulders, pulling him close.

He couldn't believe this was happening to him. The beautiful women usually went for the good-looking muscular guys, not the ones who were too skinny and had missing teeth, like him. To have one, even one he hadn't seen before, want him this badly was too much for him to resist. Brent started kissing her neck. He wrapped his arms around her and squeezed her butt hard. It had been a long time since he had been with a woman. His sword lay on the ground, forgotten.

Shyanne saw her brother appear over the edge of the rock. He eased up behind Brent and tapped him several times on his back. The sentry jumped and glanced over his shoulder, thinking he was in trouble. He expected to see Ruben standing there. Instead, he saw Drayco.

"Who are you?" he demanded.

Before Brent could recover from his surprise, Drayco threw an arm around his neck and covered his mouth to prevent him from yelling out a warning. Shyanne punched him in the stomach. The sentry collapsed in her brother's arms, gasping for a breath. Drayco continued to keep his hand over Brent's mouth as he lowered him to the ground. Shyanne squat down in front of him, her face close to his, deadly intent thick in her tone when she spoke.

"We require some information, Brent, and you're going to give it to us. Understand?" Brent's eyes became as large as saucers, he nodded his head yes. "Now, we're going to get down from here and talk. If you make one false move, my brother here will break your neck. Got it?" Again Brent nodded his head yes.

The trio slid from the top of the rock to the ground below. Drayco kept a firm grip on the man during the move to prevent him from escaping or shouting out.

They walked a short distance from the watch post and hid behind a group of rocks varying in size from as small as a box to as big as a two story building. Drayco removed the hand covering Brent's mouth and forced the prisoner into a sitting position. The dark man crouched behind him, gripping the thin upper arms tight.

"Don't make a sound unless it's to answer a question," Drayco warned.

Shyanne faced Brent, and asked, "Have you heard about a man traveling with a big cat in this area?"

"Please don't hurt me. I haven't done anything to you," Brent pleaded. "I won't tell the others. I'll just turn my back and pretend I never saw you."

"Shut up, you wimp of a man." Drayco squeezed the thin arms hard enough to cause the skin over the bones to shift beneath his grip.

Brent yelped then shut his mouth tight in remembrance of the warning given earlier. He knew if he yelled the dark one holding him would kill him without a second thought. He wanted to warn the others about these intruders, but also wanted to save his own hide. Maybe if he came across like he was being helpful, they wouldn't kill him and he could find a way to get free.

Shyanne brought his attention back by grabbing his chin with her hand. She leaned very close and asked again, "Have you heard of a man traveling in the company of a big cat? I will not repeat myself." Her soft blue eyes became as cold as ice as she glared into his brown ones.

Brent gulped hard, causing his protruding Adams apple to go up and down. He carefully shook his head yes.

Shyanne's heart skipped a beat. She kept her facial expression blank, though, not wanting either man to see her reaction. Drayco saw the flash in her eyes and remained silent. He was pretty sure he knew the reason for it.

"Have either of them been hurt?"

Again, Brent shook his head yes.

"Are they dead?" The question made her heart ache, but she knew she had to ask it.

He shook his head no. He tried to say something. Shyanne's grip on his chin muffled the words. She let go and sat back.

"We caught the pair sneaking up on the camp. They gave us a humdinger of a fight and that cat killed five of our people before we were able to put an arrow into it." Brent watched Shyanne tense with his last statement. *How interesting,* he thought. *I wonder how I can use that to my advantage.*

"The man swung his sword around screaming like a banshee the whole time. Kept yell'n somethin about killin his family and friends and what not. We hit him on the back of the head after we got a lucky break. The only reason they didn't get killed right away was because of Ruben. He said the cat looked a lot like the one traveling with the girl we're look'n for."

Shyanne inhaled sharply. Drayco shot her a stern look. She recovered her composure quickly.

Brent noticed the second loss of control. *This must be the girl Ruben's after. If I can bring her to him, he'll reward me greatly for it.*

"Who is this Ruben fellow and why does he want the girl?" Drayco asked.

"He's our leader. He brought us together and showed us how to do the kind of jobs no one else wanted, and to make us lots of money."

"What kind of jobs?"

Brent smiled a wicked smile, "Why...hunting and killing, of course."

"Hunting?"

"Yea—like the girl. Ruben promised us lots of gold for find'n a girl with a big cat. He even showed us the gold before we left." A glint filled his eyes. "He didn't say how he came across it and we didn't ask. All we was interested in was the payment...and the fun." Brent winched because the grip on his arms had tightened during the conversation.

"How many of you are there?" Shyanne hoped the man's guard was down enough for him to answer the question without thinking.

Brent hesitated. He knew better than to say too much. "There are 15 of us left after the cat made a mess of things." There were really 25, but he wasn't going to tell that to these two. "I can take you to the ones you look'n for. I know where they are in the camp." The restrained man looked at Shyanne, hope in his eyes.

"We'll get back with you on that, Brent." Shyanne punched him hard across the jaw, causing his head to rock back and forth, effectively knocking him out.

Drayco let go and watched as Brent fell over on his side. "What do you want to do? He took too long to answer. That tells me he's lying."

Shyanne walked a few paces away from the unconscious man. Drayco followed. "I think we should check out the camp before daylight. Our chances of getting caught are less with the darkness covering us."

"I agree." He tipped his head in Brent's direction. "What about him?"

"We tie him up and hide him. His boss will think he fell asleep somewhere."

While the twins were talking, Brent had revived. He lay still, listening to the pair talk. If he could overhear something important, he could take that information to Ruben.

He wasn't sure if he could get the girl into the camp, but, if he could bring Ruben to her, that was just as good.

"I wonder who this boss is and why he's going through all this trouble to find you," Drayco pondered.

"Right now, all I want to do is find Drizzle and Joseph." Shyanne sighed heavily, rubbing her eyes. She was exhausted from the long ride and the lack of sleep thereafter. "Let's scout out the camp. We can get some rest after we're done. If they move before we return, we can shadow them and wait for a chance to free our friends."

"I'll tie him up first. Then we'll go."

Brent had slowly risen to his feet while the twins planned. He was almost around a large group of rocks when Drayco turned toward him. He shuddered as the dark man's eyes locked onto his, and ran. He had to get away; he had to tell Ruben the girl they sought was here.

"Help me! Help me! The girl's over here! Over here!"

"Damn!" Drayco growled. He started after the fleeing man, Shyanne right behind him. "We have to shut him up! Fast!"

They could hear the sentry as he wove his way ahead of them. The twins were gaining, but not quick enough. Drayco scrambled up onto the rocks to try to cut him off. Shyanne continued on the ground, increasing her speed as she ran. They had to shut him up or the camp would know they were there. She rounded a large stone and saw her prey directly ahead. He was about to disappear from sight when Drayco landed in front of him, blocking him.

Brent slid to an abrupt stop and yelled at the top of his lungs, "HELP! I need help!"

Drayco snarled and leaped at the man. Brent ducked down and flipped Drayco into the wall behind him. He stood up to continue his forward momentum toward camp. Shyanne was on his back before he could move. She pounded on his head and upper body as hard as she could.

Drayco recovered immediately from the unexpected toss. His already dark appearance seemed to take on a new level of darkness. His eyes smoldered with anger at being fooled so easily by this worthless bit of a man. He walked up to Brent, grabbed his hair, and yanked hard, knocking him off his feet. Brent and Shyanne went down in a tumble of arms and legs.

The dark man threw himself onto the struggling man's body, pinning him to the ground. Shyanne saw what was coming and was unable to get away. She was trapped beneath Brent. Her eyes widened with fear as she watched Drayco snarl like a feral beast. He sank his teeth deep into the soft exposed neck and pulled out a large chunk of flesh. The only sound from Brent was a quick intake of breath when the pain from his ravaged neck registered in his brain.

Blood splattered all over Shyanne's face and upper body. Drayco latched onto the spurting wound created by his teeth, cutting off the flow. She wanted to get it out of her eyes; her arms were pinned by the two men on top of her. The metallic taste of blood coated her mouth; it made her gag with disgust. Her breath came in ragged gasps. She wanted to cry out. It was difficult enough to breathe because of the weight on her, much less cry out. She tried to control the rising panic. Her fever crazed nightmare after the rizbak attack returned in full force. The only difference was Drayco wasn't biting her.

The blood running in her eyes temporarily blinded her. Unfortunately, her hearing was working all to well. The sound of sucking and slurping filled her every being. The fear at what might happen when the blood flow stopped was almost unbearable. Her heart raced faster and faster.

With his eyes closed, Drayco quenched his inner need with a thirst powered by hatred, hatred for these who were after Shyanne. He savored every drop from the severed artery; it filled him with a sense of euphoria. Lost as he was in the blood drinking frenzy, he failed to notice his sister's agony. The man under him quit fighting as his lifeblood drained. The flow stopped when he died.

The rushing sound in Drayco's ears gradually subsided as he let go of the dead man's neck. He heard an odd sound beneath the body. Opening his eyes, he saw his sister covered with blood, a panicked look in her eyes as she tried to breathe. A bluish color surrounded her lips. He scrambled to his feet and hurled Brent's lifeless body off her.

Shyanne rolled onto her side, gasping, savoring the

sweetness of fresh air once she was free. She frantically rubbed at the blood on her face, trying to get it off. The action only smeared it. Drayco reached out to help her; she flinched away from his touch. He backed away, a hurt look etched on his face.

"I'm sorry, Shyanne. I'm so sorry. I just wanted to kill him before he got away. Before he let all the others know we were here. If I had only known... If I had only opened my eyes and seen....￼" He could tell he was rambling. He couldn't stop himself.

He knew now that the virus had come between them like nothing else ever would. Drayco turned away from Shyanne. He walked to the rock wall and curled into a small ball, his face buried in his hands. He loved his sister dearly. It had taken him so very long to find her, and now he might lose her forever. Even seeing the fear and disgust would be better than never seeing her again. He finally admitted it; he was tired of being alone.

Shyanne watched as Drayco backed off and went down into ball. Her heart broke at the sight, but she could not make herself go to him, not yet. She had to get herself under control first.

The whole attack, escape, and recapture took only a few minutes; yet, it seemed like hours had passed. No alarms sounded and no one was running around frantically searching for anything. It appeared luck was on their side. No one had heard the shouts from the doomed man.

Using the sleeve of her shirt, she wiped her eyes and face. By the time she finished, she had come to terms with her fears. The dream that haunted her was just that, a dream. It could continue to haunt her until it became a reality, or she could put it to rest. Either way, it was a matter to be dealt with on another day. Right now, her brother needed her.

She moved to Drayco's side. He gave no indication of knowing she was there. Reaching out, she placed a hand on his shoulder and felt the muscles underneath tense.

"Drayco? Are you okay? Can you look at me?"

The dark twin refused to look into his sister's eyes. He knew what he would see: the fear; the hatred; the pity. He remained curled in a tight ball, unwilling to face the inevitable.

"Drayco, please, look at me. I know you didn't mean to do what you did." Shyanne continued to touch his shoulder, "I'm sorry I acted like I did. I couldn't help myself...I was afraid. You are my brother, and I love you very much. I know you would never do anything to intentionally hurt me."

Shyanne squat next to Drayco and wrapped her arms around him. She knew if he didn't come around soon, they'd risk discovery when a replacement came for Brent. The fear at what she had just experienced was still fresh, but she had to bury it deep if she was to help her brother. Shyanne talked to him in a soft soothing voice, combing his hair with her hand while she spoke. She felt his body start to relax.

Drayco listened to his sister's words. She sounded calm, not in the least bit disgusted. *I only hope her eyes match the tone of her voice.* He slowly looked up.

A pink hue blended with her tanned skin, and the blood made sections of her hair stiff. With dread, he gazed into her blue eyes. Although they were filled with caring and love, she was unable to hide the fear he saw deep inside. He reached up and grabbed one of the hands holding him, giving it a gentle squeeze. He knew for her sake, and for the sake of the others, he had to pull himself together. With a sigh, he stood up.

He extended a hand and helped her to her feet. "We have lost companions to find."

Shyanne watched his face transform from that of a lost child to that of a steely soldier. After a brief pause, she nodded her head in agreement. "Let's go."

Drayco followed Shyanne toward the camp. His stomach was still in complete knots, but he gave no indication of the inner turmoil on his outward appearance. Through the years, he had learned to hide his feelings, even from those who thought they knew him well. The twins wove their way through the rocky terrain toward the glow seen earlier. They dropped to their bellies and crawled quietly onto a shadow-covered rock to observe the camp's activities below.

Tents were pitched in a circular pattern within a sizeable clearing amongst the rocks. About two dozen people strolled between them going about their business. Fires burned in several places, lighting up the area and accounted for the glow they had followed. In the center, a man was tied to a large wooden post standing upright from the ground. His head hung down and his arms were at a painful angle behind him.

"Joseph. Drayco, there's Joseph." Her whisper was soft; he almost didn't hear it.

Drayco put a finger to his lips and pointed over her shoulder. A guard stood on another boulder several paces away. His back faced them as he watched the outer perimeter of the camp. The man never turned around. If he had, he would have seen the twins crouched close by. They moved deeper into the shadows to avoid being seen while they continued to check out the area, and look for Drizzle.

A mountain of a man emerged from a large tent close to the captive. His long black hair was tied back to keep it away from his strong handsome face. His body appeared to be one giant muscle, not an ounce of fat showed anywhere. His arms and legs were as big tree trunks and he towered above the people around him. Shyanne and Drayco looked at each other, seeming to think the same thing. This must be Ruben.

They watched as the big man sauntered over to the prisoner. He stopped inched from Joseph, an arrogant half smile on his face and seized a handful of hair. Jerking the bowed head upward, Joseph's bruised and battered face appeared. The glare he gave the big man said he still had some fight left in him, though. Ruben let go and words were exchanged.

The prisoner must have said the wrong thing because in the next instant, Ruben backhanded him. Joseph recovered from the sudden blow and glared once more at the monster standing before him. The twins were too far away to hear what was said. They understood the body language well enough.

Shyanne's heart ached at having to watch what happened to him, knowing she was unable to stop it. At the same time, it swelled with pride at the way Joseph handled himself.

She frowned. *These conflicting feelings are becoming a nuisance.*

It was odd that she cared for Joseph almost as much as she cared for her family. What made this man so different from the others, and in such a short amount of time?

She returned her attention to the scene below. Ruben was pacing back and forth in front of Joseph. The twins could see his mouth moving.

"I wish we could hear what he's saying," Drayco whispered.

"We can't risk getting any closer. We might be discovered, and that would ruin any chance of a rescue."

"I know. But it's hard seeing this go on and do nothing about it."

"I know what you mean, Drayco." Tearing her gaze from the prisoner, she glanced around the camp. "I wonder where Drizzle is. Brent said they didn't kill him, but I don't see him anywhere."

"Ruben probably has him hidden in one of those tents. He knows you'll eventually come for your cat. When that happens, he'll have you. That's what I would do if I wanted to capture you."

"We'll meet that son of a rizbak soon enough—but on our terms, not his," Shyanne said through clenched teeth.

The big man halted once more in front of the fair-haired prisoner. He leaned close, his nose mere inches away, his arms clasped behind him in a typical military stance. Joseph met the stare with his own cold hard gaze, showing no fear. Ruben started talking again. The prisoner kept his mouth shut, refusing to answer any questions. Suddenly, Ruben straightened up and slammed his fist into the side of Joseph's head.

The hit rocked the captive sideways as far as the restraints allowed. He slumped over and did not move. Ruben observed the unconscious man, his arms folded in front of him. A sneer spread across his face. He turned and strode toward his tent when he knew nothing more would come from the one before him.

He barked some orders concerning the prisoner to the nearby guards. They jerked to attention. One guard's response time was not fast enough for Ruben. He flew over and knocked him to the ground. A kick in the rear followed.

The man leaped immediately to his feet and snapped to attention once the abusive commander backed off. With a satisfied nod at the quickness of the man's recovery, Ruben went inside his tent.

Shyanne was shocked at how quickly the big man became violent with anyone, including his own people. She glanced at her brother. Drayco's face was grim, his jaw clenched. His eyes smoldered with anger. She looked back at Joseph's unconscious form.

Drayco indicated with a hand signal that they should back off after Ruben disappeared inside his tent. They slid off the rock to the ground below, beyond the sight of the guard standing near them and crept back to where they had left Brent's body.

"He gets such a thrill out of hurting people. You could see it in his face." Shyanne's tone was as hard as the stone surrounding her.

Drayco understood the meaning behind the words. She wasn't talking about the way the guard was treated. She was talking about Joseph. His sister was getting close to Joseph, even if she didn't realize it. The small signs she gave off and some of the things she had said led him to believe it so. He wasn't sure if it was love or simply infatuation. Either way, he felt it wasn't his place to say.

"We'll make sure he understands what he did to Joseph is unforgivable, and we'll find Drizzle. This I promise you, little sis." He gripped her shoulders gently.

She glanced up at Drayco. "I promise you, brother, one day, I will kill that man." She crossed her arms in front of her and challenged him to say anything to make her change her mind.

Drayco could tell by her mannerism that she would achieve what she set out to do. He held up his hands in a gesture of defeat and pretended to cower down from her. She relaxed and returned his smile.

"We have to do something about him." she tilted her head in the direction of the dead man. "We can't just leave him like that. They'll know something's up when they come to relieve him and find him not at his post."

"I've been thinking about that," Drayco replied. "I've got a plan."

The dark man grabbed Brent under the arms and

dragged him to the boulder he had stood guard on. "Shyanne, help me get him up there." He leaned the dead man against the rock face and climbed up onto the boulder, then waited for his sister to come help lift the body up to him.

She moved to Brent's body and tugged his arms upward, placing them in her brother's outreached hands. She grabbed the man's legs and helped Drayco lift him up, wondering what her brother was up to, but didn't say anything.

Drayco could tell from the look on her face that she thought him crazy. He wasn't too sure how far off that thought was.

To keep Ruben and the camp from suspecting anyone was there, he knew he had to make Brent's death look like an accident. He maneuvered the body into a sitting position, straddled the upper torso with his legs, and grabbed either side of the head. With a quick twist of his body, he broke the man's neck. Shyanne grimaced and looked away. Drayco wrestled the body into a standing position and moved to the edge of the rock. He let Brent drop toward a group of smaller rocks lying near the base. The body fell like a lead weight and landed at an awkward angle between two of the rocks. The neck Drayco had torn open now had a large chunk of stone imbedded in it.

Drayco jumped down from the boulder to inspect his handiwork. Something tugged at him; something was missing. Suddenly, he remembered Brent's sword and ran back to get it. Returning, he stood close to the group of rocks where the body came to rest. With his back facing the edge, he tossed it. It landed at such an angle that any observer would think it actually fell with the body instead of looking staged. Satisfied with the results, the dark twin walked around the area brushing away his footprints with a gnarled tree branch he found trapped between some rocks.

"What do you think?"

Shyanne didn't say anything, at first. Her brother's ingenuity impressed her. At the same time, it disgusted her. "It looks like the real thing. Good job." She started down the pathway toward Jack's hiding spot. When she didn't hear footsteps following, she turned back to see why.

Drayco was looking in the direction of the glowing camp.

"Let's go, brother. We need to get out of here before that other guy returns. Besides, I want to wash this blood off me. I'm sick of wearing it."

Drayco grimaced at Shyanne's words. Fortunately, his reaction went unnoticed because his back faced her. "I want to see their reaction. I want to make sure they think the death was an accident instead of intentional. You go on. Wait for me at the camp."

"Do you think that's wise? Will you be able to get away if they don't think it's an accident and start hunting for whoever did this?" Shyanne stamped her foot in anger. "I already lost you once. Now that I've finally found you, I don't want to go through that again. I know you've changed, in some ways not for the better, but I still love you."

His heart broke with those words. Recent events being what they were, he thought for sure Shyanne would reject him. He rushed to her and hugged her against his body. She hugged him back with all her might.

"You have no idea how happy that makes me, little sis." His words were little more than a whisper.

"Yes I do, big brother. Yes I do."

The twins separated. Shyanne reached up and touched her brother's face. "Be careful. I don't want to go on without you."

He covered her hand. "Don't worry. You won't."

He let go and disappeared into the field of boulders to find a hiding place to watch the enemy's actions unfold. He never once looked back at his sister. To him, that would be the same as saying goodbye without hope of ever seeing her again, and that was not going to happen.

* * *

Shyanne waited until Drayco was gone before she made her way carefully through the rocks, leaving no trace of her passage. She had no desire to lead the people from the camp to her hiding spot if they suspected foul play.

The branch off for the alcove appeared in no time. Shyanne moved the brush hiding the entrance and replaced it so that it looked natural from the trail. Jack nickered as she walked up to him, and bumped her in the chest with his nose. She gave his neck an affectionate pat before making sure he had enough food and water.

I need to get this blood off. I'm sick to death of feeling so icky, she thought.

She held up bits of her bloody hair and felt the stiffness crinkle between her fingers. Letting it drop with disgust, she gathered the necessary things to wash with. A small amount of water was poured into a bowl shaped dip in the rocks worn away with the passing of time and weather. She didn't use much, though. One never knew when an opportunity would arise for more water to be found, especially in this arid terrain of rock.

She took a worn cloth out of her bag and washed the blood off her face and upper body. She tried to get it out of her hair, but there wasn't enough water in the natural bowl to do the job. She cringed at the thought of leaving it in so she scooped the filthy red tinged liquid out and refilled it.

"I know I shouldn't waste so much water, but I can't stand this mess any longer."

In short order, Shyanne had her hair clean and her clothes changed. The bloodied ones were buried in some loose dirt to hide the scent from any passing night dwellers. While putting everything away, a noise sounded near the entranceway. She picked up her sword and freed it from its scabbard with the adeptness of someone used to doing it. The noise sounded again, only this time it was closer. She hoped the mercenaries had not found her.

All kinds of wild thoughts flew through her brain as she watched the bushes covering the entrance move. Remembering the rizbak incident, and the cruelness she witnessed from Ruben, she put her back toward the wall and waited. She had been alive for 213 years and had seen many changes throughout that time; she planned on seeing more.

The bushes moved again. Shyanne crouched in response, her sword held ready before her. Just as the tension was becoming too much, a small nose poked through. It wiggled up and down several times. A long set of ears followed.

A smile crept onto her face as the creature emerged. "A Jackrabbit! All that worry over a jackrabbit." Shyanne lowered her sword.

At the sound of her voice, the rabbit whipped around to get away from her. Instead, it became ensnared in the bushes. Seeing the frantic struggles, Shyanne rushed over and lifted the mass out of the way. With the flat side of her sword, she shooed it in the right direction down the pathway before she could change her mind and make a meal out of it.

"Thanks for the scare, little one," she laughed softly to herself as she set the bushes down. "If we meet again, I will make a meal out of you."

The chilly bite in the air caused her shoulders to shake. Shyanne put her sword away and fetched her blanket. She wrapped herself in the thick material and sat down to wait for Drayco. The lack of sleep and the wild events of the night were taking their toll on her. Her eyelids became heavy. She leaned against the stone wall and thought to herself, *Drayco won't be long, I'll just close my eyes for a second.*

Soon, the only one aware of the passing night was Jack.

*   *   *

Drayco left his sister and went into the rocks to scout out a position in which to observe the body. He discovered an ideal nitch not too far from the site. The overhanging slab of rock created a dark recess that would hide him from any angle and leave the area he watched unobscured. Before crawling into his hiding spot, he made sure no evidence of his passing remained to give his position away. Half an hour went by before the man who said he would send a replacement returned.

"Brent! Brent! Where are you, you lazy bum. Have you fallen asle..."

The man stopped and gaped at the body sprawled at his feet. His mouth hung open. It stayed open as he cupped his hands around it and shouted for help. "Hey! Hey, get over here! Something's happened to Brent!"

Drayco heard the sound of running feet; the stone beneath him vibrated in response. A half dozen people ran into view, weapons bared, heads turning in several directions trying to see what was going on. The shouting man pointed to the body among the rocks. The mercenaries started talking rapidly, their voices bouncing through the gaps in the rocks. A hush fell over the group as the moon cast a huge shadow in front of Drayco's hiding spot.

Ruben strolled into sight. His manner was calm, his voice strong, his posture full of arrogance.

"What's going on here?"

"Sir, something's happened to Brent." The man jumped to attention at the same time he barked the words.

Ruben sauntered over to get a closer look at the body. After walking around as far as the rocks allowed, he stated, "Appears to me he fell and broke his neck. See the odd angle?" The mercenary bent over, grabbed a handful of the dead man's hair, and lifted. The rock fell out, exposing the wound on the neck. He let it go and stood up. "Captain, get a detail together and get rid of this trash. I have no desire to do battle with scavengers wanting this worthless thing. I don't care what you do with it, just don't leave it here."

He reinforced his words by shoving the body off the rock grouping with his boot. He stood back, crossed his arms on his chest, and watched as a group of men gathered up their fallen comrade and carried him into the darkness.

Drayco recognized the type of man Ruben was. The dark twin had seen it many times before. He was used to getting his way. If he didn't get it, he bullied everyone around him until they either gave in, or he killed them. One way or the other, he got what he wanted. A giant sword draped across Ruben's back. Drayco suspected the powerful leader knew how to use it well.

Ruben stayed after the rest of the group had gone, starring off at nothing. He appeared to be deep in thought. Drayco felt a twinge of doubt crawl into the pit of his stomach. He wasn't sure whether they had gotten away with the plan or not. He waited nervously, afraid to move even a finger lest it draw attention to his hiding place. Suddenly, the big man nodded his head, as if satisfied with something he had been debating. He spun around and started back to camp. Drayco relaxed his guard for a split second then slammed it back in place until he was certain the man was truly gone.

Drayco emerged from his hiding spot, curious as to what Ruben was up to. He worked his way to where he could see the camp. Ruben was walking up to the prisoner. He stopped in front of Joseph and said something before continuing to another tent located next to his. He pulled the flap out of the way and ducked inside. Drayco noticed a guard standing inside the tent.

Drizzle must be in there.

Ruben stayed in the tent for what seemed like only minutes before he returned to his own. Drayco backed off the rock and without leaving any traces of his presence, worked his way back to Shyanne.

The dark twin located the entrance and moved the brush out of the way. He saw Shyanne jump to her feet, her sword suddenly in her hand. A blanket fell from her shoulders.

"It's alright, sis. It's just me."

"What happened? Did they go for it?" she asked as she slid her sword into its sheath. A yawn followed.

He answered while he hid the entranceway again. "They seemed to. I was worried about that Ruben fellow, at first. He returned to the camp and went into another tent with a guard posted inside. I think Drizzle's in there."

"What do we do now?"

"We watch, and we wait. Dawn isn't too far away, and I don't think anything else will happen tonight." He fetched his blanket before continuing. "For now, we need to get some rest. We'll scout out the camp in the morning and see if we can find a way to free the others."

To stay warm against the chilly night, the twins curled up next to each other and fell into a light sleep. A watch was not needed. They knew Jack would alert them if anything came close enough to spook him.

*   *   *

Ruben heard the shouting and calmly walked toward the commotion. He saw one of the men, a captain who's name he couldn't remember, standing near a body sprawled among the rocks.

"What's going on here?"

The captain spoke about Brent and his apparent fall.

Ruben inspected the scene and gave his conclusions about what he thought happened. What he hadn't told the man was his true thoughts. After giving instructions to the onlookers, which they followed perfectly, the big man stayed behind, listening. Nothing but the usual sounds of the night echoed back to him.

The feeling of someone watching burned through his body. He looked around the area without seeming to look. The darkness of the night prevented him from seeing anything. Over time, the mercenary had developed an inner sense that he trusted well. It had saved his life on many occasions. It screamed at him now.

Brent's 'accident' disturbed him.

Where's the blood from the neck wound? Nothing but dry rock surrounded the body. I suspect someone killed him elsewhere then made it appear to be an accident.

Ruben's face showed nothing of his inner turmoil. If the one who did this were close, as his instincts led him to believe, that person would see his reaction and become overly cautious. If she remained unaware of his suspicions, she might become careless, and easily captured. Ruben was almost certain it was the girl they sought. After all, he had her cat and the male companion who was with it.

A nod of approval solidified his decision against further action. For the moment, he wanted to give the person watching a chance to become lax. Ruben turned and started back to camp.

The prisoner met his gaze with one filled with hatred when he stopped before him. The glare turned to one of confusion when the mercenary said, "Not much longer now."

Ruben moved toward the tent situated next to his. The guard inside jumped to attention as he ducked through the flap. A small lamp sitting in the corner brightened the interior. Drizzle lay in the middle, chained to a post in the ground. His mouth was tied shut to keep him from biting anyone; his feet were tied, as well. The bloody spot where the arrow had struck near his shoulder had long since become dried and crusty. Ruben looked down at the big cat, and chuckled.

"I thought you'd like to know...she's here." His words were smug. "We will capture her and bring her to the Boss, and there's nothing you can do about it. How does it feel to be so helpless, to be unable to prevent it?" Ruben laughed at the discomfort his declaration gave the cat. He left Drizzle to contemplate his inability to help his friends.

The mercenary leader returned to his tent. He wanted to make sure he had his wits about him in case the girl slipped up. Sleep would help. He had to bring her to the Boss alive, or else. That one would not tolerate any mistakes made during her capture.

Ruben sat down on his sleeping pad and peeled off his boots. They hit the ground next to the only other thing in the tent, his pack. He did not like to carry a lot of unnecessary things on his journeys; they only slowed him down when speed was of the essence. The faster he worked, the more he earned. A simple philosophy.

Removing the sword from his back, he placed it on the ground within easy reach. The big man curled under the blanket and fell into a light sleep. His dreams were filled with the capture his quarry, and the rewards he would receive for it.

Ten

The twins stirred just as the sun was sending its colorful rays across the morning sky, announcing its presence to the world. The cool air from the previous night made getting out of the blankets difficult.

"I'm not looking forward to winter. Always makes my fingers and toes feel like they're going to freeze off," Shyanne said as she snuggled deeper into her blanket.

"Better than the sweltering heat of summer," Drayco quipped.

"True. I have to agree with you there."

Shyanne got up; her blanket still draped over her shoulders, and fetched some dried meat along with some trail mix.

After Drayco finished the meager breakfast, he said, "I'm going to scout out the camp. Be ready in case they pull out this morning."

Shyanne nodded her head and started gathering their belongings.

He moved the bushes hiding the entrance to their camp and went out onto the little used trail. Hearing nothing, he made his way toward the small ledge he used yesterday.

The guards posted on the outer perimeter didn't pay much attention to the surrounding land. They couldn't imagine anyone remotely dangerous being in this part of the world except them. If there was anyone around, they couldn't imagine him or her being stupid enough as to attack a well-armed group like theirs. Because of their lax behavior, they failed to spot the dark man moving in their midst.

The other mercenaries were bored with the hunt for the woman. They had been on this mission for the better part of the summer and they wanted it done. With winter approaching, they felt it was time to get their money and go back home, where a tall mug of ale and a warm companion awaited them. Besides, she probably wasn't even in the area. They had captured a man traveling with a large cat who stumbled upon their campsite, but he denied any knowledge of the woman they sought.

None mentioned these facts to Ruben. They respected him for what he had done, making them richer and more powerful than they had ever dreamed. Each also knew better than to anger the big man. He would likely kill the one talking to him in a fit of rage before more than three sentences were spoken.

Drayco made it to the previous days hiding spot without difficulty. Today, he wanted to get closer. He wanted to be able to see and hear what was going on. Keeping an eye on a nearby guard who was daydreaming, he worked his way through the rocks. Several times, he had to duck to avoid people moving around the camp. The uneven terrain, with its nooks and ledges, gave him many places to hide.

One such nook was perfect for him to see and hear what was going on in the enemy camp. Gripping his sword to prevent any noise, he crouched low and crawled under an overhanging rock wedged next to another huge boulder. By the time he was in place, the shadows hid his body entirely.

Drayco could see Joseph still tied to the post, his head hung low. The only thing holding him upright was the ropes around his body. The dark man wanted to let him know he were there, but could not risk it.

Suddenly, two riders came barreling around a rock outcropping into camp and jumped off their mounts before the horses completely stopped. They went immediately to Ruben's tent. One of the men yelled to let the occupant inside know they were there, and to receive permission to enter. A bellow from inside told them to do so. They tossed back the flap and disappeared from sight.

Several groups formed around the cook fires to eat and to stay warm in the chilly air. Drayco watched a muscular woman dressed in fighting gear walk over to Joseph. She grabbed his hair, held his head up, and gave him a drink from a battered cup pressed against his lips. He drank eagerly, taking in every drop that touched his lips. The woman let go of his hair once he finished and watched him. He glared at her, giving no thanks for the liquid that helped his parched body.

She reached up and ran her fingers along his cheek in a sensuous manner, then traveled them down to the exposed skin of his chest. Joseph jerked his head back, disgusted, and hit the post behind him. The female mercenary smiled at the pain caused by his reaction. A hand rose to her lips as she turned and walked away. She blew him a kiss before disappearing from sight, laughing.

At least he's still alive, Drayco thought.

The dark twin lay under the rock outcropping watching the morning activities of the mercenaries. He wanted to establish a pattern to their movements in case the opportunity arose to rescue Joseph. The sound of a tent flap tossed open brought his attention back to the center of the camp. The two men who had entered earlier were leaving. They jumped on their horses and rode out of camp as quickly as they had ridden in. Drayco wondered what was going on. He didn't have long to wait before he got his answer.

Ruben stepped out from the tent and shouted to get everyone's attention. "Let's break camp! I've just received new information from the Boss. We have to go farther west." He walked over to Joseph and said in a loud calm voice, "And you, my friend, are going with us. The boss is interested in how you are connected to the female we seek, and why you are traveling with her cat."

The mercenaries put all the loose items away and pulled down the tents in a timely, organized manner. The people worked with as little sound as possible. They knew what part of the takedown process they had to do and completed it before Ruben could get frustrated. Drayco got the feeling they had performed this task many times before and was impressed with their speed and efficiency.

Horses were brought from a secret alcove that Drayco had not seen before. The Bay he acquired from the burley man was among them.

Ruben stood in the middle of the process and watched without comment. When all activity ended and the horses were ready for the journey, he went to the prisoners.

Drizzle lay on the ground next to Joseph. Drayco saw a bloody spot near his shoulder; otherwise, he looked unhurt. The cat attention was focused on the movements of the people.

Probably doing the same thing I am...looking for any opportunities or weaknesses.

The big man stared at the prisoners before he turned around to address the crowd. "Well done, people. You make me proud." The mercenaries smiled at each other then returned their full attention to Ruben. He continued. "The information just given to me is from the Boss. As you know, the Boss is the one paying us to find a woman traveling with a big cat. The purpose is of no concern to us. What matters most is that we are paid well for our services."

The last statement brought a cheer of approval from the mercenaries.

"We have the cat. Now I'm informed the woman we seek is located in a town west of here called Grandfield."

Grandfield, that's the town Moss mentioned before he died, Drayco thought as he listened.

Ruben paced back and forth in front of the group, a stern look planted on his face. "We will move out immediately to find her. When we do, we will detain her without harm...if possible." He paused in his pacing and gave a sideways smirk to the mercenaries, then resumed walking. Several of the men said lewd comments as they grinned and elbowed each other.

"The Boss also wants this man." He jerked a thumb toward Joseph. "He will be brought back alive for questioning. Anyone caught messing with him will be killed immediately. Am I making myself clear?" He stopped and gave each man and woman a look that left no doubts about what would happen if his orders were disobeyed.

The lot standing before Ruben appeared to be made up

of roughnecks, killers, fighters, and thieves, but they all must have met with the leader's wrath at some time or another. Drayco watched in fascination as each one refused to meet Ruben's stare. They all looked at the ground or fidgeted when his gaze met theirs. He could only imagine what each one had gone through, but for some reason they still respected him and stayed with him.

"Let's move out," Ruben commanded. He remained where he was while the others followed his orders.

Drayco decided it was time to get back to Shyanne so they wouldn't lose the group within the rocks. He also wanted to update her as to what was said and on how Joseph and Drizzle were doing. Sliding backwards out from under the ledge, the sword at his side made a slight chinking noise when it rubbed against the rock. He froze. No one looked in his direction. The commotion created by the group moving toward their animals overshadowed the noise.

Or so he thought.

Apparently, someone did notice. Drizzle casually moved his head around in such a way to lead anyone watching into thinking he was stretching his neck. He stopped when he spotted Drayco. Drayco met the cat's gaze and let him know through hand signals that all was well, and that they would be following when the party moved. Drizzle gave a slight nod of his head to let the dark man know he understood. He returned to the previous position.

The dark twin decided to stay where he was until after the mercenaries moved on to reduce the risk of another incident. He remembered hearing the direction the troupe were going and did not want to risk getting caught needlessly.

After everyone was ready, one of the men brought a huge black stallion with a brilliant white blaze on its forehead forward from another alcove. The power rippling from the beast was incredible. The horse sensed the excitement in the air and pranced around, making it difficult for the man leading him to keep from being trampled. Ruben walked up and stroked its forehead, calming it immediately.

"How's my big boy?"

The horse bobbed his head into the big man's chest, almost knocking him over. Ruben kept a firm grip on the bridle to prevent him from succeeding.

"Is Wind Racer ready to go for a run?"

He grabbed the reins and walked down the side of the animal, running his free hand gently against the muscular body to keep it calm. Wind Racer held steady, even though he trembled with excitement. Once the big man reached the well-worn saddle, he placed a foot in the stirrup and threw himself onto the broad back.

The big man gripped the reins and watched as two people from the group untied Joseph from the pole. He laughed as the prisoner crashed to the ground, causing a swirl of dust to puff up around his face.

Joseph lay where he fell, coughing from the effort to breathe through the cloud. His arms were forcefully pinned behind him and a knee planted square in his back to prevent him from struggling while the men retied his arms. They picked him up and dragged him to one of the horses where he was thrown into a sitting position on the animals back. One wrapped some rope around both arms and tied the ends to the saddle horn to prevent him from falling off in his weakened state.

The men picked up the big cat and attempted to place him on the same animal. The horse shied away from the scent, and would have thrown Joseph had he not been secured to it. It took several people holding the animal to get it under control before the cat came to rest behind Joseph. Afterwards, everyone leaped onto their horses and waited for Ruben to give the signal to begin the journey.

Ruben had witnessed Drizzle's reaction and without letting anyone know what he was doing, looked around while waiting for the camp to get ready. He couldn't see what the cat had spotted, but knew someone was there. A slight nod of the head told him that a message had been passed between the two.

A smile crossed his face as he prodded the black horse through the pass that led toward the open country to the west. Ruben knew his bait had been taken. Unlike himself, he felt certain the woman would never abandon her companions, and would follow them straight to Grandfield, a town well known by the gang.

If the female trailing them tried to rescue her companions, he looked forward to the fight and the ensuing capture. He knew he couldn't kill her, but a little playful groping was allowed. The Boss' order said to bring her back alive. The order did not specify in what condition.

*   *   *

Drayco waited until the last of the party had disappeared around the rocks before he moved. He weaved his way back to the hiding spot as fast as he could. When he got there, the clump of bushes blocking the entrance went sailing. He skidded to a stop with his hands in the air when the point of a sword almost pierced his chest.

"Whoa...Shyanne, it's me!"

"Drayco! That's becoming a dangerous habit with you!" She lowered her sword to the ground. "What's going on?"

"Ruben received word you were in a town called Grandfield, and has started his people toward it." He leaned over, resting his hands on his knees to catch his breath.

"Isn't that the town Moss told us about before he died?"

"Yea. Oh, I saw Drizzle. He's been hurt, but not badly. I was able to get a signal to him that we would follow."

"What about Joseph? Is he still okay?" The weird feeling in the middle of her chest returned, and she felt flushed when she said his name. Looking away, she again wondered what was it about Joseph that caused her to get so worked up.

Drayco saw the look in his sister's eyes at the mention of Joseph's name. He knew, even if she didn't, that she loved this man. He resolved that no matter what it took, he would make sure their companions were freed, and that his sister was reunited with the man who had so thoroughly stolen her heart, even if she had yet to realize it.

"He's okay. Ruben gave orders to the rest that he's to remain unharmed."

Shyanne's stiff posture relaxed. The look he saw a moment ago was gone. A look of determination replaced it.

She focused on her brother. "Let's go after them. We don't want those...mercenaries... to get too far ahead." She spat the word out like it had a bad taste.

She climbed into the saddle and extended a hand out to help her brother up. With every passing moment, Jack became more tolerant of him and remained still. Drayco grabbed the offered hand and pulled himself up behind her. Once he was settled, gentle prodding urged the horse beyond the opening of their hiding spot. She pointed him in the direction of the recently vacated camp and clicked her tongue several times to move him through the narrow winding pathway between the rocks.

They passed where the mercenary's camp used to be and continued westward. During the journey through the field of stone, silence ensued. Neither brother nor sister had much to say. Each was pondering on how they were going to get their companions back.

*   *   *

Ruben kept Wind Racer's forward momentum to a slow prance by maintaining a steady pull on the reins. The horse was thrilled to be out of the enclosed space, and it showed. The rest of the mercenaries made sure to stay with him. If they lost track of the pair in the field of stone, it meant they were not paid, and that was simply not an option this far into the mission.

Front and rear guards were posted as was customary during a move. Everything was calm, and the big man liked it that way.

Ruben thought about what he had witnessed back at the camp. The cat twitched its ears at something then slowly moved its head around until it stopped, looking at a rock outcropping toward the left. Keeping his head straight, the big man used his eyes to watch the entire process without the cat or watcher noticing. He had learned to be observe discreetly through his years as a soldier, and it was about to pay off.

The girl must be close. I knew she would come.

The sun was just past midday when the world of gray turned to one of green brushed with tan. Ruben was so tired of seeing nothing but rock that the sight of the open field ahead raised his spirit immensely. The mood of the entire group lifted, as well.

Ruben pulled Wind Racer to a stop and let the rest of the party go past into the sea of waving grass. They were shaking their heads, smiling, because they had seen this maneuver many times in the past and knew what came next. The dark horse was anxious, moving his shiny black hooves from one spot to another, like a dancer nervous before his first performance. He knew what was coming.

The big man watched until the party was nothing more than specks on the distant horizon before starting to count. When he got to fifty, he whispered to the stallion, "Now's your chance, boy, show me what you're made of."

He grabbed a handful of mane, let the reins go slack, gripped with his thighs, and leaned low in the saddle. The muscles beneath him bunched and sprang into action as the stallion responded immediately. Within seconds, they were flying across the open space.

The rhythmic sound of hooves pounding against the ground and the heaving of each breath as it rushed out of the stallion, along the wind rushing past his face all helped rid the sour feel of so much stone. He loved doing this. So did Wind Racer. The horse had been cooped up far too long. The ability to stretch in the open plains lengthened his stride to the point that it felt like he soared with wings instead of legs.

They cleared the hill and entered the vast plains beyond. The mercenaries were barely visible in the distance, but the man and horse were closing the gap rapidly. As they neared the back of the group, Ruben let go of the reins and sat up. He reached his arms out wide; fingers spread apart, and leaned his head back with his eyes closed. Wind Racer slowed his pace when his rider sat up. He knew the run was almost over.

His eyes watered freely and his face stung from the wind, but Ruben always felt exhilarated after a run. By the time they caught up, both man and animal were exhausted. Sweat lathered out from under the saddle, covering the horse's body. Ruben knew he had to walk him to cool him down. Wind Racer was the only family he had; he cared for the horse as he would his own child.

The stallion's nostrils flared and his sides heaved with every breath; but he held his head high and arched his neck gracefully while chomping at the bit in his mouth. He still had some spring in his walk. Ruben knew better than to let the horse continue running.

"I know, big guy, I know. You're a powerful horse. I would love to let you run some more, but not right now." He leaned over and gave the wet neck an affectionate pat. One of the men rode up to him while he spoke to the stallion.

"Another fulfilling ride, sir?" he asked.

"As a matter of fact it was. No better way to take your mind off things than to have it blown around a bit."

"Sorry to have to bring it back, sir. We were curious what your plans are?"

"I want to cool Wind Racer for a few more miles. After that, we'll break for the afternoon meal then start again for the west coast."

As soon as the mercenary, another captain, left to pass the message along, Ruben returned his attention to the horse. Sweat still gleamed from Wind Racer's coat, but the warm breeze was drying the exposed areas quickly. The big man knew when they stopped, a good brush down was in order.

While they continued on to Grandfield, Ruben reluctantly returned his thoughts to the girl he sought, and of what her connection to the Boss might be.

Why is he willing to put out so much gold for just one woman? What does she have that he wants so badly?

He remembered the first time he met the Boss. It had been almost five years ago.

He was sitting in a bar, minding his own business, drinking himself into oblivion, when this stranger came up to him. Ruben was startled when a shape sat down as silent as a cat next to him. The stranger was draped in a long black oversized cloak with the hood pulled up, hiding the face completely. It hung off him like there was nothing beneath it.

"Can I buy you a drink?" a soft whispery tone emitted from the cloak.

"Whatever you like, pal. It's your money. Just don't expect anything for it." Ruben's words were slurred.

"I only want a moment of your time."

The stranger held up a gloved hand and indicated for the barkeep to come over. When the man stood before them, the stranger said in the same whispery tone, "A drink for this gentleman and a mug of warm cider for me."

After the barkeep walked away to fill their order, Ruben leaned back and snickered, "What's the matter? You a pansy or something? Can't hold your drink?"

The cloaked figure remained silent, which only fueled the verbal attack.

Ruben nearly toppled off the stool laughing at his own statements. He continued to pick at the stranger in his usual cruel fashion. "You a momma's boy? Want me to call your momma for ya?"

The barkeep returned with their drinks and waited for the payment. "That will be two bits of gold."

The stranger reached into the cloak.

"You too much of a wimp to handle it? Why don't you get a mug of milk and...."

Ruben stopped in mid-sentence as he saw five shiny pieces of gold hit the bar in front of the waiting man. An additional handful was set on the counter for future purchases.

"The extra three pieces are for your continued good service. More will follow if you do well."

The barkeep picked up the gold and pocketed the three pieces indicated for him while keeping the other two out. "Yes sir, thank you, sir. You let me know when you're ready for another round and I'll bring it straight away." He was thrilled at his good fortune tonight, and hoped the other pieces resting on the counter were a sign of more to come.

"I'll let you know when we need your services again." He dismissed the barkeep with a wave of the gloved hand.

Ruben watched the bartender walk away, still fingering the three gold pieces. The big man's eyes had nearly bugged out at the sight of so much gold. However, he was a cautious man. The drinks may have made the world a bit fuzzy, but he still had the ability to think straight. He kept his mouth shut and waited for the stranger to inform him what it was he wanted.

"I have been watching you for some time, Ruben." The face remained hidden deep in the shadows of the hood.

Ruben stared at the person sitting beside him. He was surprised at the mention of his name, but kept it from showing.

"I want you to work for me. I've seen the many talents you possess, and I want to put them to a better use."

"What talents are you talking about?"

"The ability to lead men, to get from them what you desire, and the talent you possess in handling people when they get out of control."

"Other men can do that—why me?"

"Because I like your style. I like the way you enjoy your line of work. Not many people can handle the kind of pressure involved with it, and the killing that can happen." The dark hood turned toward Ruben, unnerving him with the eeriness of its depth.

"I need that for my many projects. Someone who can listen, who can follow directions and come back with results. I will pay you handsomely if you join me." He emphasized his words by patting the dark cloak. The chinking of many coins hitting each other echoed from the material.

"What makes you think I won't kill you and take that from you now?"

"Because you have standards. And killing without a reason is not one of them."

"How do you know these things?" Ruben's eyes reduced to slits as he leaned back in the chair and crossed his arms over on his chest.

"As I said before, I've been watching you."

Although the stranger intrigued him, Ruben did not like the situation in which he found himself. He had standards, as mentioned, but what good were they to the one sitting next to him?

"I want to know what jobs I'll be doing before I decide to work for you. And the cost for my services," Ruben demanded. He picked up the mug of ale in front of him took a long draw from it.

"Of course," whispered the unnerving voice from deep in the hood. "Meet me at the inn located in Grandfield and we'll talk. I like a little more privacy when we discuss business. Obtain a room after getting a bottle of whatever you want to drink. I will meet you there shortly."

"How do I know this isn't a trap or something?"

"You have nothing of value to me except your talents," the stranger said as he glided from the chair and seemed to float toward the door. "What good would they be if you were dead?"

"Who should I say is coming?

"Tell the innkeeper the Boss is coming. He'll know what to do." and was gone before Ruben could say another word.

Ruben looked back and saw the pile of gold left on the counter. "I might as well put these to good use." He became even more rip roaring drunk than before the encounter.

The big man did what he was told, more out of curiosity than anything else; he went to Grandfield.

The inn was easy to find; it was the only one in town. He informed the clerk he was there to meet the Boss and was given the key to room 130. Ruben made his way down the hallway and discovered it was the last room on the right. No other sleeping rooms were near it. A storage area of some kind was across from it and a closet sat next to it. The hallway he walked down was the only way in or out of the area.

"Kinda odd place to put a room," he muttered as he unlocked the door.

The room was dark except for the faint glow shining in from the hall. There were no windows anywhere. He discovered a set of half-used candles in holders on the small table by the door and a little pot with a hot coal in it sitting next to them, ready to light the candles when needed.

Ruben picked up the piece of coal with a set of tongs hanging on the wall. A pair of flames soon chased away the impenetrable darkness. A quick look around showed a room sparse of furniture. He put the coal back in the pot then shut the door behind him.

A soft thud filled the room as the pack over his shoulder dropped onto the floor next to the table. He picked up one of the two candleholders and moved to a small table located in the back corner. Pulling out a chair, he sat down to wait, his sword within easy reach in case it was a trap after all.

He did not have long to wait. A slight rapping noise caught his attention. Before Ruben moved to answer it, the door burst open. Two armed men carrying swords and a third holding a whip burst inside. Two went to either side of the room while the last came straight at him.

Ruben whipped out his sword and met the charge head on. The sound of metal hitting metal echoed throughout the small room. The man tried to bring his weapon around for an uppercut; Ruben's weapon was there. Every time he attempted to cut at the big man trapped in the corner, a sword was there to meet it.

As the attacker in front jumped out of the way, the sound of a whip snapped in the room. Ruben felt the sting as it bit into his chest. It pelted his body repeatedly, causing him to flinch with each hit. One such hit brought him to his knees, grimacing with pain. The first attacker saw an opportunity and tried to take advantage of it. He swung his sword high with the intent of bringing it down on Ruben's bowed head. Instead, he was looking at the big man's sword buried deep in his chest.

Ruben tugged the weapon free and stood ready for the next attacker, a snarl etched on his bleeding face. The man in front of him slid to the ground, dead. The other two attackers paced around in the room, looking for any opportunity to get at the trapped man.

The one holding the whip started hitting Ruben again. Blood from several new whelps melded with the rest on his exposed skin. The remaining attacker took advantage of the distraction and dove at Ruben. He was met with a foot in the side of the face, followed by a sword in the middle of his back as he went down.

As the second attacker fell, the third hesitated. He turned and fled out the door before Ruben could react. The big man followed, only to see the Boss standing in the hall with the third attacker lying dead at his feet. He was putting something away in the cloak.

"I had hoped for more from this one, but, as you can see, it didn't happen. The other two were expendable." The same whispery voice floated from the black hood.

"What sort of game are you playing here?" Ruben demanded. He still had his sword in hand and contemplated using it on the cloaked figure standing before him.

"It was a test to see if you were worthy of working for me."

"I thought you were watching me. If you were, you'd already know I could handle myself."

"I know through watching you spar with others. Now I know from an actual battle."

Men exited from the room across the hall and gathered the bodies. They looked and moved in an odd fashion, almost robotic like, ignoring the pair completely. Ruben watched them warily. He put his sword away when the men and bodies were gone.

The Boss indicated for Ruben to return to the room. Upon entering, the big man saw the small table was moved away from the corner and another chair had been added. Food and drink sat on it. Ruben glanced around the room, trying to figure out when the move had happened. No one had entered the room. Shrugging, he sat down in the chair against the wall.

They discussed what was required of him long into the night and gold passed between the two. That was the beginning of his rewarding involvement with the Boss.

Ruben's attention returned to the world around him when the captain guided his horse up to him again.

"Sir, we have traveled for several miles. What are your wishes?"

"Break for a meal. Plan on staying for only a short time. We still have several days ride ahead of us and I don't want to get caught out on these plains without some kind of shelter."

"If I recall, there are some ruins ahead. We could reach them before nightfall."

"Good work, Captain. Tell the group we head for those ruins after the stop."

"Yes Sir." The captain pulled around and returned to the men and women following.

The mercenaries halted their forward progress and fed their horses before eating any food themselves. Ruben watched as Drizzle and Joseph were removed from their animal. One of the men untied the cat's mouth and quickly moved away before the cat could bite. A jackrabbit, killed this morning in the stone hell, was tossed close enough for him to grab. Drizzle glared at the big man before reluctantly eating the rabbit.

As Ruben watched, a plan formed about how he was going to get the girl back to the Boss. A smile appeared on his face. He dismounted and removed the saddle so he could brush the horse down. The smile remained during the entire process.

The group was unnerved when they looked in his direction. They knew Ruben. The big man had not smiled this much in a very long time, and they hoped they were not going to pay the price because with it.

Eleven

Shyanne kept Jack's pace slow to make sure they didn't stumble upon a rear guard hidden amongst the massive stones. The pace grated on her nerves. It could not be helped, though, not if they were going to free their friends. When they came upon the open plains, nothing lay ahead except for a never-ending sea of rippling grass.

"What do we do now? If we go out into the plains, they'll see us," Shyanne asked.

"We stay on Jack and follow their tracks. If we come close to a hill, I'll scout ahead on foot. That way we're still on the move, but out of sight. On the flat plains, we just have to take our chances."

The twins kept at the jerky pace for hours, stopping to scout hills before crossing them. They were between gently rolling slopes when a light breeze brought the scent of freshly trodden grass and dirt to their noses. Shyanne inhaled deeply and leaned back on Drayco.

"I miss this. It reminds me of how good the grass smelled after a mowing." She peered up at him, changing the subject. "Do you feel a twinge of fall in the air?"

"Yes, I feel it. I hope we're all together and settled before it gets here."

"You, me, Drizzle—and Joseph, if he wants. He is a friend of ours, after all. And that silly old cat does like him." She returned her gaze to the plains.

Drayco looked at Shyanne, *She hasn't accepted the fact that she is in love with Joseph. Just like my sister—*

always the last one to know.

Before riding over the other side of the slope, Drayco slid off Jack to check out what lay beyond. This time, he fell to the ground quickly. The mercenaries were ahead, stopped for a rest. He motioned for Shyanne to stay where she was before returning his gaze to the crowd.

No tents stood among the crowd. He assumed it was a short break instead of a full stop. Seeing Ruben on the outer edge of the group brushing his horse caused his blood to boil. The sight of their friends, Joseph and Drizzle, in the center of the group brought the temperature down. After making sure they were still in good shape, he eased away from the hill and returned to Shyanne. She had dismounted and was standing next to Jack.

"They're just over that hill. It looks like a short stop so we'll have to keep an eye on them. I don't want one to stray back and find us."

"How many are there?"

"I counted 25. That Brent fellow lied when he told us there were only 15." Turning toward the direction he came, Drayco added, "You stay with Jack. I'll go back to the crest and keep an eye on the situation." He kept his voice down during the conversation so it would not carry with the breeze. Shyanne followed suit.

"Did you see Joseph and Drizzle? Are they okay?"

Drayco faced her, grabbed her shoulders, and looked into her eyes. "They're fine, little sis. Ruben was ordered to bring them back alive—both of them. I don't think he'll let anyone hurt them. I heard him say what would happen if they did back at the campsite, remember?" He pulled Shyanne close.

"Thanks, Drayco," she whispered as she snuggled against him.

"Now, let's get back to watching this gang before they sneak away and they can't see us." He stepped back and gave her a sideways glance.

Shyanne started to turn toward her horse, but stopped when she realized what he had said. She punched him in the arm. "You stop teasing me, you overgrown galoot!" She hissed.

"Owww," Drayco mouthed while rubbing his arm. At the same time, he tried to look injured.

The bad acting brought a grin to both faces before they separated for their appointed tasks. Drayco returned to the hill while Shyanne stayed with Jack to prevent him from wandering too close to the crest.

Spanning the area, she saw great beasts off in the distance. What kind, she couldn't tell. Overhead, birds flew past, calling to each other and spiraling playfully in the currents. The faint shadows of mountains with their white hats were visible farther off. They stood in a more northerly direction than where the group was heading.

Drayco came back to his sister. "Looks like they're getting ready to move. Ruben is saddling his horse and the other are putting their things away."

"Does it look like they are sending out a rear guard?"

"I don't think so. My guess is Ruben feels the openness is protection enough from any attack."

"He's an arrogant one, isn't he?"

"Or very cunning," Drayco replied. "I'm not sure what he's up to, but it's bound to be something not good. We'll have to be extra cautious from here on out."

*   *   *

Ruben signaled to pack up and move on when he finished brushing Wind Racer. In a timely fashion, the group was making their way toward the west again.

The captain rode beside Ruben while the rest of the mercenaries left the big man alone. They were afraid of his temper, and his sword, but they respected him at the same time. He took good care of them as long as they did not mess up.

"Sir, do you want to post a rear guard?"

"No, Captain, not at this time."

The officer was fearful of asking his next question, but felt it needed to be said. "Are you sure that's wise, sir?"

"Are you questioning my decision?" Ruben turned sideways in the saddle. He focused his cold blue eyes on the man riding next to him.

"N...n...no sir! I would never do that," the Captain stammered, a glint of fear showing in his eyes.

"Smart man. I knew there was a reason I made you captain." Ruben faced forward again. "Reinforce to the others that we are making for those ruins you discussed earlier. I want the shelter of walls around me when darkness settles over the land."

"Yes sir!" the Captain answered in a crisp manner. He exhaled a sigh of relief at having not incurred the wrath of the big man as he left. Ruben nodded, satisfied.

The group of mercenaries made good time across the plains. They did not want to be out after dark any more than their leader did. Things of unspeakable evil roamed through the night. Things so large, a man could be carried away easily before anyone could help.

Black sky showed above the orange and red hues of the setting sun when their intended destination came into view. The silhouette of the buildings looked ominous against the darkening horizon. Mutterings of superstitions and bad feelings were heard as the group drew closer.

Ruben stopped Wind Racer some distance from the buildings. He turned to meet his fellow mercenaries. "I understand your misgivings. However, to stay out in the open is to invite nothing but disaster. At least this way we will have a wall to put our backs against if something does arise."

The men and women grumbled about having to go into the ominous site, but they all agreed the idea of staying out in the open was far worse. Inside, there was a measure of protection. Outside, in the open plains, there was none.

"I'll go in first and check out the area. Captain, keep everyone here until I give the signal to follow."

"Shouldn't someone go with you?"

"Not this time. If something is in there, I don't want anyone in my way. Besides, I don't like it when my people get hurt by anything other than me." Ruben grinned as he prodded the black horse toward the even blacker group of buildings.

"Very well, sir. We'll wait for your signal." The captain had genuine respect in his voice.

The people around the officer spoke softly amongst themselves. They had gotten to know the big man as well as he let them. He was cold, cruel, and brutal at times, but he also allowed his fellow companions to see a calmer, more protective side, as well.

The site was not really a town or a city; it was more like a commune. There were four buildings in all. Three of the four were in shambles, their roofs long since gone and their walls partially knocked down. The fourth one, which appeared to be the main building, was for the most part intact. The glass for the long windows was missing and the front door was nowhere in sight, but the roof looked to be in good shape. A tall spire rose upward on the front leading Ruben to believe it was once a church.

He peered up and saw a thick bank of clouds rolling rapidly in their direction. At the same time, he watched a bolt of lightning spread its pointy fingers across the ever-growing mass.

Ruben guided his horse to the fourth building. He dismounted and walked up the steps to the porch. Inside, the room was vast. Several pews stood near one wall. Others were scattered throughout the space, lying on their backs, or remaining upright. The back half of the room was hidden by an impenetrable darkness. A familiar odor hung near the entranceway. He could not remember where he had smelled it before, or what caused it.

Quietly, he withdrew his sword and crept into the dark building. Nothing except for the sound of grit crunching under his boots echoed across the room. He only went as far as the light outside allowed. He did not want to fall or trip in the darkness.

A bright flash of lightning glared through the windows. It was enough to show that no animals occupied the building. Fortunately, it also showed that no light came through the roof. The sound of thunder rumbled around the room. Ruben could tell by the time between the flash and the noise that the storm was closing in fast. He backed out and shoved his sword into the sheath before returning to Wind Racer. Throwing himself into the saddle, he rode back to the waiting crowd. The massive, bloated clouds were directly overhead when he reached them.

"The main building is sound and will protect us from the coming rains. Captain, take some men and gather as much wood as you can find. You," Ruben pointed to a female in the crowd, "take the rest inside and start setting up camp. Grab some wood on the way and get a fire started immediately."

The captain and the appointed female nodded their heads. The main body of people moved toward the building while five broke away and followed the officer.

Ruben stayed where he was, watching the people who traveled with him. In his opinion, they were a worthy lot. There was no hesitation when they were told to slaughter the townspeople—all of them. They enjoyed being paid to rape, torture, and kill almost as much as he did. Glancing upward, he followed the group heading toward the main building and hoped the rain would pass quickly.

*   *   *

Drayco looked at the looming clouds rolling across the darkening sky. He saw the flash of lightning followed by the rumble of thunder. He and Shyanne had followed the mercenaries to the ruins. In the growing twilight, the twins lay flat on their bellies watching from a short distance away as the band of killers split into two groups.

"We have to find shelter before these clouds drop their deluge, or we get struck by lightning."

"The only shelter I see is the building the others are heading toward," Shyanne said as she glanced over a shoulder at the plains beyond. Nothing was visible for as far as the eye could see.

"We can't stay out here. We'll have to find something in the rest of the remains since most of the party looks like it's going to the intact one," Drayco emphasized. "But we'll have to see what that separate group is doing first."

The twins watched the six stragglers run around gathering up any wood they could find from the ruined buildings. Once they felt they had enough, they made their way to the main building.

"Now's our chance." Drayco started over the hill in a hunched over run toward the closest ruin.

"What about Jack? We can't leave him out on the plains," Shyanne whispered as she ran beside her brother.

"If we find shelter we can come back for him. Now keep running before someone comes out and sees us."

Shyanne's forward momentum had slowed with the thought of leaving her horse. It picked up again with Drayco's harsh statement.

They flattened themselves against a portion of upright wall just before a man stepped outside. The mercenary walked past them to check on the horses penned in the ruined building beside the main one. If he had looked around, he would have seen the twins easily. Drayco motioned for them to move around to the other side; the rumbling of thunder masked any sound of their retreat.

The mercenary reached out to the nearest animal. The horse nuzzled his hand and nickered. The others paced around the enclosure, pawing at the ground. Their ears twirled every which a way, as if they were trying to locate a particularly annoying noise located in a direction they could not pinpoint.

"You sure are nervous." He slapped the thick neck affectionately. "It must be the storm. It looks like it's going to be a bad one." The man looked up into the sky and saw a blue white bolt streak across the sky followed immediately by a thunderous roar. Both man and animals jumped.

"Best be getting back in before I get drowned. Be safe." He rubbed the forehead before returning the way he came, missing the twins again.

The smell of rain hung thick in the air, and the wind started whipping everything around. The twins knew they were in for a drenching, but there was no way to avoid it. The rest of the buildings were useless as a shelter.

Drayco made his way to the horses. The Bay, Bravaro, was near the back. He came to the dark man when he clucked softly. "I see they've been taking good care of you, boy. I'll come back and get you when we free the others, okay?"

Bravaro nudged him in the chest and snorted. It was as if he gave Drayco the okay to go on without him. He hugged the horse's neck then turned toward Shyanne. "I have a plan. Get Jack and bring him here. We'll put him in with the other horses. No one will be the wiser."

Do you think that's a good idea?"

"What better place to hide him and keep him safe at the same time," he answered.

Shyanne shrugged her shoulders, turned around, and ran over the hill to get her horse. A few minutes later, she returned pulling him behind her. She put him in with the other horses, but secured his reins close to the entrance so that he would be easy to find if the time came for a quick exit. Drayco brought Bravaro next to Jack and secured him. The horse had a bridle in place, but no saddle. The dark man knew that would not be a problem.

After they were finished, Drayco said, "We need to get as close as possible. I want to see if there is any way to get inside and free Joseph and Drizzle. If there is, I want you to stay outside and cover our retreat."

"Drayco, I want to go in. I can be of more help there. I can handle my sword better than most men."

"I know, Shyanne. That's why I want you there to cover our backs once we're outside running. Joseph will be weak, and who knows how Drizzle will do. He's been tied up for several days now."

Shyanne's shoulders dropped. She did not look very happy. Finally, she said, "I understand. I'll be there for you," and trotted toward the main building.

Drayco sighed and took off after her. They had gone only a couple of paces when the clouds decided to dump their precious cargo, hitting them with a torrential downpour. They were soaked in seconds.

Suddenly, Drayco was grabbed by the front of his shirt and pulled behind a section of half crumbled wall. Shyanne put a finger to her lips when he started to protest. She pointed to the front porch. He glanced at it and watched as a man and a woman walked out of the building.

"Come on, Lela, why can't we disappear someplace away from the others? The rhythm of the rain reminds me of how badly I want ya."

The man pressed himself against the woman's back and wrapped his arms around her, grabbing her breasts. Lela flung his arms off and spun around in one fluid motion, a dagger in her hand as she faced him. She grabbed a fistful of shirt to prevent him from backing away. The tip of the blade was so close to his skin, blood flowed from the nick it caused. The trickle ran down his neck.

"I told you before, you stench of a rizbak, I'm not interested. If I were, you'd know it already. Now leave me alone—or you may not wake up one morning."

"Aww, Lela, ya don't have to be like that...mak'n me bleed and all." The man wiped the blood running down his throat with his fingers. "Give me a kiss to show you're sorry." He grabbed the arm holding his shirt and received another slice across the top of his forearm.

"Why'd ya have to do that? All I wanted was to have a bit o fun with ya." He shrugged her hold off, causing blood to splatter across her shirt, and stormed back inside, nursing his bleeding parts.

Lela put her dagger away and went in after him. "I warned you before. This is what you...." The rain covered the rest of the statement as they disappeared inside.

The twins grinned broadly at each other. Shyanne gestured toward her neck, pretending to slice it as she stuck her tongue off to the side. Drayco shook his head at her warped humor and twirled his finger close to his temple, indicating she was nuts. She nodded her head in agreement.

The smile disappeared as he motioned that they needed to move closer to the building. They ran up to one of the long windows and hugged the wall on either side. Drayco leaned forward slightly and peered inside the room.

A small crackling fire burned in a dirt pit near the back wall. Men and women relaxed about the room: some sleeping, others carrying on conversations. A few of the surviving benches were being used as beds. The rest became firewood. Holes were visible here and there in the ceiling; none leaked rainwater. The foul odor noticed earlier still hung in the air. The smell of the burning wood masked it for the most part.

Ruben leaned against a wall a short distance from the rest with one foot propped up. Joseph and Drizzle lay close to him, their restraints still in use to prevent any escape.

Drizzle was upset. He kept looking up at the ceiling, ears raised then flattened alternately. The big man watched the cat with interest. The rest of the group ignored them. They were thinking about other things, like their families or the local bars that were waiting for them.

"Has Drizzle become the nervous type?" Drayco asked.

"No. He's the most rock steady creature I've ever met."

"Well, something sure has him jumpy. I don't ever remember seeing him this edgy before."

Shyanne looked inside toward the big cat. "You're right. Something sure has him uptight. I wonde..."

A strange noise started coming from the area near the entrance of the building, a sort of rustling sound. The mercenaries missed it, at first. Finally, one of the men close to the front heard it. He walked over and looked around, attempting to locate the source of the sound. It seemed to be coming from overhead, in the ceiling.

"What's that?" he asked, trying to see into the dark holes above.

Ruben straightened up. He was looking at Drizzle, not the man speaking. The cat was going wild, struggling against his bonds with all his might. His mouth was tied shut, leaving him unable to bite at the restraints holding him. He yowled in frustration. Joseph watched the struggling cat, as well.

The rustling sound grew louder, as if many, many things were brushing against each other. Men and women around the room stopped what they were doing to look first at the cat, then at the man near the front.

A bad feeling settled in the pit of Ruben's stomach. The odor had reminded him of something from the past. Unfortunately, he still could not put a finger on what it was.

The man standing under the holes shouted, "Someone bring a light over here. I want to see what's up there." He had his arm extended toward the fire.

Drayco glanced at his sister. He could tell from the look on her face that she was uneasy. He understood; he was wearing the same look. He turned his attention back to what was happening inside just as someone was getting up with a torch. It was the same woman who had argued on the porch earlier. The blood still dotted her clothes.

Lela made it to the reaching man's side when Ruben remembered what caused the disturbing smell.

"No! Wait! Get away from there. NOW!" He started to move toward the pair. It was too late.

A large black object dropped like a rock from the ceiling. It landed on the woman, knocking her off her feet with its weight. She screamed in utter terror and threw up her arms to block the thing making its way along her body toward her face.

The creature was covered with coarse spiky hairs and had large bat-like ears. Leathery wings protruded from its fat, round body. Eight spider-like legs latched onto Lela's clothing, helping to propel it along her torso. The oversized mouth filled with razor sharp teeth bit into one of her up-raised arms. The red stain of blood from the earlier argu-ment was still evident. She hadn't bothered to wash it off completely. Multiple eyes rolled back into its head as the teeth sank into her flesh repeatedly. A thin blood red tongue darted in and out, licking at the old and new mois-ture.

"*Oh God,* Drayco thought, *these creatures are after blood, just like me.*

More creatures fell from the ceiling onto the man standing below. They covered him instantly. Some broke apart from the main group to join the one already on Lela. She disappeared in the same fashion. Their screams of horror and pain sounded from the writhing mass of spiky bodies. Hers ended quickly; the man continued, more of a gurgling sound than words.

The mercenary who argued with the woman on the porch went down next. The thick scent of blood on him was more than the creatures could resist. He died before he was able to hit any of the spiderbats with the short knife in his hand.

Ruben pulled his sword free and swung it in all direc-tions as he ducked and dodged the erratic flying creatures from hell. The rest of his mercenaries were trying their best to save themselves in the same manner.

Long talons snagged clothing and cut the skin under-neath as the winged demons flew around the room looking for more food. The smell of fresh flowing blood had created a feeding frenzy, and the spiderbats were attacking any-thing in their path, including themselves.

The twins watched in horror as men and women went down under the grotesque attack. Drayco saw Ruben make his way toward the main room then stop as the number of creatures swooping at the people grew.

He nudged Shyanne, and said, "I'm going to try and free Joseph and Drizzle. With this distraction going on, no one will notice another person amongst them."

Shyanne looked at her brother, concern in her eyes. After a second, she said, "Be careful, Drayco."

She knew better than to try talking him out of it. Pre-cious time would be wasted arguing, and the spiderbats would kill their friends in the meantime. Besides, the same thought had crossed her mind, as well, but Drayco would never allow her to go into the killing melee. If Ruben saw what they were doing, he would try to stop it. She was good with a sword, but not against someone like Ruben, who where larger, stronger, and more devious.

Drayco slipped inside the window and dropped to the floor in a low crouch. He waited to see if anyone noticed the stranger amongst them before moving. They were too busy trying to survive against the spiderbats to see a tall, dark stranger in their midst.

A man covered with spiderbats ran past Drayco, yelling and thrashing, trying to get the creatures off. He fell to the floor in a heap. After only a moment, all movement stopped except for those caused by the black monsters.

The mercenaries' numbers were dropping quickly. Some had fled out the front door. Others were valiantly trying to save their fallen comrades. Over two dozen spiderbats lay about the room dead or flopping around, unable to fly.

Drayco saw Ruben across the room. He was swinging his great sword high at the creatures trying to get at him. Scrapes and cuts covered his upper body and blood dripped off his left elbow from a long gash to his upper arm. A couple of scratches were on his face. They had crusted over long ago.

The dark twin made his way to the prisoners, keeping his back flat against the wall to create as small a target as possible for the spiderbats. Joseph watched him, unable to speak due to the gag in his mouth. Drayco reached him and removed the gag.

"What are you doing here? If Ruben sees you, you're dead," Joseph whispered harshly.

"Saving your butt," Drayco muttered back while attempting to untie the bonds holding the man's arms.

"Where's your sister?"

"She's outside, waiting to help us when we get out of here."

"Don't waste time trying to untie the ropes...cut them. Hurry, before Ruben notices you're over here!"

Drayco pulled a small dagger out of his boot and sawed at the rope. He had to be careful because he did not want to cut Joseph's wrist in the process. Drizzle watched, and waited. He knew Drayco would get to him when Joseph was freed.

"When I get you loose, go to that window over there. Shyanne's waiting." Drayco tossed his head in the direction of the window he had come from.

The rope fell to the ground after a few more slices. Drayco directed the blade toward the captive's ankles. In as much time as it took to blink, the fair-haired man was free. He assisted Joseph into a standing position and made sure he was able to move toward the window before turning his attention to Drizzle.

Joseph was weak from being in the same position for too long. He hissed when the blood started circulating more freely into his numb hands and feet. It felt like a thousand tiny pins were poking into them. He managed a couple of steps before stumbling to his knees, unable to go any farther.

Drayco took a couple of steps toward Drizzle. He glanced over his shoulder and saw the difficulty his companion was having.

"I'll be back, Drizzle. I promise. I have to help Joseph first."

The cat gave him and understanding nod.

Drayco made it back to the struggling man, avoiding the spiderbats flying directly overhead. He grabbed an arm and pulled it over his shoulder as he put his own arm around Joseph's waist.

"Go help Drizzle. I can make it," Joseph insisted.

"The longer you squabble with me, the longer it takes me to get back to Drizzle. Now shut up and get moving." Drayco practically dragged the man toward the exit.

Joseph gasped as the pain intensified with each step. They were a little more than half way to the window when a shout came from across the room.

"Hey!" Ruben bellowed. "Where do you think you're going?"

Drayco urged the hurting man to go faster. They were almost to the window when he glanced over his shoulder. The powerful man was charging in their direction. Just as he thought their chance of escaping was gone, a spiderbat landed on Ruben. The big man yelled and spun around trying to get the deadly creature off. The dark twin took the opportunity given to them and moved as quickly as possible toward the exit.

The tingling in Joseph's limbs reduced to the point where he was able to bear more weight on his feet. "Drayco...let me go. The pain in going away and I can stand better."

"Then let's haul it, mister. That spiderbat won't keep him busy for long."

Shyanne was there when they made it to the window. She reached in to help Joseph crawl through. As he cleared the opening, a bellow of rage echoed throughout the room. Drayco spun around to see Ruben, free of the black monster, rushing their way. He faced the charging bull of a man, pulling his sword ceremoniously out of its sheath.

"Drayco...NO!" Shyanne shouted. She tried to enter the room but Joseph grabbed her and held her back. "What are you doing? Let go of me! He can't take that animal on by himself!"

"Shyanne, get to the horses ready. I have to free Drizzle. I promised him," Drayco said, his voice calm. "And the only way I can do that is to face this idiot once and for all. Joseph, make sure she goes. I don't need her in the way."

Grimfaced, Joseph said, "Let's go, Shyanne. We can wait for him with the horses." He moved away from the window, dragging the screaming woman with him. It was a struggle in his weakened state, but he managed.

Their retreating shouts were quickly covered by the sounds of the pounding rain, crashing thunder, and the battles raging on around the room. Drayco focused his attention on the big man barreling down on him. Ruben was twice his size in muscle mass, but they were about even in height. He wanted to go to Drizzle. Regrettably, that had to wait until he dealt with Ruben.

Their blades met with a clash of scraping steel. Drayco knew better than to try to overpower the more muscular foe. His only chance to win was to evade the blade swinging at him for as long as possible until he found a weakness or an opening. He turned aside the bigger man's steel and ducked to the right.

Ruben flew past the dark twin. He skidded to a stop and spun around to face his adversary, sword held in front of him ready to swing when an opportunity arose.

"You will not take what is mine," Ruben snarled.

"You can not claim something that is not yours to claim."

The two men faced one another, each sizing up the other. Suddenly, Ruben faked a thrust, which caused Drayco to leap sideways to avoid it. The big man's follow-through was fast. It caught Drayco off guard.

A foot planted in the middle of the dark man's stomach forced the breath out of him. The blow sent him flying through the air. He landed on his back, gasping. Ruben was on him with the speed of a striking snake. Drayco rolled out of the way, barely in time, as the sword hit the very spot he had just vacated. Ruben tried several more times to pierce the man rolling beneath him. He missed each time.

Drayco knew he could not stay down much longer and survive. He threw a leg out wide and swiped the big man's feet out from under him. Ruben hit the floor with a resounding thud. No one noticed what was happening between the two combatants; they were too busy fighting for their own lives.

Drayco scrambled to his feet. Before he could make it, Ruben was already on his knees. The big man brought his sword upward in a wide arch. The blade whipped past Drayco's face. He fell backwards to avoid it, but was not fast enough to get away clean. The blade bit deep into the flesh across his right cheek. Blood flowed down his neck and onto the front of his shirt. Drayco straightened and kicked Ruben in the face, knocking him down again. When the mercenary sat up, blood was running down his chin. His teeth had cut the inside of his mouth.

The spiderbats sensed the new flow of blood coming from the combatants, and attacked. Hoards of them converged on the two men. Drayco and Ruben were forced to divert their attention away from each other and onto the flying messengers of death instead. The glint of steel bounced off the surrounding walls as they swung their swords not at each other, but at the black creatures in the air above.

Teeth and claws that felt like tiny needles dug into Drayco's skin as he tried to get free of the mass of black bodies. Ruben was having the same problem. More and more spiderbats eager for the taste of blood forced the men against the outer wall.

The big man knew he was not going to win this battle, with either the man next to him, or the spiderbats, and decided it was time to leave. He forced his way over to the big cat and grabbed him up with one arm.

He bellowed, "Let's get out of here, people!" and ran out the front door into the downpour still going on.

Drayco was pinned against the wall by the spiderbats and could only watch in frustration as his friend, whom he had promised to free, was carried away.

"DRIZZLE!"

In a fit of rage, he yelled and swung his sword with greater power and speed. He tried to make it to the door, but was driven back by the sheer volume of spiderbats trying to get at him. The blood still flowing from his cheek was driving them mad with the need to feed.

A few of the remaining mercenaries struggled to get through the door, and made it. The rest were either unable to get away, or were dead. Drayco was completely exhausted from fending off the creatures and failed to notice the window behind him until he fell through it. Shyanne and Joseph were there to drag him away from the opening.

A couple of the black creatures came out with him, still clinging to his clothes. The main body of spiderbats refused to follow. They turned back to the dryness inside, and the feast awaiting them therein.

Joseph and Shyanne kicked the ugly things off the dark man and watched as they flopped around on the ground, unable to fly due to the moisture saturating their bodies. Two drowned in the growing number of puddles caused by the rain; one remained attached to the man sitting on the ground. He threw it off and rose to his feet. With the power of someone angry at the world, he brought his sword down hard, slicing the creature in half.

Drayco glared at the Joseph and Shyanne. "What are you doing here? I told you to wait by the horses!" He was furious at them for not following his instructions.

"We did wait by the horses," Shyanne yelled back. "When it took so long for you to come out, we knew you were going to need help, so we brought them with us." His sister pointed to where Jack and Bravaro stood a few yards away.

"What about Ruben? Did you see him? He had Drizzle with him and was probably heading toward the horses." He started that way. Shyanne called to him.

"Drayco, Wait. We saw him." Her voice grew softer, her anger reduced. "It's too late. They rode out of here just before you tumbled out the window."

"We're not even sure which direction they went. We lost sight of them after only a few paces because of the rain," Joseph said.

The dark man's shoulders sagged. He had failed, failed Drizzle miserably. That was something he would never forgive. Shyanne and Joseph moved to either side of the distraught man, they put their hands on his shoulders.

Shyanne noticed the slash on her brother's face, and the blood on his clothes. "Your cheek looks bad. It needs to be taken care of." She tried to touch his still bleeding wound; he jerked his face away.

Drayco shrugged off the hands resting on his shoulders and walked over to the horses. Bravaro nudged him in the chest once he was close enough. The dark twin automatically reached up and rubbed the animal's nose, but his thoughts were elsewhere.

He was furious, furious with everything—the spiderbats, his sister, Ruben—but mostly, with himself. He felt he had let everyone down, especially Drizzle. The frown on his face caused pain to run down the right side of his cheek. He ignored It.

Joseph started to go to Drayco. It was Shyanne's turn to hold him back.

"Let him work it out. When we were younger, all the family had to do was give him space to think. He'll talk when he's ready."

The three of them stood in the rain for what seemed like hours. In reality, it was only minutes.

The rain became less of a torrential downpour and more like a spring shower during the wait. The noise of the spiderbats feasting inside grew louder than the soft pattering of raindrops hitting the ground. Shyanne and Joseph decided it was time to move closer to the horses and get away from the sickening sound of slurping and crunching.

Drayco stood with his head tilted forward. His hair was thoroughly soaked, effectively hiding his face from the approaching couple. When he looked up, the fingers of blood winding down his face and neck made it appear as though he had a bright red lightning bolt shooting across it. A haunted determination filled his eyes. Shyanne thought it gave him an almost evil look. Her spine shivered in response.

"I promised Drizzle I would come for him, and that is exactly what I am going to do. Ruben will high tail it to the Boss with the hopes that we will follow." He paused, glaring at them as if daring them to contradict him. "I'm going to do just that. I going to Grandfield and locating this Boss. Where I find him, I find Drizzle." His fingers curled into tight fists.

"I agree. WE need to go to Grandfield and find Drizzle," Joseph said.

"But WE'LL have to be careful. A trap will be waiting for us for sure," Shyanne finished his statement.

Drayco expected an argument. He closed his eyes with relief when none came. The loss of Drizzle had left a hole that would not be filled until his return. He had grown rather fond of the old fur ball since rejoining Shyanne, and he wanted the sour puss back. Before they could leave, though, he needed to stop the blood flowing from the slice on his cheek.

He reached up and traced the cut with his fingertips. It went from the top of his cheekbone to just above the corner of his mouth. He could tell from the look on Shyanne's face, it must be bad. She handed him a cloth. He took it and pressed it firmly against the skin to staunch the flow. The grimace that flew across his face almost certainly matched hers.

"I have to drink before we go. Since I'm not familiar with the area, I don't know if we'll find anything before we reach Grandfield." The battle left him washed out. He knew he had to replenish what was lost before setting out.

"Some horses were left behind. I have a feeling that's all you'll find...unless you're interested in spiderbats," Shyanne teased.

Joseph had no idea what the twins were talking about. If Drayco needed to drink, all he had to do was fetch a waterskin. "Wait here. I'll bring you some water." His words brought such a sorrow-filled look from the dark man that he wondered what he really needed.

"It's okay, Joseph," Shyanne said softly.

Drayco gave his sister a thankful nod and walked toward the temporary stables.

After he left, Joseph turned to Shyanne. "What the hell is going on here?"

Shyanne told him the complete story—beginning with the virus, up to when she and Drayco joined forces again. It took some time, but, at the moment, time was what they had.

Joseph stood with his mouth hanging open, staring at the woman talking to him as if she came from another planet.

"You are the first person I've ever told the full story to," she said to him afterwards.

"I can see why. It's hard to believe. I'm having a hard time believing it myself."

She looked at Joseph. "Why would I lie?"

"I don't know, Shyanne, I just don't know." He shook his head back and forth.

His eyes showed the many conflicts raging inside. Caring, fear, doubt, and a few others passed by. The final emotion to stay was concern. Shyanne wondered if it was concern for himself, or for the party as a whole.

"Will you go with us?" Her heart raced a thousand beats per minute in anticipation of his response.

He paused before answering. The sound of the gently falling rain was soothing. He looked up at the dark cloud filled sky, and sighed, "I will go with you and your brother to find this Boss. I have nothing left now. The mercenaries who attacked my town are scattered, or dead."

Shyanne released the breath she had been holding and hung her head. When she looked up, he was watching her. She smiled. Joseph was beside her in an instant, scooping her close to his body. She turned her face upward to receive his affectionate lips. They held the kiss until Shyanne broke contact and turned away from him.

"I'm sorry, I shouldn't have done that. This could never be," she said, holding back the tears welling in the corners of her eyes.

"Why, why could it never be? I love you, Shyanne. I know this now." He grabbed her shoulders and tried to turn her toward him. She brushed his hands off.

"Because....because I'll just watch you die as I have all the others. I can't bear to do that again—not with you." The tears finally ran down her cheeks, blending in with the moisture from the rain. She moved away, hugging herself.

Joseph was about to follow her when Drayco returned. His color was better, save for the dark circles still present under his eyes. It shocked the fair-haired man to see the cut on his face was scabbed over.

"The rain is stopping. We have to get away from here before the spiderbats escape their cage." He stood where he was, observing the pair.

Shyanne brushed the moisture out of her eyes and went toward their horses. Joseph stayed where he was, watching as she went past him without even a glance in his direction. He opened his mouth to say something, but immediately shut it again before doing so. He faced Drayco, intent on forgetting about what had just happened, even though he knew he never would. The feel of Shyanne's soft lips was still fresh in his mind.

"Are there any horses left? I need one."

"They're over here."

Drayco returned the way he came. Joseph followed. As they disappeared around the corner of a ruined wall, he glanced back at his sister and saw her shoulders shaking, as if she was sobbing. Her face was buried in the mane of her horse. Drayco said nothing while they walked into the horse enclosure.

Joseph's step faltered and a gasp escaped as he caught sight of the two dead horses lying near to the back wall, their necks ripped open.

"I thought what she told me was outrageous. I see now it was the full truth. You do have to drink blood to survive, don't you?"

"What all were you told?"

Joseph repeated the earlier conversation. Drayco stared at the man with cold eyes. He had never told anyone what he must to do to survive, and wished Shyanne had used the same discretion.

When Joseph finished, he sighed. "I guess it had to

come out sooner or later. I trust you will keep the information to yourself—for our sake and yours."

"Drayco, I would never tell anyone. I don't want to see either you...or Shyanne...get hurt."

The dark twin heard the hesitation when he mentioned his sister's name. He knew then that something had happened between the two of them while he was replenishing himself.

Returning his attention to the enclosure, he said, "Pick a horse. That's why we came here, isn't it?"

"Yes...yes it is." Joseph reached out to one of the remaining horses. It nibbled at his hand, searching for a treat. He grabbed the halter and led it out of the enclosure.

Shyanne's composure was back in place when they rounded the corner.

"What took you guys so long? I was getting worried." She nodded her head in the direction of the main building, "The spiderbats are getting restless. Several poked their ugly faces out, until it got wet."

"We're leaving now, little sis." Drayco moved to Bravaro's side and threw himself into the saddle. He noticed the sideways glance she gave Joseph when he straightened up. The longing showed for only a moment then was gone.

"I'll need a second to get this horse ready," Joseph said. "Shyanne, can you hold the reins for me?"

Shyanne went to the front porch and hauled one of the saddles left by the mercenaries to Joseph instead of holding the reins like some handmaiden. During the handover, their hands brushed against each other. She pulled back suddenly, almost causing him to drop it, and quickly returned to Jack. She practically flew into the saddle to wait.

Joseph watched as she walked away. He sighed heavily before tossing the saddle onto the horse. While he worked, he noticed something odd about Drayco. The cut on the man's cheek was closed. A thin scar formed where under an hour ago, an open slice had been. Joseph thought the limited light from the moon shining through the clouds was playing tricks on his eyes. When he looked again, he saw the same sight.

I wonder if by having to drink blood to stay alive, it has a fantastic healing effect on the body as well.

He did not have time to think about it, though. Within minutes, the three of them were riding away from the place of terror and death in the same direction taken by the fleeing mercenaries.

The only things left alive to see them go were the spiderbats and a couple of horses.

Twelve

It took the trio six long days to cross the vast open plains. In that time, they saw no other living being except for some birds flying high in the sky. A few glided lazily on the air currents while others accompanied the riders in shifts, as if giving them an escort. None flew close enough to replenish the dwindling food supplies. The big animals seen at the beginning of the journey were long since gone. It appeared as if the trio and the flying escorts above were the only living things left on the planet.

Very little conversation transpired throughout most of the travel. Drayco tried on several occasions to get his sister to talk. She refused to say more than a few words, which was just as well since he wasn't in the mood to talk either. Joseph chatted on those occasions he was spoken to, but he also remained silent.

Shyanne avoided the fair-haired man for most of the journey, keeping Drayco between them or riding ahead. On those occasions where they were forced together, like when they camped for the night, she kept mostly to herself.

Drayco felt the steadily worsening effects of needing blood increase when the plains finally surrendered its hold on the world to the trees growing visible on the horizon. He had been feeling the weakness and ache for the last two days, but said nothing to the pair riding with him. They could not resolve the issue. Moreover, he had not wanted to weigh them down with any more worries than they already had.

"Finally!" Shyanne yelled when she sighted of the trees. Her mood picked up substantially, as did that of Joseph. Drayco wanted to share in their excitement. His body hurt too much to let him.

The waterskins hung limp from the saddles with only a few drops remaining. Because of the shortage, the horses had been rationed along with the people on them. Some kind of water must have been close because they picked up speed as the scent of the badly needed moisture reached their nostrils.

Joseph and Shyanne could barely keep their animals from breaking away. They grinned, winked at each other, and finally gave in, letting the animals run.

Drayco smiled as he watched the others bridge the gap between the open field and the trees ahead. With a slight prod, Bravaro leaped to follow. A few feet into the run, however, Drayco was hit with an intense pain to his abdominal region. It forced him to double over and grasp a handful of mane to stay in the saddle. Sweat broke out on his forehead; it ran into his eyes, causing them to sting, adding more insult to an already abused body. He grimaced as another wave more intense than the first hit him. This time, he wasn't able to stay in the saddle.

Bravaro was running at a brisk pace when Drayco's grip finally gave way. He fell sideways off the horse and hit the ground, hard. His right shoulder dislocated with the impact, and the back of his head bounced a couple of times while he rolled like a broken rag doll on the grassy plain. He vaguely noticed the new pains due to the other pain still holding him in a vice grip, refusing to give up its hold. When he finally stopped rolling, he was face down on the ground. His right shoulder was at an awkward angle and he couldn't catch his breath.

Shyanne made it to the edge of the woods and pulled Jack around, halting his mad dash across the open area. A wide smile covered her face; it was the first one in many days. Thin wisps of hair stood out in complete disarray. Joseph pulled his horse up beside her, laughing.

"You should see yourself. It's hilarious the way your hair is sticking out. It makes you look like a giant sunflower."

Shyanne laughed. "You should see yourself."

Pushing her hair down, she glanced back to see how her brother fared. Her face changed in an instant. Where joy and pleasure glowed over every inch of her, fear and dread replaced it.

"DRAYCO!"

She was looking over his shoulder in the direction they had just come. Joseph turned in the saddle and saw Bravaro running their way, riderless. A dark patch lay sprawled on the ground in the distance, half buried by the waving sea of greens and yellows. His smile faded as quickly as hers had. Shyanne spurred Jack toward her brother's still form. He jerked his horse around and kicked it in the sides. At first, the animal fought, its thirst strong, but the will of the man on its back was stronger.

In seconds, they were racing back to where Drayco lay.

Shyanne reached him first and leaped off her horse before it had completely stopped. Joseph was right behind her. When he reached out to move the wounded man, she motioned for him not to. She had seen the odd angle of his shoulder. Instead, she brushed lightly against his face with her fingers. Drayco gave no indication that he knew they were there.

He's breathing. Oh dear god, thank you.

Beneath her fingers, his skin was so pale, almost as if he had no pigmentation left.

Why didn't I notice this before? Why didn't he say something about needing to drink?

Shyanne knew why. They could have done nothing about it.

"Drayco? Can you hear me?"

"Ohhhh..." A moan escaped from the wounded man as he tried to rise up.

"Drayco, don't move. We need to see where you're injured." She leaned closer to make sure he heard what she said. He must have, because he stopped. Guiding her hands gently over his body, she felt no other breaks. Sitting up, she looked at Joseph. "He has a bump on the back of his head. Other than that, his shoulder looks to be the only thing out of place. We need to put it back."

Joseph nodded his head. "I'll help where I can."

Shyanne met his eyes. She could see the love shining

from within. The same longing ached within her, but she knew it would never work, not with the cruel hand dealt to her by the virus. She turned her attention back to her brother.

Drayco, we need to put your shoulder back in place, it's been dislocated from the fall. Do you understand me?"

His eyes remained shut, though he managed to croak out one word: "Y...yes..."

"Are you hurt any where else?"

"My head hurts...and my gut feels like it has a hot poker sticking in it." He barely got the statement out before the pain, which had brought him out of the saddle, hit again. He curled into a ball on his right side, retching, ignoring the injured shoulder completely.

"Drayco, I'm here with you, just hang on." Joseph placed a hand on the dark man's side, preventing his from rolling back and forth and injuring himself further.

Watching her brother writhe in pain cut into Shyanne as sure as a knife would. She knew what had to be done to end his suffering, and hated it. A look at Joseph told her that he knew this too. With grim determination, she sat next to Drayco's left side and indicated for Joseph to do likewise on the right.

"Once I have him on his back, I want you to take the injured arm and pull it away from his body with all your might until you feel the shoulder slip back in place. I'll do my best to keep him from thrashing about." He nodded his head and waited for the signal to begin.

"Drayco," Shyanne spoke into his ear, "I need to lay you on your back. It's the only way we can fix your shoulder." She tried to roll him onto his back, but a loud hiss of pain escaped from his lips, stopping her.

"Brother, keep your knees bent to take some of the pressure off your gut. We can't do this without your help."

She started to move him again. This time she succeeded in rolling him onto his back.

Shyanne indicated for Joseph to pick up the dislocated right arm. He did so in a slow, easy manner, straightening it out as best he could during the move. The dark twin cried out. With his teeth clenched tight, he managed to stay on his back and even help.

"Drayco, we're going to try to fix your shoulder now.

I'm sorry for hurting you like this, but it's necessary. I love you, big brother."

She kissed him on his sweaty forehead then wrapped her arms around his upper torso, firmly pinning his left arm between their bodies. Drayco tossed his head back and forth as the pain attacking his body worsened. He made no attempt to move away, even though every muscle on his body indicated he wanted to. She glanced up at Joseph and nodded for him to get the job done as quickly as possible. He grabbed the forearm with both hands and leaned back as far as he could go, pushing with his foot on the side of Drayco's chest.

With the first pull, the dark man tilted his head back and let out a blood-curdling scream. He started struggling. Shyanne wasn't sure if she could hold him. Fortunately, before it became an issue, he passed out. Joseph slacked off for a second; she told him to continue. With renewed effort, he pulled until he felt the shoulder slip into place. The arm moved freely in all directions.

Sitting up, Shyanne said, "We have to secure the arm to his body so it can have time to heal. Let's try to get this finished before he wakes up."

Joseph placed the repaired arm across Drayco's chest and positioned himself above his head. By sliding his hands underneath and lifting, he shifted the dark man carefully into a sitting position. Drayco's head dropped onto his chest. The black hair fell to one side, revealing a large bump on the upper aspect of the neck. Further proof of the hard landing he had suffered.

Shyanne bandaged the arm in a sling and wrapped a rope around his chest to prevent both the sling and arm from moving freely. She inspected the welt and discovered it to be superficial only, not life threatening. The lack of blood, on the other hand, would be if was not resolved quickly. Joseph was laying Drayco back on the soft bed of grass when he roused. Shyanne went to her horse and returned with the little bit of water that they had left.

"Drink this. I know it's not what you need. It will have to do until we can find what you do need." She lifted his head and brought the skin to his lips, slowly pouring some water in his mouth so he didn't choke.

He tried to reach up with his right arm. A sharp bolt of

pain reminded him of the foolishness of such a move. He reached up with his left arm instead. The hand was shaking badly and would have spilled the contents if Shyanne had not been holding the waterskin as well.

Drayco swallowed only a tiny amount before he indicated he had had enough. "I can't take any more. It'll only set off the cramps again." His voice was almost too soft to be heard. Closing his eyes, he laid his head back on the ground. "I already hurt enough as it is."

Joseph had heard enough. He leaped to his feet, and declared, "I'm going to get you what you need, Drayco. It's the least I can do for causing this much trouble. If it hadn't been for me, you two would be fine right now."

Shyanne scrambled to her feet. "You have no idea how to bring back what he needs...I do. I can't let you jeopardize my brother's life like that. I can't!" Her feet were shoulder width apart and her arms, straight at her sides, had her hands clenched into tight balls. She looked like she was ready to take on someone four times her size. A glint of fire shined in her eyes.

Joseph matched her glare with one of his own. "I can do this, Shyanne. Believe me when I say I will do everything that I can to help your brother."

A groan escaped from Drayco as he struggled into a sitting position. Shyanne instantly dropped to his side. She tried to get him to lie back again.

"Drayco, you have to rest. You don't have much strength and I won't have you wasting it needlessly."

He looked into her eyes. "Let him do this, little sis. As long as you tell him what he needs to know, I believe he can do it."

"But Drayco..."

"No, Shyanne. Tell him what he needs to do. It's been a long time since I let this curse given to me by the virus go this far. I still remember the pain and want you here with me. I don't have much longer."

Drayco started to fall over. Shyanne caught him and hugged him tight against her body. When she looked up at Joseph, tears welled in her eyes. She tried to hold them back; they rolled down her cheeks as he watched. His heart broke with each tear.

She gave Joseph detailed instructions about having to

catch something and bring it back alive for her brother to drink from. If the creature died, it would be of no use. He took in all the information given to him like a sponge.

When she was finished, he said, "I have it. I'll be back before dark—or as sooner if I can."

Drayco reached up to the man standing a short distance away. For the moment, the pain had subsided. Joseph came over and knelt down. He grasped the outstretched hand with both his. It felt so cold.

"Thank you, Joseph. My life is in your hands. I trust you."

Those words, scarcely spoken above a whisper, hit Joseph harder than anything else in his life ever had. He barely knew Drayco and Shyanne, but it already felt like they were family. He knew the trouble he caused could never be forgotten, or forgiven, but he could attempt to make amends now.

"I will not fail you. I will return as soon as I possibly can." He rose to his feet and walked toward the horses grazing a little way off. Shyanne stood and followed.

"Take Bravaro. He knows you and is a sturdy beast. I would offer Jack, but he's still too temperamental." Shyanne was about to say something else when Joseph leaned down and kissed her softly on the lips.

As they separated, he said, "Take care of Drayco until I get back." He leaped into the saddle and started toward the woods.

*   *   *

Bravaro was just as fast as he remembered. The horse reacted instantly to knee pressures and turned on a dime when indicated. Joseph guided him to a path that became visible once they drew close to the vast forest. He dared not look back when he entered for fear his heart would break at having to leave Shyanne. He sighed with the remembrance of her lips on his and wished the feeling could go on.

Suddenly, his thoughts were brought back to the present when a small, low hanging branch hit him on the face, almost knocking him off the horse.

"Whoa! Bravaro, you silly beast, watch where you're

going." He quipped as he rubbed where the branch had hit. The horse never faltered in its forward motion, ignoring the man on its back.

"I guess that's what I get for daydreaming, huh guy." He leaned over and gave the broad neck a pat. "Back to business. We have to trap something fast."

He followed the path deeper into the trees. Nothing moved. No crashing through the underbrush; no chittering sounded from above; nothing. Joseph decided to get off and look around for tracks. He saw some, but they were old.

Another mile or so down the path, a particularly thick patch of growth stood before him. Rays of sunlight shined through the trees at the entrance; they disappeared a few paces inside the tunnel. It looked more like a cave than a forest. No other paths led from the main one. Joseph considered not going in until he remembered his parting words, and the pair waiting for his return. The only other option available was to backtrack and find another path. That was not something he had time for right now.

"I guess we go in, boy," he said to the horse. With a slight tug of the reins, he led him into the darkness.

Day became night in a matter of seconds. Joseph knew about some of the creatures that roamed in the night and hoped none of them was here. He looked back the way they had come. Daylight shined brightly through the opening in the trees. He considered leaving the horse behind, but ditched that thought. If he needed a quick exit, he wanted the animal near.

Faint rays of light tried to weave its way through the dense foliage above. A few made it as far as the lower branches, allowing Joseph to see where he was going. He could barely make out the path and the surrounding trees, but that was about all.

Unlike the other section, he heard creatures moving deep in the forest. None came close enough for him to trap. He also heard the flittering of wings as birds flew from branch to branch. Again, none came close enough for him to capture. While he cursed every living creature on the planet, the light shining through the trees grew darker. Night was coming. Joseph wasn't looking forward to spending it in these woods.

He still had not captured, much less spotted anything before the last rays of the sun disappeared. With a heavy heart, he considered going back. Just as he chided himself for being so weak, an orangish-yellow glow bounced off the trees ahead. He stopped, trying to see what caused it.

A fire. Someone's got a fire going ahead. Joseph tied Bravaro's reins to a tree branch and moved forward to investigate.

The flashes of yellow and orange danced through the dark trees, beckoning him to come join in. He saw a break ahead and crouched low. The path opened into a small clearing with the remnants of a hunter's shack in the far corner. One wall of stone was still upright; the other three were gone. Rubble lay all over. Part of the mess had been cleared and six people, two women and four men, sat around a fire burning in the center. Horses were hobbled close by to prevent them from wandering away.

"What are we going to do now? We've lost track of Ruben," a woman asked.

"I don't know, Viola. I do know we have to wait until morning to try and find the trail," one of the men answered.

"He'll be going to Grandfield. That's where we always go after we've trashed a town, or had a bit of fun, if you get what I mean," another man sitting next to her said.

"Of course he will, stupid. Seth, you amaze me sometimes." Viola shook her head.

Seth made a move to grab his knife. Another man reached up and stopped him. "Don't do it, Seth, you know she can tear you apart."

"Probably with one arm tied behind my back," Viola mumbled sarcastically.

Seth glared at the man who had stopped him, then at Viola. With a snarl, he pushed the man out of the way and fell onto the woman. They wrestled on the ground for a couple of seconds before getting up and returning to their seats, laughing.

"You two are worse than kids," a quiet man with black hair said.

"Like you're any better, Garth"

Joseph recognized the people sitting by the fire. *These are the people who killed my friends and family.* He remained calm, even though his blood boiled. *If I could get my hands on one of them, I could take him or her back for interrogation. Then Drayco can finish up from there.* He listened in as they continued with their conversation.

"We best get some rest. We have a long ride ahead of us, and a lot of explaining to do when we catch up with the rest. Viola, you take first watch. Seth, you relieve her. I'll follow you. We'll each take two hours." Garth watched to make sure his orders were followed before getting into his blankets.

Viola muttered under her breath, "Don't know who died and left you in charge." She followed the instructions given to her anyway.

The night wore on. Joseph hoped the other two were faring okay, especially Drayco. He was plotting how to get one of the people separated from the others when a noise sounded in the woods off to his left. Seth was on duty and hadn't appeared to notice. He was sitting near the fire. A couple of times his head fell forward then jerked upright. A yawn and a stretch always followed those incidences.

SNAP!

Joseph jerked his head around and focused on the area. Whatever caused the noise was circling around the other side of the camp. He glimpsed a darker shadow moving with stealth in the darkness. He hugged as close to the tree as possible and kept an eye on the area where he last saw the movement.

Seth had finally heard the sounds coming from the woods and rose to investigate. He moved past the outer edge of the ruined building, away from the sleeping men and women. He never stood a chance.

A large ill-proportion beast raced out of the forest and hit Seth in the chest, knocking the wind out of him before he could let out warning. The creature looked like it might have been a German Sheppard at one time. Unluckily, for the mercenary, it had mutated into something that was no longer man's best friend.

Front legs that were longer than the back joined with the muscular upper body. Claws extended past the paws like those of a bear. Spiky hair covered the entire body, including the long curved tail. Its heavy bulk kept the man pinned against the ground while the oversized mouth filled with razor sharp fangs tried to latch onto his throat.

Seth blocked the creature's attempts with his arms. He had not had time to drawn his weapon because of the suddenness of the attack. Instead, his thoughts were on how to get away from the gaping jaws snapping at him.

A Grangoor, Joseph thought as he watched in horror. *The beast must have been focused on the group in the clearing, which was why it missed the easier target close by.*

Fortunately, the grangoor were loners. Unfortunately, for their victims, they were very aggressive and cunning. They could gut a man in seconds with its claws and drag the victim off where they could dine in privacy; a thing a grangoor liked best.

The beast tried again to get at the throat; flailing arms kept getting in the way. It bit one of the upraised arms and dug its claws into the soft exposed abdomen, ripping it wide open. Seth tossed his head back and screamed. The Grangoor saw its opportunity and lunged for the now visible neck. The scream ended abruptly.

By now, the rest of the camp was up and moving. But it was too late for Seth. The Grangoor had him by the throat and was dragging him toward the blackness of the woods, away from the annoying light caused by the fire.

Garth drew his sword and ran after the huge monster. "You'll not eat one of my people, you ugly beast!"

The others remained by the fire, unwilling to help. Seth had always been a pain with all his wisecracks and practical jokes. With him gone, they could split the gold pieces he had stashed in his bag.

"Come back, Garth, it's too late for him," Sheena shouted.

Garth was hell bent on killing the grangoor. The rest of the mercenaries may not have liked Seth, but he had. And he wanted revenge for his friend's death. He barreled across the clearing after the beast that had disappeared into the forest. He stopped at the edge and listened. A noise that sounded like something heavy being dragged deeper in the darkness echoed through the trees. He was beyond thinking about his safety. He wanted blood and dove into the thick growth.

Joseph saw the mercenary enter the woods behind the

grangoor. He decided to take the opportunity handed to him and moved in that direction. Dragging noises sounded in the woods to his left. He worked his way over until he was close enough to make out the dark shape of the man. Joseph waited. He knew the intended victim would follow and he hoped to capture him with little or no difficulty.

Garth listened to the shouts from the others, but ignored them. Seth was dead and he was going to make sure the beast that killed him would not going to enjoy its kill. He heard the dragging sound come from his left and started toward it. As he passed a tree, a large black shape leaped at him. Pain followed and the world surrounding him cascaded into oblivion.

Joseph hit Garth hard on the back of the head and watched as he crumpled to the ground. The dragging sound hesitated, it continued within seconds. The grangoor had its meal and had no desire to bother the men close by, as long as they did not try to take its food.

The four remaining people grabbed their things up quickly and headed toward their horses. They shouted for Garth; no answer came back. They assumed he was either dead, killed by the beast that took Seth, or crazy. Whatever the reason, they were not waiting around to find out. Minutes later, they were riding hard into the night, leaving the fire still burning and two horses hobbled in the ruins.

The sound of dragging and the pounding of hooves grew distant. Joseph decided it was safe to retrieve one of the horses to carry his prisoner back on. He worked his way toward the fire, making sure to avoid the huge bloody smear in the grass.

Speaking in a soft voice, he walked slowly up to the horses with an outstretched arm. One, then the other, nibbled at his hand, looking for a treat. He grabbed the dangling reins, guided the animals to the only standing wall and secured their reins to prevent them from leaving before removing the hobbles. The bridle from one of the horses dropped to the ground. A resounding smack on the rump sent it toward home, wherever home was. The other horse darted around as far as the reins would let it, but calmed down when Joseph cooed to it.

Joseph pulled the horse to where the unconscious man lay and secured the reins to a low hanging branch. He had no fear that the grangoor would return; it was busy with its present meal. The fair-haired man wrestled Garth across the broad back and made sure he was equally positioned to prevent him from sliding off when the horse walked. Once he made it back to where Bravaro was stashed, he would secure Garth with some rope so they could travel at a faster pace.

They reached Bravaro before the unconscious man woke. Joseph grabbed some rope from the saddle pack and secured the captive's hands and feet. Another rope wrapped tight under the horse's belly, forcing the secured limbs to hug the rounded body. Joseph knew time was of the essence. He had to get back to Drayco before it was too late and did not want his prize to slip off during the return trip. They were well on their way when Garth recovered his senses.

"Wha...What's going on here?" he demanded. "Who are you?"

"I'm the only one to survive the slaughter you and your filthy kind did."

"You! I know you! You're the one we captured with that cat, aren't you?"

"Yes."

"What are you going to do with me? I won't give you any information if that's what you're after."

"You don't have to yell. There's no one left to hear you. They packed up right after you disappeared."

Garth quieted down after that.

Joseph turned his attention to the path ahead. In the darkness, he did not want to lose his way, no matter how unlikely that was. The ride lasted another hour before he caught sight of the opening in the trees, and the moonlight shining down on the open plains beyond.

"We're here. Don't get any ideas. I'll have no problems killing you rather than listen to you rant on about how you were treated."

Shyanne was sitting next to her brother, head hung low, as Joseph rode up. She tilted her head upward at the sound of his approach. He could see the dark circles of worry under her eyes. His heart wrenched in his chest. A bandage hid her left wrist; he wondered what she had done while he was gone.

"I had to give him something. He was dying," she explained when she saw where his gaze stopped. "I couldn't let that happen, so I gave him some of my blood to hold him until you returned."

Drayco lay on the ground covered with blankets to help keep him warm. He was so pale. Joseph had never seen anyone with skin as white as his and still live. He watched to make sure the chest actually rose and fell to prove life continued within.

"I captured one of the mercenaries." He jerked a thumb toward the horse following his. "They became separated from the main party and were camped when a grangoor attacked. I took the gift handed to me and ran with it."

Shyanne looked at the restrained man lying on the back of the horse. She stood and walked over to him, stopping when she was close enough to see his face. She crossed her arms on her chest.

"We need to ask you some questions. If you do not answer them, we will kill you." Shyanne knew he was dead already, but did not want to inform the man of this.

"Go spit on yourself, lady. You'll get nothing outta me."

"Joseph, could you bring this...man...closer to Drayco please?" Shyanne moved back to her brother's side.

Joseph walked over and cut the ropes holding Garth to the horse. He left the restraints to the extremities tied. The prisoner slid to the ground and landed hard. He lay there, gasping for a breath. Joseph grabbed a handful of shirt and dragged him over to the pale twin. Drayco made no attempt to move. He was too weak from lack of blood to do anything more than watch. Even the simple task of moving his head brought pain and an overwhelming weakness.

"What do we do next?" Joseph asked as he deposited the prisoner next to Shyanne.

"Are you going to answer any of our questions?" she asked.

"No! Nothing! I'm not afraid of you! You can torture me and I'll still not talk!"

"So be it." She stood, drew her short knife, and brought it toward Garth's neck. Shyanne usually had no problems killing. In this instant, against an opponent who could not defend himself, she hesitated. When she looked into Garth's eyes, she saw defiance...but, also, fear, though none of this showed on his rock steady face. She held the gaze for a second before looking down. The knife followed.

"I can't do it. I just can't do it. I know Drayco will die without it but..."

Garth stared at the woman in front of him, a look of contemptuous triumph etched on his face.

"You'd let this trash live and your own flesh and blood die?" Joseph was shocked by Shyanne's lack of action. "Well, I'm not going to allow that to happen!"

He grabbed the prisoner by the hair and pulled his head back. The horses with their ripped throats flashed though his mind. He also remembered the instructions given to him prior to leaving; about whatever was brought back had to be alive. Because of this, he put two and two together and knew what came next.

The knife from his boot appeared and the sharp blade slashed the exposed throat quickly. Blood spurt from the cut artery while Joseph put the dying man's throat as close to Drayco's mouth as he could. The shocked look on Garth's face was replaced with one of horror at the sight of his blood being consumed by another. It was too much for him to handle.

Joseph refused to allow the struggling man to pull away. He held Garth with the strength of a man intent on helping his friend survive.

Drayco watched the exchange between the three, unable to talk or move during the entire process because of his extreme weakness. He received the gift given to him with the eagerness of a man anxious on living.

Shyanne closed her eyes and turned her head away while Drayco swallowed each drop that poured into his mouth. She could not bear to watch the restrained man's struggles, or see her brother's look of contentment as he drank. She moved several paces away, sat down, and put her face between her pulled up knees.

Garth's eyes haunted her more than she would have ever thought. To have him die in such a degrading manner ate at her. She was ashamed at not helping her brother, but she had morals and standards, standards that she could not compromise for anyone, even her family. She loved her brother dearly and hoped, one day, he would forgive her for what she was not able to do.

The struggles reduced in their intensity as the man slowly died in Joseph's grasp. The lifeblood flowing from one became the life giver for another. When the flow stopped, Drayco reached up and wiped his lips with the back of his sleeve. He plopped the arm down on his chest, glad he was able to make that small movement with little pain. Color returned to the dark man's face as the blood ran its course through his system, but he was still pale. He dared not sit up yet. He knew his limits. For the moment, that was one of them.

Drayco turned his head toward his sister. She was sitting a few paces from him completely withdrawn in on herself, her head bowed, her golden hair glowing in the dim moonlight.

"Shyanne," he managed to croak. "Shyanne, look at me."

She kept her head low and refused to look.

Drayco kept at her. "Shyanne...please. I want you to look at me. Sister...please...look at me."

The effort involved with drinking the blood, after having gone without for so long, was catching up to him. His body needed to sleep. He tried to fight it off so he could continue to reassure Shyanne. Her forehead stayed against her knees; she refused to acknowledge his pleas.

"Shyanne, I love you very much and will never hold anything you do, or don't do, against you. Ever."

Joseph was not sure if she heard the last words, they were spoken so softly. He watched as Drayco's battle to stay awake was finally lost. He slipped into a deep peaceful sleep.

He made sure Drayco was okay before carrying Garth's body into the woods, away from where the trio was staying. He moved to Shyanne upon his return. She remained bunched in on herself. Kneeling beside her, he reached out to put a hand on her shoulder. She twisted away before he could touch her.

"Shyanne...he said he's not holding it against you, and neither am I. I wish you would not hold it against yourself either. He's going to be okay." Joseph sighed heavily before he continued. "Shyanne, I love you. I never thought I would have the courage to say this, but I do. I realized it back at the mercenaries' camp when I didn't have you there and thought I wasn't going to see you again."

He moved in front of the woman all scrunched into a ball, making sure not to touch her until she was ready. As the words hit her, she lifted her head. Her eyes met his; they began to fill with tears. His heart wrenched again. All he wanted to do was wrap his arms around her and hold her close.

"You helped Drayco survive by giving him some of your own blood. That's a sacrifice most people would not make. But you did." Joseph pleaded. "Drayco still loves you very much. And so do I."

Shyanne listened to the sincerity in his voice. She put her arms around his neck and kissed him on the lips. Joseph responded with his own passion.

"I love you, Joseph. I love you so very much. I have from the very start," she said between kisses.

The couple reluctantly separated and walked a few yards away, their fingers intertwined. They wanted to sit and talk without disturbing the sleeping man. Yet, they wanted to be in the vicinity when he did wake.

Once they were settled, Joseph repeated, "I love you, Shyanne." Cupping her hand with his, he continued, "I want to spend the rest of my life with you. Will you grant me that pleasure?"

"I love you too. But this relationship can't possibly work. I will stay young and vigorous while you will grow old and wither away. I can't ask you to live with that cold hard reality."

"My love for you is not based on whether you outlive me. It based on the time I have with you. Quality of time, not quantity. That's what's important to me. Can you say the same?"

The passion with which he spoke took her breath away. She gazed deep into his eyes and saw the sincerity and love in his words. "Oh Joseph... yes, yes I can. I want to spend as much time with you as I can. I have been alone for so long." Shyanne started to cry again. Joseph wrapped his arms around her, pulling her against his body.

He rocked her back and forth. With his hand, he reached up and brushed away the loose strands of hair, gently kissing the supple neck beneath. Her sobs subsided as she closed her eyes. She fell asleep in his arms, comforted by his touch. He lay her down and rose to check on Drayco. The dark man was breathing easier and did not show any signs of distress. Joseph moved the blanket covering the sleeping man higher before returning to Shyanne.

He had grabbed a blanket before coming back and covered both of them with it as he lay down beside the sleeping woman. Joseph put his arm over her. She snuggled against him. Thoughts of Shyanne danced through his mind. He couldn't believe how lucky he was to have her. He only wished his mother had lived long enough to see her dreams fulfilled. He fell asleep as the stars above twinkled.

*   *   *

Drayco woke to the stars twinkling down at him from the heavens above. He blinked several times to make sure it was still nighttime, and not because he was dead. When he decided he was alive, he realized the pain in his body was gone. He recalled what happened: how he had gone for too long without blood, which caused him to become painfully weak and fall off his horse, dislocating his shoulder in the process.

The feeling of impending death, which had hung above him for far too long, was becoming a distant memory. The image of his sister putting a knife to her wrist, cutting it to give him some of her blood, was still foremost in his thoughts. He also remembered the torment he had put her through by needing to kill a defenseless man. The indecisiveness when she held the knife at Garth's neck struck Drayco hard. He never wanted to put her through that again.

He turned his head and saw the other two snuggled together under a blanket, asleep. A feeling that someone was standing uncomfortably close caused him to turn his head quickly to the other side, making the world spin as if he was flying in a tornado. After the world stopped its mad race, he saw a large ominous shadow standing an arms distance from him. He was too weak to fight off anything, especially something that big, and was about to call out when he was hit in the face with a warm moist breath.

"Bravaro, you god forsaken beast from hell...you nearly put me in my grave," he whispered to the horse towering above him.

He attempted to reach up with his right arm. The sling, and the pain that followed, reminded him of the injury to his body. Sweat broke out on his forehead and upper lip as the throbbing inched its way through his body, laughing at his discomfort. He exhaled the breath he held through pursed lips once the pain ebbed to a dull ache.

"Come here, Bravaro, I need your help to get up." He kept his voice low so as not to wake the others only a few paces away.

Drayco extended the left arm. To his relief, no monstrous pain arose from the movement. He gripped the reins hanging from the bridle and, with teeth clenched firmly together, pulled himself into a sitting position. The lack of blood reared its ugly head. It caused the world surrounding him to revolve in a sick fashion. After a couple of deep breaths, the blinding haze and sickening spin faded.

Bravaro had been trained well by the burley man. He stood firm as the dark twin grabbed the bridle and worked his way into a kneeling position. Drayco bowed his head after achieving that small feat because the pain to his right shoulder had increased with the awkward movement. After a lot of resolve, he wobbled into an upright position. The horse glanced back at the man standing on very unsteady appendages as if to ask—now what?

Drayco whispered to himself, "Well, I'm up. Now all I have to do is get into the saddle."

Once the ground wasn't going to rush up to meet him, he gripped the reins in his right hand and inched his way down Bravaro's side. At the saddle, he tried to lift his left leg into the stirrup, but was unable to hold his balance long enough. The only thing that kept him from falling was the death grip he had on the saddle horn.

That won't work, he thought. *I'll have to find another way.* He clung to the horse and tried to figure out how to solve his dilemma.

The woods were in his peripheral vision. Looking at them, he came up with an idea on how to get aboard the horse and started toward them. Halfway there, he had to stop and catch his breath.

He leaned against the horse, panting, his lungs screaming for more air. A sharp pain knifed through his sides with each intake of breath, and his thigh muscles burned. They calmed a little during the short break.

"I feel like I've just run a marathon. I haven't let myself get this bad ever. I don't plan on doing it again if I can help it."

The pain subsided to a dull ache and his breathing slowed to a more manageable rate when he continued toward his objective. He made it to the forest line without having to stop again, but had to lean against a tree before he could do much of anything else.

This had better not last much longer, Drayco thought as he paused. *I've got to free Drizzle. I've let him down once already and I'm not about to leave him in the hands of that moron Ruben.*

Drayco's thoughts grew darker, darker than they had with the pair that kidnapped him. A frown appeared, making him look cold and menacing. The heart in his chest sped up at the thought of the things he would do to Ruben when he got his hands on him, him and the Boss. He clenched his hand around the reins, imagining he was gripping something else. His teeth grinded with each movement of his jaw and a distant look entered his eyes, as if he could see into the future.

"Don't worry, Ruben. You will know soon enough how I feel about the way you conduct business." Determination filled his words.

An instant later, his heart skipped several beats, similar to a rock thrown across a pond. It split in half as he once again remembered the look in Shyanne's eyes. Utter sorrow replaced the deadly hatred he felt moments ago. His left hand fell limp beside his body. The right remained in the sling, unmoving.

"I'm so sorry, Shyanne. I hope you will forgive me for leaving you like this. What we once had is as gone as the past. I'm doing what I feel is best to protect you from any more harm...because of me."

He was leaving in the cover of darkness because he did not want to see that look again. It hurt too much. It brought back memories of the bad times, the times where the virus had caused so much suffering.

"The old adage was right...you can never go home," he whispered softly to himself.

He looked in the direction of the sleeping couple. With his strength somewhat returned, he turned away, pulling Bravaro behind him. He found what he was looking for a couple of paces away. A majestic tree that once stood tall and proud, reaching for the sea of blue above, now lay withered and dead, the base of the trunk eaten away by termites.

Drayco brought the horse alongside and while using the animal as a support stepped up on the crumbling trunk. The maneuver was hard enough. With one arm out of commission, and in his weakened state, it was all the more difficult. He hoped the tree was strong enough to hold his weight. Bark broke away under his boots, almost causing him to crash to the ground. He managed to stay on and slowly make it up the side of the horse. Carefully balancing himself, he got into the saddle.

He vaguely remembered the direction Joseph had gone when he left to fulfill the task given and rode toward it. In the faint moonlight, he strained to see the ground below. Eventually, Bravaro's distinctive hoof mark stood out in the soft dirt. They led to a trail that disappeared into the woods. He guided the horse inside. No other path large enough for man and rider led from this one. It made it easy for the dark twin to continue in the right direction.

He found the area with the ruined building where Joseph must have encountered the mercenaries. A bloody smear in the grass stood out like a sore, leading him to wonder what happened. The clearing was large, without any discernable breaks in the foliage. Not knowing which way to go, he needed to check the area for tracks, but dared not get off Bravaro in his weakened state. Instead, he guided the horse around the clearing until he located the tracks he sought.

"They sure took off in a hurry." He could tell by the distance between one set of hoof prints and the others. "They must have fled as if their lives depended on it."

The tracks led from the ruined building toward a clump of bushes wedged between two large trees. Drayco tapped Bravaro with his heels, guiding the horse through the broken branches. When they emerged on the other side, a path almost too small to use met them. He was able to see several horse prints and knew this was the right direction. It disappeared deeper into the thick overgrown wall of green.

The path widened to the width of two horses after an hour of riding. Drayco started feeling the weakness creep up again. It was not to the point it had been earlier, before Garth's blood. But he knew another source had to be found soon or he would be in trouble. Ignoring the weakness, he kept going. He had to find the people ahead of him. They would lead him to Drizzle, and to Ruben. This he was certain.

"Hold on, Drizzle. I said I'd come for you and I will." Drayco prodded Bravaro to greater speed and vanished into the dark cover caused by the trees and the night.

Thirteen

Ruben ran to his horse after fleeing the ruins. The bridle was still in place. The saddle, which he had grabbed from the porch, was strapped on quickly. The other people who ran out when he yelled were getting their horses ready with the same amount of haste.

He tossed Drizzle over the saddle in front of him. Long slashes lined the big man's back where the cat had dug his claws in after being flung over a broad shoulder. Ruben hit the cat on the head, knocking it out before it could do any more damage. He could not afford to draw the deadly spiderbats outside with the strong smell of fresh blood. Moments later, he and the survivors were riding hard into the plains. He held on to the cat to make sure he was not lost during their mad dash.

Five days later, Drizzle continued to ride in front of the big man. His feet were padded to prevent another slashing. The red lines on Ruben's back were scabbed over. They itched terribly.

"I'm going to enjoy turning you into a nice rug to lie on once I have the Boss' okay to kill you," Ruben said. "For now, that is the only thing keeping you alive."

Six people rode with him. All were men. The women who made it out were lost in the woods with other members of the party. They became separated during the hasty departure and Ruben had not waited for them. He particularly missed Viola. She had wonderful fingers, which would have helped immensely with his itchy back. That, plus her many other attributes that he loved to explore.

Something else lost during the mad dash was their supplies and food. They were back with the lousy creatures from hell, forcing the survivors to live by whatever the land had to offer.

A sigh of relief escaped from one of the men behind Ruben when the trees ahead thinned and a dirt road became visible. Whispers about the joys civilization had to offer started. Somewhere to the right, the faint clanking of metal objects echoed to the riders, ending all conversation. The mercenaries remained hidden and watched as a wagon covered in bright cheerful material pulled by a pair of white horses passed by.

"Damn Wanderers. Never could stand them," Ruben muttered more to himself than to anyone in particular. He might be a thief and a murderer, but he had standards, and being a show off was not one of them.

Three wagons in all went by, each with a pair of white horses in front. Men and women dressed in equally bright and cheerful clothes sat on the seats. Some held instruments. Others clapped their hands or accompanied the tune that filled the air with their voice. Songs and laughter floated back to the mercenaries. A milk goat pulled by the last wagon brought up the rear. Several children leaned out the back and watched it, laughing like the adults.

Ruben and his men remained out of sight. They did not want to explain their presence to anyone, much less this band of useless vagabonds. None of his group was in a talking mood right now anyway.

"Where do we go from here?" a stocky man with a deep tan named Romero asked. His long flowing hair was like Ruben's only it was wavy, and he was a half a foot shorter than the big man.

"We go to Grandfield, as planned," Ruben stated. "The Boss will be waiting for us there."

"How do you know the Boss will be there?" another man with short curly blonde hair named Paul questioned. "How does the Boss know where we are?"

"He knows."

"Are you sure this is the right road?" Paul watched the Wanderers disappear from sight with contempt.

"This is the right road. We have another day's ride

ahead of us. By late tomorrow or early the next day we
will have a tall mug of ale before us and a fine woman to
hold." His wide grin was infectious.

Grinning in return, the men sifted their positions in the
saddle, anxious to get underway.

Ruben looked down at the cat in front of him. "And you,
my friend, will be the bait to a well laid trap." He reached
down and scratched the fur between the big cat's shoulders.

Drizzle wanted to move away from such a disgusting
touch, but his position and the restraints holding him
would not allow it. He swore that when this nightmare was
over, no matter how much he hated water, he was going
to soak for a month.

"Maybe I'll have your hide tanned into a blanket instead. I like the feel of it." He saw the discomfort his touch
gave the cat, and smiled.

Ruben guided Wind Racer out of the woods and onto
the road. With a backward glance at the group following,
he said, "Let's not go too fast. That way we give our comrades a chance to catch up and avoid the unwelcome company moving ahead of us. Plus, I have a particular fond-
ness for a blonde with the missing slowpokes." He gave
them a sly smile and a wink.

The men murmured their agreement as they started
toward the west, toward the town called Grandfield.

*   *   *

Drayco rode through the rest of the night, ignoring the
needs that wracked his body. The need for sleep, the need
for blood, he wasn't sure which was worse. On several occasions, the reins almost slipped out of his cold hand and
he nearly toppled out of the saddle when he closed his
eyes. Strong determination to find Drizzle and keep the
promise he made kept him on the horse.

He was coming to a bend in the path when a noise re-
verberated from ahead. It sounded like a female humming.
The trees and the underlying brush were thick and made it
difficult for him to see the source. He slowed, cautiously
rounding the corner.

A woman stood off to the side of the path. She was

coming out from behind a bush with her back facing him and had not noticed his arrival. Drayco pulled on Bravaro's reins, backing him out of sight.

"What's taking you so long, Viola?" a man shouted from farther up the path.

"Hey! Back off! It takes a lady time to get herself back together!"

"Ha! You...a lady! That's a good one. When you become a lady, I'll become a Rizbak. Catch up to us when you're done...your majesty. We're moving on." The sound of hooves hitting the ground faded in the distance. Viola muttered to herself about them leaving without her.

"Wait until I tell Ruben that you left me, you stinking Rizbak butt. You'll wish you had stayed then." She knew full well the big man liked her. It showed in the many nights they had been together and the way he made love. A smile creased her face when she pictured Ruben smashing in Brey's face.

Drayco watched Viola straighten her clothes as she walked in the direction of her horse. She was small in stature, yet stocky in muscularity. Her long blonde hair shined like honey in the sun's rays. Tight pants hugged her shapely hips. The ties for her shirt were open, revealing far more than any respectable woman should. A sword that reminded Drayco of the kind used in medieval times hung from her side. She would have been inviting to the dark man if he had not already known what kind of a person she really was.

The need to drink grew stronger with the sight of the woman. A twinge of pain started in his abdomen. It crept from one side to the other and back. Drayco decided now was the time to make the most of the opportunity handed to him.

He urged Bravaro forward. Viola heard the movement and whirled around to see who approached. A hand gripped the hilt of her impressive sword. From the way she held her stance, he was certain she knew how to use it. Fortunately, she kept it in the sheath. He kept Bravaro's forward pace steady and unthreatening. The sun was shining over Drayco's shoulder, forcing Viola to put a hand up to block its brightness.

Viola frowned as she watched him ride toward her.

"Who are you? What do you want?" she demanded.

"Nothing, my fair lady. I only want to continue on to Grandfield."

She moved to block his way. "And what business would you have there?" She tightened her grip on the sword resting on her hip.

"My business is my own, but you're more than welcome to ride with me if you wish. From what I can see," he made a show of looking her up and down, "I think we could get to know each other very well during the journey." Bravaro was almost to Viola when Drayco pulled on the reins, stopping him short.

Viola moved her hand away from her sword. She still could not get a good look at the man on the horse because of the sun shining in her eyes, but she liked what he said. *At least he knows a lady when he sees one, unlike those ungrateful slugs who left me behind.* She gave the stranger one of her winning smiles and closed the gap between them in a sensuous manner.

With the stranger's body between her and the sun, Viola could see his features better. His black hair against such white skin gave him an ominous look; the dark circles under his piercing eyes didn't help. She was beginning to think it had been a bad idea to be left behind.

"You look kind of familiar. Have we met before?"

Viola did not like the look that entered the stranger's eyes with her question. It had the look of death. Through the years, she had learned to listen to her instinct. It was screaming at her now. She decided to end this conversation quickly and get the hell out of there.

"Look, I'm moving on now. Maybe next time we can have a bit of fun and..." Recognition washed over her face, causing her to pause mid-sentence. "Hey, wait a minute...I remember you. You're the man from the ruins. I knew there was something about you that bugged me!"

Viola's stance went from a relaxed one to a guarded one in the blink of an eye. She spun around to put some distance between her and the horse. Drayco's hand shot out and grabbed a handful of hair before she could move. He fell out of the saddle on top of her, forcing her to land face first into the soft dirt, knocking the wind out of her. She felt her head wrenched back and to the left as she gasped for a breath. The cloud of dirt that rose from her hitting the ground filled her mouth with every intake of air. She started to cough.

The sword she desperately wanted was pinned underneath her body, digging into her heaving ribs. She couldn't get to it. And no matter which way she tried to roll, he was there putting his weight on her to prevent it.

She coughed out a mouthful of dirt, and pleaded, "Why are you doing this? I didn't do anything to you."

"No...not to me. But you did hurt someone close to me. The captive you had in your midst lost all that was dear to him and that hurts me," he answered her in a quiet menacing voice.

Drayco could feel Viola building up for a major struggle and decided to end this encounter before his weakness showed itself. He yanked her golden hair backward, forcing her head up to expose the neck. He immediately leaned over and bit deep into the soft tissue. Viola inhaled sharply then screamed. She tried to throw Drayco off, but he had a hold on her that nothing could break.

He closed his eyes and savored every spurt of blood flowing from the supple neck. Drayco sucked on the wound to help the flow speed up before the woman died. He needed every drop if he was going to banish the weakness for a while. The screaming stopped as soon as the woman realized nobody would hear her.

Viola knew her instincts had finally failed. The look of death she had seen in Drayco's eyes moments ago now filled her own as her lifeblood continued to flow into his waiting mouth. The last thing she heard before the angel of death came was the sound of slurping from a man who showed her the same mercy she had shown the slaughtered townspeople.

The pulse under his lips stopped; he let go. No more blood would come from the dead woman now. He sat up with his shoulders slumped and tilted his face skyward, soaking in the warmth of the sunlight. A trickle of blood ran down from the corner of his mouth. He automatically wiped it off with the back of his hand. He was lost in the rapture of the replenishment flowing through his veins. It caused him to miss the man sitting on horseback, a look of total shock on his face as he watched what happened to

Viola.

Randolf could not believe what he had just witnessed. He had come back because he felt guilty at having left Viola alone. Brey said she would be along soon. When she didn't, he decided to go looking for her. As Viola took her last breath, the trance freezing him like a statue broke. He snarled with rage and kicked the horse hard. It leapt toward the man sitting on the ground.

Drayco felt the vibrations through the ground before he heard the pounding hooves. He rolled his head toward whatever was making its way through the haziness and saw a man on horseback bearing down on him fast. A blade flashed in the light. He tried to roll out of the way but was too slow. He felt the blunt side of the sword hit his head, causing the world around him to disappear. He spun backwards and landed on Viola's dead body, unconscious.

The mercenary swung his sword and felt it hit as he flew past. He glanced over his shoulder and watched the dark man slump onto the woman's body. He had used the blunt side because he wanted the killer alive. He wanted to make this guy suffer for what he had done to Viola.

Randolf jerked the reins to the right and spun the horse back toward Drayco. He jumped off when he was beside the downed man and kicked him off Viola. A nasty purple welt was rising on the left temple near the hairline, attesting to where the sword hit. Kneeling beside her, the ugly wound on her neck made it plain that she was dead.

What manner of creature would kill like this? He peered at Drayco, expecting to see a monster. All he saw was a man.

Bravaro stood a few paces away from his rider. When Randolf moved toward him, the animal bolted in the opposite direction.

"Pity, you would have made a great addition to my stock."

Randolf retrieved Viola's horse. Returning to the dark man, he removed the sling holding the right arm. It did not matter why it was there, or if by removing it, it would cause pain. He only knew it wouldn't matter after Ruben was finished with him. Picking up Drayco's limp body, he tossed him onto its back. The hands and feet of the stranger who killed in such a grotesque manner were secured to prevent him from escaping.

Viola was buried quickly to prevent scavengers from finding her. When he finished, he leaped into the saddle and urged his horse closer to the other animal. Grabbing the reins, he dug his heels in and started up the path at a ground-eating pace, Drayco's animal pulled along behind him.

*   *   *

Shyanne woke the next morning and saw an empty blanket where her brother should have been. She shook Joseph awake and pointed toward the bare spot.

"What was that fool thinking? He's in no shape to go anywhere."

"His horse is gone." Joseph noticed only two animals grazing nearby.

"We have to find him. He's not strong enough to have gone far." Shyanne looked around, frantically trying to see every direction at once.

"Shyanne, he was on horseback. He didn't need to be strong enough to go far. The horse will do that for him."

She scrambled to her feet. "Why would he leave like that? Why? I bet it was because I couldn't kill for him. That's what drove him off. We have to go after him. I'll never forgive myself if he dies out there all alone."

Joseph rose and grabbed Shyanne by the shoulders. Shaking her gently, he forced her to pay attention to what he said. "Shyanne my love, we will go after him. You have to remain calm to help, though." He looked straight into her scared blue eyes to make sure his message was getting through.

Shyanne reached up and grabbed his hands, giving them a squeeze. "You're right love. I'm okay now. My emotions took over before my brain could catch up." The reply was calm and decisive. "Let's get our things together and go after him."

She gave Joseph a grateful smile and broke away to get the horses ready. He watched to make sure she was okay before turning toward the woods.

"I'm going to look for his tracks."

"Drayco said his horse has a distinctive print. It's supposed to resemble a vee."

Everything about Shyanne's mannerisms was down to business now, for which he was glad. Joseph walked slowly toward the wall of green and brown, keeping an eye on the ground for the unusual print. He had an idea where to head, but wanted to confirm it prior to saying anything.

He angled his direction toward the path taken yesterday and was almost to the entrance when he noticed something that might be what he sought. He squat down to get a closer look. A hoof print with a notch shaped like a vee was deep in the soft ground. The prints of the animal disappeared with the path into the trees. Making his way back, he also noticed the freshly loosened bark lying on the ground next to a downed tree.

"Damn. Just as I thought." Joseph frowned and ran to Shyanne.

"What did you find?"

"He's gone in the direction I went yesterday. I can only guess that he's going after the people I found."

"That idiot brother of mine! What does he hope to accomplish?"

"Remember, Shyanne, they have Drizzle," he reinforced softly. "Drayco promised to come back for him and failed. That's got to be eating at him."

"Yes....he doesn't like to fail." Shyanne remembered all the tantrums he used to have as a child.

"Are you ready to go love?" Joseph walked up and wrapped his arms around her.

She nuzzled into his chest, and said, "Yes."

He bent over and kissed her before they separated toward their horses.

"We will find him. That is my promise to you, Shyanne." Joseph moved the animals toward the path leading into the trees. He started into the dimness ahead. Shyanne followed on his heels.

*   *   *

When he awoke, Drayco found himself tied to a horse he did not recognize. The path was gone. A main thoroughfare with deep ruts made by wagons during the past rainy seasons replaced it. One person was ahead, while two more followed behind. The weakness he felt before drinking Viola's blood was reduced. But he had been depleted for far too long for that small amount to do any good. He had to have more.

His head and right shoulder throbbed with every step the animal took. A moan escaped his lips when the animal stumbled in one of the ruts, causing the throbbing to become an avalanche of pain.

"Well, sleeping beauty is awake. I bet you have one hell of a headache, don't you." The man leading his horse laughed at his own corny joke.

Drayco kept quiet. He moved his head carefully to glance around at his surroundings, trying not to set off another avalanche. They were traveling on the open road. No other travelers were in sight. He wondered where they were going when the man leading him seemed to read him mind.

"I bet you're wondering where we're going. We're trying to catch up with Ruben. He's ahead of us, making his way to Grandfield."

"Brey, shut up! You're already in enough trouble. Don't add more to it."

"What are you talking about, Randolf? I didn't do anything."

"Tell that to Ruben when you tell him about Viola." Randolf shook his head while making a tisking sound with his tongue against the roof of his mouth, "I'm glad I'm not in your boots."

Brey frowned and faced forward again. Drayco could see the man's shoulders hunch. He appeared to be pouting. The others remained silent. The woman riding behind Drayco glared at him as if she could kill with her eyes alone. He let his head hang, his eyes closed, as the trio continued after the party they had become separated from.

The group rode for another four long and grueling hours before they saw any sign of the party they were chasing. The sun reflected off something laying on the side of the road, causing it to cast bright rays of light in the eyes of the man in the lead.

Brey shouted to the other riders, "Hey, something's here! Sheena, come check it out!"

Sheena nudged her horse toward where Brey pointed

and leaped to the ground in one fluid motion. An earring made of gold was among the sprouts of grass growing on the side of the road. She bent over and picked it up, holding it this way and that before saying, "It's Andrew's. I saw him wearing it during our last ride together."

"Your last ride together, eh?" Brey had a devilish smirk on his face.

Sheena gave Brey a look of disgust. "Only someone as sick and deprived as you would think up something like that."

"You want me. I can see it all over you," he cooed as he leaned over in her direction.

Sheena was a hands span away from Brey. She closed the gap in an instant and grabbed him by the front of his shirt, pulling him off the animal with little effort. He hit the ground in a cloud of dust; a look of surprise spread across his face. She started kicking the downed man in the ribs. Brey grabbed her leg as she swung it and tossed her to the ground. He was on top of her before she could roll out of the way. Brey started kissing her. His hand strayed to other parts of her body. A foot hit him in his side, knocking him off Sheena.

Sheena jumped up and snarled at the man lying on his back. She pulled a knife out of her belt and dove at Brey with the intent of slitting his throat. She was met with a shove before she reached him. It caused her to go reeling into the grass. Both combatants were so focused on each other that they had failed to see Randolf come up beside them.

"That's enough! If you two want to continue this on a later day, that's your business. For now, we have a mission to complete." He glared at the two, causing them to stop before he brought the sword he carried on his back into play.

"Now get up and get on your horses! We've wasted enough time here." He moved toward the horse Drayco was on and grabbed the reins, "I'll take over this job. You seem too preoccupied to handle the duty." He pulled the animal closer to his own horse then got up into the saddle. He continued to glare at the others while waiting for them to move. When they still scowled at each other instead of getting on their animals, he bellowed, "NOW!"

That broke the staring contest. With a lot of grumbling, they got on their animals and started down the road. Randolf brought up the rear so he could keep an eye on the two ahead. If they decided to fight again, he would end it quickly.

I don't know how this band ever managed to stay together without killing each other. Drayco thought.

Three more hours passed. Dried jerky was passed out, but none was offered to Drayco. The tension from the fight had dissipated and everyone was calm again.

"I can't wait to get to Grandfield. I'm going to get me a woman and bed her until she screams for mercy," Brey boasted.

"More like shudders in terror and revulsion," Sheena whispered to herself.

"I heard that. If you were woman enough, you'd try my wares and scream with utmost pleasure too."

"Brey..." Randolf warned.

"Well she would," he challenged.

Sheena rolled her eyes and leaned over, pretending to throw up.

Randolf broke out into a hearty laugh, "You two are worse than children. In fact, you two are worse than any brat I've ever met."

Sheena smiled at Randolf's statement. Suddenly, she stood up in her stirrups and squinted, trying to see what was ahead in the vast openness. Randolf and Brey saw her action and sat up straighter to look. A group of horses was standing off to the side of the road near a clump of trees. The tall shadowy remains of a city were on the horizon beyond. As they rode closer, a look of overwhelming happiness covered Sheena's face.

"It's them! I'd recognize that big horse anywhere! It's Ruben's!"

She energetically kicked her horse into a full run and flew away. In a flash, Brey was on her heels. Randolf prodded his animal into a gallop, pulling Drayco along. The dark man's throbbing headache had become a dull ache. It returned in full force with the pounding he received. He groaned with every step of the horse, unable to hold it back. By the time Sheena was halfway cross the field, she was yelling like an Indian from an old west film Drayco remembered.

"Ayeee-yee-yee! We finally caught up to you!" Her sword was in her hand. She raised it in salute to the group waiting for them.

The people separated as she barreled through their midst. They did not want to be trampled by the crazy woman on horseback. She circled around and came to a halt. In one fluid motion, she slid off the horse and put her sword away. Brey was already amongst the comrades. Randolf was arriving with Drayco.

Ruben walked up to Sheena, a frown covering his face. He flashed a smile and picked her up in a huge bear hug. She kicked and laughed, making it hard for the big man to keep hold of her. He let go and started toward the other two.

"Good to have you back with us, Brey. You too, Randolf. Where's Viola?" Looking around, he finally noticed the man tied to the trailing horse. "What have you brought us?"

Randolf walked over to Drayco, glad to distract the big man from thinking about the missing women. He grabbed a fistful of hair and jerked the prisoner's head up so Ruben could see his face.

"You! I never thought I'd see you so soon—especially after our recent encounter—and in this manner. How wonderful this day has become." Ruben smiled. "Randolf, I want a full report. Andrew, see that his horse is taken care of. Romero, put this trash somewhere close so we can keep an eye on him. We'll camp here for the night instead moving on."

The band of mercenaries relocated to the opposite side of the trees, out of the direct view of the road. No fire was started to attract passersby and the horses were tethered to keep them from wandering.

Ruben led Randolf out of earshot from the rest. He could tell by his mannerism that Randolf needed to talk privately. They spoke of the events that had transpired since the smaller group became separated from the larger, and about how Drayco had killed Viola by drinking her blood. A couple of times the two looked toward Brey, but he never noticed. He was too busy trying to get Sheena to disappear with him into the trees.

Later, before darkness covered everything, the mercenaries sat in a circle talking. Drayco, secured in both hand and foot, sat on a fallen log next to Ruben. Drizzle lay behind the group, secured in the same fashion. He looked a bit thin, but seemed to be holding up well under the circumstances.

"Look, kitty, a new plaything for us to have fun with. Don't you wish you could play too?" Ruben smiled slyly at the cat. "Too bad, though. All you can do is watch."

The leader of the mercenaries stood up and faced Drayco. "I've been given orders not to kill you. Nothing was said about what condition you had to be in when I turned you over. I plan on having a bit of fun first."

He pulled a small thin knife out of his boot and held it up for the all to see. They started cheering the big man on.

"Let him have it for Viola... Cut him, cut him good... Make him bleed... Cut a finger off..." On and on the words flew. The crowd leaned in close; anxious to watch the suffering about to be inflicted on the man they felt had caused them so much pain.

Drayco sat perfectly still, showing no fear. He watched with cold eyes, his head held high in defiance, as Ruben advanced. The big man stopped the knife inches from Drayco's face. With a flick of the wrist, a small seam led from the corner of the left eye to the area beside the nose. Small streams of blood ran down his cheek and onto his shirt.

"Oops. Did I do that? I hope it didn't hurt...much." He chuckled with the rest of the mercenaries. "I've made such a mess of your shirt. I guess we'll just have to get it out of the way."

The knife started cutting again. Ruben made no attempt to prevent the slim sharp blade from coming in contact with the skin underneath. The shirt hung in tatters around the dark man's waist by the time he was finished. Several streams of blood flowed freely on his chest and back. None of the wounds was deep.

Drizzle squirmed against his restraints. A sound of utter frustration escaped from the cat at his inability to help his friend. Drayco remained quiet throughout the entire session. He had not flinched or made a sound as the blade cut into his flesh.

"My, we are a tough one, aren't we? Now what can I do to get you to scream. Hummmm, I think I have it."

He put the tip on the knife one-quarter of an inch into the right side of Drayco's neck and dragged the weapon down over the nipple of the left breast, slicing the tip in two. Drayco was unable to hold back this time. He screamed as the pain enveloped him. Blood shot from the neck wound causing the people nearest that side to be sprayed. Drayco paled and almost fainted, but Ruben dropped the knife and grabbed his hair. He slapped the bloody face back and forth several times.

"You will not pass out on me!"

The flying blood hit Brey in the eyes. He shouted, "Hey! Watch what you're doing!" and reached up to wipe it off with his shirtsleeve.

Ruben let go of the prisoner and was upon Brey in seconds. He grabbed the unsuspecting man by his hair and dragged him over to Drayco, where he forced his face against the bleeding neck. Randolf kept the dark man upright.

Ruben bellowed, "Drink! Drink you ass-wipe of a dog! Drink like your life depended on it, because it does!"

Brey tried to push away, but the powerful hand holding him would not relent. He felt his jaw forced open and the taste of something salty flow into his mouth. He gagged and tried to spit out the sticky substance. He wanted to get away, to force the hand off his jaw, but other hands were holding his arms, preventing him from doing so.

Ruben pulled Brey away from Drayco and instructed Randolf to hold pressure to the neck wound. He indicated for Romero to hold Brey as he let go.

"Why are you doing this to me? What did I do?" Brey cried.

Ruben leaned in close, and said, "You left another of our party alone and she died because of it."

He glanced in Drayco's direction. Drayco had his eyes shut. The flow of blood from the neck wound was slowed thanks to the pressure held on it. His skin had whitened considerably and was wrinkling. The hair on his head had pale streaks running through it. It was graying at the temples. He looked like he had aged 20 years in minutes.

"How was I supposed to know he was going to come

along and kill her?"

"You didn't. But you should have planned on it. We NEVER leave one of ours alone." The next sentence came out low and menacing. "Don't worry, though; you'll not have to concern yourself about it again."

Brey's eyes widened and he started thrashing about. Sheena assisted Romero in holding the struggling man, a look of smug satisfaction on their faces. The thin knife appeared once more. Ruben reached up and neatly slit the neck of the man he considered offensive. Blood spurt out of the wound like a geyser. He grabbed the back of Brey's head and lowered it to Drayco's mouth.

The dark man had not seen what transpired between the mercenaries. The pain to his body was so intense, he forgot about the world around him. The blood loss from the knifing was substantial, but not life threatening, even in his weakened state.

Drayco felt something pressed against his lips and tried to pull back. Hands prevented it. Suddenly, the taste of blood hit his tongue. He drank tentatively until the needs of his body took over. He latched onto the neck like a leech and sucked as hard as he could before the offered life form died.

Randolf continued to hold the wound on Drayco's neck as instructed. He remembered watching this done to Viola and wished he could get away from this disgusting being. He turned his face away with revolt. The rest of the mercenaries were looking disgusted as well.

Ruben indicated it was okay to release his hold on the neck. He did so and backed away as fast as possible. Drayco's never knew it; the world was lost in the need to drink. The bleeding to his neck and body had stopped. Romero and Sheena continued to hold Brey in case the dying man attempted something.

Color returned to the ash-white skin and the wrinkles disappeared. The hair lost all of the gray color, returning to its black sheen. Drayco continued to suck on the neck long after the pulse quit. Ruben finally pulled him off and slammed him to the ground.

"Enough, dark one, he's dead."

Drayco lay there gasping. He felt every ounce of the pain to his body return full force. The gash to his neck re-opened; Ruben indicated for one of the men to hold it. Andrew reluctantly came forward.

"I want the wounds on this man dressed immediately. I want no more blood loss to occur. Do I make myself clear?"

Eight voices rang out as one. "Yes Sir!"

Ruben walked toward Wind Racer. He heard the mutterings of the others, but chose to ignore them. They knew they had it good and would do nothing to mess it up.

*   *   *

Shyanne and Joseph entered the clearing with the ruined hut. A saddled horse was grazing in the grassy field surrounding it.

"Joseph! That's Drayco's horse!" Shyanne gasped when she got a better look at the animal.

The horse raised his head as they neared. Joseph slowly dismounted and made his way to the creature whose full attention was on him.

"Bravaro, remember me? We had a great adventure together."

The ears flipped back and forth. Joseph continued to work his way toward the horse, his arm extended, talking softly as he moved. Shyanne stayed where she was and watched in silence. If she made a move now, she might drive the animal away.

Joseph reached Bravaro and grasped the dangling reins. He gave the horse a pat on its damp neck. The horse calmed under his rubbing hands. Sweat ran from underneath the saddle, covering his body. It looked like he had run a long way. Joseph led the animal to the ruined hut. He removed the saddle, grabbed a brush out of a saddlebag, and started brushing him down. Shyanne dismounted and moved to his side.

"What do you think happened? He would never leave Drayco unless he was forced to." She looked the horse over.

"I don't know. He must have run for several hours to get in this kind of shape. Look at the amount of sweat on him." He continued to rub the horse down as he spoke. "What I'm wondering is what happened to Drayco?"

When silence was his reply, he looked at her. Her head was down. Joseph walked to her and pulled her against his body. She looked up at him; tears filled her eyes.

"I hope he's alright. I will never forgive myself for not helping him if anything has happened."

"I haven't known him all that long, but I get the feeling he is a very resilient man. No matter what the situation is, he'll be okay. I know it." Joseph spoke with such conviction.

Shyanne smiled, "Thanks, Joseph."

"Let's get the rest of the animals bedded down before it gets too dark. It's already hard enough to see." The pair gathered the other horses and secured them next to Bravaro.

The fair-haired man removed the blanket rolls from the back of the saddles and spread them out afterwards. All three horses were given grain and water before he sat down next to Shyanne.

She admired how he reacted to each crisis. He was calm and under control where she was chaotic and reckless. All she could think about was finding her brother. He was so weak when they went to sleep last night. He might be laying somewhere, dying, or worse...dead.

As if Joseph was reading her mind, he said, "We'll take off at first light and find out where Bravaro came from." He sat up and looked around when he remembered the grangoor. "By the way, this is the spot where the mercenaries met with ill-fortune."

The crickets sang and night birds sounded off in the darkness. If the grangoor were close, all would be quiet. He relaxed and leaned back onto his arms. The air had a cool bite to it. The woman next to him shivered. He picked up one of the blankets and draped it over her shoulders. She snuggled into it.

"I want to thank you, Joseph, for being the wonderful person you are. Without you, I would be lost." She sighed and lowered her eyes. "I know Drayco will be found and that he'll be okay. I can feel it in my bones."

"We will find him." Deep inside, he was not sure if he would be alive or not.

Shyanne looked into Joseph's never-ending blue eyes. She reached up and put her arms over his shoulders. The blanket dropped to the ground behind her. She leaned in and gave him a soft tentative kiss on the right side of his lips, followed by a kiss to the left side.

Joseph was not sure how he should respond. Shyanne answered the question for him. Her next kiss was on the lips. At first, the kiss was soft. The passionate love she felt inside did not keep it that way. He responded to her growing need with an emotion he had not felt in a long time.

Joseph kissed her face, her cheeks, her lips, then moved down to her neck. Shyanne leaned her head back, her eyes closed with pleasure. He pulled away, holding her at arms length. She looked at him questioningly. He simply smiled. He reached up to the strings keeping her shirt closed and untied them slowly. She smiled back and watched his actions with longing. When the strings were undone, he lifted the shirt. She reached her arms up, causing the man in front of her to disappear until the shirt was out of the way.

Her creamy skin shined in the moonlight. Joseph leaned over and kissed her exposed body. She wrapped her arms around his head, running her fingers through his hair. A moan escaped from Shyanne's lips as she pulled his face harder into her chest. Joseph sat up and took his own shirt off. He watched her for a second, observing Shyanne's beauty before helping her to lie back on the blankets. They kissed again, their need for each other growing with each stroke of their lips, with each touch on one another's body.

Shyanne helped Joseph undo and remove the rest of his clothes. He in turn rose to his knees and helped her. Their eyes met in the faint glow of the moonlight. The love he saw in them yesterday shined as bright tonight as it did then.

He moved up and down Shyanne's body, tasting everything as he went. It had been a long time since she had been with anyone. She relished the touch of his lips on her skin. Ripples of ecstasy washed over her like an ocean wave on a sandy shoreline. As they flipped the blankets over themselves, they became one not just in body, but in mind and soul as well.

*   *   *

Drayco lay still long into the night. He was exhausted, but sleep eluded him. The slices to his neck and chest were bandaged. He could not shift his head far without feeling as if the wounds would rip open. The other cuts were minor, and the incredible healing powers of his body were already hard at work. He turned his head and looked at Drizzle. The big cat was awake, watching him.

The rest of the party was asleep except for the one standing guard. Ruben lay next to Drayco, his back facing him. As he watched, the big man rose to his feet and went to the lone individual standing watch.

"Get some sleep. I'll take over from here." Paul murmured his thanks and moved toward the other sleeping forms.

After watching Paul lie down and roll into his blanket, Ruben returned to Drayco. He squat next to him and whispered, "Let's walk."

He cut the bonds securing Drayco's legs, but left the ones on his wrists intact. Ruben supported him while he walked several yards from the main group before stopping. Drayco was still weak from his experience and nearly went down as his legs gave out. Ruben grabbed him, preventing it from happening. He set the dark man down carefully before sitting across from him.

The wind coming from the open plains had a bite of cool air to it. Fall was just around the corner. The leaves of the surrounding trees would change colors before long, and winter would arrive shortly thereafter, covering everything with a snow-white blanket. Travel would slow down considerably once that happened.

Ruben glanced sideways at Drayco, "What is it about you and the girl that the Boss wants?"

Drayco stared into the night, refusing to talk.

"I wanted to let you know how much I admire your courage and devotion to your friend." He pointed at the big cat with a long piece of field grass. "Most people, including the ones I travel with, would not have been able to take what I gave you without breaking down. And they would not even consider doing it for a humecat."

Drayco wondered why the one person in this entire post virus world he intensely hated was telling him this.

"I'm talking to you like this because I wanted to let you

know it's nothing personal. I've been paid to do a job, and I do it, regardless of who it involves. If the circumstances were different, we could be friends. I just wanted to let you know that.

Drayco could hear the sincerity in Ruben's voice, but knew better than to trust him. The man was a paid killer and he could probably talk an old miser into giving him gold just because he asked for it.

"Well, I just wanted to let you know." The big man sighed. "What I'm curious about is what the Boss wants from you? Can you tell me that much?"

The dark twin considered not answering; he decided there was no harm in doing so. "I don't know what the Boss wants." He shrugged his shoulders. The movement brought on a wave of pain, causing him to wince.

Ruben saw the facial expression. "Sorry about that, had to do my job. If I let you get away with whatever you wanted, I'd lose face." He gave Drayco a half smile. Assuming a thoughtful pose, he continued. "What is it that the Boss wants? Do you have special powers? Are you a demon? What?"

"I don't know." Drayco's thoughts were racing. What was so special about him and his sister? He and Shyanne were nothing. They didn't have money or power, so what was it that made the Boss want them so badly.

"Oh well. Thought I'd ask. Just have to wait until tomorrow to find out. We'll reach Grandfield by noon. Then you'll be in the hands of the Boss." Ruben shrugged his own shoulders in the same fashion Drayco had and got up.

"Have to take you back and tie you up again. Can't have you running off on me. Big money involved here." He winked at Drayco grabbed the back of his shirt, lifting him off the ground with one arm as if he was a feather.

The shirt pressed hard into the bandaged areas covering his neck and upper chest. Drayco gasped with pain. Ruben's smile broadened. A hint of the evil hidden inside showed itself in the twinkle of his eyes. Ruben held the shirt tight for a little longer than necessary before letting it relax. Drayco's legs felt like rubber. They wanted to buckle out from under him, but he concentrated on keeping upright and they held. The pain subsided as the shirt relaxed. He let out the breath he had been holding.

Ruben thumped him on the back. "Glad we had this chat. I wish it would have been more informative but...oh well."

The pat on the back did him in; he fell to his knees. Pain rippled through his body once more. The mercenary leader picked him up by his shirt and dragged him to where he lay prior to their chat. He threw the dark man to the ground. Drayco landed on his left side, the wind knocked out of him. Ruben bent over to inspect the bandages. After making sure no fresh blood showed, he secured his legs.

"You should have talked to me. I could have helped you. Now you'll have to deal with the Boss, and he's not going to be as nice. I've seen his work. By the time he's done with you, you'll wish you had chatted with me instead."

Ruben stood and looked down at the gasping prisoner, a stern look on his face. A moment later, he threw his hands in the air. "Maybe it was for the better." He walked away, shaking his head as he went. "Who knows what I would have done with the information anyway."

Drayco lay there wishing the pain would go away so he could think about what Ruben had said, but it continued to make his life a living hell long into the night.

Fourteen

The sky overhead was overcast as they drew near the town of Grandfield. The clouds were fat and gray, floating slowly to the east. No rain fell yet. Ruben was in the lead, Drayco's animal close behind him.

They did not bother to tie his limbs together. It would have been too conspicuous and brought unwanted questions to the group. In his present state, Drayco would not have been able to do much anyway. His right arm was strapped against his body again to prevent the wound to his neck and chest from opening, and all his strength was being used to keep himself upright in the saddle. The cut Ruben had put on his face was scabbed over and itched.

"Finally! We're home!" Sheena waved her arms over her head. A huge grin covered her face.

"I can't wait to get to the bar for a drink," Paul said. "And the company of a fine woman." He glanced at Sheena as he spoke. She turned a deep crimson.

Andrew glared at Paul. He stated," Back off, man, she's mine."

The two men made a move for their weapons simultaneously. Laughter broke out and they released their grip on their swords. Sheena moved her horse next to Andrew. She leaned over to give him a kiss. He turned his head away then turned back quickly, giving her the kiss she sought before she could become offended. They had apparently played this game before because everyone groaned and rolled their eyes while the two would-be lovers acted out their parts.

Ruben looked back with a half-cocked grin on his face, "You two need to get a room or something. Take out your frustrations on each other in the sack. We're sick of seeing it."

The other mercenaries murmured agreement with his statement. Sheena and Andrew scoffed at everyone. They leaned over and kissed again.

Drayco looked back at a horse behind the main group. It had a blanket draped over its back, covering its precious cargo. The cover shifted occasionally. Unlike Drayco, Drizzle had his extremities tied. Ruben did not want the cat to escape before he could put his plans into action.

The group of mercenaries rode down the dusty road toward town. Bit and pieces of past technology lay about, taken from the nearby ruined city. The hood of a rusted automobile was a roof for a rickety wooden shed. Drayco saw what might have been a sign from a fast food place where chicken was sold used by a merchant to advertise his goods, a couple of cages filled with live chickens sat nearby. Other signs advertised tools, household wares and mostly... women.

The buildings had a dull dingy look to them; most were run down and in need of repairs. Paint was peeling off and bare wood exposed to the elements. Some of the people had haunted looks in their eyes. Others openly glared at everyone that passed.

A few of the women hollered at them. "Hey Ruben, glad to see you back! Randolf, I have something for you. When are you coming to see me? Romero, you owe me money from the last time you were here!"

Some of the merchants liked to see this group come into town because they brought lots of gold with them. Other merchants scowled because they knew the trouble that usually followed this group, as well.

This was Grandfield's seedier part of town, a haven for people not looking to be found. A haven for murderers, thieves, and bandits. Unsuspecting people who entered for the first time usually left empty-handed after meeting one of the local bands of rowdies.

On a few occasions, rich persons accompanied by mean looking bodyguards came to hire someone for a job they needed done with stealth and quickness. These people went no farther than the inn, enquiring from the barkeep which person was best for their particular job. Gold was exchanged and information given and all parties went away happy. Law enforcement was not a part of this postvirus world, but vengeful families could make one's life a living hell until they finally decided which way to kill you.

This was Ruben's home away from home. He did not reside here full time, but was here often enough to be know by most of the locals. His name was mentioned more often than any other as someone who could get the job done correctly. A few of the mercenaries with him were from around here. Ruben paid them well for their skills and bloodthirsty love of killing.

He led the group to the stables. A stableman came out to greet them. The clothes on his back were old and worn. He had short brown hair peppered with gray that seemed to have a mind of its own, going whatever direction it wanted regardless of what he did to it. His skin was wrinkled and looked as tough as leather due to too much exposure to the hot glaring sun. He squinted when he looked up, even though the sun was not shining in his eyes. Drayco knew right away that the man was unable to see much.

"Who there and what can I do for you?" he asked while reaching out ahead of him with his hand. He held a long stick in the other.

"Old man, I have returned from a long journey and want the usual locations for my horses," a deep raspy voice replied.

"Ruben! You crazy hoot, I'd know that voice anywhere, no matter how much you try to disguise it.

"I should have known better than to try to pull one over on you, Crusty."

The old man grinned and Drayco could see why he got the name. His teeth, what was left of them, were black and crusty, as was his skin with several layers of dirt.

The party got off their horses; Drayco was left on his. Ruben indicated for Paul to lead the injured man to the stalls reserved for them. "I have an errand to see to. I'll be back in about ten minutes. Take care of him until I return."

As they passed the old man, Drayco had to hold his

breath to keep from gagging. The stench reminded him of meat that had been left to spoil in the trashcans during the hot summer months when he forgot to take it down for pickup a long time ago. He exhaled only after they had entered the dark hay-smelling building.

"Pretty rank isn't he. For as long as I've been riding with Ruben, he's always stunk like that." Paul put two fingers to his nose and squeezed it shut. He released it with a grin, "But he sure can take care of the horses."

Drayco agreed on the stench part, but kept his mouth shut. He did not feel like talking at the moment. His wounds ached and he was exhausted from the abuse he had received from these people.

"You sure are a quiet one aren't you, mystery man? Don't see what all the fuss is about. Oh well, a job is a job." He shrugged his shoulders and led the animal into the back of a stall then exited. He made no attempt to help the injured man down.

Drayco clenched his teeth and moved to get off the horse. A wave of pain and nausea shot through him. His face paled even more than it already was and sweat broke out on his forehead. With his right arm incapacitated, it was a difficult maneuver, but he finally made it down. He held on to the saddle horn until he knew he was not going to collapse. The pain slowly reduced. Ruben strolled up behind him and slapped him on the back, close to the right shoulder, causing the pain to intensify once more. Drayco shot the big man a look filled with intense hatred.

"How are you doing now that you're on solid ground? Oh, did that hurt? My goodness, I forgot about that nasty cut, didn't I." He gripped Drayco's right shoulder and squeezed, "I just wanted to remind you not to try anything while we're at the Inn. I'm expecting company and I don't want you to spoil the night." He gave Drayco a smile and relaxed his grip. The smile contained nothing akin to warmth in it. The big man squeezed the shoulder several more times, causing Drayco to take it a sharp breath. "Let's get ready shall we?" He steered the prisoner toward the exit.

The rest of the group was already waiting outside after making sure their horses were taken care of. They were discussing what they planned to do next.

"I'm going to get me a drink of cold ale and a soft bed to sleep in," Paul said.

Andrew had his arm over Sheena's shoulder. "I plan on doing the same thing, but I don't know how much sleep I'll get." He winked at her. She elbowed him in the ribs.

"Shut up, you maniac!"

"You'll just have to make me, sweetie." He grabbed her and held her against him, kissing her neck in several places.

"Will you two cut it out," Ruben said as he exited the stables with Drayco beside him. His face was serious. It broke into a huge grin after the others quieted down, their smiles gone. "Like I said before...take it to a room, we're sick of seeing it." The mercenaries burst out laughing; the tension in the air dissolved.

"Let's divvy up the pay for this fine job." He pulled a large bag out from under his shirt and untied the drawstrings. The sound of many coins clinking together rang out as he walked to a small barrel located next to the building, his arm over Drayco's shoulder to keep him close. The contents were poured out and the glint of sunlight reflected off many shiny objects.

"There's enough gold for each one of you to get 20 pieces. I want you to take your share and go enjoy yourselves. When another job comes up, I'll be in contact."

Eight people strode up to Ruben. He handed each of them 20 pieces of gold. As the last person walked up, Ruben said, "Randolf, I want to thank you for bringing me this prize. Here is an extra 5 pieces for your quick thinking." The rest had already left, so they missed the extra transaction.

Randolf looked at the big man. He said, "I only hope he gets the same fate as Viola." He crossed his arms in front of his chest and glared at Drayco standing beside Ruben. "I wish I could be there to see it happen."

"Maybe you can. I need someone to bring the cat to the Inn. I will add more gold to your pockets if you help me."

"It would be my greatest pleasure to see him suffer and scream like a little girl." A sneer crept onto Randolf's face as he asked, "Can I help him scream?"

"Of course. Like I said, I need help and I appreciate it

far greater when it comes from a skilled professional like yourself," Ruben purred. Drayco wondered what the big man was up to. His type never needed help from anyone, much less from this wannabe tough guy. He was still wondering when he was painfully steered back to the front of the stables. A bundle waited there; Drizzle was inside.

"I need you to carry the cat. I have to keep an eye on this one in case he tries something. When we get to the room, you can have first crack at him."

Randolf grinned wickedly and picked up the cumbersome package. The three men started down the road toward the Inn located in the center of town. Ruben had his arm casually draped over Drayco's shoulder to make it look like they were the best of chums. People murmured their hellos as they passed.

"So what do you think of my little town? Friendly isn't it?"

Drayco said nothing. He was too busy looking around, trying to memorize the direction they came, just in case. It would come in handy if he was able to get Drizzle and himself free.

The wounded shoulder suddenly sent messages of pain to his brain as Ruben grasped it. "I asked you a question. It is only polite to answer."

Drayco glared with deadly intent at the man beside him. He replied, "Yea...friendly."

"I knew you'd see it my way."

Randolf snickered at Ruben's comments. He added, "Yea, real friendly."

The trio made it to the Inn without any difficulty. Most of the thugs who hung out in the shady areas knew better than to mess with Ruben. They lived longer that way. His size, reputation, and sword made him a formidable opponent.

The Inn was located on the right side of the road. It was neat and well kept, one of the few on the street that was. Plants in pots were on either side of the entrance. The paint was fresh and new, the windows clean and shiny. A bench sat on the front porch and the door was propped open, inviting all to enter.

Ruben led the way up the single step and entered the open door. He pulled Drayco inside. Randolf shifted his burden and followed. They stopped in the front foyer until their eyes adjusted to the darker interior.

The inside was as neat and orderly as the outside, a stark contrast to the rest of the town. A man standing behind a counter looked up when he heard them enter. He had the appearance of a bank manager from the old west era with his prim and proper clothing. His short blonde hair was slicked back, not a hair out of place and he had a slender face. Any woman who walked in would have been instantly smitten by his charm and good looks.

"Ruben! It's good to see you again. I heard you were back, and had company, so I took the liberty of preparing the appointed room. You're things have already been delivered."

"Louis, like always, so punctual. I'll be going to the bar first with my friend here." He threw an arm on Drayco's shoulder, causing the dark man to flinch. "Would you be so kind as to show Randolf here where to put his burdensome load?"

"Of course. Will you require anything else?"

"If I know you, Louis, everything is in order."

A slight nod of the head and a look that passed between the two men did not go unnoticed. Drayco caught it. He wondered for a second time what Ruben was up to. Randolf was looking down the hall leading to the rooms. He was oblivious to the exchange.

"Follow me sir." Louis departed from behind the counter and indicated for Randolf to follow him down a hall to the right.

Randolf stopped and turned back to Ruben before going out of sight. "I'll meet you at the bar."

"See you there."

Ruben faced a doorway to the left. A dimly lit room was visible beyond the opening. "Drayco, my man, we have hit the jackpot." He indicated for him to lead the way in.

Drayco entered the room and stopped. He was surprised by what he saw. It had a shiny bar against the far wall made out of mahogany. A glowing stone fireplace in the center of the left wall provided some of the lighting, and a chandelier made out of spun glass hung from the ceiling by a shiny copper chain, candles burning in its many holders, provided the rest of the light. No windows were visible throughout the room.

Tables were located in the main area, their tops covered with white cloths. Booths wrapped around two walls, some of them covered in a silky material with heaver drapes underneath in case the occupants wanted privacy during their stay. Paintings from before the virus hung on the walls. Drayco was curious where they came from, and how they had survived the ravages of time.

"Takes your breath away, doesn't it."

Ruben indicated for Drayco to take one of the booths near the fireplace. He pushed him onto the bench and moved in beside him, pinning him against the wall. The drapes were left open, allowing them to get service. A woman in a tastefully cut outfit that fit her slim voluptuous body well came up to them.

"Ruben, how are you sweetie." She bent over and gave him a kiss on the cheek.

Ruben reached up and grabbed the slim waist, pulling her onto his lap. "I'm fine, Rachael, but I'll be even better if we can get together real soon."

"I'm working right now," she pouted. "We can meet up afterwards."

"I'll be busy tonight. How about tomorrow?"

"I'm off. We can play all day." She lowered Ruben's face to her chest. He nuzzled what was in front of him with delight.

Drayco looked away, disgusted, trying to avoid having to watch the spectacle going on beside him.

Ruben sat up and pushed Rachael off his lap. He held on to her hand, turning her toward him as she stood. "Take this to buy yourself something nice for our party." He reached up and shoved several pieces of gold between her breasts. A pat followed for each one.

Rachael smiled at his actions, and asked, "What do you want to drink?" She left the gold where it was.

"I will have a tall mug of refreshing ale, and my friend here will have the same."

Drayco turned his head away from the wall and toward the woman standing at the end of the table. He glared at her, causing the wound on his cheek to turn a deep crimson. Her smile faded as she looked at the scar then his eyes. Ruben frowned at her reaction. He glanced over his shoulder at the man sitting next to him. An elbow firmly planted in Drayco's ribs caused the dark man to wince with pain and avert his eyes.

"Be nice to the lady or you won't be able to play later." Ruben's back was turned toward Rachael so she could not see his face. It became cold and threatening, giving Drayco a firm understanding as to what would follow if he did not listen. Drayco continued to glare in defiance. Ruben turned back toward the woman and smiled. "Please excuse him, Rachael. It's been a long hard ride for him."

Her smile returned. She put her hand under Ruben's chin and slid it away as she started toward the bar to get their drinks. "I'll be right back with your order, lover."

After she was gone, Ruben slowly turned his head toward Drayco. "That was foolish and unnecessary. You better learn to behave." He spoke softly but his words carried meaning. "I can make things very, very unpleasant for you if you don't." He emphasized his point by grabbing Drayco's side near the long wound and pulling the skin taut.

The dark twin tried to pull away, but the wall ended his progress. A groaned escaped. Ruben heard footsteps approaching their booth. He let go of both the shirt and the skin beneath it. His body prevented anyone coming their way from seeing what he did. He straightened and flashed one of his most charming smiles as Rachael returned with their drinks. He took one of the mugs and drank a good part of its content before thumping it down with a smack of the lips.

"Rachael, you are a god send."

"I bet you say that to all the women.

"All the time...but only to you."

"Yea, right. I'll see you tomorrow, wise guy." She smirked and turned away to help other patrons.

Ruben stood and went to the side of the booth that was unoccupied. He pulled the heavy drapes shut then returned to his own seat, leaving his side open.

"Why did you do that?"

"You'll see soon enough. I said I have business tonight and I'm expecting him to show up any time now. He'll want privacy."

"Who is coming?"

"My employer."

Ruben lifted the mug to his lips again. He downed the remaining contents in one swallow and looked at the mug sitting in front of Drayco.

"You going to drink that? No? Then I guess I'll have to do it for you." He reached over and grabbed the handle, bringing the mug to his lips. This time he only sipped at the contents.

Fifteen minutes later the booth was still unoccupied on one side. Drayco leaned against the wall. "I thought your employer was going to show up."

"He will, when he is good and ready. Rachael! Bring me one more." He held up the almost empty mug for her to see. She acknowledged his request and went toward the bar. She returned immediately with the ale. Ruben stuffed more gold between her breasts and gave each a pat, followed by an appreciative kiss on the cheek from the woman. Drayco could tell Rachael was used to this game and knew how to keep the gold coming.

Ruben watched her hips sway as she left. "Nice. Can't wait to get a piece of that."

Drayco wished he had his sword so he could slash the lewd look off Ruben's face. He was sick of this man and the way he treated people, as if they were toys. When he got the chance, he was going to show him what it meant to be toyed with.

The room was almost empty now. Most of the other patrons had finished and went on about their business or had gone home. Ruben leaned back, calmly sipping on his ale.

More than an hour had passed since the drapes were lowered. Drayco was surprised that the big man stayed so composed, especially after having to wait so long. He was almost asleep, his head leaned against the wall, when the curtain rustled and a black robed figure slid quietly into the booth.

"Nice to see you again," Ruben stated before taking another sip.

Drayco noticed the hint of fear in the big man's tone. This caused him to sit up and look more closely at the figure sitting quietly across the table. Nothing could be seen of the person under the robes. Even the hands were hidden. Drayco felt the hairs on the back of his neck rise.

This must be the Boss I heard so much about, the one that wants Shyanne so badly.

"Always a pleasure to see you too, Ruben," the figure whispered.

Drayco had to strain to hear the voice; it was so soft. Ruben reached up, pulled the rope holding the drapes on his side of the booth, and overlapped the two, enclosing their seating area completely. When the drapes were shut, the bar's staff knew not to interrupt the occupants inside unless called for.

"I see you have brought a friend with you."

"Drayco, meet the Boss. This is the employer who hired me to find that girl you ride with."

Drayco looked at the person sitting across from him. The thick black cloak hid the body, but he could tell the Boss was not a large person. There seemed to be nothing extraordinary about him.

How could this little bit of a person cause a big powerful man like Ruben to show fear? I'll have to be careful with this one. He continued to watch the cloaked one and say nothing.

"I've brought both the cat and him here. With these two as hostages, it will bring the girl for sure, ensuring she will be captured as agreed upon." Ruben kept his voice low to make sure no one overheard what was discussed.

"Well done. I will wait for you in the room. We will carry on this discussion in privacy." The mysterious Boss rose and left the table in the same quiet manner he had entered.

"Awe inspiring, isn't it? It can be a bit overwhelming for a first timer like you. Happened to me the first time I saw him."

Drayco realized he had been holding his breath and slowly exhaled through pursed lips. Ruben chuckled. He slapped Drayco on the back, again causing pain to run through his body.

"Let's go."

Ruben flipped back the drapes, got up, and grabbed Drayco by his shirt collar, dragging him to his feet. He let go once the dark man was upright, indicating for him to return to the front lobby. When they entered the main room, Ruben told him to go toward the hallway beside the counter where Louis stood; the same one Randolf went down earlier. The man looked up as the two entered, then returned his gaze to the paperwork in front of him. All niceties disappeared once Drayco was in the hall, out of sight of the open front door.

The big man reached up and grabbed a handful of Drayco's hair, pulling him to a stop. He forced the dark man's head back and whispered, "You better be on your best behavior from now on. I may not be able to kill you but the Boss won't hesitate."

He kept a firm grip on Drayco's hair as he dragged him down the hall to a door with the number 130 on it. Ruben opened it and tossed Drayco inside before entering himself. Unable to stop himself, his arm strapped to his side, Drayco fell hard. Ruben grinned at the man lying on the floor. He turned and bolted the door behind him.

Drayco managed to get to his feet and looked around the room. A small table with a chair was in a corner and a bed was close to the opposite wall. That was all the furnishings in it. The room had a coolness to it due to the lack of any heating apparatus. And, like in the bar area, there were no windows. A rug covered part of the floor to muffle sounds and to ward off some of the chill. A small candle on the table and another on the wall mount near the door were the only lights in the room. The rest was covered in shadows.

Drayco inhaled sharply when he saw Drizzle on the bed, still tied up. A man was lying gagged and hogtied next to it on the floor. It was Randolf. He wondered what had happened when the mercenary had not showed up. Now he understood. A bruise covered the side of his head. It looked like he had been knocked out. He was awake now, staring at Ruben, eyes filled with questions.

Ruben came up behind Drayco, grabbed a handful of hair, and propelled him to the wall beside the table. The world spun and his back met solid material as he was slammed against it, knocking the wind from his body. Rope hung embedded in the wall. The dark man felt it wrap around his left wrist. The big man cut the strap holding the right arm and tied it against the wall, as well.

Drayco's feet were secured in the same manner, pinning him effectively. When Ruben straightened, he backhanded the prisoner several times across the face.

"That will do," a voice whispered from the dark shadows near the bed. The Boss emerged and glided across the floor to the captive tied to the wall; his robes made almost no sound when he moved. "You can have your fun when he is of no more use to me."

A small, gloved hand reached out from the robe and came to rest on Ruben's shoulder. He jumped at the touch, as if he had been hit with lightening. He recovered quickly and turned toward the Boss.

"I have something of interest to show you."

He turned back to Drayco and firmly grasped the front of his shirt. With one powerful yank, he tore it open, revealing the skin underneath. A long freshly healed scar ran from around the right side of the neck to the left nipple.

"Yesterday afternoon, I put this wound here. Today, it's healed like it has been there for weeks. I first noticed it when we were sitting at the table. I have an idea, but I need your permission to prove my theory."

The Boss observed the scar on Drayco's chest. With a slight nod of the hood, he gave Ruben the permission he needed. "As long as it doesn't kill him."

Ruben pulled out the same slim knife he used on Drayco yesterday and advanced on the restrained man. Drayco kept an eye on the blade. He had no idea what Ruben planned but knew he was not going to like it. Ruben reached up and put the knife tip into the exposed skin close to the left clavicle bone. He pulled it smoothly across the new scar to just below the breastbone. Another slice followed two inches from the first. Blood ran down Drayco's chest, pooling at his feet.

The dark twin held back with the first cut. He was unable with the second. A blood-curdling scream echoed across the room. The last thing he heard before passing out was Ruben laughing as he admired his handy work.

In the front lobby, Louis heard a faint scream echo down the long hallway. He'd heard that sound before and ignored it as he had previously. He was paid handsomely to hear nothing. He followed those directions very well. He glanced at the paper in his hand then turned it over onto an orderly stack in front of him. He picked up another and sighed. He hated doing paperwork but someone had to do it.

*   *   *

The sun was just clearing the treetops when Shyanne and Joseph woke, their arms wrapped around each other, her head resting on his warm chest. The blanket only half covered them. It was kicked off during the night by their activities. She wasn't concerned, though; she was warm against Joseph's body. Shyanne looked up at the man holding her and smiled. He was awake, watching her. He had the look of a man who had been awake for many hours.

"Good morning, my love. Did you sleep well?"

She stretched before returning her head to his chest. "When I finally did...yes."

He kissed the top of her hair and hugged her. It had been a love-filled night for the both of them. Because of it, he felt truly alive for the first time since the death of his family and friends, instead of merely existing.

Joseph thought about his mother while Shyanne slept. If she had lived, she would have liked this half-pint spunky whip of a girl. Shyanne sat up and stretched again. He watched as her long strawberry blonde hair fell down her back like a waterfall. He reached up and ran his fingers through it, enjoying the silky feel.

"Hey, silly! That's for my brush to do." She smiled as she swatted his hand away. "It does a better job too."

He grabbed her around the waist and pulled her down beside him. His lips met hers and they kissed long and passionately. When they broke apart, Shyanne sat up again.

"Joseph, my love, we need to get going. I want to stay and make sweet love to you again and again, but I don't want Drayco to get too far ahead of us. Who knows what kind of shape he's in."

He sat up, encircling his arms around her, "You right, my dear. We need to find your brother first. I shouldn't be so selfish."

"I don't know how to explain it...but deep inside here,"

she tapped her chest with her fingers, "I know he's okay. I've been able to sense him for some time, even before we found each other. It took me so long to find him, and I don't want to lose him aga..."

Joseph turned her face toward him and put a finger over her lips. "Shhh. We won't lose him." He kissed her then stood up. Reaching his hand out, he offered it to her, "Let's get going before something does happen, something that won't involve searching for Drayco."

Shyanne smiled as she grabbed the offered hand, rising to her feet. The two dressed quickly. They moved to the horses afterward. Joseph decided to ride Bravaro instead of the horse from the mercenaries.

"It would only slow us up. Bravaro and Jack can move faster.

Joseph removed the bridle and gave the backside of the freed horse a swat. It jerked away from him and darted around the ruins, running across the open area toward a small clump of bushes.

"I wonder if that horse will lead us to where the mercenaries have gone," Shyanne asked as they watched it disappear.

"Damn. I didn't think of that. Let's move!"

Shyanne and Joseph flung themselves into their saddles and hurried after the smaller horse. Joseph was in the lead. He pulled Bravaro to a sudden stop when they were close to the bushes. Shyanne yanked Jack's reins to the side before he rammed into the lead animal.

"Joseph! What are you trying to do, get killed?"

Near the bushes, the grass was sparse and the ground soft. A gap between them showed prints in the middle of a pathway leading deeper into the woods. The path widened beyond the bushes to hold two horses side by side.

He got off and walked to the gap. "Shyanne, I don't think this is the way Bravaro came. There is only one set of tracks here. If Drayco's horse came this way, the prints would still be visible."

"What do you want to do?

"Stay where you are. I want to walk the perimeter."

He moved around the field but did not find any other horse tracks leading away from it. Some parts of the perimeter were thick with undergrowth, making it difficult to see anything. He returned to where he started and walked up to Shyanne.

"Nothing. No other prints. I guess we have no other option. We follow these tracks and hope they lead us in the right direction. I remember the other mercenaries leaving, but it was too dark to see which way they went. And I was focused on capturing that Garth fellow. Damn it all to hell!" He slammed a fist into the other hand.

"It's okay, Joseph. Everything will be all right. We'll find them. You'll see."

Joseph returned to Bravaro. He paused before getting into the saddle. "Shyanne, I will not fail you. I will find your family before anything happens to them." He got up, jerked on the reins, and turned Bravaro onto the trail. With a nudge, the horse started into the thick woods.

They rode for half a day, their forward progress slow for fear of losing the tracks they followed. Just before the trail took a sharp turn to the right, they found what they were looking for. Another path joined the one they were on. It bore a print matching Bravaro's hoof. Joseph smiled back to Shyanne. He gave her a thumb up then pointed to the ground. She smiled when she saw the vee mark in the dirt.

Several miles later, Joseph started to go around a bend in the path but pulled Bravaro to a sudden halt before going completely around. Shyanne had to pull hard on Jack once more to prevent a collision.

"What's the..." she started to ask. Joseph waved his arm for silence. She stopped and listened.

Joseph was already getting off his horse, his hand reaching for the sword on his back. Shyanne wondered what was ahead to make him so concerned. His face had a harsh look and his stance was stiff and guarded. Everything she saw indicated he was ready for a fight. She wanted to ask what was going on, but did not want to distract him. He was concentrating hard on what lay ahead.

Shyanne started to get off Jack. Another wave halted her in mid swing. Suddenly, a snuffling noise sounded. Joseph's gaze locked on hers for a split second before returning to whatever was on the path ahead. She saw fear shining in those eyes, but determination as well. The undergrowth made it impossible to see what was making the noise. As if on request, a light breeze shifted the bushes. A huge shape became visible. The greenery blocked the way again when the breeze ceased.

Shyanne started to get off her horse again. This time it was not Joseph who halted her in mid-swing. It was a high-pitched squeal. It came from whatever creature was around the bend. The sound caused all the hairs on her neck to stand straight up. She looked at Joseph. He was crouched low, ready. His entire attention focused on what was ahead. She got off Jack and moved to his side, slowly taking her sword out as she went. She crouched beside him and looked down the trail. What she saw took her breath away.

It was huge, monstrous in fact; and there was more than one. The creatures filled the path that was wide enough for a wagon to use. At that moment, they were standing upright on their back legs. Their heads, append-ages, and backs were bald, with only tufts of hair sticking out sporadically. The underbelly was the only place where it was thick. They were about ten feet tall.

The creatures faces were like something out of a long ago science fiction movie.

Eight eyes peered from different areas of the head, al-lowing it to view many angles simultaneously. No nose was discernible where one should have been and the mouth was a large gaping hole with fangs jutting upward. The hunched shoulders had four powerful arms protruding from the upper torso. The legs were short and stocky. They looked strong enough to kill with a single kick. The hair covered any distinguishing features, which would have al-lowed anyone to recognize a male from a female.

The two lumbering creatures were fighting over what appeared to be the remains of a woman. The bigger of the two had the body in its mouth. It swiped at the smaller creature with a heavily clawed appendage. The body was filthy. A nearby pit showed where it had been put to rest, but these creatures found her and dug her up. At seeing what was happening, Shyanne felt sick to her stomach.

"What are those things?" she asked softly.

"Scavengers," Joseph whispered without taking his eyes off them. "They live off the dead and won't attack us unless we try to take their meal away." He paused. "And they're very aggressive when provoked. I don't want to take any chances. We'll have to work our way around them somehow.

"We can't just let them eat that poor girl."

"That poor girl doesn't feel a thing; she's already gone."

Disgusted, she whispered, "Well if you're not going to do anything about it...I will." Her tone was harsh. Shyanne raced down the path toward the creatures before Joseph could reach out and stop her.

"Shyanne! Stop! You don't know what you're dealing with!" Shocked by her odd behavior, he ran after her, hoping to catch her before she reached them. Unfortunately, she had a large head start on him. "Shyanne!"

Shyanne refused to listen. The thought of those beasts ripping that woman apart and eating her was too much to bear. Even if she was dead, Shyanne was not going to let her body be desecrated in such a fashion.

As she reached them, she brought her sword up and swung it with all her might at the nearest beast. The smaller scavenger was trying to get at the body. It missed seeing the threat until it was too late.

Shyanne's sword cut deep into the outstretched arm. The creature screamed and drew its appendage back, almost wrestling the sword out of her hands. She managed to keep a hold of it and freed the blade as she went past. It turned swiftly, reaching with razor sharp claws. It would have gotten Shyanne if Joseph had not reached it first.

He buried his sword almost to the hilt in the exposed area between the shoulder blades. He immediately pulled it out and swung at the neck. The blade sliced deep into the skin, causing the creature to scream again. It grasp at its neck with one paw while reaching for the being causing it so much pain with another. Shyanne buried her sword into a thigh before it could snag him. Blood ran everywhere.

The ground became saturated and muddy, causing the lumbering creature to lose its footing and crash onto its back. Joseph took advantage of the opportunity and plunged his sword deep into the exposed chest. An ear-piercing wail emitted from the mouth, similar to a fingernail raked across a chalkboard. It caused the human combatants' to wince. The sound gradually stopped as the creature died.

Joseph was leaning on his sword next to the smaller creature's body, panting from the effort of killing it, when the bigger creature made its move.

"Joseph! Watch out!"

The larger beast threw the female's body aside and lunged at the two people standing near the dead one. Both dove out of the furious creature's path and into the shelter of the surrounding trees, winding up on opposite sides of the path. The creature stopped at the other's side. It looked around with its many eyes before it bent over and smelled the matted bloody mess lying on the ground. Shyanne and Joseph observed the situation without moving.

With a high-pitched squeal that ran up the spines of the both watching, it picked up the dead creature, threw it over a shoulder, and ran down the path until it disappeared from view. The sound of the creature fleeing through the trees was heard long after the pair lost sight of it.

"What do you make of that?" Shyanne asked. When nothing was said, she looked at Joseph. He was standing next to the road, anger written all over his body.

"Do you know what that was?" he shouted at her. "That was a Zindrell! They are very, very dangerous when messed with."

"We beat it, though. And we did it easily."

"We were damn lucky. The one we killed must have been its mate. That's the only reason I can think of as to why it didn't shred us apart instead of running away. I've seen just one tear a group of ten well armed men apart with ease." Joseph shook his head at Shyanne's folly. "And we were facing two."

"I'm sorry, Joseph." She shuddered at the picture that came to her mind. "But I wasn't going to let them rend that poor woman's body apart."

Joseph sheathed his sword as he walked up to Shyanne. He grabbed her shoulders and shook her gently to emphasize his words. "I didn't want to see them rend the bodies of the living apart."

She looked into his blue eyes and saw the fear mixed with concern in them. She looked down at the ground.

"I'm sorry."

"Don't be sorry. Just don't do that again. I don't know if we'll be as lucky the next time." He hugged her close before releasing her. "Now, let's see to the body. We'll have to go deeper into the underbrush to give her a safer burial place."

Joseph moved toward the body lying in a heap where the scavenger had thrown it. He rolled it over and discovered it was a young woman maybe in her early twenties. It was hard to be sure because of the shape of the body. The extremities were intact, as was the head; but the abdomen area was gone. Dull blonde hair, caked with dirt, stuck out in several directions. Shyanne walked up behind him after sheathing her weapon. She gasped when she glanced over his shoulder. Joseph looked up at her shocked expression, thinking it was due to the condition of the body. She pointed at a large ragged hole in the woman's neck.

"What do you think?"

Joseph didn't think, he knew. He had seen a wound just like that before, back at the ruins with the spiderbats, where the horses were kept, when Drayco fed.

"Drayco."

Shyanne bent over for a closer look at the neck wound. "He must have stumbled upon this woman and attacked her to replenish his lost blood. We are definitely on the right path."

She stood up and looked around. A glint of light reflected off something several paces down the path. She walked over to it. A sword, partway in its scabbard, lay just off the road in a section of tall weeds.

"Joseph! It's Drayco's sword!" She picked up the weapon and held it high for him to see.

He rushed over and looked at the ancient weapon. "Are you sure? It may have been the woman's."

"I'm sure. Our grandfather gave it to him a long time ago. We used to spar together. He always used this sword."

"Then we are definitely on the right path. I wonder what happened to cause him to leave his weapon behind."

"I have no idea. I don't think it was something good. He never let anyone touch it, much less left it lying about, discarded like this. It meant too much to him."

"Do you think the mercenaries have him?"

"I don't know. What I do know is that we're not going to find out by standing here. Several horse prints go off in that direction." She pointed down the path. "One of them must have Drayco on its back."

Shyanne ran back to Jack and threw herself into the saddle. Joseph was hot on her heels and in his own saddle a split second behind her. Both spurred their horses into a run as soon as their feet hit the stirrups.

The body of the woman they had fought so hard to save from the scavengers lay where it was, forgotten.

Fifteen

The prisoner hung from the wall, a bloody mess. The black hair hanging from his head had gray streaks where none had previously been. His face had aged quite a few years and wrinkles were still forming as the two standing in front of him watched. Two fresh diagonal cuts ran across the scar on the dark man's chest, a scar placed there by a monster named Ruben. His pants and boots were covered with red because of the streams flowing from those wounds.

Drayco was awake, but no longer had the strength to stand. The events of the past few days had sapped all the reserve energy his body possessed. He'd never felt this bad before. Not after he was inflicted with the curse given by the virus, nor when he fell off the horse from lack of drinking blood. Every inch of his body hurt more than he could ever imagine.

Two people stood close by. One was tall, dark tanned and muscular. The other was a mystery. A black hooded cloak covered every part of the person underneath. Nothing was exposed. Gloves covered the hands when they appeared out of the flowing sleeves.

"I hope there is a point to this, Ruben."

"There is, just watch."

Ruben walked over to the man tied up next to the bed. Drizzle watched, unable to help his companion's brother. His tail whipped about wildly, showing his displeasure at what was going on before him.

"Don't worry, kitty, I won't kill him. He has to be here to bait the trap." Ruben scratched Drizzle on the head.

He bent over and grabbed Randolf by the arms, lifting him to his knees. He dragged the bound man over close to Drayco and dropped him. The gag prevented Randolf from crying out when he hit the floor.

Ruben pulled out the thin knife from his boot. He cut the bonds holding Drayco against the wall and watched as the dark man landed face-first on the floor.

The Boss observed Ruben's actions quietly. He was waiting for whatever it was the big man was so anxious for him to see. However, he was quickly losing patience with the entire process.

The big man looked at the Boss. "I want you to see what I discovered. I think it will interest you greatly."

He grabbed a handful of Randolf's hair and pulled up-ward. Randolf's eyes enlarged to their farthest extent when he saw the thin blade advancing toward his exposed throat. He started to struggle, but the strong grasp and a well-placed knee prevented much. Ruben slid the knife into the soft skin under the jaw line, but only enough to get the man's blood trickling down his neck. The slice was inten-tionally non-lethal. He put the blade away then grabbed Drayco. Some of the precious fluid was smeared into the weakened man's mouth and his lips were placed on the bleeding slice.

As soon as the blood hit Drayco's tongue, instinct took over. He reached up and held Randolf's head like a vice grip. The cut was not deep enough to cause a large enough flow, so Drayco sank his teeth into the surrounding skin and bit deep. A large chunk of flesh hit the floor. He was not interested in it; he was more interested in what flowed underneath.

Randolf stopped struggling as the pain from the torn flesh hit his brain. He knew what happened next. He had witnessed it when Brey was the target. If he had been able to pray for mercy, he would have. It was too late.

The blood flowed freely now. A growling noise began as Drayco returned his mouth to the open wound. He latched onto the neck and began to suck; pulling everything he could from the wound. His animal instinct for survival was in full motion. The two men standing nearby were forgotten. All that was important was the blood, and ridding himself of the pain.

Ruben and the Boss watched. No reaction could be seen beneath the shrouded cloak of the mysterious one, but the reaction on Ruben's face was clear. He was revolted. He wanted nothing more than to end this abomination's life. The Boss wanted Drayco kept alive, unfortunately, so he could get his intended target—Shyanne.

"I see nothing interesting about one man killing another," the Boss whispered.

"Keep watching," Ruben insisted.

Drayco rolled on top of Randolf to hold him better and to prevent any struggling. His face was turned away so the onlookers could not see it. As the men watched, the gray in Drayco's hair faded, replaced by a color as dark as the midnight sky. The skin on the visible hand became taunt and young again. Randolf's eyes glazed over as death took him. Drayco stayed where he was until he was sure no more blood would could, then he let go and rolled onto his back.

His face looked as young as it had when Ruben first met him. A small streak of gray remained above his left eye, leaving him with a slightly wiser and older look. Drayco closed his eyes and went into a peaceful sleep, allowing his body to absorb the life giving fuel he had taken from Randolf.

"See what I mean? Interesting isn't it?" Ruben beamed as he looked at the Boss.

The shrouded figure remained quiet for a moment before responding softly, "Yes... yes it is...a prize indeed. See that you take great care of him. If what I think is true, I may not need the other we seek." The Boss moved toward the door, but stopped when he reached its entrance. He turned back and added, "I will send word as to whether you need to continue seeking the female or not. In the mean time, make sure these two don't escape or become excessively damaged." The cloaked arm waved toward the prisoners. "If either happens, you will not have to worry about anything else again. Have I made myself abundantly clear?"

Ruben jerked his head around and stared at the cloaked person hovering by the doorway. "Don't worry. I haven't let you down in all our years of association. I'm not about to start."

The hood nodded once then the Boss disappeared out the door as if he had never been there. No sounds were heard beyond. Ruben walked to the open door and looked outside. The hallway was empty.

"I hate when he does that," he muttered as he shut the door.

Drayco had not moved from where he fell asleep. Randolf's body, with its ravaged neck visible from across the room, lay next to him. Ruben shuddered as he looked at the bloodless wound.

Unconsciously, he reached up and rubbed the side of his neck. *That will never happen to me.*

He glanced over to the bed and saw the cat watching with intent eyes. "Don't get any ideas, cat. If I get the word that you're not needed, I will kill you where you lay." The big man reinforced his words by moving his hand from his neck to the sword handle sticking out of its sheath on his back.

Ruben looked back at the dark man lying on the floor. A shudder ran up his spine, causing him to clench his teeth. Returning to Randolf's body, he grabbed a handful of shirt, dragged it over to the doorway, and dropped it. The ravaged neck was now facing away from him, which suited him just fine. He made his way back to Drayco and bound his extremities, just in case the sleeping man woke.

The room reeked with the stench of blood. Being a mercenary, he was used to it. The chair next to the table scraped across the floor as he pulled it out and sat down. With both arms crossed on his chest, Ruben leaned back against the wall. The small table stood close by so he threw a leg on top of it. Within minutes, he fell into a light sleep.

While he slept, the door opened silently. Two cloaked figures emerged. Without bending over, they brought Randolf's body up between them. They left as silently, closing the door behind them. Only one being in the room witnessed anything. Drizzle lay on the bed, thinking. There was something about the way they moved that nagged at him. He could not remember it presently, but knew, in time, it would come to him.

*   *   *

Shyanne and Joseph made their way into town just before sunup. They rode all night with only short rests for the horses. They had not slept. After leaving the dead woman to follow Drayco's trail, they found the main road and the camp left by the mercenaries. A body, or what was left of one, was discovered near the edge of the woods. Joseph had made Shyanne stay back until he was sure it was not her brother. Closer inspection showed it wasn't. It had been one of the mercenaries.

"We need to find a stable. Who knows how long we'll have to stay here," Shyanne said.

"I hope we find the inn. I'm beat. Sleep is in order before we hunt for Drayco."

"We have to find him," Shyanne insisted. "I want him safe again."

"I know, but in our present state, we would be of no good if things went sour. We're both exhausted and need to rest."

Shyanne remained silent. Much she hated to admit it, his argument made sense. The events of the last few days were starting to blend together and the lack of sleep only made matters worse. Even now, she was having a hard time keeping her eyes open. As bad as she wanted to find her brother, her body was telling her it needed to stop.

The pair rode farther into town until the stables appeared. They brought the horses to a stop in front of the building and dismounted. An old man came out of the building to greet them.

"What do we have here, early birds out before the sun comes up, or late bloomers coming in before the sun rises? I wonder which one they are... hummm," the old man mumbled.

"We've been riding all night, sir, and were hoping you could direct us to a place to stay. We're very tired," Joseph said.

Shyanne stood a little off to the side, holding Jack's reins in her hand. She was using every ounce of her remaining strength to stay upright.

"Sure...sure...come right in." The old man turned

around and started back into the shadows, waving for them to follow. Horses nickered inside the building. "I'm the stable master here. I care for the horses as if they were my own children.

The travelers followed the man into the building. A faint light glowed in the corner away from the stalls, probably from his sleeping area. The old man led Joseph to stall number 14 and opened the gate.

"Just put your animal in here and don't worry about him. I'll take the saddle off and brush him down. You too, young missy," he said to Shyanne. He led her and Jack to stall number 9. She guided the big horse in and shut the gate behind him.

"I appreciate it more than you know, but I think I should take care of him myself."

"No trouble, missy. Like I said, I treat the beasties like I would my own, if I had any." He walked up to the stall holding Jack and leaned on the gate.

"Be careful, sir. He usually doesn't like strangers...especially the male version."

"My mother, god rest her soul, called me Abraham, but most people just call me Crusty. It's easier to remember."

Shyanne could understand why. He was dirty and stank to high heaven. She kept her comments to herself, though. "Be careful, Crusty. My horse has a problem with men coming too close."

"He wouldn't hurt little ole' Crusty."

Before Shyanne could stop him, he entered the stall. Jack had his ears pointed forward and watched the approaching man with interest. What happened next caused her mouth to hang open.

The old man walked right up to the towering animal and started petting his neck, cooing nonsense statements softly as he ran his hands up and down the curve of the neck. Jack nudged him in greeting then went back to eating the grain out of a bucket hanging on the wall. In her whole association with the horse, she had never seen him behave like that with any male.

"See. I told you he wouldn't hurt this poor little runt."

Crusty reached up and removed the saddle and pad. Both were tossed onto the top rail to air out. He removed the bridle and hung it on a peg poking out of one of the support poles. Then he picked up a brush and returned to the animal's side where he started working on the coat.

Shyanne wasn't able to say a thing, at first. She stared, totally amazed that her horse allowed Crusty to get this close, yet behave as if he wasn't there. When she finally said something, her voice betrayed her amazement.

"Well I'll be. Jack, I guess you've finally gone soft on me." She smiled.

Joseph came up behind her, resting his hands on her shoulders. "Maybe being around us two hooligans has softened him."

She elbowed him in the ribs, and smirked, "Being around you two bad influences would give anyone serious cause for alarm."

Crusty listened as the two bantered back and forth. He decided to butt in when his curiosity would not let him take anymore. "Who is this other person you are talking about? All I've seen come in today were the two of you."

"We're sorry," Shyanne said to the squat little man. "The third person being discussed is my brother. Maybe you've seen him recently. He's tall and has dark hair down to his shoulders, almost the color of night. His skin is tanned and he has a slim muscular build. He would have come in yesterday."

"He'd be in the company of another man named Ruben," Joseph added.

"Nope, haven't seen 'em. I know Ruben, though. He's a regular in this town. He left a few weeks back on some job he was hired out to do and hasn't come back yet."

The hope Shyanne felt building was dashed with the old man's words. Her shoulders sagged and her heart felt like it had been smashed with a hammer. Joseph turned her around to face him.

"Maybe we beat them here. Let's give it another day. If they don't show up, we'll backtrack and try to locate their trail."

"But if they don't come, we will have lost tha..." Her voice choked with emotion.

"Shhh. They'll come. I think he's trying to use Drayco to get to you. That will be his means of survival. As long as we keep you safe, your brother will be too.

"I hope so, Joseph. I hope so." Shyanne turned back to

the elderly man. "Can you direct us to the Inn? We're very tired and want to get something to eat. Does the Inn have a restaurant?"

"Yup. The restaurant is on one side of the building and the sleeping area is on the other. Just follow this here road outside to the next intersection then turn right." Crusty led the pair outside after they picked up their packs. He pointed to where they needed to go. "It's a short way down from there. You can't miss it, it's the only nicely place on the street."

Shyanne called back to the old man watching them as the walked away. "Thanks, Abraham. Until we meet again, take care of yourself. And don't let Jack get too soft on me, okay?" Crusty waved in response before he disappeared inside.

He stood where he was for a second or two, thinking, before hurrying past the outstretched necks of the horses and exiting through the back. He turned left and entered an alley running behind the buildings. It was filled with trash from the various businesses. It also had some of the living trash hanging out there as well.

"Hey Crusty! Where's the fire? Where ya go'n in such a hurry? Got a hot date wait'n?"

Crusty ignored the teasing comments tossed his way as he passed the 'trash' milling in the alley. This town has been his home for more than 30 years. He was well known and left alone by the local ruffians. He took good care of their horses, whether they were at the stables or at their homes, it didn't matter to Crusty. He loved horses and the people loved him in their own gruff kind of way.

He had to get to the inn fast and warn Ruben of these people trying to find him. He purposely gave the man and woman directions for the long way so he could beat them to their destination. He had helped the big man before, and was well compensated for it. He looked forward to being compensated again. The inn came into his blurry sights within moments of leaving the stables. Crusty let himself in through the back door.

A little used room where excess items for the inn and restaurant were stored greeted him. Crusty made his way through the crowded space to the opposite side. He stood by another door, listening. When nothing was heard, he opened it and ducked into the hallway.

It was early. The few patrons in the building were still asleep or had not left their rooms yet. The old man crept down the hall to the front lobby. Louis stood at his usual post, the stack of papers left from yesterday before him. He tried to sneak up on the man while he worked.

"What do you want this time, Crusty?"

"How' you know I was here?"

"I could smell you a mile away." Louis put the paper in his hand down and turned toward the old man. "I repeat, what do you want?"

"I came with information for Ruben."

"I'll give him the information for you."

"I have to tell him myself," Crusty insisted.

Louis crossed his arms and waited. Crusty tried to convince the manager to take him to Ruben, but he wouldn't budge. Time was running out so he decided to tell him what he knew.

"A man and a woman came into town this morning. They were hunting for Ruben and the fella he brought in. They looked like they could be trouble, with their swords and all, so I wanted to let Ruben know. They're on their way here now."

"Thank you for the information, Crusty. Ruben will be happy to hear it. Here's something for having to come all the way here to inform him."

Louis reached under his counter and pulled out a small bag. He tossed it to the old man who caught it with ease. He knew the old codger's vision was bad, but it always seemed to work fine when money was involved. Coins clinked in the pouch as the old man tossed it into the air and caught it again before stashing it in his clothes.

"Much obliged. Tell Ruben to watch out for himself. The guy looks like a handful."

Crusty went back down the long hall and cut through the storage room to the alleyway. He returned to the stables the same way he had come. A door stood across the hall from the storage place. On it was the number 130.

* * *

Drayco came awake from what had felt like an eternity

of sleep. He was lost for a moment when he did not recognize his surroundings. All of a sudden, he recalled where he was.

Ruben...the Boss...where are they now?

The last thing he remembered he was tied to the wall and Ruben was slicing into his chest with a knife. After that, the pain took over and everything disappeared. He tried to move his arms, but found they were tied behind him. His feet were also tied.

He lifted his head slowly and looked around the room. Ruben sat in a chair with his feet propped up on a small table, his chin resting on his chest. Drayco could hear faint snoring. Drizzle lay restrained on the bed across the room, watching, his eyes glowing in the faint candlelight. Drayco met those eyes for a brief moment then continued looking around the room. Upon seeing nothing else, he focused on his body.

He should have felt weaker than he did and wondered what had happened to cause its reduction. He vaguely remembered images of a neck in front of his face and drinking from it, but it was all a blur. The picture of Randolf tied up near the bed flashed into his mind.

Randolf, you poor pathetic fool, you should have known better than to trust someone like Ruben. Now you're probably dead. That's the only explanation I can think of as to why I feel better than I should.

He tried to shift his position without making too much noise but was unsuccessful. Ruben raised his head and looked at the man lying on the floor.

"Awake are we? Glad to see it."

The big man sat up just as a light rapping on the door started, drawing his attention away from the prisoner. Ruben slid his sword out of its scabbard and advanced toward the door. He was reaching for the handle when a voice sounded through the wood.

"Master Ruben, sorry to wake you but I must. I have some important news to deliver."

The voice belonged to Louis. Ruben relaxed. He opened the door for the man.

Louis saw the blade. He replied, "I don't think that will be necessary, do you?"

"I wasn't sure who was here...or if you were alone."

Ruben returned the sword to its sheath. "What do you have to tell me?"

"I think the privacy of your room would be better, don't you, Master Ruben?"

Ruben moved out of the way, allowing the smaller man to enter. After the door was closed, Louis faced the big man.

"I've just received word that there are two people in town enquiring about you and your associate here. He pointed to Drayco lying on the floor. Drayco remained still, his undivided attention focused on the thin clerk from the front desk.

"I was told it was a man and a woman. They are well armed and apparently able to handle themselves."

"Fabulous!" Ruben replied. Pleasure filled his tone. "The bait has been taken. It's now time to spring the trap. Get everything we discussed earlier together. I'll make sure everything here is ready."

"Understood, Master Ruben. It shall be done." Louis walked out of the room, closing the door behind him.

Ruben started to chuckle. He glanced over his shoulder toward Drayco. "Now the fun begins."

The big man walked over to the prisoner and grabbed an arm. He dragged him across the floor to the bed where he threw him down next to Drizzle. Drayco winched in pain. Before he could say anything, a wad of cloth was shoved inside his mouth and secured with some rope.

Ruben straightened. "Can't have you shouting out a warning to your friends, now can we. That would spoil all the fun."

The rope bit into the corners of his mouth. Drayco tried repositioning it, but the tightness of the rope would not allow it.

Ruben finally realized that Randolf's body had disappeared and wondered where it went, but not for long. He had things to do. "Sorry to go, but I have a trap to set in motion. We'll be back together real soon...and this time we'll have company." He winked at Drayco and gave Drizzle a pat on the head. The dark man felt his blood begin to boil.

Ruben moved to the door. He paused, "I always love company, especially the right kind." He winked again and shut the door behind him.

Drayco immediately went into action. He wiggled on the bed so that his back was close to Drizzle and indicated with hand signals for the cat to let his claws out. The cat understood what he needed to do. Five razor sharp instruments of death emerged from one of the tawny front extremities shaped like hands. Drayco carefully positioned his arms next to the claws and started rubbing the bonds back and forth.

A few strands severed but not enough to break free. Drayco did not get a chance to finish before he heard voices coming down the hall, toward this room. He recognized one of the voices. It was one he would never forget. It belonged to his sister.

*   *   *

The weary pair made their way through town, toward the direction the old man had indicated. They reached the intersection without incidence and turned right. Even though it was early, the sun barely above the treetops, patrons were about their business. A group of young men hung out just past the intersection, watching the newcomers with interest. They looked like troublemakers from the moment Shyanne laid eyes on them.

Each one was wearing black pants and a shirt with the sleeves missing. A sword hung at their side. All three were young, in their late teens or early twenties, but one was larger than the rest. He appeared to be the leader of the group.

Shyanne was holding Joseph's hand while they walked; she gave it a gentle squeeze when she spotted the trio. When he glanced at her, she tilted her head in their direction.

The men straightened and started toward them. One shouted, "Look at the lovers! Got any money lovers?" Another added, "Wow, look at the babe. Can I have some of her too?" The third quipped, "Why share, let's just enjoy her for ourselves." All three were pulling out their swords as they advanced.

Joseph and Shyanne stopped. They watched the men advance, their faces grim. The overzealous hotheads surrounded the couple and began moving in a circular motion, their swords held loosely before them. A few people stopped to watch, but none interfered. Smirks were on more than a few of the faces. They were used to seeing fights in this part of town and hoped today was going to start with a good one. They wanted something interesting to gossip about.

Shyanne turned her back toward Joseph. Her posture was calm and relaxed, as was his. Joseph glanced over his shoulder at her and smiled. They returned their attention to the antics of the three circling them.

"What do you think, Shyanne?"

"About these three?"

"Yes...these poor little boys who think they know how to play with knives. I don't know if they want to mess with us"

"Maybe they'll wise up and we won't have to find out."

"You think you can take us on?" shouted one whose dark facial hair grew in blotches. "You and your fanciness and all?"

"Then let's find out!" shouted another, his blonde hair tied back in a ponytail.

The biggest of the three bolted toward Shyanne. A sneer of triumph covered his face as the sword swung in a wide arch, intent more on scaring her than hurting her. She raised the pack she carried and threw it into the face of the charging man, effectively wiping the sneer off his face and knocking him off balance. His arms pinwheeled wildly, but he somehow managed to recover his balance before falling. His buddies froze in their tracks. These men were used to getting their way; they were not used to having opposition.

"You bitch!" He screamed while rubbing his nose. "How dare you do that to me! I own this part of town! You pass through only after paying me with money, or favors, your choice!"

Shyanne remained where she was, smiling. This infuriated the young man further.

"I'll teach you what it means to come into my part of town and mock me!" This time he charged full force at Shyanne. He wasn't holding anything back. This wench had embarrassed him in front of his gang, in fact the whole town, and he was going to make her pay the hard way.

Again, he swung his sword. This time he did so in an upward motion. He intended on gutting the woman all the way up to her chin. Joseph spun around to help Shyanne, but she did not need it. She stepped to one side, her sword out of its sheath in one fluid motion. The move was so sudden and so unexpected that the young man did not have time to react. He barreled past her. The exposed blade sliced into his side. She had purposefully held the weapon low to avoid hitting any vital organs.

His forward momentum carried him past her. He landed on the ground, a look of shock planted on his face. Shyanne gripped her blade with both hands. She held it ready in case the wounded man decided he hadn't had enough, or one of his fellow hagglers tried something.

Joseph moved to her side, casually holding his pack over his shoulder. "I told you to reconsider messing with us. Now look at what happened."

"What's this 'us' thing you're talking about. What 'us'? I did all the work. All you did was stand there," Shyanne retorted. She put her sword away and faced him, her hands resting in her hips in indignation.

The other two watched the strangers banter back and forth, mouths hanging open. Their leader lay on the ground, hugging his side, groaning with pain. A small puddle of blood spread beneath him, but it wasn't enough to cause great concern. They moved quickly to his side and helped him to his feet. The wounded man groaned even louder. He leaned heavily on their shoulders as they walked away from the still arguing couple. Every few steps one glanced back to make sure their exit went unnoticed.

"I was going to help you, but you ended all the fun before I could even draw my sword," Joseph snapped.

"That's because you were too..."

Shyanne stopped and looked around. The three hooligans were gone. The rest of the crowd was watching them with keen interest. The first fight had been a complete washout. Maybe this one would pan out better.

She broke into gut-splitting laughter. Joseph looked around then joined her. After wiping the tears from their eyes and putting away their swords, they started down the road toward the inn, an arm around each other as they walked.

"Did you see their faces? They were priceless," Shyanne managed to get out between giggles.

"Honey, that's why I love you, you always see the humor in everything. It keeps life fresh. I know we haven't known each other long, but it feels like many years of wonderful bliss."

"You sweet talking devil you." She reached up and kissed him before turning her attention back to the task at hand. "I wonder where that inn is. I'm starved and tired and I want to catch up on some sleep before Drayco gets here.

As if appearing magically, just by discussing it, the inn stood in front of them. The old man had been correct in his description. It was the only business on the street that looked like someone cared. Joseph and Shyanne made their way up the step and into the main lobby. The check in counter across the room was vacant. A door to the left had wonderful smells wafting from it. They moved closer to check out what lay beyond.

"This must be the restaurant Crusty talked about. I hope the food is as good as it smells," Joseph said with a note of hopefulness in his voice.

"Just like a man, always thinking with his stomach."

They looked in the doorway. Tables were throughout the room, and booths lined on the outer edges. The pair made their way to one of the booths. After they plopped onto the benches, weary from the long travel and morning event, an older woman with gray speckled hair walked up to the table. She informed them of what was available from the kitchen. The days of hand held menus, with a large selection to choose from, were long gone, thanks to the virus.

When they placed their orders and the woman was gone, Joseph leaned against the back wall. He stretched his legs out under the table and extended his arms to either side, resting them on the ledge behind him. A huge yawn followed the stretch.

"Boy am I beat. I hope the food gets here soon. I don't know how much longer I can stay awake."

"I know what you mean. I'm so tired I'm almost

tempted to get the room now instead of eating." Shyanne leaned back, assuming the same relaxed position as Joseph.

"No way, woman. My stomach would never forgive me if I did that to it. It's been begging for some real food for a while now." He paused, an aggrieved look flashed across his face. He leaned forward; resting his elbows on the table and gazed at the back wall, but did not really see it.

Shyanne leaned forward and cupped his hands with hers. "I wish I could have met her. She must have been some kind of woman, your mom."

"You're a lot like her...stubborn, pigheaded, thoughtful, kind. I guess that's why I'm drawn to you like I am. Yet, you're also your own unique person, and I love that part as well. He raised his eyes to hers. "Shyanne, my love, when this is over, I want to be with you forever, to have you as my wife." He bent over and planted a long and enduring kiss on her lips, which she returned passionately. They broke apart, blushing, when the older woman returned with their food and beverages.

Silence, except for the occasional groan of pleasure due to the wonderful flavors of the food, filled the booth during the meal. Other people came in for a morning meal. None paid any attention to the two sitting off to the side.

When the food was devoured and the hot cider all but gone, they both leaned back. Joseph rubbed his stomach. "Boy that was a great meal. I am definitely ready for that bed now." His eyes were heavy with sleep. He yawned again.

"I can't remember the last time I had something so fabulous," Shyanne murmured. A yawn followed her statement as well.

The old woman returned to pick up the dirty dishes and the payment. Joseph handed her an extra gold coin as a tip for her services.

"Thank you, fine sir. Come again, come again," she said as the coin disappeared into a pocket. She smiled and left to attend to the other patrons in the room.

Joseph stood. He helped Shyanne to her feet then moved to the door leading into the main lobby. The packs they carried felt like stones filled them instead of clothing and trail items. Both had the same thought; the sooner we put these heavy things down the better. The fatigue, which engulfed their bodies and minds, caused them to move slowly.

As they entered the lobby, a thin, proper looking man stood behind the counter. His clothes were fancy, reminding Shyanne of an old-time bank teller from western movies seen as a child. His just beyond shoulder length brown hair was slicked back into a neat ponytail.

The man glanced up from his stack of papers when they approached. "Can I be of service?"

"We need a room," Joseph replied. "We may need it for more than a day. Will that be a problem?"

"No sir, no problem at all. Have you traveled far?"

"Not far, only from the next town over."

The two had agreed earlier to give false information if questioned. They wanted to play it safe.

"That would be Radnor. It's a nice place to visit, but I wouldn't care to live there. Rough people, you know. My name is Louis. I'll be the one showing you to your room, or will it be rooms?"

"Just one room. We're married." Joseph hugged Shyanne close during the conversation. She smiled at Louis and nodded her head in agreement.

Louis smiled back. He opened the registry book located next to the stack of papers. Shyanne leaned over and looked with him. She wanted to see if the names of her brother or Ruben were listed. They weren't. To her, that could be either a good thing or a bad thing. She hoped it was the foremost. If they had chosen the wrong path and the mercenaries went another way, who knows what shape Drayco would be in, or how long it would take to find him.

"Excuse me but has a man named Ruben been here recently?" Shyanne asked.

Louis looked up from the book. "I haven't seen Ruben in a few weeks. Why do you ask?"

"We're friends of his. We haven't seen him in a while either and knew he stayed here sometimes. Just wanted to give our greetings."

"Ah, well, when I see him again, who should I say was asking?"

Louis wasn't sure if these were the ones Crusty warned

him about until the woman asked the question she had. He kept his face bland, but his mind was racing. He was aware of Ruben's mission and knew what he had to do.

"Kitchens. Mr. and Mrs. Kitchens," Joseph answered.

"Very good. When Mr. Ruben returns, I will pass the message along."

Louis looked at the ledger again and made it appear to those watching as if he was looking for a room. In actuality, it had already been chosen. He ran his finger down the page and stopped at a number. "Ah, here's a good one. Room 130. That room is available and quiet. I assume you'll want to rest without being disturbed?" He tilted his head up and lifted an eyebrow in inquiry.

"Definitely," Joseph sighed.

Shyanne looked at him wearily. "Yes please, we definitely need to rest."

"I'll just get the key then." Louis reached under the counter. He pushed a button located near the side wall before grabbing the room key. With a wave of his hand, he indicated for the tired couple to accompany him. They shifted the weight of their packs and followed.

They passed other rooms as they made their way down the seemingly endless hallway. No sounds came from any of them.

"What about these other rooms? Is anyone else staying in them?" Joseph asked.

"I'm afraid not, sir. They are shut down for renovation. We're putting down new floor coverings to keep the cold out during wintertime. Only a couple of rooms near the entrance are in use. You came at an awkward but convenient time. We're not that busy yet."

"At least you have something available for us. We appreciate that," Shyanne said.

When they reached their destination, room 130, it seemed odd to Joseph that there was not a window or another patron room nearby. The only rooms located around this one appeared to be a storage room and a cleaning room. He had a bad feeling but was too tired to think about it.

"Here we are." Louis halted in front of the door. He started to reach toward the lock with the key and stopped. He turned toward the waiting couple, "I hope these accommodations will be adequate. This is the best room in commodations will be adequate. This is the best room in the inn for what you are wanting.

"I'm sure it will be fine," Shyanne responded. She felt like she was already asleep, only in an upright position.

"Good. Then let me show you in."

The key went into the lock. With a twist of the wrist, it unlatched. Louis stood back as he pushed the door open wide enough for them to enter.

Shyanne entered first, followed closely by Joseph. The area inside was dark except for the light shining in from the hall. She stopped a couple of feet inside until her eyes adjusted to the darkness. When they did, she drew in a sharp intake of breath. On the bed, in the partial shadows, lay her brother and her companion, Drizzle.

Sixteen

A gasp escaped from Shyanne when she realized who was lying on the bed. Joseph could not see who was there yet.

"Shyanne, what is it?"

"It's Drayco...and Drizzle!"

"What! They're here? I thought they hadn't arrived yet."

Before either could recover from the shock, the door across the hall opened. Ruben leaped out and hit Joseph hard on the back of his head. The blow caused him to crumple to the floor, stunned. Ruben grabbed Shyanne before she could react. A hand swung up and backhanded her across the face. She spun around, slammed into the wall, and fell to the floor, unconscious.

The big man bent over and picked her up, tossing her over his shoulder with ease. On his way out, he kicked Joseph in his abdomen, knocking the wind out of him. He wanted to make sure the downed man could not follow too quickly. Joseph lay there, curled in a ball, moaning, trying to get his breath back, when Ruben shut the door. The departing laughter echoed long after the man from hell disappeared, taking Shyanne with him.

Drayco squirmed frantically, trying to cut his bonds with the big cat's claws. He was able to do so, but only after receiving several gashes in the process. He sat up quickly and removed the gag. The rope holding his legs followed. In an instant, he swung the door open and darted into the hall. It was empty. Ruben and his sister were nowhere in sight.

"Damn!"

He hurried back to Joseph. "Are you okay?"

"Yea..." Joseph managed to gasp. "Where's Shyanne?" His breath was finally returning after the brutal kick. He sat up and leaned back against the wall, his knees bent to relieve the tension to his tender abdominal area.

"I don't know. The hall was empty by the time I got to it." Drayco stood. "Stay here, I'll be right back." He returned to Drizzle and removed the ropes that bound the cat's mouth and extremities.

"Good to see you again, old friend."

"And you." He stretched his legs to loosen them from the long period of restraints. "It feels good to finally be free."

"Are you able to move?" Drayco sat on the edge of the bed rubbing the animal's extremities to better help circulation flow through them again. "Can you help us track Shyanne?"

The cat shrugged the man's hands off. He tried to get up, but his legs gave out. He flopped down on the mattress.

"I'm afraid it will be a minute or two before I can do that," Drizzle said.

He struggled to stand several more time before he finally succeeded. Drayco watched. He knew better than to help the big cat. Drizzle was just as independent as he was.

"Who did this? I didn't see who it was before I was hit," Joseph asked as he stood up gingerly. Only one word was uttered. It was said with such hatred that he paused to look at the dark man.

"Ruben."

Drizzle curled his lip at the sound of the name. A low grumbling emitted from his throat. "I'll make him pay for what he has done."

"First," Drayco reminded the cat, "you and I need to replenish ourselves. Neither of us will be of any use right now in the shape we're in." When the cat started to say something, Drayco added, "Ruben won't have gone far with Shyanne. With your nose, we will find him quickly."

"What can I do to help?" Joseph asked.

"Find that Louis fellow. He may be able to give us some information that could be useful."

"We wouldn't be lucky enough for him to be at the front desk. That would be too easy." He made his way to the door. "I'll go see what I can find out. You two stay here and conserve your strength."

Before he could get there, Drizzle laid his ears back and stared at the entrance to the room. A low growl escaped from him. Joseph crept to the door and grasped the handle, yanking it open suddenly. He reached into the hall, seized the shirt of a man standing with his ear pressed against the door, and threw him to the floor inside. The stained apron over his clothing showed he worked in the kitchen.

"Don't hurt me, don't hurt me," he cried out. He was bent over on his knees with his hands held open over his head, waving them in the air.

Joseph walked over the kneeling man, and asked, "Who are you? What do you want here?"

"I'm Wally, one of the kitchen hands. I just came to get some supplies from across the way. I was almost finished and had everything stacked by the door when Ruben ran in, knocking everything over, including me."

Drayco straightened up at the mention of Ruben. Wally cringed when he saw the intense look of hatred coming from such a young face. Drayco returned his gaze to the floor, deep in thought. Wally wasn't sure what to make of it.

"He had a woman slung over his shoulder. When I shouted at him for messing up my work, he ignored me and disappeared around some boxes. I thought it was a bit odd when he didn't come out so I went to investigate. He was gone, nowhere to be found. I don't know where he went, but he was gone." Wally looked up at the man towering over him. "I heard voices coming from this room so I leaned over to hear what was being said. I was curious what Ruben was up to."

"Joseph, check out the other room. See if you can locate the secret hidden inside," Drayco said in a voice almost too soft to hear. He was leaning forward, his elbows resting on his upper legs, his hair hanging in front of his face, hiding his features from view.

"What are you planning?"

"I want to have a private chat with this person here. Drizzle, you stay with me."

The big cat sat back on his haunches, watching Drayco's hunched form. The dark man lifted his head. Both Joseph and Wally gasp at the sight that met their eyes. The color of Drayco's eyes was almost entirely black, as black as the hair on his head. A look of undisguised hunger was written all over him.

"Drayco, wha..."

"I said go. NOW!"

Wally looked at Joseph, then back at Drayco. He whined, "What is he going to do?" He scooted back against the far wall. "I promise to leave and never tell anyone about this. Promise!"

Drizzle yawned at the pathetic human being squirming against the wall.

Drayco stood slowly with his hands balled into tight fists. "Joseph, please. This is not something you want to watch."

Dread filled Joseph as he moved toward the entrance. He paused, glanced at the dark man half hidden by the shadows and turned back. Grasping the handle leading out, he said, "I'll be waiting for you in the other room." With that, he left.

Drayco could feel the hunger rising to an agonizing level. He felt sorry for the innocent man who had stumbled into the wrong place at the wrong time, but could not prevent what was going to happen next even if he had wanted to. The needs of his body were taking over.

A groan of anguish escaped from his lips as the dark man made his way to the one sitting on the floor. Wally glanced up with trepidation. He didn't move as Drayco squat next to him and reached out to brush a hand across his neck. Fear had him frozen in place.

"I'm sorry for killing you. It is not something I would have done any other time, but today I must."

Wally locked eyes with Drayco, a tear started down his cheek. "I haven't done anything to you. Why, why are you doing this?"

"Because I must," Drayco whispered. He bent over and sank his teeth into the soft flesh of the neck. He bit deep.

The skin gave way, allowing the blood to flow. But it wasn't enough. He bit again and found what he was seeking, the jugular. Now the blood gushed out of the ravaged neck into Drayco's mouth. Wally's breath hissed in, but he never cried out. The shock of what was happening was enough to keep the man silent. Wally's eyes rolled back into his head.

Drayco closed his eyes, unable to look at his victim. He sucked on the neck until he felt nothing more come out. Releasing his hold, he sat up. Wally's eyes were staring at the ceiling, his mouth hanging open. A look of extreme sadness had settled on his face. It remained there even after death.

The dark twin hung his head in sorrow, sorrow at the loss of this unfortunate man. He whispered, "Ruben, here is another death I will kill you for. When I find you, I will make sure your death is agonizingly long in coming."

He stood and removed Wally's shirt. His had been ruined when Ruben ripped it off his body. The wounds on his chest, put there by the sharp knife, were pink and healing. Quite an amazing thing considering they were put there only a few hours ago. The gray streak in his hair was still there. The abuse his body endured the last few days had left its mark.

His strength was almost at full capacity. The blood he had received earlier, and again just now, had helped in bringing it back. Drizzle continued to watch what Drayco did. He was interested in knowing what his companion's brother was going to do next. It took him by surprise.

Drayco finished undressing Wally's body. He picked it up and carried it to Drizzle where he set it down carefully and backed away. "Here is the nourishment that will help you gain strength, my friend. I suggest you make the most of it. One never knows when the next meal will happen." He turned his back to the cat and walked to the exit. As he put a hand on the handle, he stated, "Don't take too long, though, Shyanne needs us." He went out the door without looking back.

The room across the hall was only a few steps away, but it felt as vast as the Grand Canyon. Drayco shuddered at what he had done. Unfortunately, it was necessary if he was to help Shyanne.

He opened the door to the storage area and shut it quietly behind him. The things Ruben had knocked over in his haste were still spread out on the floor. All kinds of wares, including boxes full of restaurant items, were stacked against the walls, leaving little space available in the room. Drayco stayed by the door, looking for Joseph. He wasn't anywhere.

"Joseph? Are you in here? Where are you?" No answer.

Without warning, the sound of whooshing air came from an area off to his left. He reached where his sword should have been and found it missing. The dark man felt a momentary pang of loss. He banished it from his thoughts.

No sense in mourning over things you can't bring back.

He crouched behind a stack of boxes, intent on taking down whoever came into sight. A long shadow stretched before him. Drayco started to attack but pulled up abruptly when he saw who it was.

"Joseph, where the hell have you been?"

"You would not believe what I found. It's a passageway hidden behind a secret door. I found the trigger for it totally by accident." A huge grin covered his face. "Come. Let me show you." Joseph reached for Drayco's arm. The dark man pulled it back abruptly.

"I can make it on my own."

"Oh...okay. Here. This way...over here."

Joseph sounded like a small child who had discovered a secret treasure trove of toys stashed away for the holidays. He retraced his steps to a wall located behind some boxes filled with eating utensils. No door or seams were visible in the area. Reaching up, he touched what looked like a dot up near the ceiling, hidden in the shadows.

A whoosh of air, similar to the type Drayco heard earlier, occurred. Three seams appeared on the wall then a small section slid into itself. The air beyond was stale but breathable. A stairway cut in the stone disappeared downward into the darkness. A thin layer of dust covered the floor and several sets of footprints marred the smooth surface.

"These go on for only a short distance then level out. I couldn't go any farther because I didn't have a light."

Joseph beamed at Drayco, the incident next door temporarily forgotten. Drayco frowned as he looked at the floor. Three sets of footprints were present, two heading into the darkness beyond with only one set coming out. Ruben must have gone this way. And from the looks of it, He's still down there.

"Help me look through this stuff. Maybe we can find something to create a light source while we wait for Drizzle to finish."

The smile evaporated from Joseph's face. A shiver ran up his spine at the picture that entered his thoughts. Turning to the nearest stack of boxes, he began going through them. Distraction would help him from thinking about what was going on in the room across the hall, or so he hoped.

Drayco moved to another stack and started opening their lids. Nothing but dried foodstuff and things for the restaurant were in them. Just as he was about to give up hope on finding anything, Joseph called out.

"I found something. I'm not sure what it is but it lights up when I push this." He held up a silver cylinder for Drayco to see.

"It's something from a time long ago, something I never thought I'd see again, not a working one at least."

"What do you mean? What is it?"

Drayco walked over the Joseph and took the object from his hand. He turned it over until he found the button then pushed it. A circular glow hit the wall, driving the growing shadows away. "It's a flashlight."

"A flashlight? What's a flashlight? Is it dangerous? Is it a weapon? Can we use it?"

Drayco smiled for the first time in a long time, "No my friend, it's not a weapon, and it won't hurt anyone. It provides light for us to see with in the dark, that's all. Are there any more of them?"

Joseph looked at the flashlight with wonder and a bit of skepticism. Drayco watched the man, his amazement at the lost technology refreshing.

"Joseph..."

"Humm.? Oh...no, there aren't any more, just the one."

Drayco turned it off to conserve the batteries and returned the light to Joseph. They were about to look in the last couple of boxes when the door to the hallway opened. Both men spun around to face the intruder.

Drizzle crept quietly into the room. He observed the two men across the way and the thing in Joseph's hand. His expression never changed, but Drayco could see the interest in his eyes. "A flashlight. How amazing."

"Am I the only one who hasn't ever seen a flashlight?" Joseph groaned.

"Have you finished with your task?"

"If you mean have I made full use of what was left me, the answer is yes. My strength has returned."

"Good. Because we need you to track Ruben. We've wasted enough time." The smile on Drayco face faded. "Joseph, did you find any weapons while you were going through the boxes?"

"No. But I did find these." He held up two batteries. Their outer coating was dry and intact; no signs of corrosion were on them. "I think they go with this." He held up the flashlight.

"They do, bring them along. Hopefully we'll find more along the way." Drayco moved to the open stairwell. He stopped just inside and turned back to the others. "Well?"

Joseph and Drizzle looked at each other before following the dark man through the opening. The big cat slid past and disappeared into the darkness beyond.

"Don't get too far ahead, Drizzle. We don't want to loose you."

"You won't."

Joseph still had the light in his hand. He flicked it on as they made their way down, away from the light shining in. A small landing carved out of the surrounding stone appeared. The small circle of light from the flashlight showed nothing except more walls.

A few paces away, another set of steps led further underground. The air grew thick with humidity the deeper they went. The lack of air currents made it feel like a sauna in the small, enclosed space. This fact did not make sense to Drayco. Every time he and his family went spelunking in caves, those many years ago, the air was always cool.

The two men were drenched with sweat by the time they made it to the bottom of the stairs. With nothing to show the passing of time, it felt like they had been walking for hours. Drizzle was nowhere in sight.

I wonder where that cat has gotten to, Drayco pondered. *I told him not to go far.*

He touched Joseph on the shoulder and indicated for him to shine the light around. Joseph pointed it in all directions, but could not pierce the seeming endless darkness ahead. The room beyond was vast.

"Where do you suppose we are," Joseph whispered. Even with the softness of his voice, the sound echoed across the open space.

"I don't know, somewhere underneath the inn."

"This must have taken years to do. Why would someone take the time to cut such a vast space in the stone?"

"Again, I don't know. Let's follow the wall around. Maybe we'll find another exit, or at least the way Ruben or that fool cat went."

Joseph led because the light was still in his hands. They had gone about 100 paces when the wall of stone was replaced with a wall of some unknown substance. Drayco reached out, putting his hand on it. It felt cool, even in the stifling warmth of the room, and was seamless for as far as they could see with the light.

"Odd," Drayco said. "This situation is getting stranger and stranger with each step,"

"I agree. I've never seen material like this before. Do you know what it is?"

"At first I thought it was steel, but now that I've touched it, I'm not sure what it is."

"Some more things from the past?" Joseph questioned

"It must be. Nothing like this exists nowadays."

They continued following the strange wall. After another 150 paces, they discovered something even more interesting to Drayco, and more disconcerting to Joseph. The wall stopped at a corner before it continued around, disappearing into the darkness once more. Parked in the corner was an ancient vehicle.

"It's a golf cart! And in mint condition no less!" Drayco rushed up to the vehicle and jumped into the driver seat.

Joseph remained at a distance. He had never seen an object like this in his entire life. It was a white box with round things attached to it that looked like wheels. It reminded him of a small cart ponies pulled. Something that looked like a smooth rope came out of the wall behind it. It was stuck in the back of the box.

Drayco leaned over, squinting to see the dashboard. "Joseph, come over here with the light. I need to see."

Joseph remained where he stood. He wanted no part of whatever this thing was. He had heard about the items created from the past, and about how they had destroyed the lives of so many people. He was not about to let this contraption destroy him.

Drayco glanced up. The wary look on Joseph's face caused the dark man from the past to return to the present. He went to his friend's side.

"I'm sorry about that. I forgot you haven't seen one of these things before. Come on; let me show it to you." Drayco started walking back to the cart but stopped when he realized Joseph was not following. He said, "I promise, it won't hurt you."

"You're sure?"

"I'm sure."

Joseph made his way warily to the cart. He stayed in front of it, out of reach, just in case. When it made no move against him, he relaxed, but not much. Drayco kept his face straight. He did not want to insult the man trying to help him find his sister by laughing at him.

The dark man returned to the seat he had vacated and indicated for Joseph to sit next to him. He refused. He might have allowed himself to get this close to the thing from the past, but he was not going to be stupid enough to get into the damn thing.

This time Drayco could not hold back. He snickered, "Joseph, it's only a machine from long ago. All it did was carry people from point A to point B, just like a wagon does today. The driver told it where to go by steering this wheel." Drayco put his hands on the big circular object in front of him.

Joseph continued to watch the man inside the cart from a distance.

"Oh well, if you won't sit down, would you at least hold the light over here so I can see what I'm doing?"

Joseph moved to the side with much apprehension. He focused the light where Drayco indicated and lit up the control panel for the vehicle. Circular shaped things with little numbers in them were in front of the wheel. A shiny metal object with a round ring hanging from it reflected the light back as soon as it hit it. The object was partially sticking out of the inside wall of the box. Joseph leaned over to have a closer look.

Drayco saw what caught the man's interest. He shouted, "Aha! There is a key." He reached up, grabbed the shiny metal thing, and gave it a twist. The white box on wheels vibrated and a humming noise sounded. They both stopped within moments. Joseph shot backward, pulling his sword out at the same time. The flashlight fell to the floor.

"It's a demon thing, Drayco! Get out of there before it eats you!"

Drayco looked up at Joseph, his face a mask of utter shock. Seconds later, he was laughing so hard tears ran down his cheeks. He leaned over onto the wheel and accidentally honked the horn. Joseph responded by swinging his sword in one fluid motion and hitting the hood of the cart as hard as he could. The resounding thud of metal hitting fiberglass echoed throughout the vast space.

That did it. Drayco fell out of the cart. He landed on the floor, rolling, holding his sides and howled.

Joseph was hard pressed to watch both the box and his friend, whom he thought was either loosing his mind or wounded before he escaped the contraption. His head swung back and forth like those watching a tennis match. After what felt like an eternity to the fair-haired man, Drayco finally regained his composure.

He sat up, wiped his eyes, and glanced up at the man still holding his sword toward the cart. "Joseph, give me a hand up will you?" He reached up, waiting for Joseph to decide what to do.

Joseph took one more look at the cart then shifted the sword to his left hand. He reached down and pulled Drayco to his feet. Once the dark man was standing, he returned both hands to the sword, ready to do battle with the mechanical beast.

The dark twin faced the cart and put his hands on his hips. He knew now he would never get Joseph into the thing, not after what he had just witnessed.

"I want to thank you," Drayco said with a sideways glance at the man standing next to him. "I haven't laughed that much in a very long time."

"Glad to be so entertaining," Joseph replied sarcastically. He relaxed his pose only when the box continued to sit still, as if it was dead.

"We better move on. Since I doubt you will ride in this, we'll have to leave it. Let me look around first. I might find something we can use from it."

Drayco picked up the light and went to the rear of the cart. He lifted the lid to a compartment and rummaged around, finding another working flashlight and a pack to carry things in, but nothing more. He put the spare light in the bag then slung it over his shoulder.

I don't want to use this light until absolutely necessary, especially since there are not enough spare batteries to go around.

When the dark man was finished, Joseph put his sword away and took back the flashlight. He followed the wall leading away from the cart with utmost speed. Drayco walked him, smiling. The light again barely pierced the gloom. They had walked for about 75 paces when the end of the wall came into view. Unlike the last corner, this one was empty. The two men continued in the same direction until they returned to the point they first entered from, the stairs.

"Great. Now what?" Joseph threw his arms up in total exasperation.

"We wait. We didn't run into Drizzle during the entire circumference of the area, and we only found one way in so he must have found another."

Drayco sat down on the steps. He leaned back against the wall and crossed his arms over his chest. As Joseph watched, the dark man shut his eyes and relaxed, his chin resting on his chest.

"You can try and sleep at a time like this! We have to find Shyanne before something bad happens to her. First you make a game out of the contraption from hell, now you sit down and do nothing!" Joseph started to pace back and forth, the light waving around like a ray gun from an old movie.

"Sit down, Joseph. All your pacing isn't going to solve a thing except make you tired. And I need you to be strong when the time comes."

"And when it that going to be?"

"When Drizzle returns."

Joseph let out a long slow exhalation. He knew Drayco was right, but it burned in his gut. To just sit around and do nothing was very frustrating; it was something he was not used to doing. Hard work was a way of life for him. He was not likely to change any time in the near future.

He walked over to the stairs and flopped down above Drayco. He did not lean against the wall. Instead, he leaned forward, resting his elbows on his knees, his face in his hands, staring into the darkness, and waited for the cat to return.

"Put the light out. We need to conserve the batteries."

"You think that's wise. Something could creep up on us without us even knowing it."

Drayco looked up and stated in a matter of fact tone, "Something could do that now."

"You're right."

Joseph saw that the smiling boyish look which had appeared on the dark man's face when he was toying with the cart was now gone. It had been replaced with the seriousness of a man aged well beyond his years.

Before the lifeline to the world of light was switched off, he saw Drayco's eyes. They were filled with pain, a pain so intense; he wondered for a long time what had happened to this man from the past to give him such a look.

Seventeen

Drizzle ran ahead of the two men. He knew Drayco would be upset with him for doing so, especially after he was told not to, but he never listened to him anyway. Shyanne was his main purpose in life, not her twin. He left the sound of their footsteps far behind as he made his way down. The only noise heard now was the occasional scrape of his claws on the warm moist stone stairs. He flew down with the speed and agility of the cat he was. Unlike the men, the blackness of the stairway was not a problem for him; he had the ability to see in the dark.

He made it to the bottom of the long sloping stairs without incident. A vast room made of stone and some other substance stood before him; a faint, long faded smell of gasoline powered vehicles hung in the air. Dark spots, where oil had dripped from them onto the pavement below, were visible.

The cat carefully advanced into the room, using the outer wall as his guide. He wanted no part of the open middle until he had a chance to explore the rest of the vast space. He found a vehicle tucked in a far corner, one he did not think he would ever see again in his lifetime. It was a golf cart. Because he had no use for it, he bypassed it completely and continued exploring.

The only entrance or exit he found was the one he had come down. Drizzle sat on his haunches and pondered. Ruben definitely came this way. The cat had smelled the man's scent, intermingled with Shyanne's, all the way to the bottom. It went into the vast space. An idea came to his brain and he acted on it.

Going directly to the center of the expansive room, he lifted his nose and took in several deep breaths. The scents of Ruben and Shyanne were still fresh. They were easy to find. He crouched with his nose close to the ground and followed the trail to where it disappeared into a wall. No door was visible, but Drizzle knew one had to be there, just like at the top of the stairs. The scent of the people he tracked could not have just disappeared.

The cat stared at the wall. It was smooth, made of some kind of material unknown in the present world. No seams or creases showed. Even with his cat sight, he could not see any kind of opening mechanism. In frustration, he glanced up one more time and spotted what he had missed before. A small indentation the width of a straw was barely noticeable halfway up. He stood on his hind legs, put his front hands on either side of the indent, and sniffed. The scent of Ruben was strong, so strong it made the lips of the cat curl into a snarl.

This is where they went inside, and so shall I.

He tried to put one of his digits into the indent; it would not fit. He tried each one on both hands and came up with the same results. They were too fat and stubby. He rumbled with frustration at not being able to get in, and sat on his haunches staring at the spot as if the power of his will alone would force it to open.

He started pacing back and forth to release some pent up frustration, and to think. Abruptly, he stopped, reached one of his hands upward and fanned it wide. A claw extended out from one of his digits. He looked at it, then at the indentation.

Standing on his hind legs once more, he poked the claw into the indentation. A seam slowly appeared next to the spot where Drizzle had put the claw. A matching one appeared a short distance away from the original. In an instant, the door disappeared into the wall. A shaft of light lit up the vast room, confirming it was empty except for the golf cart.

A long wide hall with many doors showed beyond the opening. A slight humming filled his ears and a vibration almost too faint to notice ran throughout. This place had a familiar feel to it, a feel that the cat did not care to re-member. It was the lab where he had been kept prisoner until the twin's father brought him home. Drizzle remained outside the hall, watching and listening. When he heard no other sounds except the initial ones, he slid inside.

The door, which had remained open while he was near it, slid closed with a faint puff of air after he had gone a few paces down the hall. He spun around, ready for an at-tack. Nothing occurred so he turned back the way he was heading and started past the doors. These doors were eas-ily seen, each with the same indentations. No sound came from any of the room he passed. Whoever had lived here appeared to be gone now.

Another door similar to the one he entered through was at the opposite end of the hall. Drizzle put his claw in and the door opened in a similar fashion. The humming sound was louder. It reminded the cat of something from a long time ago, the sound of machinery working. That seemed impossible for this day and age. Anyone he knew who possessed the knowledge to run them, much less do the maintenance on them, was dead. The last person died 200 years ago. So who was running them now?

The room was as vast as the empty one, with two ex-ceptions: it wasn't empty and there were doors on three of the four walls. Boxes of various sizes were haphazardly piled near the wall closest to the cat. More boxes of vary-ing size were spread about the rest of the room. A genera-tor the size of a small house stood in the middle. A large belt similar to the kind used by cars long ago ran along the side of the generator on large metal wheels with groves molded in them to hold it.

Drizzle followed its progress and saw the belt caused another smaller belt that reached toward the distant ceil-ing above to spin around its own set of wheels. His asso-ciation with Shyanne's family during the time before the virus allowed him to recall the similarities between this machine and the ones used by automobiles. He remem-bered seeing her father work on his truck many times, jumping up on the fender to watch whenever the young ones tried to help.

Drizzle was still pondering how the machine was run-ning since he could not smell any traces of gasoline when he heard a door across the room slide open. Ruben entered with another being next to him. The cat ducked behind a stack of boxes before he was spotted. He watched as they approached.

"What do we do now? Are you going to be able to use the girl to your advantage?"

"That remains to be seen, doesn't it?" whispered the stranger draped in a long flowing black cape with the hood pulled up to hide the face.

"We've got a good association going here and I'd hate to see it come to an end."

"Don't be so hasty into thinking it's going to end soon. We have the girl, and with that, the means to find a solution to my problem."

"I hope so. Is it going to take much longer?"

"That also remains to be seen."

The pair made their way to another door on the opposite wall. The robed figure reached out with an object, a thin rod extending from it, and put it into the indentation. The door slid silently inside the wall, closing behind them once they were through. Before it did, the cat caught a glimpse of what lay beyond. It was filled with machines that looked like the ones used in the lab where he was born: the medical ones.

Drizzle pondered on the odd conversation between Ruben and the stranger and tried to make sense of it, but could not. What he had witnessed in the other room was disturbing, as well. The cat was about to return to Drayco so he could discuss the situation with him when a whirring noise halted him in his tracks. He looked up to see a flying silver object that looked like a ball with a camera mounted on it float into the room. It entered through the door the men had used when they first came in.

The large round lens spun as the machine flew around the room focusing on different objects. No visible means of flight was evident as it hovered near his hiding spot. The cat remained as still as a statue. The boxes surrounding him saved him from detection, so far. If it flew around the stack, he would be out in the open.

All of a sudden, a crash came from another set of boxes stacked along the opposite wall. The floating camera shot in that direction, away from the cats hiding place. A couple of smaller boxes, which had been stacked on bigger ones, rolled across the floor. Drizzle raised his head enough to see a huge rat like creature slink around the bigger boxes toward the smaller ones.

The floating camera hovered over it, watching. The rat thing looked up, wriggled its nose, and moved on after deeming it was not a food item. One side of the ball opened and a small jointed robotic arm unfolded from inside. The arm focused on the rat. A bright ray of light shot from its end. Where the creature had been a second ago, nothing but a small pile of ash remained.

Drizzle could hear the whirring of the lens as the floating ball hovered over the pile. When nothing moved, it floated off toward the door Ruben and the strange person had disappeared through.

It put the tip of the arm into the indentation, causing the door open. Again, Drizzle could see what appeared to be medical equipment beyond. This time he noticed something else. Before the door closed, cutting off any further views, he glimpsed the head of a person with strawberry blonde hair lying on a table.

Shyanne.

The big cat waited until he was certain the floating ball was gone before moving out from behind the boxes. He crossed the room and inspected the ash pile. Nothing discernible of the creature remained. He decided it would be too risky to enter the other room alone, especially with the floating orb of death inside.

He retraced his steps down the hall with many doors to the big empty space with the golf cart. Darkness enveloped him as the door closed, but he was already heading toward the stairs leading to the inn. As he neared, a voice came out of the darkness. It was Drayco.

"Did you find her, Drizzle?"

He remained silent.

"Are you sure he's there?" Joseph asked.

"He's there. I ask again, did you find her?"

"Yes. She is in the company of the mercenary leader and a stranger dressed in a cloak that hides all from view."

"Anything else?"

"A strange floating ball that kills with a ray of light protects them."

"What did you say? A ball that floats? Are you mad?" Joseph flicked on the flashlight. The sudden light caused the men to look away until their eyes adjusted to the brightness.

The cat emitted a low guttural growl at Joseph.

"Enough," Drayco said. "Anything else?"

"It looks like they have her in a room attached to some kind of medical machines."

"What! We have to get her out of there, now, before they kill her!" Joseph jumped to his feet, dropping the flashlight in his haste to get up, causing it to go out. Both Drayco and the cat could hear him shuffling around in the darkness trying to find it.

"Joseph, stop. If they wanted to, they could have killed her a long time ago. They have some reason for needing her and she has to be alive."

Drayco's voice was soft but firm. He picked up the dropped flashlight, which had rolled to a stop at his feet, turned it on and pointed it toward the distraught man. Joseph held his hand up to shield his eyes from the sudden brightness. Once his vision adjusted, he moved next to the dark man and sat down.

"What do you want to do?" The man had a wild look in his eyes, but he was under control enough to listen to Drayco.

"We need to check out this floating ball first. If it is as deadly as Drizzle says, we need to find a way to take it out. Drizzle, tell me everything you witnessed."

The cat sat on his haunches and told the men all he had heard from Ruben, the Boss, and about the floating orb. When he finished, Drayco leaned back and interlocked his fingers behind his head.

"I wonder what he meant by Shyanne being the solution to his problem?"

"Drayco...what is all this stuff? The cylinder that shines light...the flashlight, the box with wheels, the floating ball, the generator, machines. I've never heard of these things." He shook his head, "I can't help but think they are all creations of demons." The look on Joseph's face indicated he was on the verge of becoming overwhelmed by all the information he had received.

"At one time these things were commonplace. It was

called technology. Moving pictures were shown on something called a television, food could be put in a box and heated in minutes, and a person could travel across a vast body of water to another land in hours instead of weeks or months." A far away look filled his eyes as he spoke about the things of the past. "But all that became obsolete after some people created an infection, a virus, that killed a lot of innocent people along with everyone who knew how to build or repair the technology. Life became what it is today thanks to the stupidity of a few idiots trying to look out for our best interest."

"I like the life I lead, or did lead until those mercenaries came to town and wiped it out." Joseph hung his head but raised it up after only a few seconds. "And I want to start that life again with Shyanne at my side. Drayco, I hope you won't be upset, but I love your sister."

"I know. I've known long before either of you two did. I saw it in your eyes."

"You're not mad?"

"I can't think of another person I would rather see her with." Drayco slapped the man on his back, nearly knocking him off the steps. Joseph grinned at the dark twin and slapped his back in return.

"If you two are finished with this manly human ritual, can we get back to helping Shyanne?" Drizzle stared at one man, then the other as he spoke, his tone filled with sarcasm.

"You're right. What do you have in mind?" Drayco asked.

The cat went over what he had planned while he made his way to this room.

"Drizzle, you sly old cat, that is a great plan. Let's move out to this hidden door you spoke of and return our family and friend to us." The dark man looked at Joseph.

The smile on Joseph's face faded and one of grim determination replaced it.

Drizzle went to a smooth metal wall a short distance from the golf cart. Nothing even remotely looking like a door was on it. Joseph and Drayco watched with interest as he stood on his back legs and exposed a long sharp claw. He inserted it into a small indentation about halfway up. The men jumped to either side when the door slid neatly into the wall, exposing the well-lit hall Drizzle had described earlier. Nothing moved. The three entered and started toward the door at the far end.

Before they could reach it, it opened to reveal the floating silver ball. It hovered in the entranceway, the circular lens on the front whirling at a high rate of speed. It zoomed into the hall. The three dove in different directions to avoid the laser shooting from the exposed robotic arm.

Drayco dove to the left while Joseph rolled beyond the speeding ball to come up behind it. The ball focused its attention on the dark man, the laser coming dangerously close each time it shot forth. He kept moving and managed to stay just ahead of it in the confined hallway, but he was running out of tricks. Joseph held up his sword. He tried to hit the ball; it was too fast. It whipped around and almost sliced him in half. Thankfully, he had rolled out of the way.

Drizzle stood by one of the doors. He inserted a claw to open it. It refused to budge, frozen shut over time. He went from door to door until he found one that opened and yelled for the humans to follow before disappearing inside. Drayco fell in behind the cat. Joseph had the ball in the way. He crouched low and waited for it to shoot the laser .After it did, he ran under it and ducked inside the opening. The door started closing behind them at an agonizingly slow pace. The three were not waiting for it to shut.

They moved across the dimly lit room quickly, toward another door located off to the side. At one time, it had been a living space. Dust now covered everything. Drizzle was already at the door inserting his claw. Joseph stood behind him, urging him on.

Drayco kept an eye on the main door, willing it to shut faster. He wished again for his sword, but knew it was gone. He had not seen it since he had killed Viola so many days ago. An inner pang of loss filled him. It was forgotten when the silver ball flew into the room before the outer door closed.

"Get inside now!"

Drizzle was already in the room beyond when Drayco shoved the man standing next to him through the partially open door. A bright light filled the area where Joseph had been, forcing the dark man to dive out of the way to avoid being severed in half. The door started closing; a black streak marred the smooth surface from side to side. The laser had damaged the indentation on the wall, which explained why the door reacted the way it did.

Joseph leaned out to help the dark man. He had to pull back inside to avoid being crushed. The doors closed with Drayco still on the same side as the ball, his companions shut away on the other side.

Damn...now what?

The dark man heard pounding and the muffled voices of his companions while he crouched in the shadows. The only light in the room, a small fluorescent light located near the bed, was not strong enough to reach where Drayco stood. The ball hovered with its lens spinning, as if confused by the noise distracting it.

Maybe I can get out of here before it decides what to do next, or finds me. He was able to go several paces before having to freeze again.

The ball started making a faster whirring sound and a yellow beam of light shot from the lens, lighting up the corner near the black-streaked door. It began panning around the room. It had almost reached Drayco when the inner door opened. Drizzle darted into the room, followed closely by Joseph, sword in hand.

"Drayco! Nothing's in there but a dead end. We have to go back the way we came."

The floating ball spun toward the swift moving cat. The laser lit up the room. Thankfully, the ray hit empty space. Drizzle was already beyond where it had aimed.

Drayco took advantage of the distraction and grabbed the blanket off the bed. He threw it over the ball, effectively blinding it before he ran past to the exit. They left while the ball crashed around the room, shooting the laser in all directions.

"Where do we go?" Joseph asked.

"Drizzle...open another door...now! We have to get out of sight before it frees itself."

The cat padded to the door closest to the generator room and tried it. It slid open without any difficulty. They ducked inside and within seconds of the door sliding shut, the silver ball emerged. It paused, turning first one way then the other, its camera lens spinning in a wild fashion. After a moment, it glided down the hall toward the large vacant room with the golf cart, pausing at each door to scan for sounds before starting toward the opposite end.

"Drayco...wha..." Joseph stood to one side, his sword held ready.

The dark twin held a finger to his lips, indicating the need for silence. The whirring sound made by the floating lens was getting closer. He hugged the wall and held his breath. Joseph held his, as well. Drizzle crouched close to him, watching the door.

The whirring noise held steady in front of their door. It became softer as the ball moved on. It had lost track of them and decided to check the generator room. With the robotic arm, it opened the entranceway and was gone.

Drayco stayed where he was until he was positive it was truly gone. He relaxed against the wall, letting his breath out. Joseph did the same.

"Boy that was close. I thought you were a goner when that door shut before you could get through."

"You and me both," Drayco responded.

"What do you want to do now? That thing knows we're here and has probably gone to alert its masters."

"We get Shyanne," The cat answered as he moved to open the door.

"I'm afraid Drizzle's right. We can't wait and give them a chance to set up a defense. But we do need to make some kind of plan. The one we discussed earlier is now null and void."

Joseph put his sword away. He looked at the dark man, then the big cat. "What do you propose?"

"We need to get past the floating sentry. That is where you come in Drizzle. You're the quickest at getting through the doors and the fastest runner." The cat nodded his head in agreement. "You can draw it away so Joseph and I can get into that room and free Shyanne."

"What about Ruben and this mysterious person?" Joseph asked.

"If they get in the way, we take care of them. Shyanne is the important issue here. I won't tolerate her being in their hands anymore." The look on Drayco's face echoed his words.

"Let's go then."

Drizzle opened the door to the hall and looked out, "All clear."

The three walked to the door leading into the generator room and listened. The whirring sound caused by the flying ball was not heard so Drizzle inserted his claw and opened it. The cat was though the door in an instant. The two men hung back in case the generator disguised the floating ball's noise. Before the door could shut and lock them out, they flung themselves inside, rolling on the ground to either side. The ball was nowhere in sight.

Joseph stood up and glanced toward the center of the room. What he saw made his eyes open wide and his jaw drop. The huge generator with its rolling belts and humming motor stood before him. He moved next to Drayco, unable, or unwilling, to take his eyes off the machinery the entire time.

"What is that?"

"It's a generator, a source of power," Drayco said as he rose to his feet. He was near the stack of boxes Drizzle had hidden behind earlier. "I'm assuming that's what is keeping this facility going. It's old though, even for my time."

"This place is full of so many strange surprises. Some I like, while others are demon possessed." Joseph looked up just to make sure the floating ball was not hovering overhead. "I wish we had more time to check it out."

"Shyanne comes first."

"Agreed."

Joseph moved around the boxes and started toward the generator to see what else was in the room. A whirring noise different from the humming of the machine started getting louder. He dove behind the boxes, pulling the dark man down with him.

Just as they disappeared from view, the floating sentry ball appeared through a door to the right. Drizzle stepped out from behind another set of boxes and moved toward the door to the left, away from the men. The ball turned its camera on the cat and the whirring sound became faster. Before the robotic arm could be extended, Drizzle had the door open and was gone. The floating sentry flew after him. Both disappeared from sight when the door slid shut.

"Do you think he'll be okay?"

"That cat has survived Shyanne's tortures and mine; he can make it through anything."

Joseph smiled at the thought. He turned his attention to the three doors in the room, "Which door was it Shyanne was supposed to be behind?" The smile left at the mention of the woman's name.

"This one over here," Drayco said. He moved toward the door to their right.

The pair positioned themselves on either side and listened. Drayco had Joseph's boot knife in hand and looked at the indent on the wall. He glanced at the fair-haired man and nodded his head as he put the tip in and pressed. The door slid neatly into the wall, exposing the room beyond. Joseph again stood with his eyes wide and his mouth hanging open.

Equipment filled every wall except where the doors were. Other pieces stood scattered about the room, their lights blinking like those on a Christmas tree. Two TV monitors hung near a hospital bed, their screens blank. The bed was empty. Another hospital bed a few paces away was occupied. The monitors next to it showed the occupants heart rate, breathing pattern, oxygen levels, blood pressure and various other thing Drayco did not recognize. Joseph saw the woman lying on the bed and ran to her side.

"Shyanne, can you hear me?" Joseph's hands hovered above her body. He was afraid to touch her because of the condition he found her. After much hesitation, he decided a safe place to grab was her hand.

Her eyes were taped shut and a tube disappeared into her mouth and down her throat. Her chest rose and fell in a smooth pattern with each hiss of the machine. Needles were inserted into her arms and bags of fluid, some yellow, some clear, dripped through thin tubing to provide her with nutrition and hydration.

Drayco made his way across the room and handed Joseph his knife. Looking at the monitors, then at his sister, he remembered how his father had looked when the paramedics took him away; squeezing a bag attached to the tube in his mouth, and knew the hissing apparatus next to her was helping Shyanne breath. He reached out, grabbed

grabbed his sister's restrained arm and gave it a gentle squeeze. Shyanne gave no indication she knew he was there.

Joseph reached over to pull the tube out of the unconscious woman's throat. Drayco caught his arm. He looked up, his eyes filled with agony at having to see his beloved like this.

"We need to help her. I can't bear to see her like this." Joseph's voice broke.

"If we pull that tube out now, we could kill her. It's helping her to breath."

"Correct."

The two men spun around and saw a black robed figure standing a short distance away, one covered arm raised in their direction. Before either could react, a crackling noise sounded and a bolt of light shot out. It hit Joseph in the chest. He flew backwards, smashed into the machines behind him, and crumpled to the floor, unconscious. Drayco threw himself sideways. He rolled behind a piece of equipment and crouched there waiting.

What did he use to knock Joseph out with?

His thoughts were racing. Whatever it was, it sounded electrical. How was it powered? If it was a battery pack, how long would it last before it ran out?

"You are an interesting young man. I've been watching you. Your knowledge of technology is impressive." The voice was soft, barely above a whisper, but it carried across the room as if it was a shout.

Drayco glanced quickly around the equipment. The robed figure had not moved and the arm remained upraised. A faint humming sound emitted from within the fabric. He glanced at Joseph and was glad to see the man's chest rise and fall. He was still alive. A trickle of blood ran down the side of his face. Otherwise, he appeared unharmed.

The dark man darted another look around the machinery and was surprised to see the strange robed person almost seeming to float across the room in his direction. In a crouched position, he ran behind the freestanding equipment to the unoccupied bed. Using his right arm as a support, he threw himself to the other side just as the crackling noise sounded.

He was in mid-swing when he felt the hair on his right arm rise. Even though the shot missed, the arm became numb when the bolt of light grazed past it. It buckled out from under him, causing him to hit the floor at an awkward angle. He lay there trying to catch the breath that had been knocked out of him by the fall.

"You are a mystery that I'd love to solve, but I don't have the time right now. I have to return to my work and you're preventing that from happening."

Drayco took several deep breaths before speaking. "What does that have to do with the woman?"

"Ahh...so you can speak when spoken to, you do have manners after all."

The dark twin struggled to a sitting position behind the bed, its solid base hiding him from view. He held his useless arm against his body. "You didn't answer the question."

"I need her to fulfill my research. That's all you need to know. What I'm curious about is why she is so important to you?"

"She's his sister."

The answer came from across the room. Ruben entered through the door leading from the generator room. He walked over to stand next to the Boss.

"So...that explains much...the fast healing wounds...the reversal of aging. It appears the mystery about you has been solved. Now I can kill you without losing any sleep over it, especially since I have your sister."

Drayco looked around but could not see a way out. He had inadvertently trapped himself in a part of the room without an exit. Joseph's sword was still in its sheath strapped to his back. If he could somehow get to it, he could use it to break free. His sword arm was not working, but he could use the left. He was glad now for all the years of practice he had had to endure.

Somehow I have to get to Joseph, grab his sword, avoid Ruben and the Boss's weapons, draw them away from both Shyanne and Joseph AND do it with a bum arm...this ought to be fun.

He would have to leave his companions for his plan to work. Much as he hated doing so, it had to be done if they were going to make it out of here.

A noise brought him back the scene at hand. Drayco glanced over the bed and saw Ruben making his way around the equipment toward him from the left, sword in hand. He saw the Boss coming toward him from the right. An idea developed as he watched the others move. He ducked down and tucked his useless right arm inside his shirt to keep it from flopping all over. He did not need it in the way.

He waited only a breath before jumping over the bed between the two oncoming people. The Boss turned his upraised arm toward the fleeing man and the crackling intensified. A light shot out just as Ruben faced toward Drayco on the opposite side.

The dark man dropped to the floor and the light went past him, hitting the big man square in the chest. The look of shock on Ruben's face as he went down would have been priceless if Drayco had not been so busy trying to recover from the close proximity of the beam. His vision was fuzzy and his head hurt.

He looked toward the Boss and saw the other arm reach up to adjust whatever it was in his hand. He was unable to make out what the object was due to the fuzziness, but he heard something click. The Boss began to raise the unknown weapon again.

"You have delayed me far too long and I've grown tired of this. I must finish my work before it's too late. This weapon is now set to kill. I promise you, it will be quick and painless." The Boss straightened the robed arm.

Drayco heard the crackling grow louder, more intense. Just as he thought he was dead, the door behind him slid open. A blur of tawny fur shot into the room. Both people had been so focused on each other that they had failed to notice the whirring sound as it neared.

The floating sentry shot into the room on the heels of the big cat, its robotic arm extended, the deadly light firing from its tip. Drizzle ran past Drayco and toward the robed figure. At the last possible second, the cat veered away to avoid running into him. The Boss was so startled by the animal's actions that his shot went wide and hit the floating ball, which in turn, caused its shot to go wild and slice him across the mid-section.

The floating ball fell to the floor with a thud, its power

drained and the camera lifeless; the laser silenced forever.

The Boss dropped to his knees, holding his abdomen with both arms. A large pool of blood spread out around the robes. Drayco struggled to his feet. He staggered toward the wounded enemy. As he neared, the Boss's head went up and the hood turned in his direction. He tried to raise an arm, to point the weapon in his grasp at Drayco, but was unable. He was losing blood fast, and his strength was going with it.

"Why? Why did you do this?" Drayco asked.

"I wanted the secrets the girl carried in her genes, the secret to long life. I could have been young and beautiful again. I could have lived forever." A blood filled cough escaped from the darkness of the hood, splattering red moisture across front of the robe. "I didn't have much time. The machines used to keep me alive were failing. Now I will never find what I was looking for."

The hood fell back to reveal an ancient woman. Wrinkles riddled with tiny blue veins covered her pale bony face. Her hair was thin and wispy and the color was as white as a snow-covered mountaintop. Drayco could not tell for sure how old she was, but knew from her appearance and the way that she spoke, it was a considerable number. She leaned her head forward, hiding her face in her bloody gloved hands. Drayco could hear crying. He almost felt sorry for this retched old woman. Then he remembered all the people who had died because of her.

"What did you do to my sister?"

The Boss remained silent, her head down. Drayco almost thought she had died until a ragged gasp escaped from the thin pale lips. She lowered her hands to her lap and said, "She has been drugged. Stop the fluids running into her and you will stop the medicine."

"How long will it take to wear off?"

"I only wanted to live forever...is that so bad? Now look at what's happened. Why...why did this have to happen? I didn't do anything wrong." The old woman ranted to herself, the dark man standing next to her forgotten.

Drayco kneeled down in front of the Boss and grabbed her shoulder with his good hand. He shook the old woman lightly to try to rouse her from her rambling.

"How long? How long will it take?"

"I only wanted to live forever..." The old woman looked up at Drayco but did not see him. She was in a place far away. As the dark twin watched, her eyes glazed over and her head fell back. She was dead.

"How do I help my sister? How do I get the tube out of her throat? How?" Drayco yelled as he shook the body harder and harder even though he knew it would not help.

He threw the Boss aside and stumbled over to Shyanne. Grabbing her hand, he bowed his head and took several deep raspy breaths to prevent himself from loosing control. He looked up at her sleeping face. Tears ran down his face for the first time since they were kids.

She's so beautiful. I have to find a way to help her. I have to.

After getting his emotions under control and wiping the tears off his face, he went to check on Joseph. Joseph remained unconscious. The head wound had stopped bleeding. Since he was not in any distress, Drayco went to check on Ruben. He glared at the big man and thought about ridding the world of this slimy being, but the idea of drinking anything from this man made his stomach curl with disgust.

Drizzle had watched the entire scene between the dark twin and the Boss while it unfolded. When Drayco shook the dead woman, then tossed her aside to make his way to Shyanne, he followed.

Drayco reached up with his good hand and rolled the clamps for the IV tubes shut. With Drizzle's help, he disconnected them from his sister's arms. He looked at the machine beside her, but had no idea how to take the breathing tube out. The Boss had given him no information or clues. He knew that if he pulled it out without taking the proper precautions, he could do more damage than good. He had never felt so helpless.

His vision was still blurry. It was getting better, though, and his head hurt less. He looked up at the monitors. The green line against the dark background flowed steady across the screen, showing Shyanne's heartbeat. In frustration, he glanced around the room and saw a desktop computer tucked in a corner, almost hidden by some equipment.

"Maybe that will have the information I need. Drizzle,

stay with Shyanne." The cat nodded his head.

Drayco moved to the corner, pulled the chair out, and sat down. The computer was on. Unfortunately, the mouse was meant for a right-handed person. At the present, his right hand was useless. It tingled, but he still had no control over it. He moved the mouse to the other side of the keyboard and operated it as best he could with his left hand.

Watching the monitor come to life, he muttered to himself, "This brings back memories."

He saw several icons on the left side of screen. He recognized the medical one and double clicked on it. The screen changed to reveal information about medicine and medical equipment. He scanned through it and found all the information he could on the extubation of people from a ventilator. He read everything thoroughly to make sure he would do the job right. He was about to return to Shyanne when he saw a symbol he recognized. It was the one put on trucks a long time ago when they hauled hazardous material.

He was curious what it contained so he clicked on it. The file opened without a password, allowing him to read the entire contents. His expression became cold and hard the further he read. When he was finished, he paused. Now he understood what had happened and how the virus had escaped. He also thought he understood what the Boss was after and how she had survived all these years.

The Boss was one of the original scientists who helped create the virus. Her name was Francine Jacobs. She had worked with their father. Early on, through gossip, she had heard about some of the changes people who survived had undergone and wanted it for herself. She had hoped that by working with the blood of one of the survivors, in particular, Shyanne, she could discover the secret of her youthfulness and longevity of life and use it for her own aging body. Unfortunately, for her, she never got the chance.

Drayco hit the delete button and watched the dreadful information disappear. He stood up and was about to return to Shyanne but had a feeling something wasn't right, something was out of place. He could not place a finger on it. A glance toward Drizzle and his sister showed nothing out of the ordinary. Both were asleep. He looked around the rest of the room. After a couple of passes, he discovered what it was. Ruben was gone. The big man must have awakened while he was busy and slipped out without notice. He searched the room just to make sure. Ruben was gone.

A moan escaped from Joseph. Drayco went to his side. He was sitting up holding his chest and his head at the same time.

"Son of a rizbak's butt my chest hurts. My head hurts too." He ran his fingers over his face and discovered the dried blood, "What happened?"

"You took a pretty good hit there."

"I'm feeling every inch of it."

"I need your help."

"What can I do?" Joseph looked at the dark man; he noticed his arm. "You okay?"

"Yea. I need you to pick up a piece of equipment for me and smash it apart."

Joseph looked up at the large equipment behind him and said sarcastically, "Yea, right"

Drayco ignored his comment. He returned to the computer he had recently vacated. "This is what I want smashed. Can you do it?" He touched the tower with his foot.

"That I can do. Are you sure you want me to?"

"I'm sure."

Drayco shuddered when he thought about what he had just read. The idea of the virus getting loose again was an all too real possibility as long as the information remained available. He wanted to make sure it could never be retrieved, even though he had deleted it. He stood back and watched as Joseph rose to his feet and wobbled his way.

With a grimace, Joseph picked up the tower and smashed it against the ground, causing the outer casing to shatter. At Drayco's insistence, he pulled out his sword and sliced at the mess of wires and circuitry on the floor, cutting up everything until nothing was left together. Breathless from the effort, he put his sword away after Drayco indicated for him to stop.

"Thanks. You have no idea what you just helped prevent."

Looking at the broken computer, he said, "I think this world is not ready for whatever is down here. I know I'm not." He turned and caught sight of his love. "Shyanne..." He ran to her side and picked up her hand. "Drayco, can we help her?"

"Yes, but I'm going to need your assistance again. I can't do it with my arm like it is."

"You've got it. Tell me what I have to do."

Joseph's expression grew serious. His eyes filled with determination, driving out the pain his body kept reminding him about. After making sure Shyanne was able to breathe on her own, Drayco directed Joseph's movements and the breathing tube was removed safely.

"Now we have to wait until she wakes up to see if anything else was done to her."

Drayco walked over to the other hospital bed and sat down on it. Joseph followed. Drizzle remained with Shyanne. She was his long time companion and the cat wanted to make sure she was going to be okay.

"What happened after I was knocked out?"

Drayco informed Joseph about how the Boss had been tricked into killing the floating ball, using the same weapon he was hit with. And bout how, in return, the ball had killed the boss with its deadly ray. He pointed to the heap of robes lying on the floor with a pool of blood surrounding it.

"Ruben was here too, but he got away when I was busy trying to figure out how to get that blasted tube out of Shyanne."

"When we see him again, I'm going to kill him without even a second thought." Joseph's tone was laced with deadly intent.

"The surprising thing was the Boss. I expected a man under those robed. It was nothing more than a very old woman who had lived longer than she should have."

"A woman! Well—I don't care who she was—or how old she was, I'm just glad to be rid of her."

"I'm with you there." Drayco reached up and put a hand on the other man's shoulder. He thought again about what he had read concerning the virus and the Boss. He knew he would never tell the others any of it. It was not something that needed to be dredged up.

Joseph could see from the dark man's eyes that he was hiding something, something that gave them a haunted look, but he did not ask. He knew Drayco would tell him in due time if he was meant to know.

Over by Shyanne, Drizzle stirred. The two men got up and return to her side. She was moving her head back and forth.

Joseph leaned close and whispered, "Can you hear me, my love?"

"Of course I can, you nut," Her eyes fluttered open as she turned her head toward him. She smiled.

Joseph smiled back, kissing her softly on the nose. "I missed you. I'm glad you're back with us."

"Me too." Drizzle said as he stood up on his back legs. He licked her hand resting on the bed.

She reached up and gave his cheek a scratch. "Missed you too, you big galoot." A loud purring echoed from the cat's throat.

Drayco stayed back. He let the ones closest to his sister finish. He loved her very much and was glad she was with them again, but he knew he was third in this group.

Shyanne frowned. She looked to either side, trying to see where Drayco was. She reached with her arm when she finally located him, indicating for him to come over.

He moved to her side and grasped her hand, holding it tight. "I'm glad we arrived in time."

She reached up and touched the gray streak of hair above his left eye. "I love you, brother."

"I love you too, little sis."

She smiled again and closed her eyes. She fell into a deep restful sleep. The men and the cat watched to make sure it was not a deadly leftover response to the drugs.

They decided to dispose of the Boss' corpse before settling down to rest. The thought of having it in the same room while they slept was unnerving. A section of the robe shifted while the two men rolled the body over. It revealed a small lump underneath, close to the area that had been cut. Joseph opened the robes to discover a belt of some kind attached to a compact box covered with knobs.

"Do you know what that's for?" he queried when he saw it.

"It looks familiar, but I can't remember right off what

it's for. It will come to me sooner or later."

They picked up the little bit of a woman and carried her into another room adjacent to theirs. It was filled with cleaning supplies. Some of the towels stored there were brought back and used to soak up the blood spilled on the floor.

"You need some rest. I'll take first watch," Drayco said once they finished. "I'll wake you up in three hours. Drizzle, you can do the final watch."

"Do we really need to post a watch?"

"With Ruben's whereabouts unknown, I'd feel better with one," Drayco answered.

Joseph nodded his head to those words. "I see your point."

Drayco walked over to the door leading to the generator, and stopped. He watched Joseph throw himself on the spare bed and fall asleep almost before his eyes closed. Drizzle stretched out on the floor next to Shyanne and shut his eyes.

I bet that cat won't sleep an ounce. He's just humoring me so I'll leave him alone...can't say as I blame him though.

He left the room and sat by the generator to think about what had happened in the last few hours. He kept part of his senses on alert, though. With Ruben loose, the dark twin did not want either him or another of those floating sentry death-balls to catch him off guard.

Suddenly, he sat forward. "Now I know what that belt was for. It was an anti-gravity belt." The look of surprise on his face was replaced by one of wonder. "Well I'll be damned. I thought those things were found only in comic books. Looks like those books had some basis in fact to them after all."

He sat back and began thinking about the other item he had seen when they moved the body. The weapon used during the battle was still clutched in the dead woman's hand when they rolled her over. Neither of them touched it for fear of accidentally firing it and killing someone in their party.

The more he thought about it, the more the whole situation reminded him of the science fiction comics he read as a child: the weapon, the anti-gravity belt, the really old villain trying to find secrets beyond her comprehension. Drayco had a feeling that if he took the time to search around, he would find the very comics he had read stashed away somewhere.

As the night wore on, Drayco knew what he had to do. He had been without technological advances for 200 years. The idea of having to be without it again did not fill him with as much regret as he thought it would. He missed a few things, like fast food and television, but the times had changed, and he had changed with them.

It was hard to tell if it night or day in the world above because the lights were always on and their bodies were weary from all the recent action. Time had lost all meaning down in this haven of the past. After what he assumed was about three hours, he returned to the room and woke Joseph for his turn. He crawled onto the still warm, recently vacated bed, curled onto his side and was entered the land of slumber.

The next day, or what was assumed to be the next day because of the lack of sunlight, everyone was up and moving. Shyanne had dark bruises on her arms from the needles, and her throat was sore, but otherwise she felt like a new person. Joseph was sore and bruised from when he was thrown into the machinery by the Boss' weapon. He was stretching to loosen up the tight muscles when Drayco told the trio what he had planned during his watch.

Shyanne agreed it was a good one, although she had mixed feeling like Drayco. She missed the comforts technology offered. Even so, it felt weird to use it after doing without for so long. Joseph simply claimed that everything in the underground complex was an abomination.

By now, the dark man's arm had returned to normal and would work fully when it came time for the equipment to be busted up beyond repair and the generator destroyed.

The group accomplished what was needed, first by light shining down from the ceiling, then by the glow of the flashlights found during their journey. The doors leading from their present position to the large empty room were propped open to prevent the group from being trapped after power was lost. With everything destroyed, the four made their way to the big empty room with the stairs leading upward.

"That about takes care of everything." Joseph shined a light in Drayco's direction, "What now?"

"We go to the stables, get our horses, and ride the hell out of this town. I'm sick of this place."

"Boy I couldn't agree with you more," Shyanne added.

"Drizzle, lead the way."

The big cat started up the stairs. Joseph put an arm around Shyanne's waist and together they started up. Drayco paused, glanced back at the vast darkness and followed, the light in his hand turned off to conserve the batteries.

It seemed like an eternity had passed when they finally reached the top of the stairs. The batteries for Joseph's light gave out as the group stood looking at the door, trying to figure out how to open it. Drayco turned his on. Without the generator, the door would not respond to the Drizzle's claw. That was when they realized the spare batteries brought with them were down in the destroyed room below, along with the pouch.

"Great! Now what do we do?" The frustration felt by Joseph was evident in his voice. "First we had to deal with some old hag and her muscle bound crony, now we have to find a way to get out of this tomb. Man, all I want to do is to go home!"

"It's okay Joseph; we'll get out of this." Shyanne reached up and put her hand lightly on his arm.

He grabbed it, gave it a soft squeeze, and smiled. "I'll be fine; I just miss my simpler way of life, that's all."

"Joseph, give me your sword," the dark man interrupted. He handed the light to the other man and took the blade. "Shine it here so I can see what I'm doing." He pointed to the faint seam located near the stone wall.

With the light shining at the wall, Drayco put the tip of the sword into the seam and twisted the blade back and forth, forcing the door open wide enough to get a hold on it. He placed his fingers in the gap and leaned back to prevent it from closing. Joseph quickly grabbed the sword, allowing Drayco to use both hands. With one foot planted on the wall, he let out a huge groan while he attempted to pull the gap wider.

The door was halfway open when the remaining light

gave out, its batteries spent. Joseph tossed the useless tube down the stairs. It rolled all the way to the landing below. The noise it caused on the way down echoed back to them, causing the party to flinch at its loudness. He looked at Shyanne; his face took on the appearance of a child who had been caught by his parents in the middle doing something wrong. Giggles broke out. Drayco shook his head and began pulling again. There was not enough room for more than one to pull together.

The door finally opened far enough for the four of them to get into the storage room beyond. Joseph went to the door leading to the back alley. Shyanne and Drizzle followed. They turned back when the dark man stayed behind.

"Go on. I'll meet you at the stables. I have unfinished business here."

"What are you going to do?" Shyanne asked, her voice thick with apprehension.

"Don't worry. I won't be long."

"But Drayco..."

"Don't worry, Shyanne. I'll be fine. Go on; get the horses ready."

Joseph could tell the dark man had made up his mind. "Come on, Shyanne, let's go." She hesitated. Joseph moved to her side. "It's okay, love. He'll be fine. Come on." He put an arm around her and gently guided her toward the door.

She glanced at her brother. "You had better meet us."

"I'll be there, don't worry."

All of a sudden, her eyes opened wide. "Wait...wait here, I need to get something for Drayco before we go."

She darted across the room, opened the door leading to the hall and ran across to where they had first encountered Ruben. Drayco looked at Joseph. He shrugged his shoulders. Neither knew what she was after. Within moments, she reappeared with her bag clutched in her arms. A long object protruded from it. Drayco saw it and his heart soared. It was his sword.

"I just remembered your sword. We found it in some grass near the body of a woman and brought it with us. The pack was knocked off me when Ruben hit me and I forgot about it until now."

Drayco came over to his sister and took the weapon, his hands shaking. He never thought he would see the sword again. Before tears welled in his eyes and embarrass him, he hugged her close. "Thank you."

Joseph walked up to the pair and touched Shyanne on the shoulder. "We'd better leave. We need to be as far away from here as possible before it's discovered we escaped the Boss, if Ruben hasn't told everyone already."

Drayco frowned at the mention of the big mercenary's name. "He's right, Shyanne. Get to the horses. I'll be there shortly."

She moved toward the door with Joseph, giving him a knowing look. "Good luck, brother. I know I'll see you soon." Both disappeared into the alley before either could change their minds.

"You too, Drizzle." The cat was lying quietly by the exit.

"I can help."

"Not this time, my friend. I need to do this one alone." Drayco buckled his sword to his belt while he spoke. It felt good to have it back in place.

"Are you sure?"

"Positive."

The cat stared at Drayco. He sighed. "You always were an independent cuss, even when you were little. I'm glad to see you haven't changed one ounce in that department." The cat shook his head back and forth. He turned toward the door, "If you're not back in a reasonable amount of time, I'm coming to find you."

"Thanks Drizzle...that means a lot to me."

"Don't let it go to your head. I'm only doing it because of Shyanne." He disappeared out the door, not allowing Drayco time to respond.

He smiled at the cats words. Most would have thought they were an insult. He took them as a compliment. Turning toward the door leading to the hall, the smile faded. The dark twin walked out of the room and toward the lobby. As he entered the main area, he spotted Louis standing in his usual spot behind the desk. The man looked up. He gasped when he saw who was standing there.

Before the man could recover from the shock of seeing what he thought was a ghost, the dark twin was over the counter and standing next to him, a hand covering his mouth to prevent any shouting.

Wrenching an arm behind him, Drayco forced the clerk down the hall to the room he had been tortured in: room 130. Louis tried vainly to resist, but the former prisoner had the strength of a long unvented anger on his side. He decided against any further attempts after the dark man wrenched his arm painfully higher up his back.

Drayco forced the clerk inside and kicked it shut behind him. Tall candles burned in their holders, as if they were freshly lit. Drayco wondered about it, but not for long. He had other things to complete rather than worry about candles. He led Louis to the wall with the straps hanging from it and slammed the clerk against it, stunning him before tying his arms and legs.

Louis wasn't able to yell out earlier because of the hand covering his mouth. He yelled long and loud now. "Help! Help me someone!"

"No one will come. You of all people should know that. This room is ignored completely, remember?"

"Help! Please help me!"

Drayco slapped the shouting man hard across the face. A small amount of blood ran from the corner of his mouth, his teeth had cut the inside of the lower lip. Fear filled the eyes watching him.

"What are you going to do?"

"Repay you for all the kindness you've showed me during my stay." Drayco put his face as close to the frightened man's as possible without actually touching it. Louis tried to pull back; the wall prevented it. "It's the least I can do."

With a calculated slowness, Drayco leaned forward and licked the blood off Louis' face. He immediately grabbed the face and forced it sideway. Teeth sank into the exposed neck, biting deep. The life-giving blood poured from the gaping wound into the waiting mouth.

Louis gasped. His eyes went wide. What Drayco did so shocked him that he forgot to fight back. By the time he thought to do so, it was too late. The world went from gray to black and he died hanging on the wall the same way so many before him had.

Drayco released his hold when he felt the blood flow cease. He stepped several paces away from the dead man and leaned his head back, arms reaching out at his sides, hands clenched into fists. A roar from deep within his chest echoed throughout the room, releasing much of the pent up anger held inside. He straightened up after the intense feeling ebbed. Without looking back, he left death behind and returned to the storage room.

Rummaging through the things stored in the room, Drayco found what he needed to finish his task. In a corner, he started a small fire. A wooden rod taken from one of the boxes dipped into the flames. Carrying it like a torch, he walked into the hall. The blaze in the storage room grew larger as it reached the boxes stacked nearby, licking hungrily at them.

The intense heat forced him to move farther down the hall. He lit several tapestries along the way before tossing the burning stick behind the front desk. The papers and the cloth furnishings surrounding the counter caught fire quickly. Seconds later, the main lobby was fully ablaze. Patrons ran past him, some screaming, some partially dressed, to keep from being burned alive.

Drayco walked across the porch to the road. He never looked back. Thick billowing clouds of black smoke poured out the open door. Windows shattered from the intense heat generated by the fire. Flames broke through the roof as it burned the wooden covering. People from all over town rushed toward the smoke to see what was happening. Some saw the dark man walk away; none was brave enough to stop him. The look on his face and the menacing dark air about him, along with the sword hanging at his side was warning enough to stay away.

He had calmed down by the time he reached the stables. Joseph. Shyanne and Drizzle were waiting for him, the horses ready.

"You look very pleased with yourself." The look of concern on his sister's face left. A warm smile replaced it.

"Very."

"Care to elaborate?" Joseph asked.

"No."

"Is everything okay?" Shyanne inquired.

"It is now."

Drayco made his way to Bravaro. He gave the animal a pat on the neck. The horse nudged him in the shoulder in response.

"We're out of here, boy."

The dark twin moved to the horse's side and threw himself into the saddle. He looked at the others. "What's taking you two so long? Let's get going." He gave the reins a tug and started down the road, away from the stables and the town.

Joseph and Shyanne grinned at each other then scrambled onto Jack. The man who had lost everything gave the woman from the past a kiss on the neck. He hugged her tight and gripped the reins, prodding the horse into action.

Drizzle paused to look back at the dark plume of smoke filling the blue sky above the inn's location. He knew what Drayco had done and was filled with a sense of pride.

"Maybe there's hope for that man after all," he purred.

The cat disappeared with the others over the horizon as the sun continued its trek over the treetops, the beginning of a new day announcing its presence before them.

About the Author

Janet started writing while trying to help her son find his own words. From that moment on, the passion for letting her imagination run rampid took over. Most times, she is pounding on a keyboard creating new worlds for her characters to explore. Other times, she can be found sitting on the back porch wreaking havoc on her laptop. Her genre includes sci-fi and horror/thriller. Janet resides in the warm state of Florida with her son, furry companions known as cats, and a couple of neurotic dogs.

To learn more about what is available from this author check out www.janetdurbin.com.

Don't miss the next book in the
Journey of Twins Series,

Stolen

Enjoy the following excerpt.

Joey ran around Drizzle's sleeping form, laughing and giggling. Occasionally, he would reach out and tap on the cat as he ran past.

"Tag! You're it," echoed across the open field.

Drizzle ignored the bothersome child until he could not take any more. "Will you stop? I'm trying to sleep."

This only enticed the child more. He ran past several additional times, smacking the humecat on the ears, nose and rump each time.

As Joey made another pass, the cat reached out and snagged the youngsters pants with a claw, causing him to fall. Joey landed with a huff, the smile wiped off his face in an instant.

"I told you to stop."

The child's hazel eyes filled with tears. He yelled, "I only wanted to play! I don't have any friends to play with, you big meanie!"

Drizzle looked at the pint size version of Joseph. The boy glared at the cat in open defiance. Both held their stares for a moment longer before a chuckle escaped from the cat.

"You know, you may look like your father, but you're a carbon copy of your mother when it comes to attitude— won't back down from anything."

A growl rumbled from the cat's throat. It was neither threatening nor serious. The tail started swishing back and forth in a rapid fashion. Suddenly, Drizzle pounced on the boy. He play wrestled with him, pretending to bite him but never doing so.

This was the part Joey loved best. He never fully understood what the cat meant by the other stuff, but he always loved the playing that followed.

Shyanne watched from the window in the kitchen. Joey and Drizzle had played this game so many times. It always brought a smile to her face every time she watched it. She saw the pair run off toward the woods. This part of the game was over. Now, the hide and seek part began. She returned her attention to the task at hand.

Material lay on the table. Several pieces sat off to the side already cut out, waiting for her to sew them together. She picked up the scissors. They were from a time before the virus. Holding them up, she remembered the time when she and Joseph had found them in some rubble. The metal was protected from the elements by a carrying pouch and it was shear blind luck that they were found at all. Shyanne had tripped over a chunk of stone and nearly smashed her knee on them. Since then, they have been a useful addition to her life.

The soft material cut easily with the sharp scissors. A low humming sound emitted from her as she eyed which way to cut next. It was a pleasant song from long ago.

First, I'll go this way, then that. In no time, I'll have another outfit ready for the baby.

Some clothes were available from when Joey was a baby. On the other hand, if this one was a girl—then what? To make sure she was ready, either way, she embroidered several touches to the jumpers. A flower here, a hummingbird there. Joseph just shook his head whenever he saw her embroidering. He knew better than to tell his wife not to do it.

An hour later, she straightened up. With a groan, she arched her back as far as her swollen belly would let her. Her pregnancy was going along without any difficulty, just like the first one. She was happy that she had not experienced the nausea and swelling most women experienced, or any other problems for that matter.

It was almost over now. The only thing that bothered her was an ever-present tiredness. A nap usually resolved that.

The chair scraped against the wood floor as she slid it back. Going to the window, she looked for her son and Drizzle. They were nowhere to be seen.

Drizzle was a godsend. The cat was created by her father's workplace before the virus, a virus that escaped its creators and almost wiped out every human on the planet. With his ability to think and speak like a human, hence the designation humecat, he kept Joey well occupied.

Must be off on another adventure. Those two are hopeless together. Shyanne stretched again. An eye-scrunching yawn accompanied the stretch. *I'm going to take a short nap. Drizzle will keep Joey safe.* As she moved down the hall, she thought, *I hope Joseph gets home soon. I sure could use a back massage.*

The bed looked so inviting. Pulling back the covers, she crawled under them. She snuggled her head deeper into the feather pillow and drifted into what she hoped would be a restful nap.

Joey ran into the woods to hide from the cat chasing him. They played this game of hide and seek often. It usually ended with him hiding somewhere in the house and the cat finding him. The boy remembered the times he had hid in great places, only to be sniffed out by Drizzle highly sensitive nose. He found better places now, places the cat could not sniff.

Once he had rubbed onions all over his body to mask his scent. When he presented himself to his parents later that evening, they tried to wash the smell off, but nothing worked. His skin was raw after so much scrubbing and he stunk for about a week before the scent finally dissipated.

This time he wanted to try something new. He watched as Drizzle ducked into the trees then ran with all the speed his little legs could muster back to the house. He made it without being spotted. With a snicker, he darted inside, ran quietly to his room and crawled out his window. He crept around the house to the cellar doors. Reaching out, he touched them then backtracked to his window.

Furball will think I'm hiding in the cellar. Ha! Let him, he thought as he crawled inside.

Joey ran back to the woods, sprinkling some of the precious spices he took from the kitchen behind him to cover his tracks. His parents may be overprotective, and, in his opinion, too busy to play with him, but they had at least taken the time to teach him how to cover his tracks if he was hunted. Additionally they had taught him how to survive if he got lost in the woods. At the young age of five, he knew more about how to stay alive in the wilderness than most grown men did.

Let old furball try and find me now. He'll sneeze and sneeze and sneeze. Maybe I'll hide so I can see it. I bet it'll look real funny. Joey hid a giggle behind a small hand.

He entered the dense undergrowth and began looking for a good place to hide so he could watch the fun. He did not see the tall man with dark hair watching him until he almost bumped into him. With boyhood innocence, and a little bit of suspicion, he stared up at the stranger.

"Be careful there, young man, you don't want to hurt yourself."

"Who are you?"

"I'm an old friend of the family."

"Yea?"

"Yea." The big man squat low, resting one knee on the ground so he could be eye level with the boy. "Who are you?"

"Joey."

The youngster gawked at the man. He had never seen anybody like him. Most people he saw were like his parents. This man was huge, his body all bumpy with muscles, and the sword on his back...wow.

"Joey, huh. Well Joey, how's your mom?"

"She okay."

"Her names Shyanne, right?"

"How'd you know?" The boy's eyes widened.

"Remember, I'm an old friend of the family."

"Oh yea. You want to come to the house? Mom's inside, probably napping."

"Is your dad home?"

"He's gone right now. He had to go get some things from town. What's your name?"

"Ruben."

The big man extended a hand to shake with; he made no attempt to come nearer.

Joey looked at it. He hesitated, not sure if he should shake it or run away. He remembered the few times his parents had had friends over and the way they had scolded him for not being polite, so he moved forward. He grasped the huge hand with his tiny one and pumped his arm up and down as he had seen his dad do when greeting other men.

Ruben could not believe his luck. He had been watching the house for some time, avoiding the blasted cats ranging area, wondering how he was going to get the boy away from everyone long enough to take him. Now he was here, before him, alone, so innocent and trusting.

"Come say hi to mom, she'll be happy to see you." The boy tugged on the big hand.

"Joey, I can't stay. I've got to go to town myself." Ruben let go of the hand and started walking away. He turned toward the youngster after a couple of steps. "Say, did you want to come with me? We can meet up with your dad."

The boy's big hazel eyes lit up. The thought of going to town was wonderful. He had been there only a few times, and remembered all the exciting things he had seen. Upset when his father had not taken him, he was going to get the chance to see them after all.

"Really? I can go with you?"

"Only if you think your mom won't mind."

"She won't care. I'll be with a friend, and they always said it was okay to stay with their friends."

"Well then, let's go." Ruben smiled as he reached out and took the boys hand in his.

They walked to another clearing a short distance from the house where a black horse with a white blaze on its forehead grazed on the grass.

"Is that your horse?" Joey was awestruck by the size of the creature. It was huge, like the man standing next to him.

"His name is Wind Racer."

"We're going to ride on him?"

"Are you afraid?"

Joey stammered, "N-n-n—no."

"It's okay, Joey." Ruben leaned over closer to the boy. "To tell you the truth, I was a little afraid when I rode him the first time."

Joey glanced sideways at the big man, "You're teasing me...aren't you?"

"No way, I would never do that to you." Ruben held up his hands.

The five year old smiled. "Does he go fast?"

"As fast as the wind. That's why I called him Wind Racer."

The horse must have heard Ruben's voice because he looked up at the two standing near the edge of the woods. With a nicker and a toss of his head, he trotted over to them, his mane flowing like silk, the tail held high.

Joey hid behind the big man. He had never been this close to something so massive before. It was scary, but also thrilling at the same time. Ruben reached up and gave the animal a firm pat on the neck.

"Joey, let me introduce you to my horse. Wind Racer, this is the young man who is going to accompany us on our journey."

The horse looked at Joey and seemed to bob his head in greeting, or at least that was what it looked like to an excited five year old.

"You ready to go?"

When he bobbed his own head yes, Ruben picked him up and placed him in the saddle. Joey watched as the big man, who said he was a friend of his parents, got up behind him. He grabbed the saddle horn when the horse shifted his weight from one foot to the other. The ground seemed so far down.

"Don't worry, Joey, I won't let you fall."

The youngster gave the big man a sheepish look before he peered at the horse again. "I'm not afraid. I think he's wonderful."

"He's my best friend," Ruben replied. "He'll take good care of us."

The man gripped the reins, hugged the child close, and tapped Wind Racer in the sides. The horse responded immediately. They flew across the clearing and in a short amount of time; they were on a dirt road, heading east.

Joey was having so much fun; he failed to notice that they were heading in the opposite direction, away from the town where his father was located.

"Has Drizzle become the nervous type?" Drayco asked.

"No. He's the most rock steady creature I've ever met."

"Well, something sure has him jumpy. I don't ever remember seeing him this edgy before."

Shyanne looked inside toward the big cat. "You're right. Something sure has him uptight. I wonde..."

A strange noise started coming from the area near the entrance of the building, a sort of rustling sound. The mercenaries missed it, at first. Finally, one of the men close to the front heard it. He walked over and looked around, attempting to locate the source of the sound. It seemed to be coming from overhead, in the ceiling.

"What's that?" he asked, trying to see into the dark holes above.

Ruben straightened up. He was looking at Drizzle, not the man speaking. The cat was going wild, struggling against his bonds with all his might. His mouth was tied shut, leaving him unable to bite at the restraints holding him. He yowled in frustration. Joseph watched the struggling cat, as well.

The rustling sound grew louder, as if many, many things were brushing against each other. Men and women around the room stopped what they were doing to look first at the cat, then at the man near the front.

A bad feeling settled in the pit of Ruben's stomach. The odor had reminded him of something from the past. Unfortunately, he still could not put a finger on what it was.

The man standing under the holes shouted, "Someone bring a light over here. I want to see what's up there." He had his arm extended toward the fire.

Drayco glanced at his sister. He could tell from the look on her face that she was uneasy. He understood; he was wearing the same look. He turned his attention back to what was happening inside just as someone was getting up with a torch. It was the same woman who had argued on the porch earlier. The blood still dotted her clothes.

Lela made it to the reaching man's side when Ruben remembered what caused the disturbing smell.

"No! Wait! Get away from there. NOW!" He started to move toward the pair. It was too late.